ACCLAIM FOR JEFF SMITH'S

★*"This is first-class kid lit: exciting, funny, scary, and resonant enough that it will stick with readers for a long time."* —**Publishers Weekly**, *starred review*

"One of the best kids' comics ever." —Vibe *magazine*

*"***BONE*** is storytelling at its best, full of endearing, flawed characters whose adventures run the gamut from hilarious whimsy . . . to thrilling drama."* —**Entertainment Weekly**

"[This] sprawling, mythic comic is spectacular." —**SPIN** *magazine*

"As sweeping as the 'Lord of the Rings' cycle, but much funnier." —*Andrew Arnold,* **Time** *magazine*

"Jeff Smith's cartoons are irresistible. Every gorgeous sweep of his brush speaks volumes." —*Frank Miller, creator of* Sin City

"Jeff Smith can pace a joke better than almost anyone in comics." —*Neil Gaiman, author of* **Coraline**

"*I love* **BONE! BONE** *is great!*"

—*Matt Groening, creator of* **The Simpsons**

"*Every one of the zillion characters has a unique set of personality traits and flaws and dreams that are developed amid the pandemonium.*"

—*Kyle Baker,* **Plastic Man** *cartoonist*

"**BONE** *moves from brash humor to gripping adventure in a single panel.*" —*ALA* **Booklist**

"*Jeff Smith's* **BONE** *series . . . takes itself seriously enough to make you cry for puffy-nosed creatures . . . , but gives in to its funnybook and fantasy roots so wholeheartedly you'll spend the rest of the time laughing or holding your breath.* **Bone,** *in short, is unlike any other comic.*"

—**Star-Tribune**

"**BONE** *is a comic-book sensation. . . . [It] is a classic of writer-artist craftsmanship not to be missed.*"

—**Comics Buyer's Guide**

Eyes of the Storm

OTHER **BONE** BOOKS

Out from Boneville

The Great Cow Race

EYES OF THE STORM

BY JEFF SMITH

WITH COLOR BY STEVE HAMAKER

An Imprint of

SCHOLASTIC

New York   Toronto   London   Auckland   Sydney   Mexico City   New Delhi   Hong Kong   Buenos Aires

Library of Congress Catalog Card Number 95068403.
ISBN 0-439-70625-4 (hardcover) — ISBN 0-439-70638-6 (paperback)

ACKNOWLEDGMENTS
Harvestar Family Crest designed by Charles Vess
Map of *The Valley* by Mark Crilley
Color by Steve Hamaker

10 9 8 7 6 5 4 3 2 1   06 07 08 09
First Scholastic edition, February 2006
Book design by David Saylor
Printed in Singapore 46

This book is for my parents,

Barbara Goodsell and William Earl Smith

CONTENTS

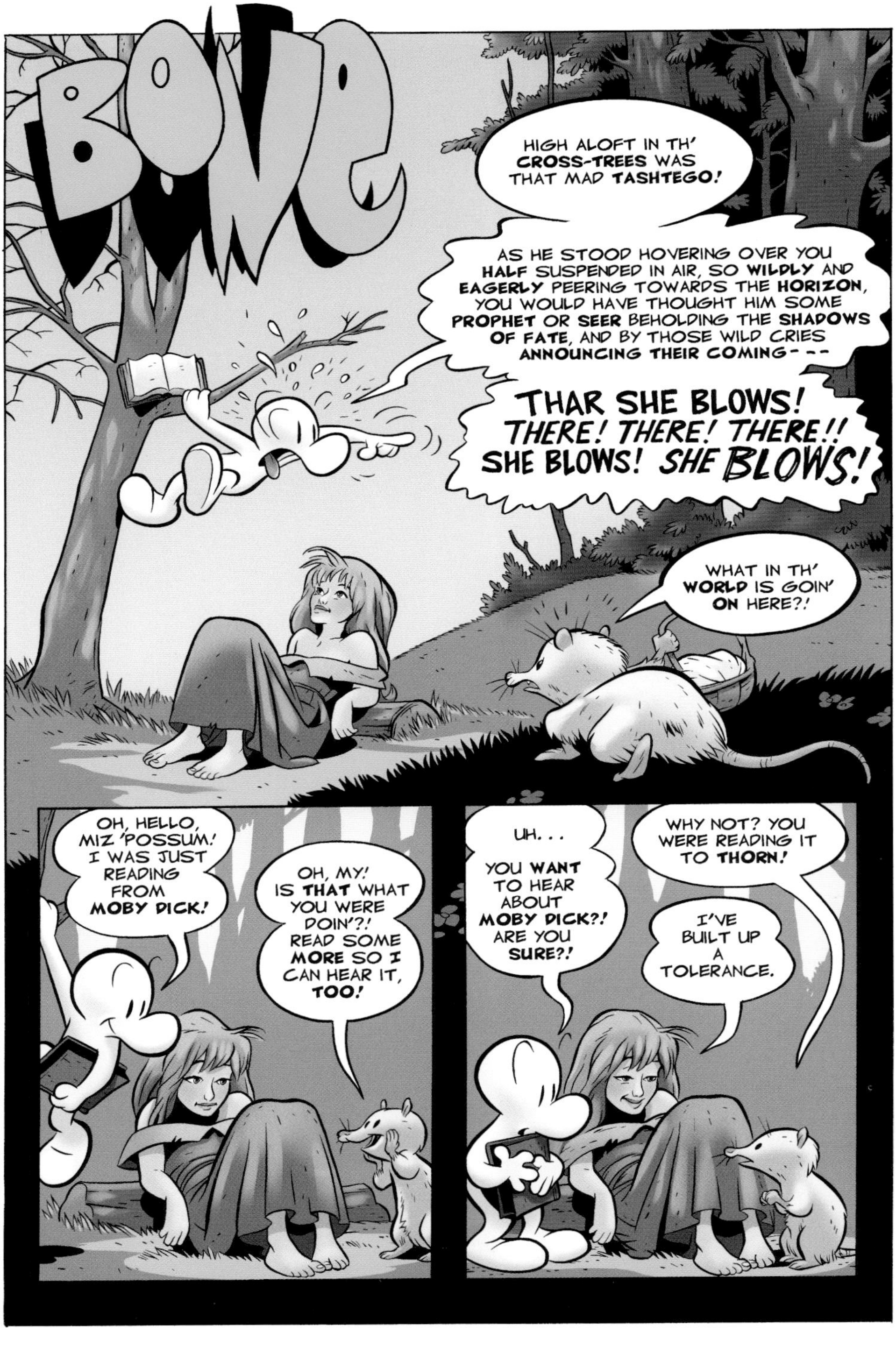
BONE
HIGH ALOFT IN TH' CROSS-TREES WAS THAT MAD TASHTEGO!
AS HE STOOD HOVERING OVER YOU HALF SUSPENDED IN AIR, SO WILDLY AND EAGERLY PEERING TOWARDS THE HORIZON, YOU WOULD HAVE THOUGHT HIM SOME PROPHET OR SEER BEHOLDING THE SHADOWS OF FATE, AND BY THOSE WILD CRIES ANNOUNCING THEIR COMING---
THAR SHE BLOWS! THERE! THERE! THERE!! SHE BLOWS! SHE BLOWS!
WHAT IN TH' WORLD IS GOIN' ON HERE?!
OH, HELLO, MIZ 'POSSUM! I WAS JUST READING FROM MOBY DICK!
OH, MY! IS THAT WHAT YOU WERE DOIN'?! READ SOME MORE SO I CAN HEAR IT, TOO!
UH. . .
YOU WANT TO HEAR ABOUT MOBY DICK?! ARE YOU SURE?!
WHY NOT? YOU WERE READING IT TO THORN!
I'VE BUILT UP A TOLERANCE.

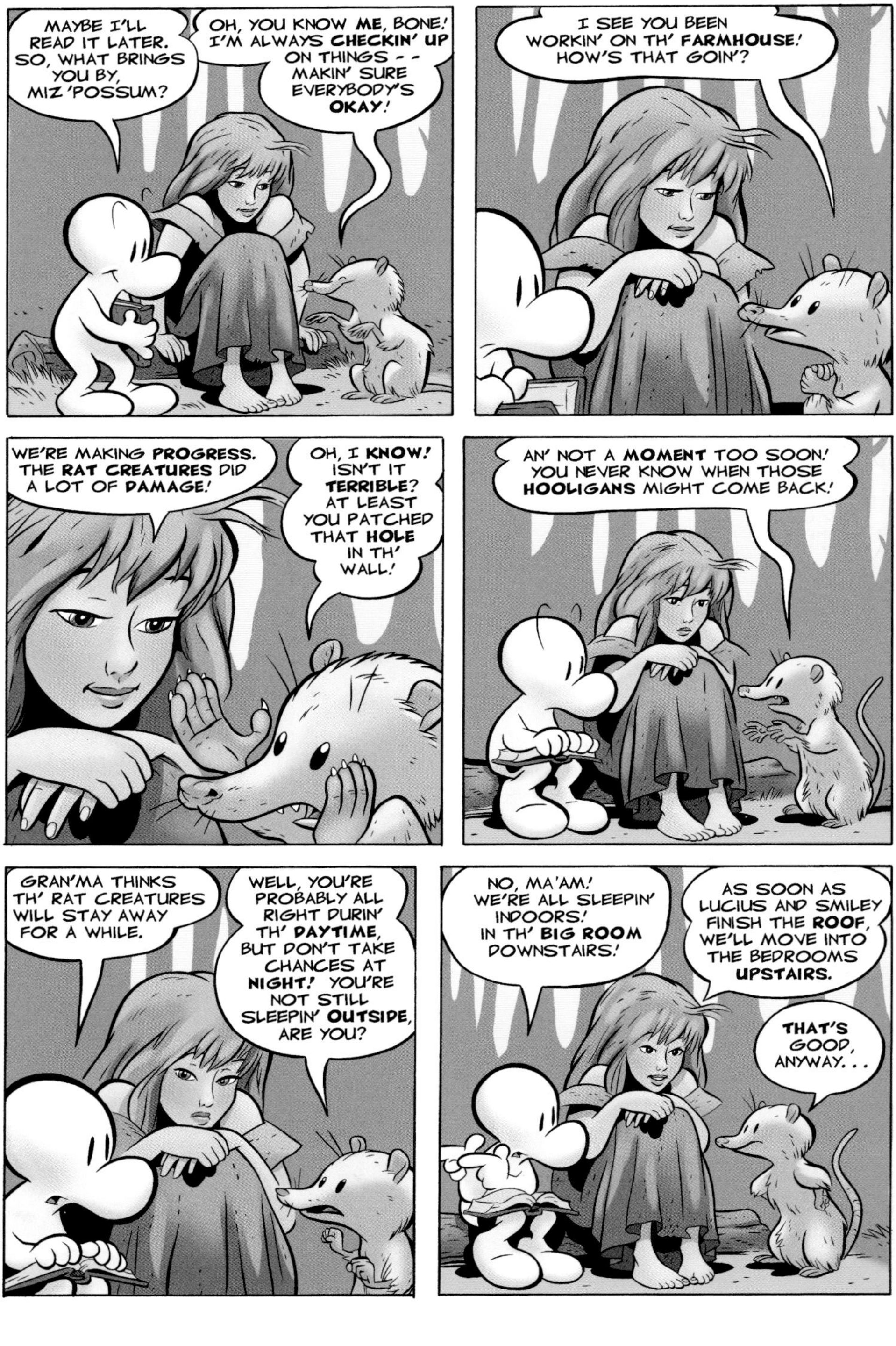
MAYBE I'LL READ IT LATER. SO, WHAT BRINGS YOU BY, MIZ 'POSSUM?
OH, YOU KNOW ME, BONE! I'M ALWAYS CHECKIN' UP ON THINGS - - MAKIN' SURE EVERYBODY'S OKAY!
I SEE YOU BEEN WORKIN' ON TH' FARMHOUSE! HOW'S THAT GOIN'?
WE'RE MAKING PROGRESS. THE RAT CREATURES DID A LOT OF DAMAGE!
OH, I KNOW! ISN'T IT TERRIBLE? AT LEAST YOU PATCHED THAT HOLE IN TH' WALL!
AN' NOT A MOMENT TOO SOON! YOU NEVER KNOW WHEN THOSE HOOLIGANS MIGHT COME BACK!
GRAN'MA THINKS TH' RAT CREATURES WILL STAY AWAY FOR A WHILE.
WELL, YOU'RE PROBABLY ALL RIGHT DURIN' TH' DAYTIME, BUT DON'T TAKE CHANCES AT NIGHT! YOU'RE NOT STILL SLEEPIN' OUTSIDE, ARE YOU?
NO, MA'AM! WE'RE ALL SLEEPIN' INDOORS! IN TH' BIG ROOM DOWNSTAIRS!
AS SOON AS LUCIUS AND SMILEY FINISH THE ROOF, WE'LL MOVE INTO THE BEDROOMS UPSTAIRS.
THAT'S GOOD, ANYWAY. . .

WATCH DUTY

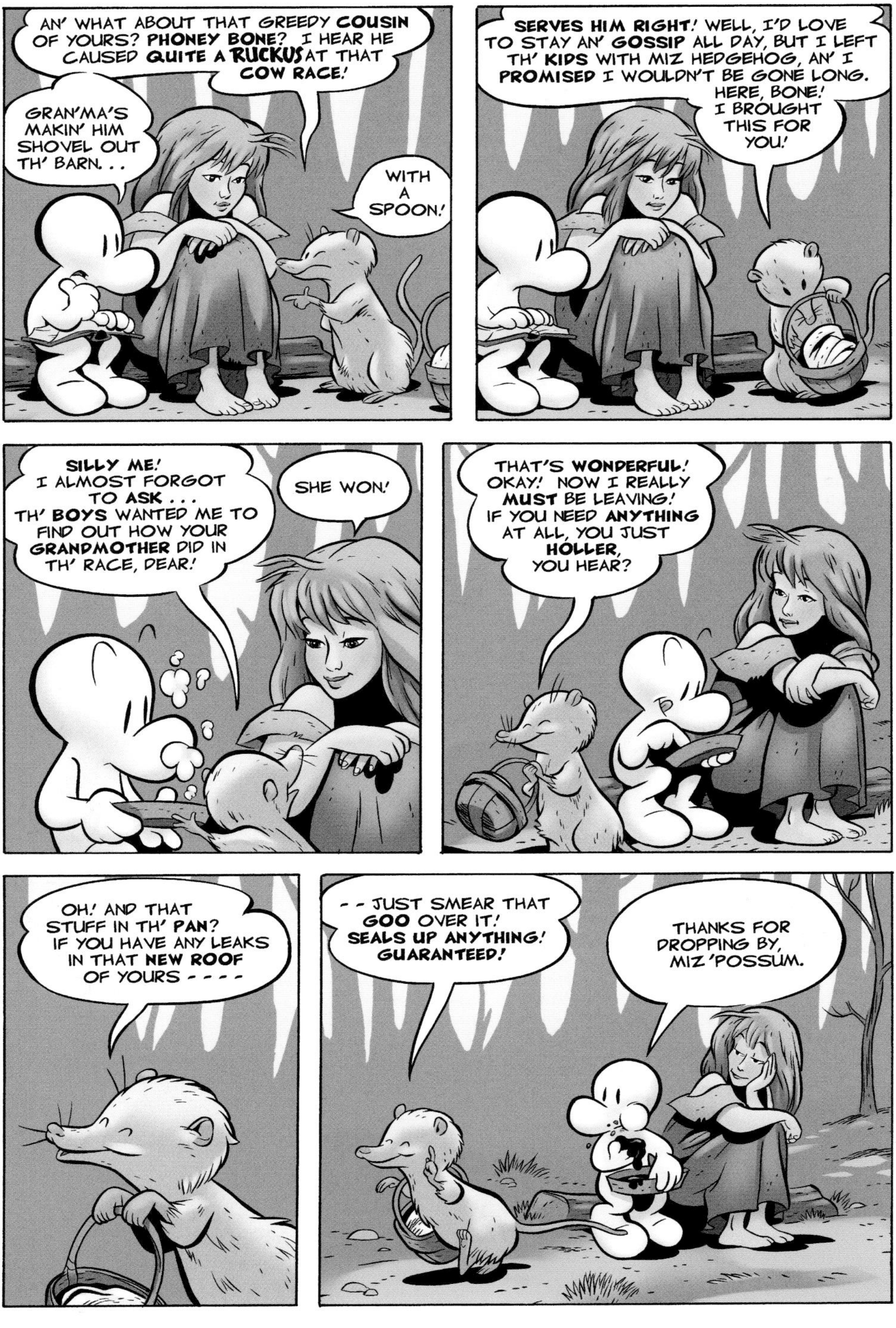
AN' WHAT ABOUT THAT GREEDY COUSIN OF YOURS? PHONEY BONE? I HEAR HE CAUSED QUITE A RUCKUS AT THAT COW RACE!
GRAN'MA'S MAKIN' HIM SHOVEL OUT TH' BARN. . .
WITH A SPOON!
SERVES HIM RIGHT! WELL, I'D LOVE TO STAY AN' GOSSIP ALL DAY, BUT I LEFT TH' KIDS WITH MIZ HEDGEHOG, AN' I PROMISED I WOULDN'T BE GONE LONG.
HERE, BONE! I BROUGHT THIS FOR YOU!
SILLY ME! I ALMOST FORGOT TO ASK . . . TH' BOYS WANTED ME TO FIND OUT HOW YOUR GRANDMOTHER DID IN TH' RACE, DEAR!
SHE WON!
THAT'S WONDERFUL! OKAY! NOW I REALLY MUST BE LEAVING! IF YOU NEED ANYTHING AT ALL, YOU JUST HOLLER, YOU HEAR?
OH! AND THAT STUFF IN TH' PAN? IF YOU HAVE ANY LEAKS IN THAT NEW ROOF OF YOURS - - - -
- - JUST SMEAR THAT GOO OVER IT! SEALS UP ANYTHING! GUARANTEED!
THANKS FOR DROPPING BY, MIZ 'POSSUM.

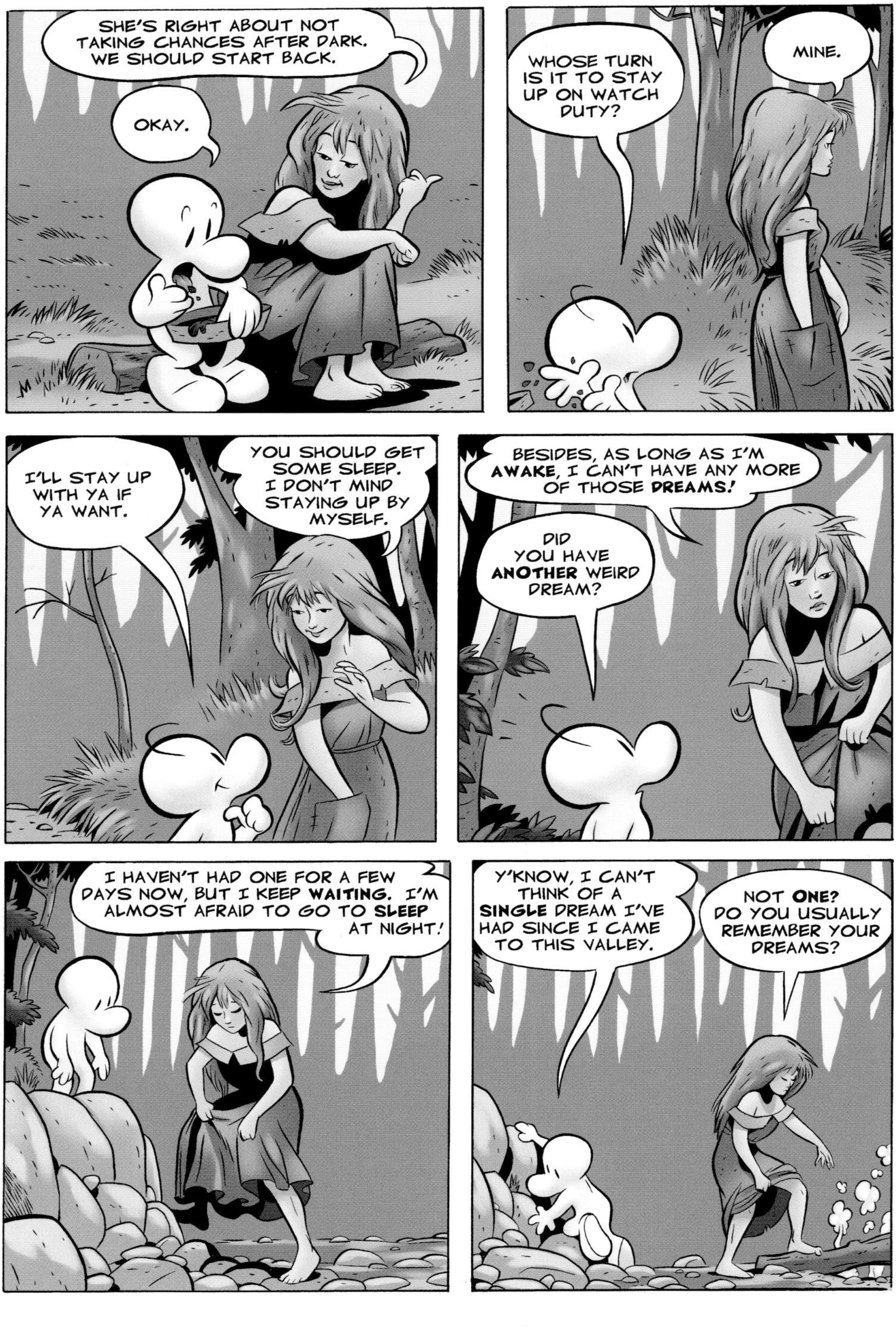
SHE'S RIGHT ABOUT NOT TAKING CHANCES AFTER DARK. WE SHOULD START BACK.
OKAY.
WHOSE TURN IS IT TO STAY UP ON WATCH DUTY?
MINE.
I'LL STAY UP WITH YA IF YA WANT.
YOU SHOULD GET SOME SLEEP. I DON'T MIND STAYING UP BY MYSELF.
BESIDES, AS LONG AS I'M AWAKE, I CAN'T HAVE ANY MORE OF THOSE DREAMS!
DID YOU HAVE ANOTHER WEIRD DREAM?
I HAVEN'T HAD ONE FOR A FEW DAYS NOW, BUT I KEEP WAITING. I'M ALMOST AFRAID TO GO TO SLEEP AT NIGHT!
Y'KNOW, I CAN'T THINK OF A SINGLE DREAM I'VE HAD SINCE I CAME TO THIS VALLEY.
NOT ONE? DO YOU USUALLY REMEMBER YOUR DREAMS?

WATCH DUTY

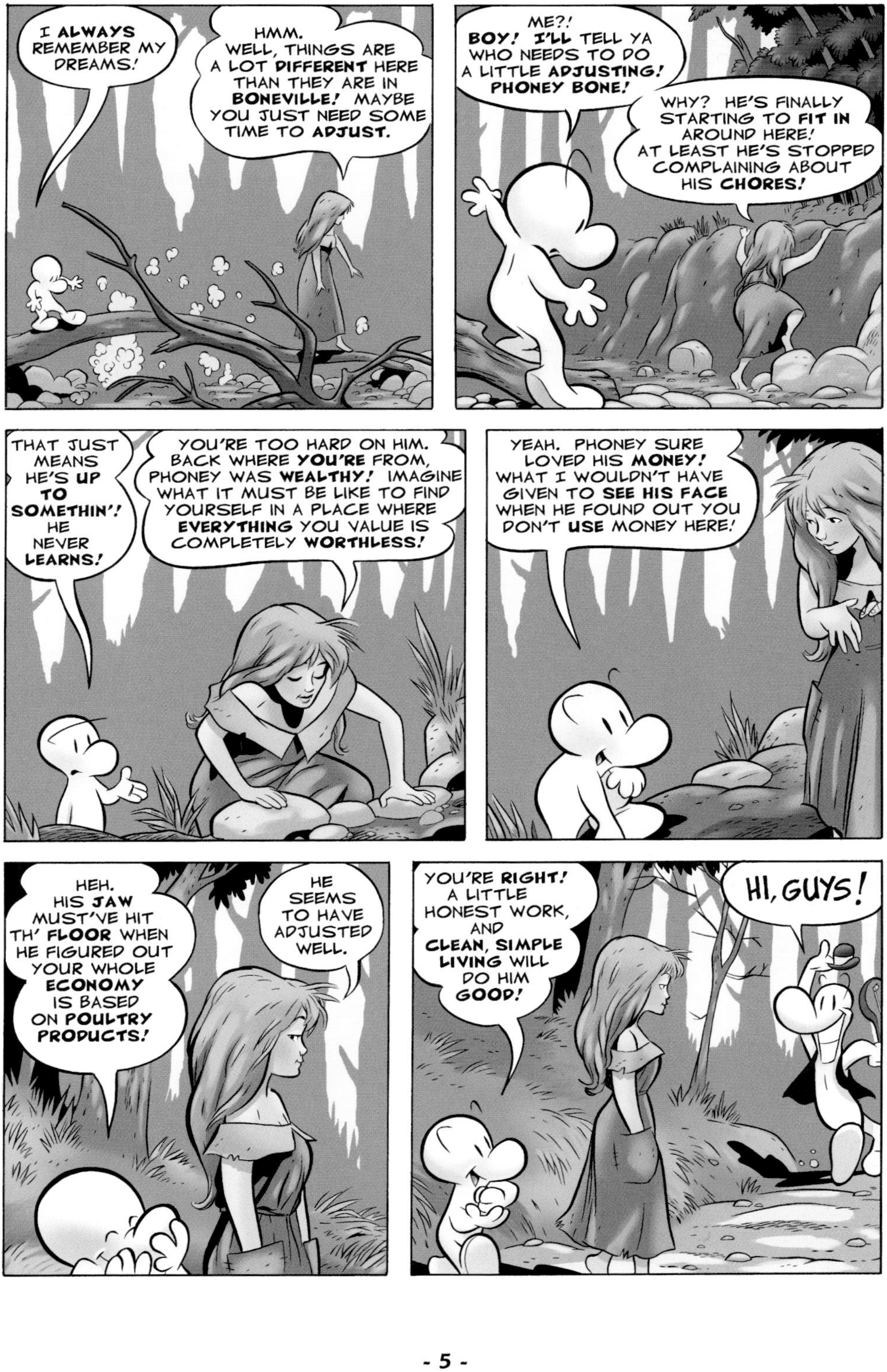

I ALWAYS REMEMBER MY DREAMS!
HMM. WELL, THINGS ARE A LOT DIFFERENT HERE THAN THEY ARE IN BONEVILLE! MAYBE YOU JUST NEED SOME TIME TO ADJUST.
ME?! BOY! I'LL TELL YA WHO NEEDS TO DO A LITTLE ADJUSTING! PHONEY BONE!
WHY? HE'S FINALLY STARTING TO FIT IN AROUND HERE! AT LEAST HE'S STOPPED COMPLAINING ABOUT HIS CHORES!
THAT JUST MEANS HE'S UP TO SOMETHIN'! HE NEVER LEARNS!
YOU'RE TOO HARD ON HIM. BACK WHERE YOU'RE FROM, PHONEY WAS WEALTHY! IMAGINE WHAT IT MUST BE LIKE TO FIND YOURSELF IN A PLACE WHERE EVERYTHING YOU VALUE IS COMPLETELY WORTHLESS!
YEAH. PHONEY SURE LOVED HIS MONEY! WHAT I WOULDN'T HAVE GIVEN TO SEE HIS FACE WHEN HE FOUND OUT YOU DON'T USE MONEY HERE!
HEH. HIS JAW MUST'VE HIT TH' FLOOR WHEN HE FIGURED OUT YOUR WHOLE ECONOMY IS BASED ON POULTRY PRODUCTS!
HE SEEMS TO HAVE ADJUSTED WELL.
YOU'RE RIGHT! A LITTLE HONEST WORK, AND CLEAN, SIMPLE LIVING WILL DO HIM GOOD!
HI, GUYS!

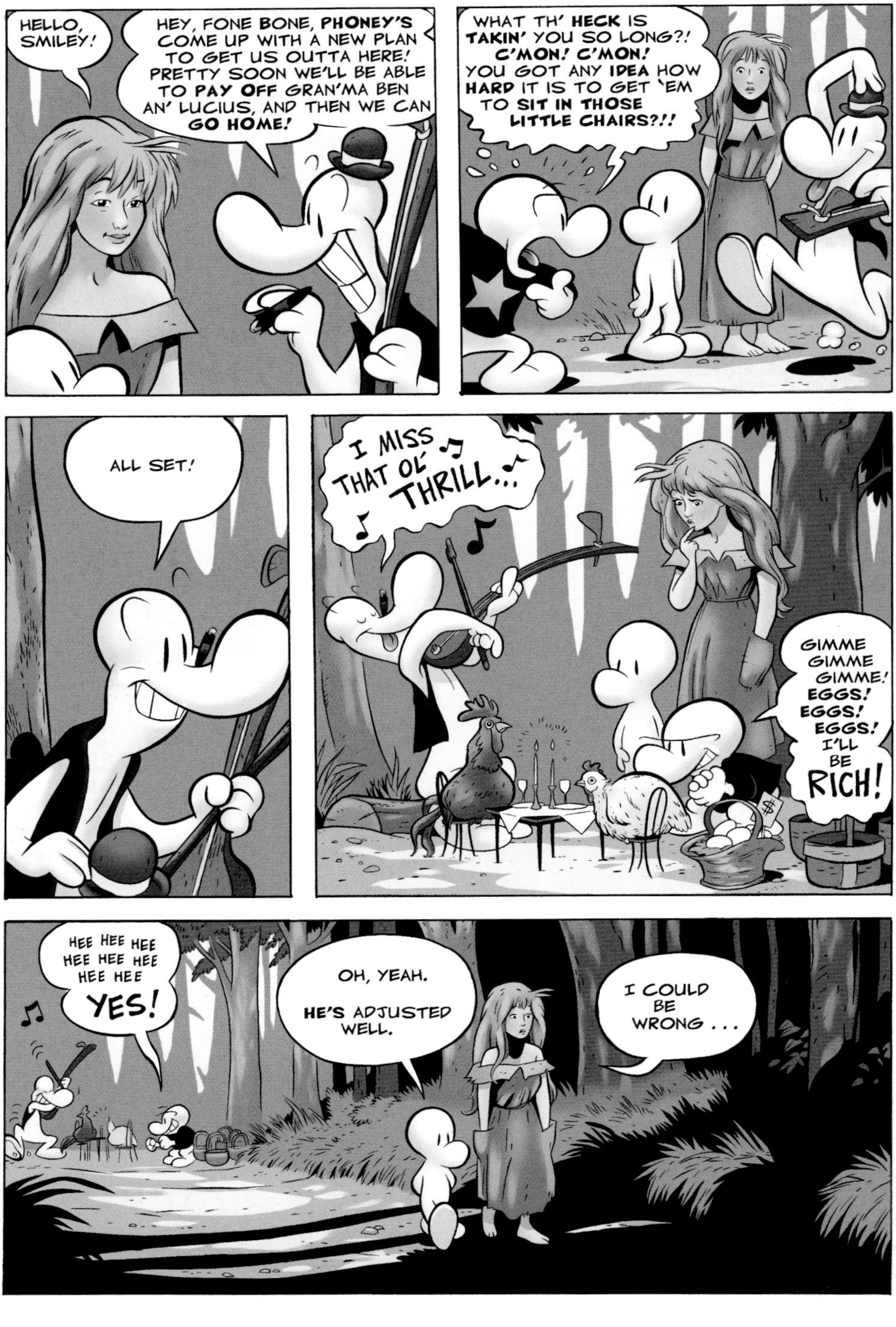
HELLO, SMILEY!
HEY, FONE BONE, PHONEY'S COME UP WITH A NEW PLAN TO GET US OUTTA HERE! PRETTY SOON WE'LL BE ABLE TO PAY OFF GRAN'MA BEN AN' LUCIUS, AND THEN WE CAN GO HOME!
WHAT TH' HECK IS TAKIN' YOU SO LONG?! C'MON! C'MON! YOU GOT ANY IDEA HOW HARD IT IS TO GET 'EM TO SIT IN THOSE LITTLE CHAIRS?!!
ALL SET!
I MISS THAT OL' THRILL...
GIMME GIMME GIMME! EGGS! EGGS! EGGS! I'LL BE RICH!
HEE HEE HEE HEE HEE HEE HEE HEE YES!
OH, YEAH. HE'S ADJUSTED WELL.
I COULD BE WRONG . . .

WATCH DUTY

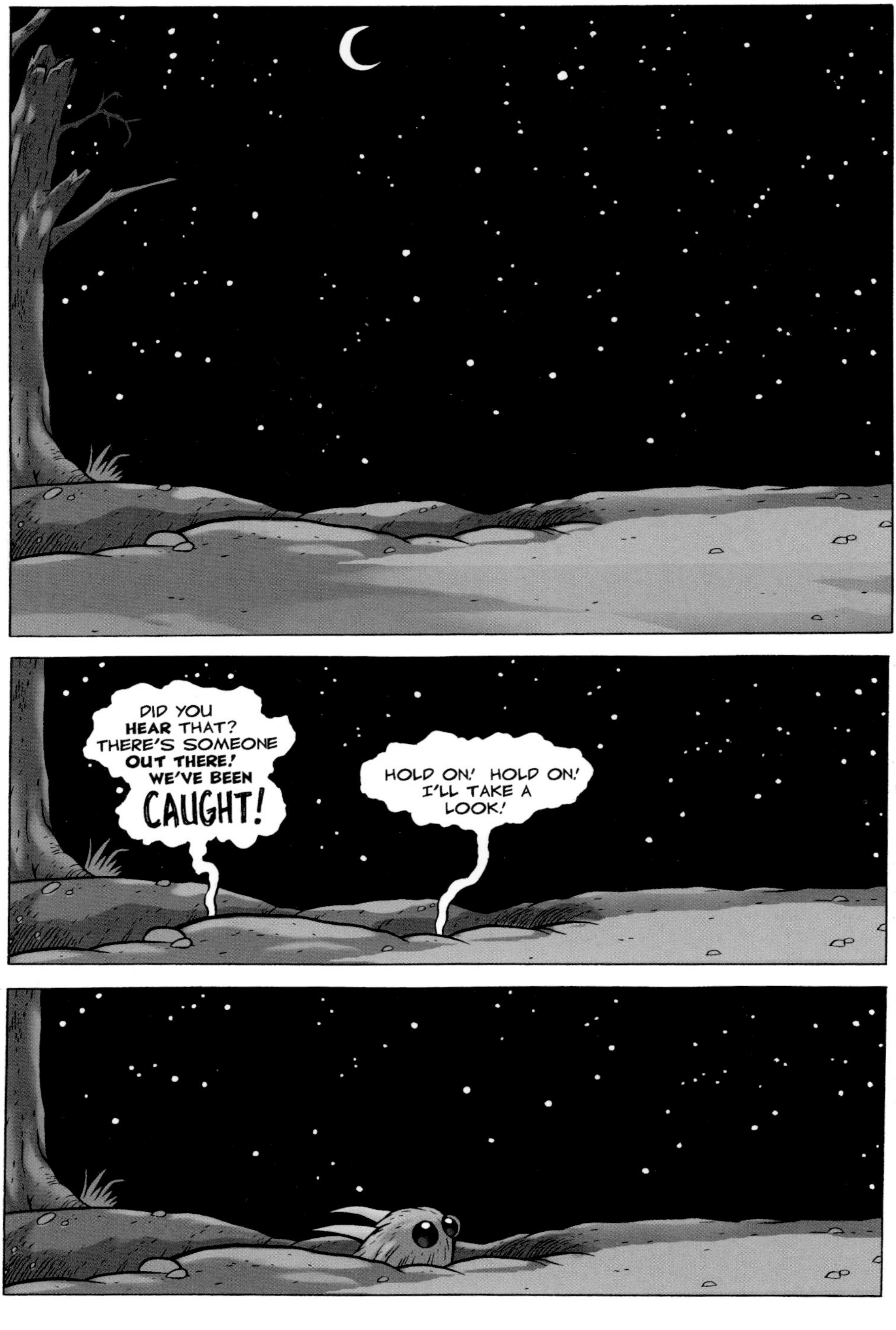

DID YOU HEAR THAT? THERE'S SOMEONE OUT THERE! WE'VE BEEN CAUGHT!
HOLD ON! HOLD ON! I'LL TAKE A LOOK!

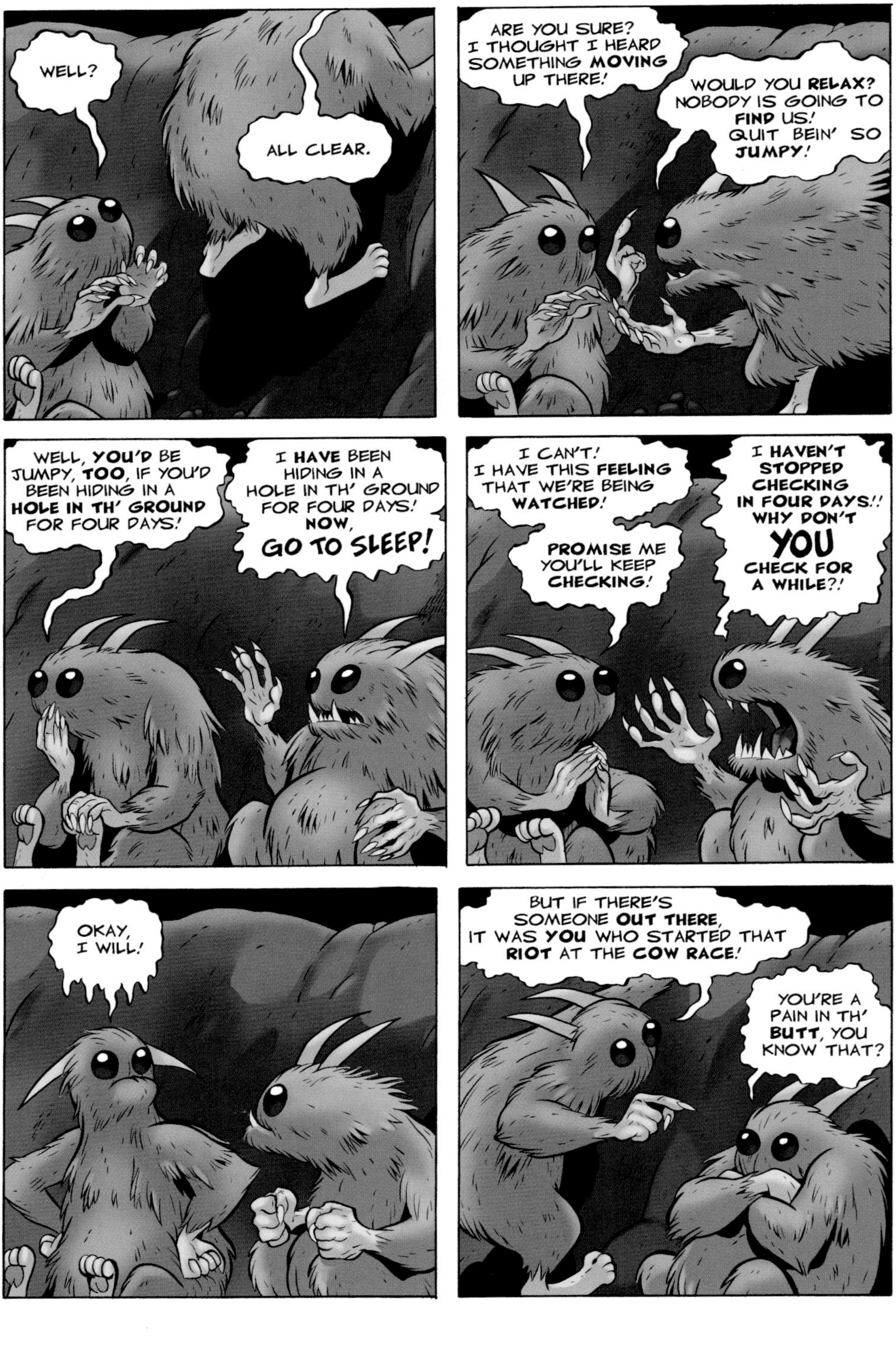
WELL?
ALL CLEAR.
ARE YOU SURE? I THOUGHT I HEARD SOMETHING MOVING UP THERE!
WOULD YOU RELAX? NOBODY IS GOING TO FIND US! QUIT BEIN' SO JUMPY!
WELL, YOU'D BE JUMPY, TOO, IF YOU'D BEEN HIDING IN A HOLE IN TH' GROUND FOR FOUR DAYS!
I HAVE BEEN HIDING IN A HOLE IN TH' GROUND FOR FOUR DAYS! NOW, GO TO SLEEP!
I CAN'T! I HAVE THIS FEELING THAT WE'RE BEING WATCHED!
PROMISE ME YOU'LL KEEP CHECKING!
I HAVEN'T STOPPED CHECKING IN FOUR DAYS!! WHY DON'T YOU CHECK FOR A WHILE?!
OKAY, I WILL!
BUT IF THERE'S SOMEONE OUT THERE, IT WAS YOU WHO STARTED THAT RIOT AT THE COW RACE!
YOU'RE A PAIN IN TH' BUTT, YOU KNOW THAT?

WATCH DUTY

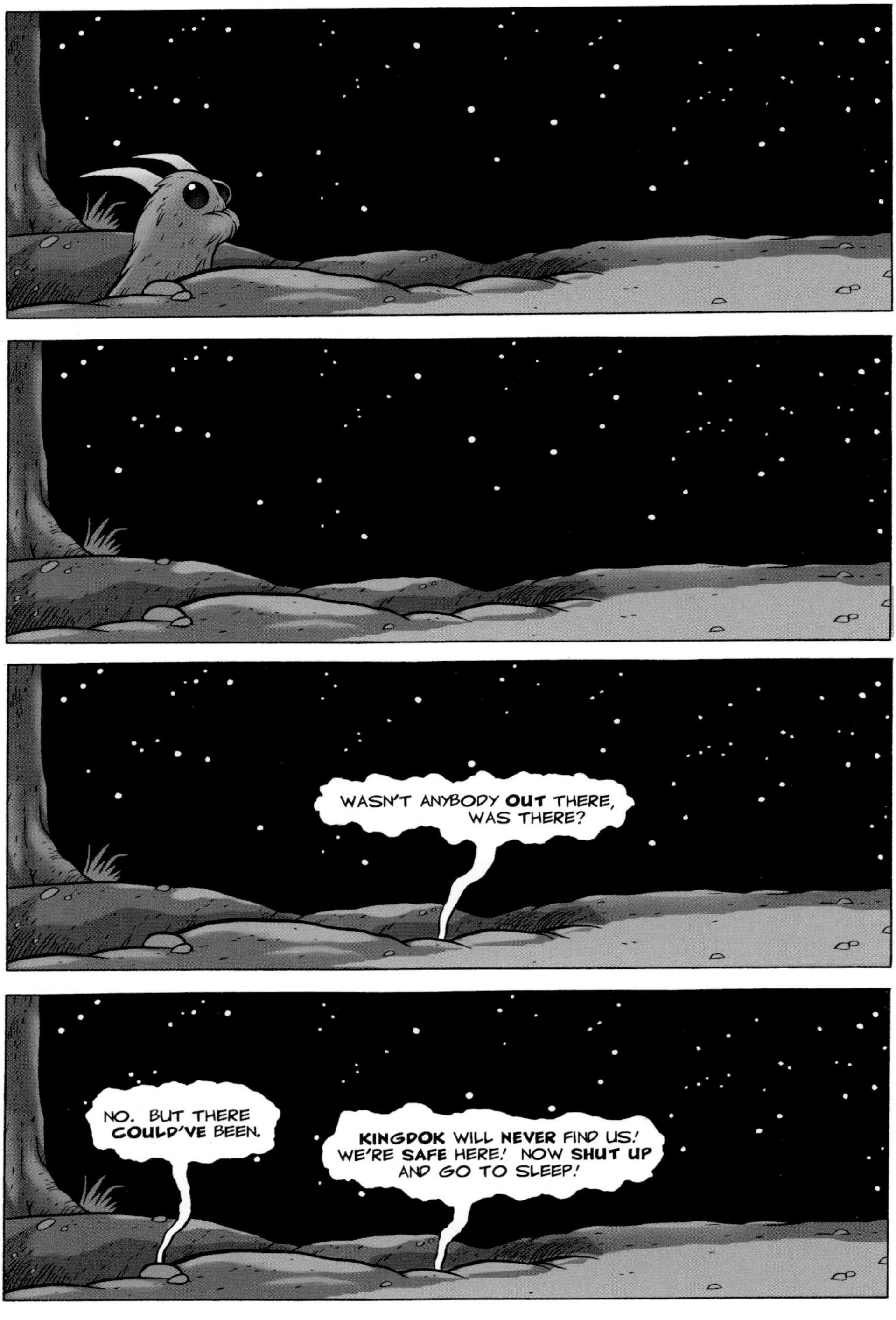
WASN'T ANYBODY OUT THERE, WAS THERE?
NO. BUT THERE COULD'VE BEEN.
KINGDOK WILL NEVER FIND US! WE'RE SAFE HERE! NOW SHUT UP AND GO TO SLEEP!

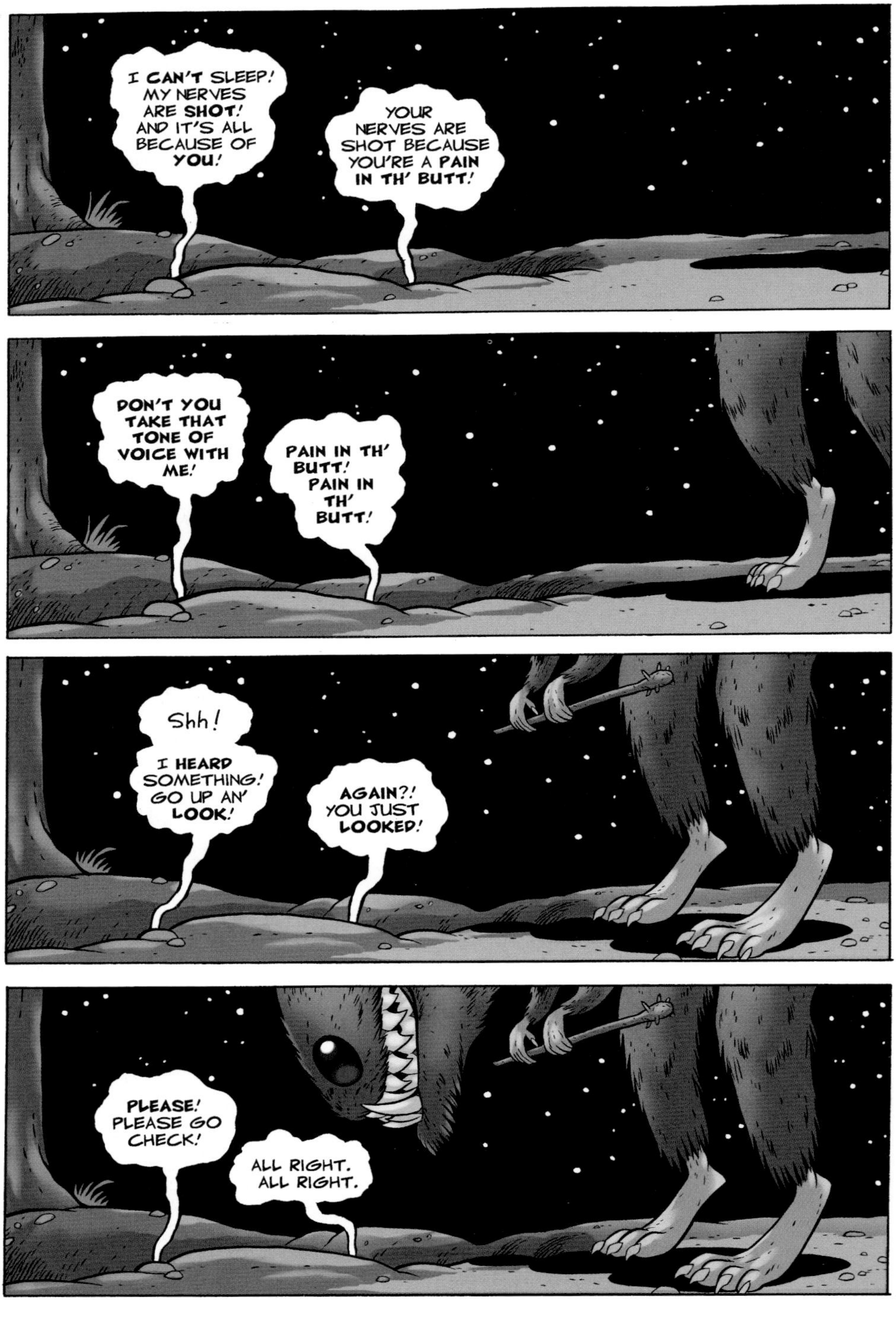
I CAN'T SLEEP! MY NERVES ARE SHOT! AND IT'S ALL BECAUSE OF YOU!
YOUR NERVES ARE SHOT BECAUSE YOU'RE A PAIN IN TH' BUTT!
DON'T YOU TAKE THAT TONE OF VOICE WITH ME!
PAIN IN TH' BUTT! PAIN IN TH' BUTT!
Shh!
I HEARD SOMETHING! GO UP AN' LOOK!
AGAIN?! YOU JUST LOOKED!
PLEASE! PLEASE GO CHECK!
ALL RIGHT. ALL RIGHT.

WATCH DUTY

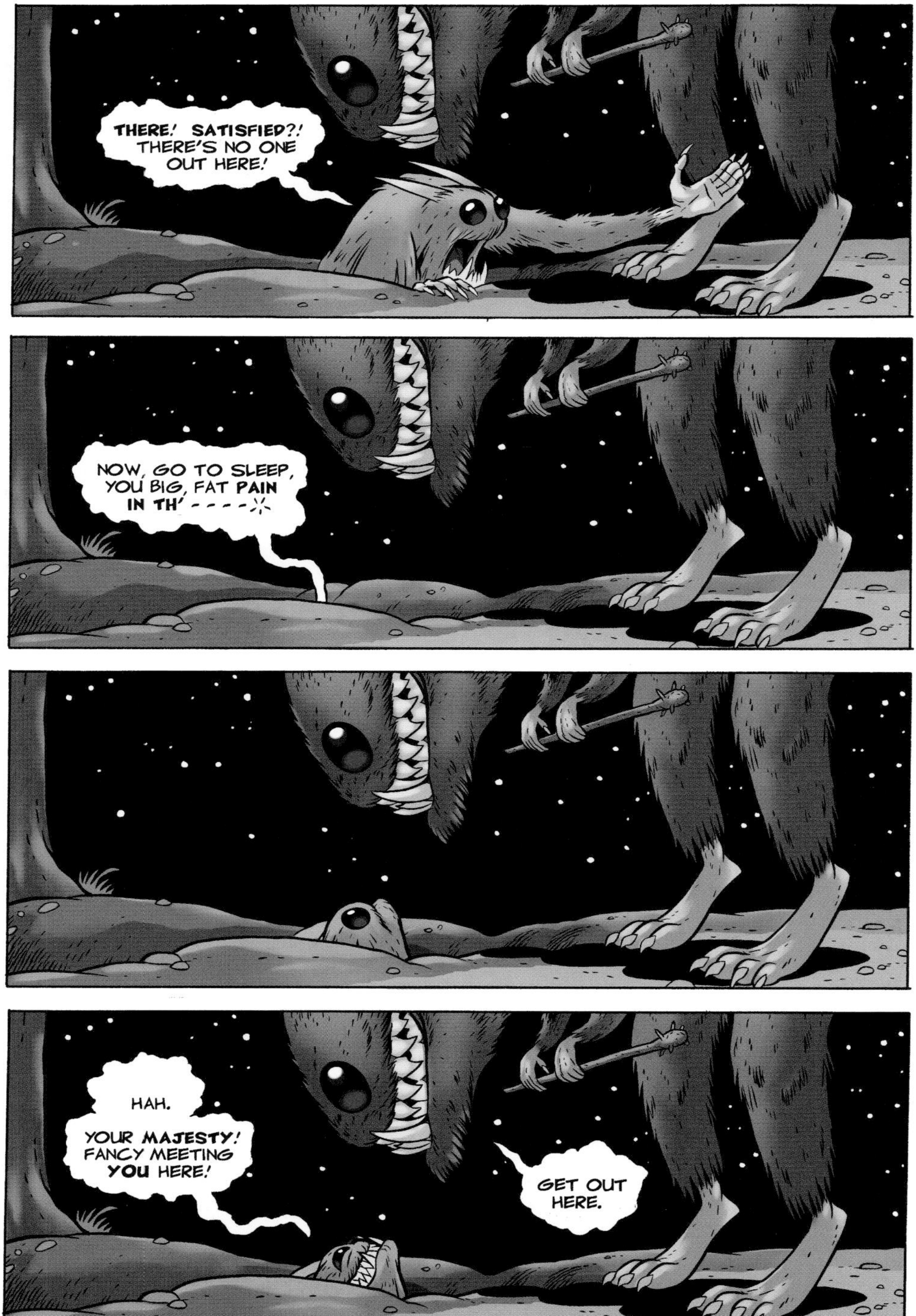
THERE! SATISFIED?! THERE'S NO ONE OUT HERE!
NOW, GO TO SLEEP, YOU BIG, FAT PAIN IN TH' - - - -
HAH.
YOUR MAJESTY! FANCY MEETING YOU HERE!
GET OUT HERE.

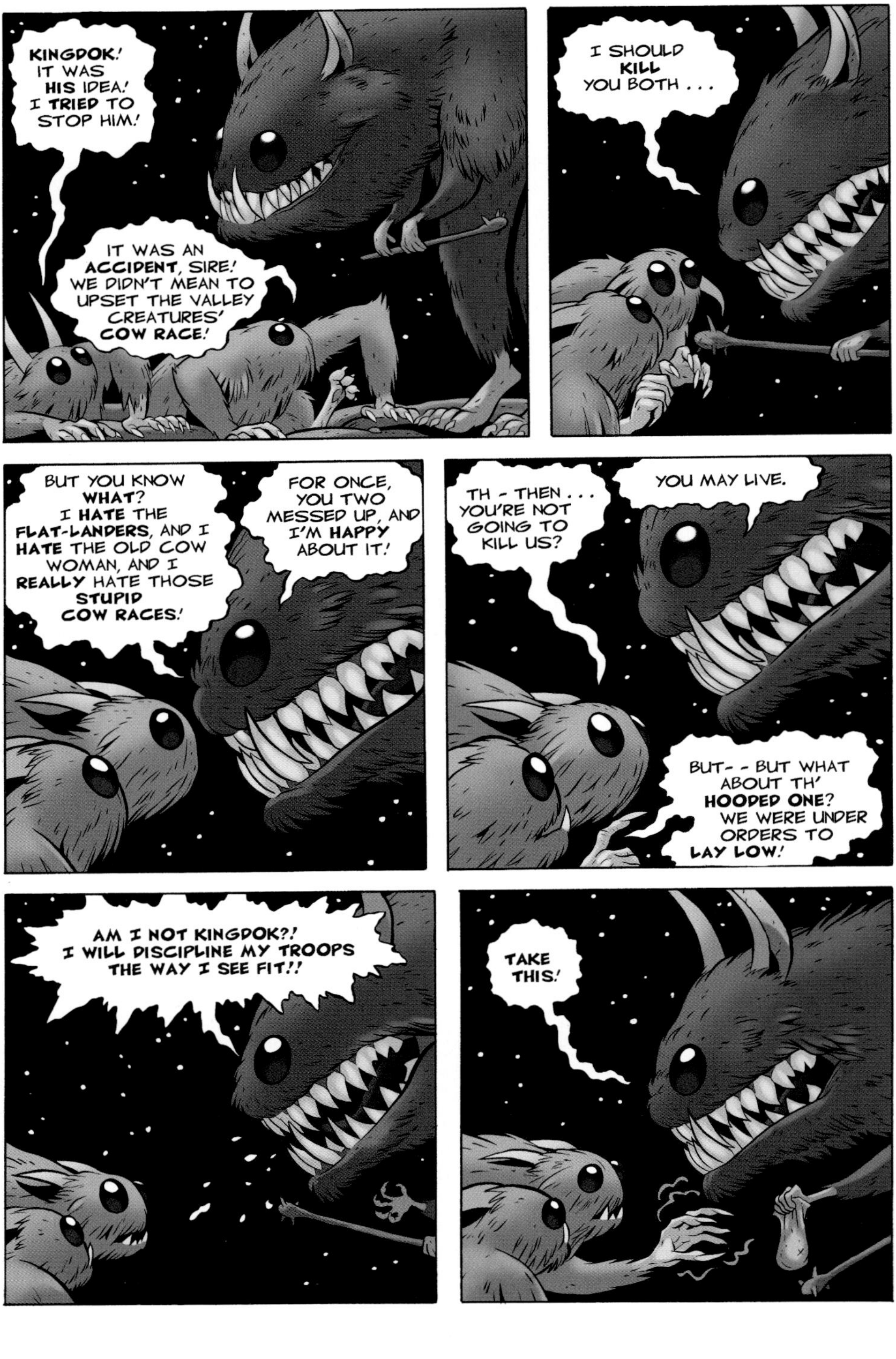
KINGDOK! IT WAS HIS IDEA! I TRIED TO STOP HIM!
IT WAS AN ACCIDENT, SIRE! WE DIDN'T MEAN TO UPSET THE VALLEY CREATURES' COW RACE!
I SHOULD KILL YOU BOTH . . .
BUT YOU KNOW WHAT? I HATE THE FLAT-LANDERS, AND I HATE THE OLD COW WOMAN, AND I REALLY HATE THOSE STUPID COW RACES!
FOR ONCE, YOU TWO MESSED UP, AND I'M HAPPY ABOUT IT!
TH - THEN . . . YOU'RE NOT GOING TO KILL US?
YOU MAY LIVE.
BUT- - BUT WHAT ABOUT TH' HOODED ONE? WE WERE UNDER ORDERS TO LAY LOW!
AM I NOT KINGDOK?! I WILL DISCIPLINE MY TROOPS THE WAY I SEE FIT!!
TAKE THIS!

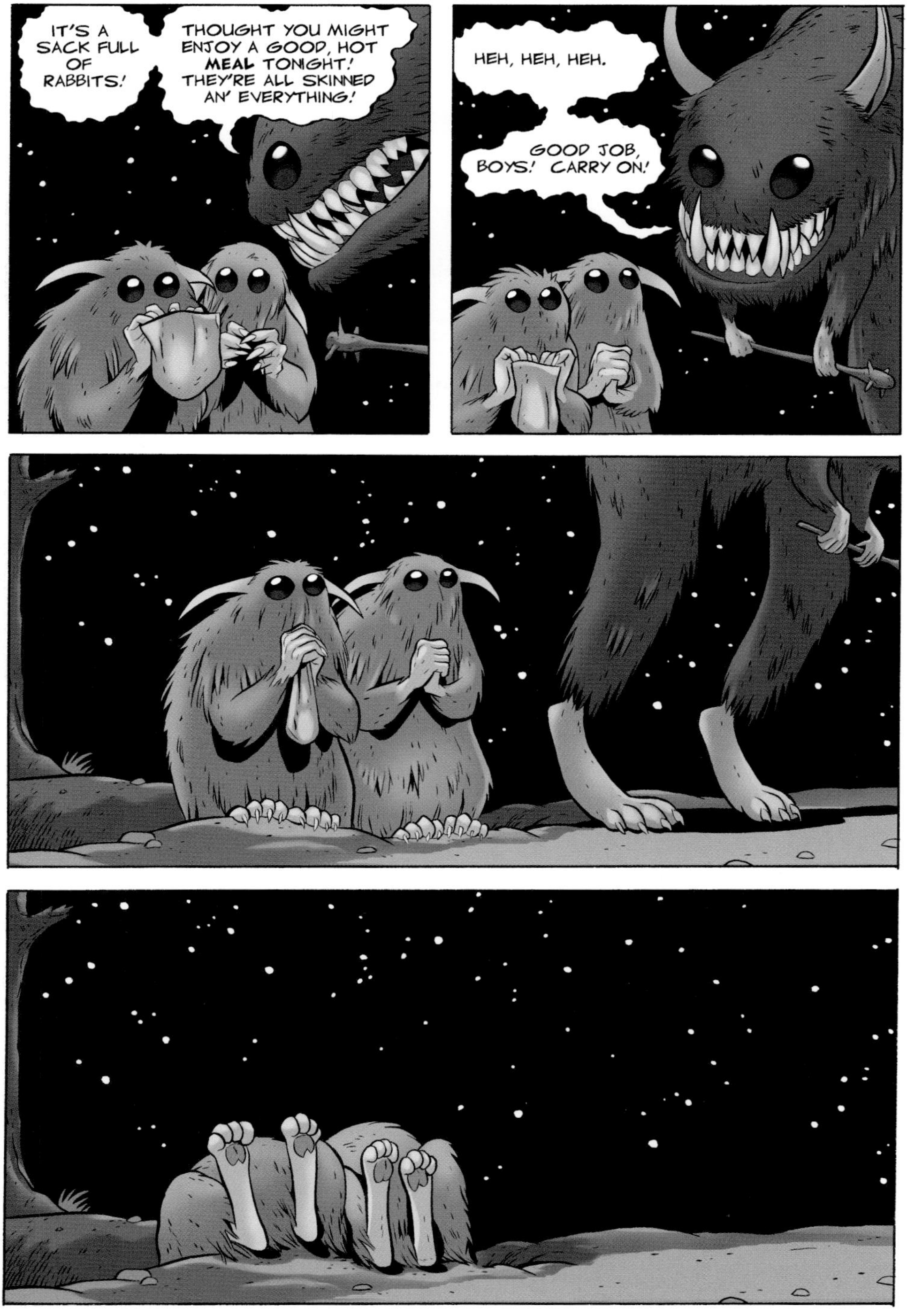
IT'S A SACK FULL OF RABBITS!
THOUGHT YOU MIGHT ENJOY A GOOD, HOT MEAL TONIGHT! THEY'RE ALL SKINNED AN' EVERYTHING!
HEH, HEH, HEH.
GOOD JOB, BOYS! CARRY ON!

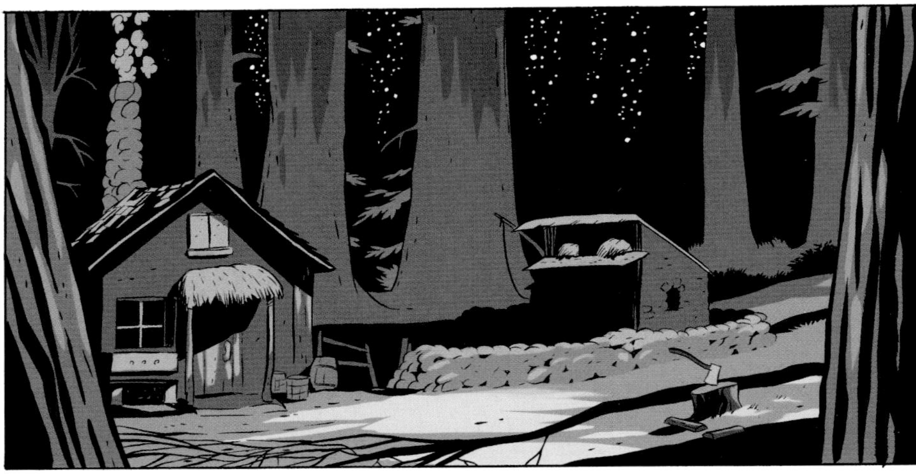

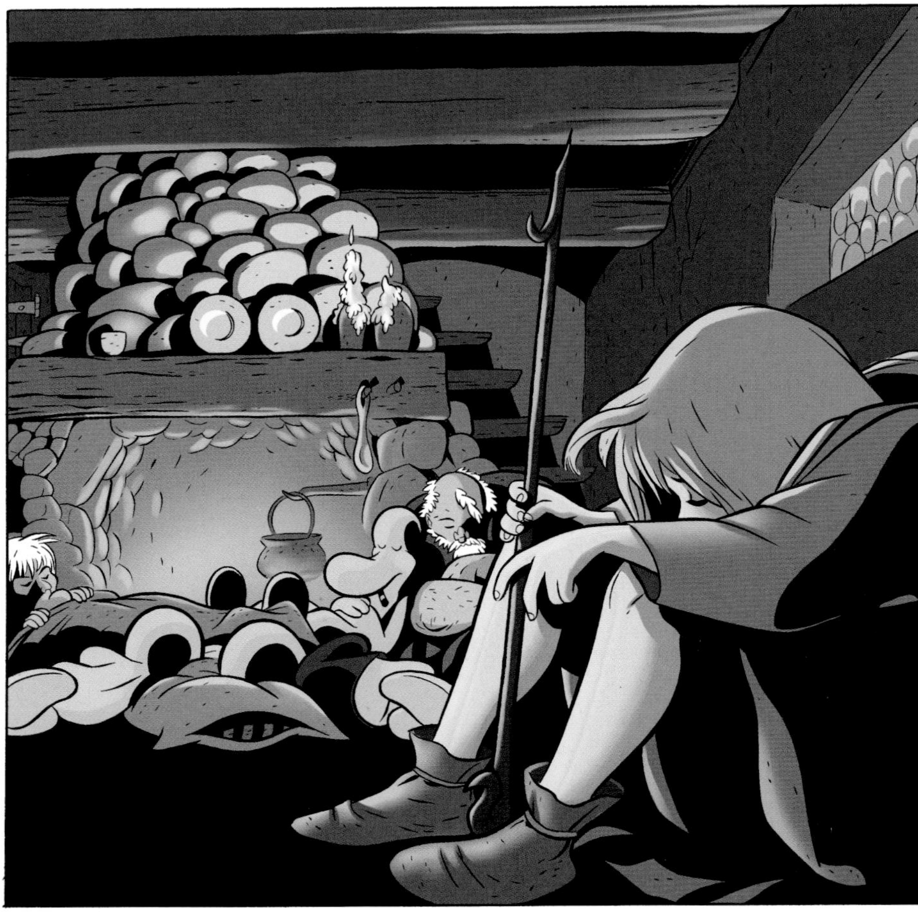

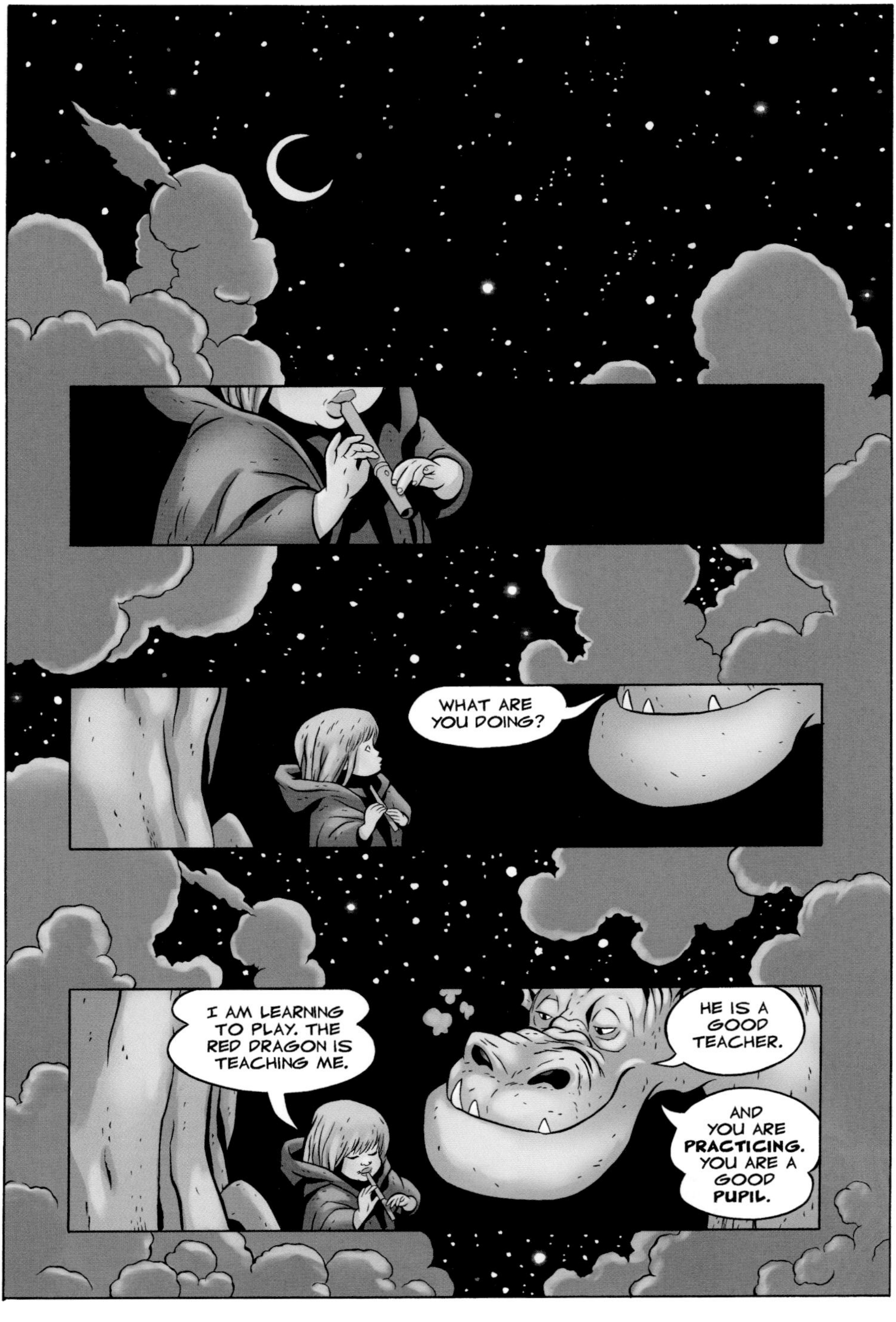
WHAT ARE YOU DOING?
I AM LEARNING TO PLAY. THE RED DRAGON IS TEACHING ME.
HE IS A GOOD TEACHER.
AND YOU ARE PRACTICING. YOU ARE A GOOD PUPIL.

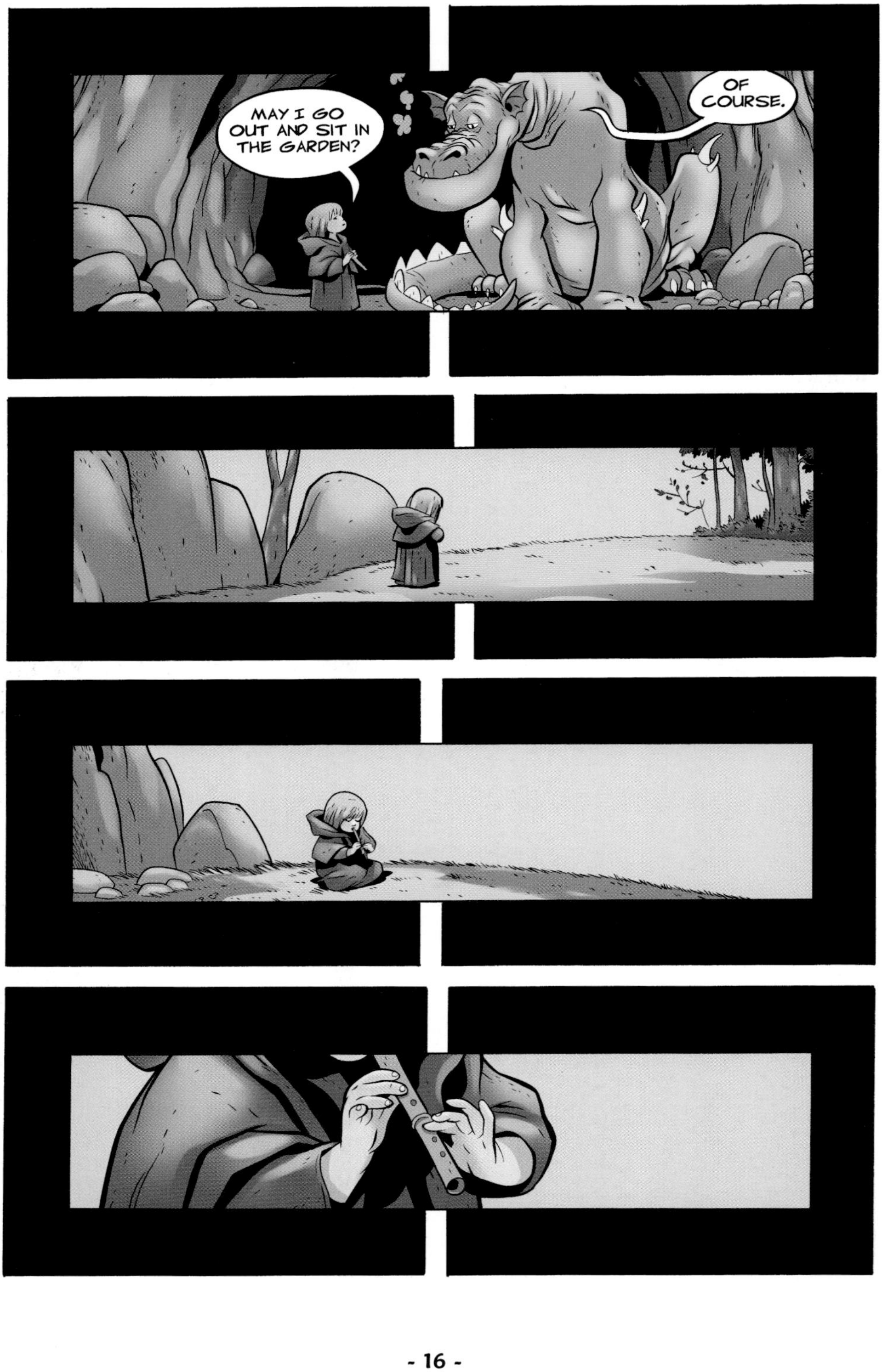
MAY I GO OUT AND SIT IN THE GARDEN?
OF COURSE.

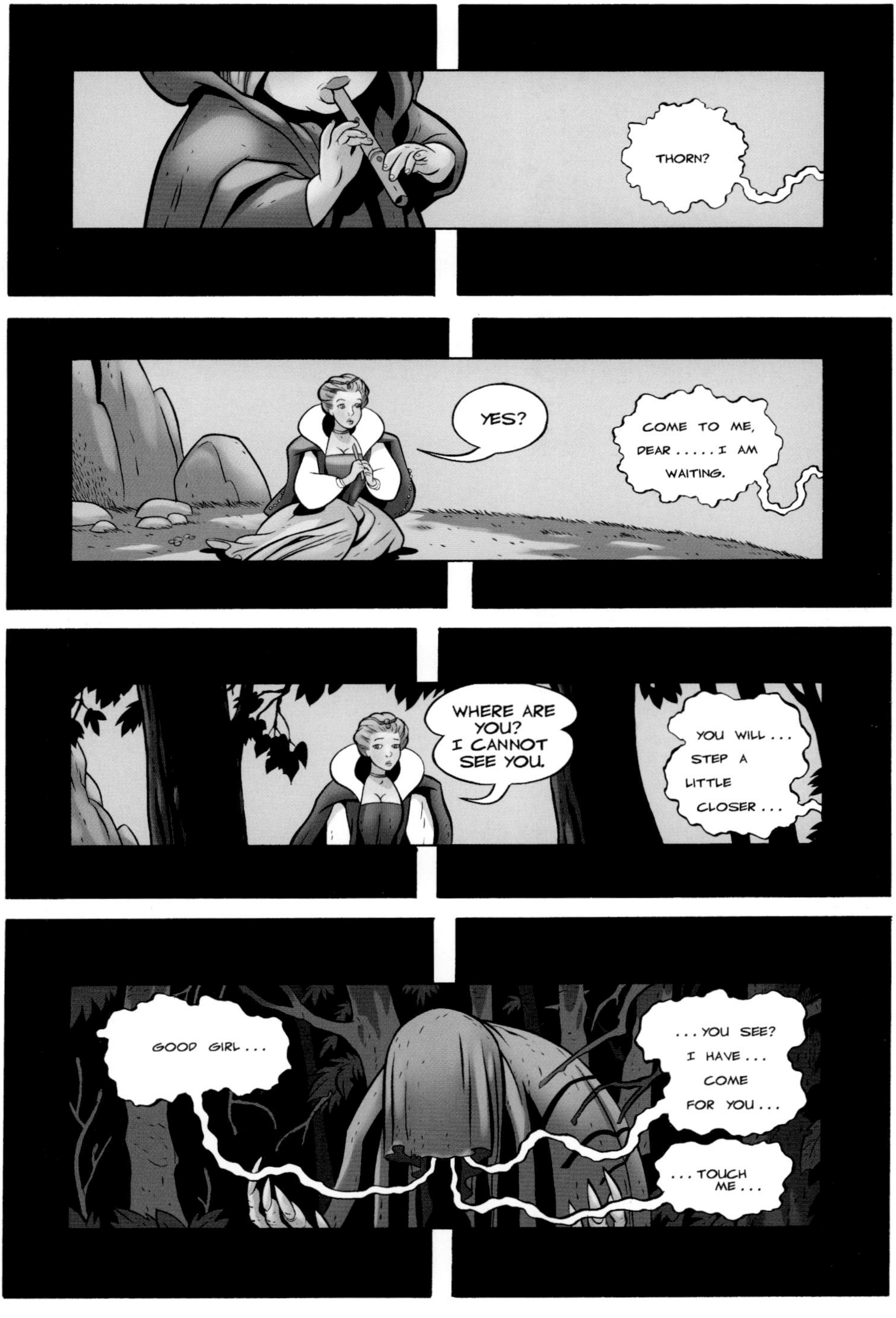
THORN?
YES?
COME TO ME, DEAR . . . . . I AM WAITING.
WHERE ARE YOU? I CANNOT SEE YOU.
YOU WILL . . . STEP A LITTLE CLOSER . . .
GOOD GIRL . . .
. . . YOU SEE? I HAVE . . . COME FOR YOU . . .
. . . TOUCH ME . . .

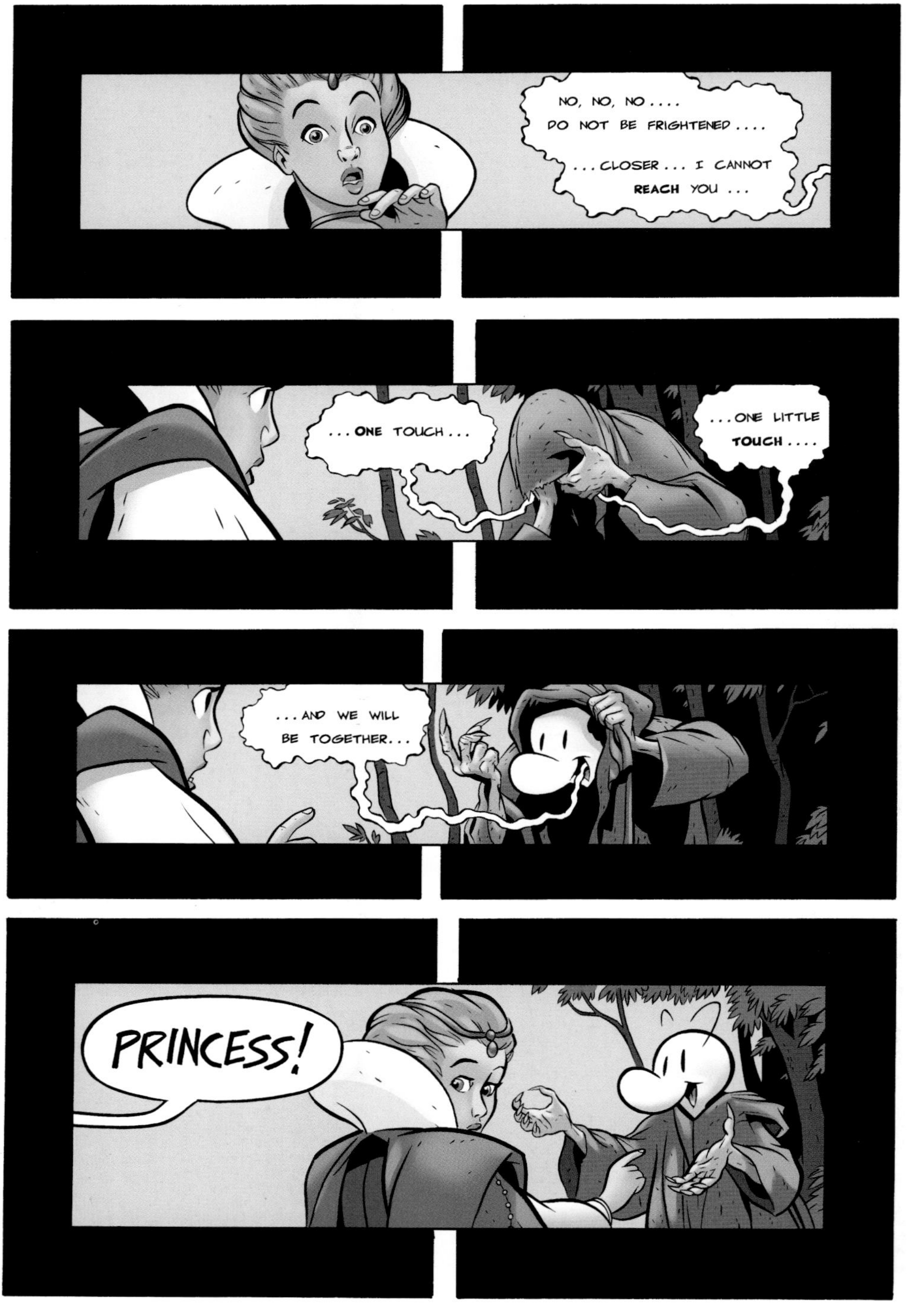
NO, NO, NO....
DO NOT BE FRIGHTENED....
...CLOSER... I CANNOT REACH YOU...
...ONE TOUCH...
...ONE LITTLE TOUCH....
...AND WE WILL BE TOGETHER...
PRINCESS!

WATCH DUTY

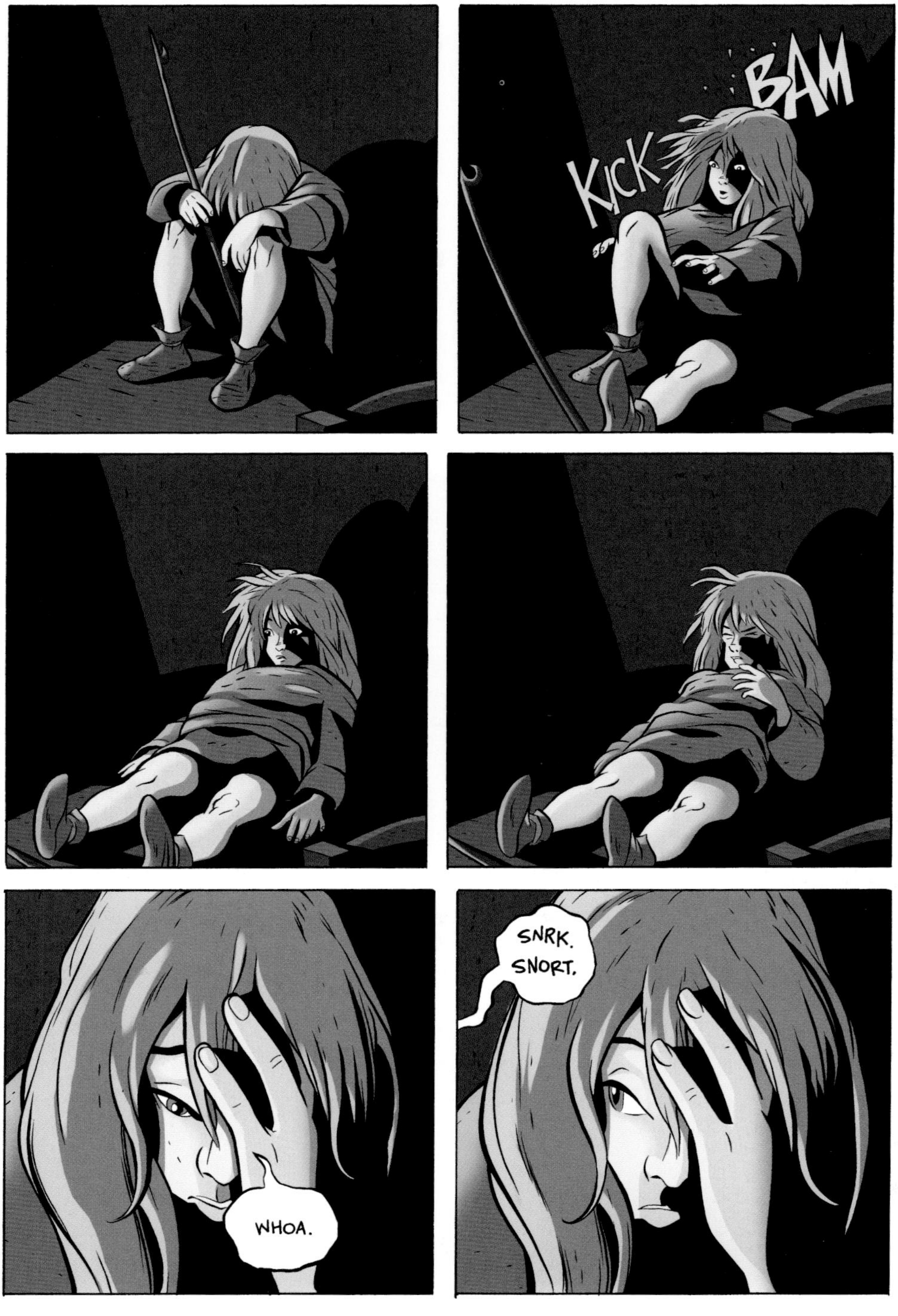
KICK
BAM
SNRK. SNORT.
WHOA.

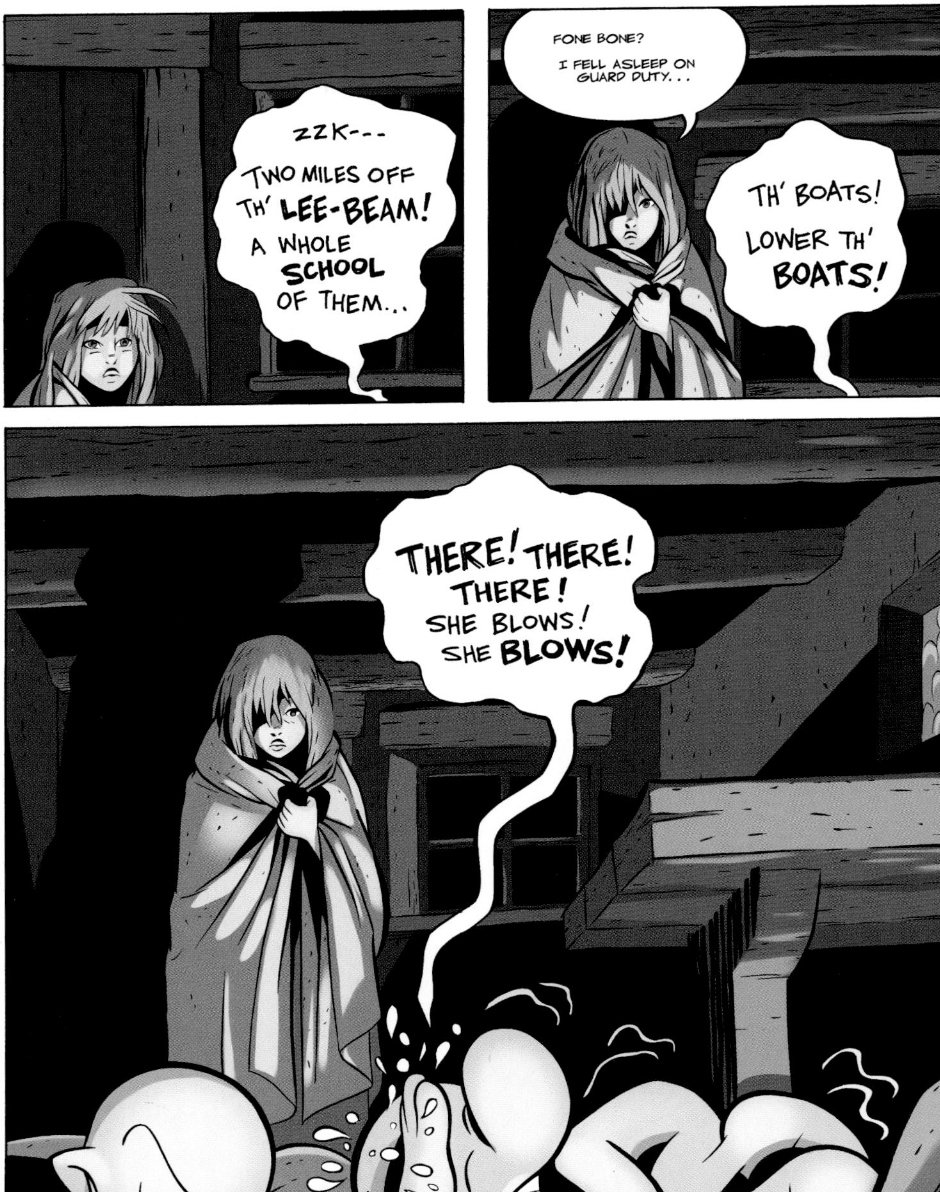
ZZK---
TWO MILES OFF TH' LEE-BEAM! A WHOLE SCHOOL OF THEM...
FONE BONE? I FELL ASLEEP ON GUARD DUTY...
TH' BOATS! LOWER TH' BOATS!
THERE! THERE! THERE! SHE BLOWS! SHE BLOWS!

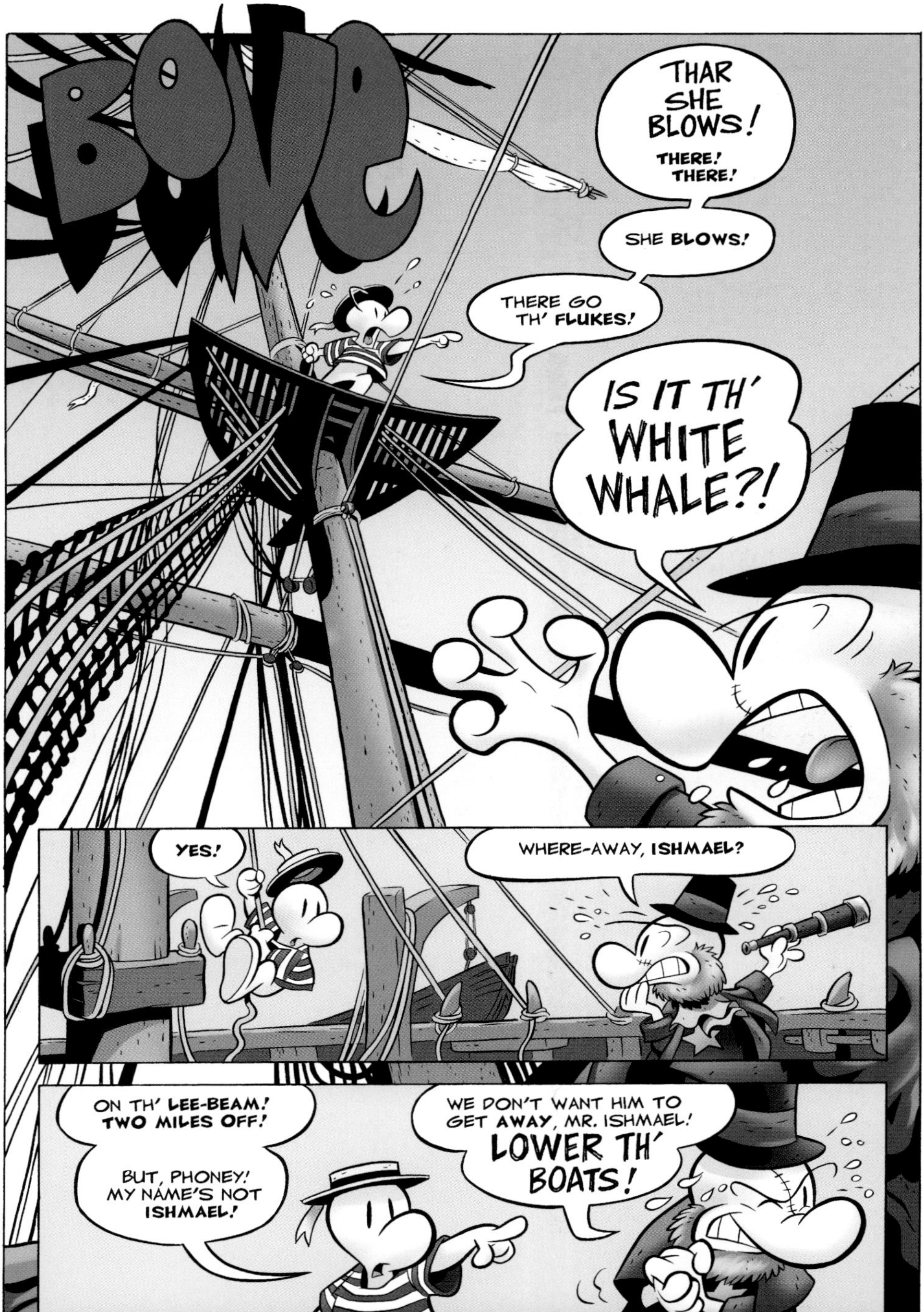
BONE
THAR SHE BLOWS!
THERE! THERE!
SHE BLOWS!
THERE GO TH' FLUKES!
IS IT TH' WHITE WHALE?!
YES!
WHERE-AWAY, ISHMAEL?
ON TH' LEE-BEAM! TWO MILES OFF!
BUT, PHONEY! MY NAME'S NOT ISHMAEL!
WE DON'T WANT HIM TO GET AWAY, MR. ISHMAEL!
LOWER TH' BOATS!

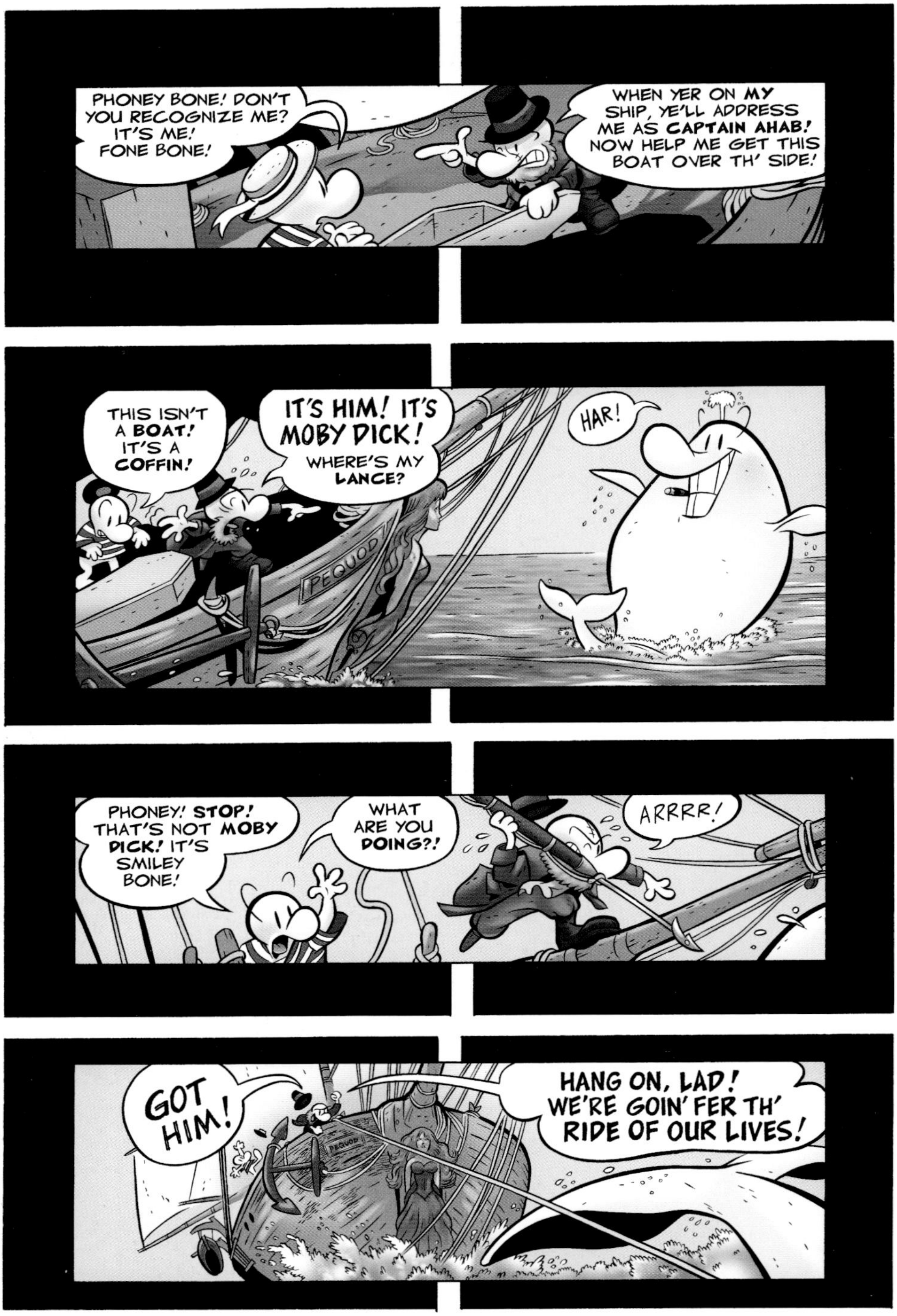
PHONEY BONE! DON'T YOU RECOGNIZE ME? IT'S ME! FONE BONE!
WHEN YER ON MY SHIP, YE'LL ADDRESS ME AS CAPTAIN AHAB! NOW HELP ME GET THIS BOAT OVER TH' SIDE!
THIS ISN'T A BOAT! IT'S A COFFIN!
IT'S HIM! IT'S MOBY DICK! WHERE'S MY LANCE?
HAR!
PEQUOD
PHONEY! STOP! THAT'S NOT MOBY DICK! IT'S SMILEY BONE!
WHAT ARE YOU DOING?!
ARRRR!
GOT HIM!
HANG ON, LAD! WE'RE GOIN' FER TH' RIDE OF OUR LIVES!

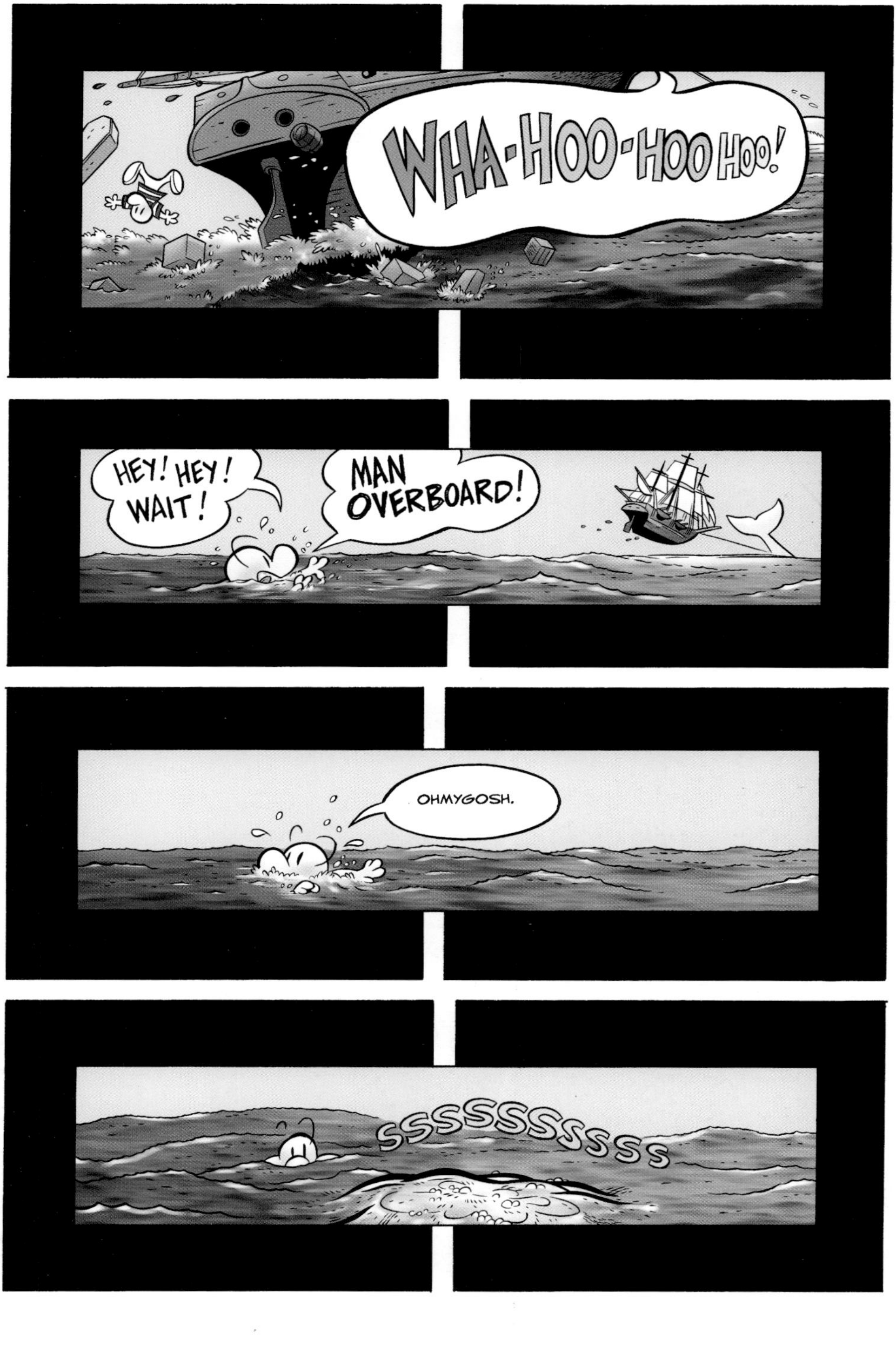
WHA-HOO-HOO HOO!
HEY! HEY! WAIT!
MAN OVERBOARD!
OHMYGOSH.
SSSSSSSSSSS

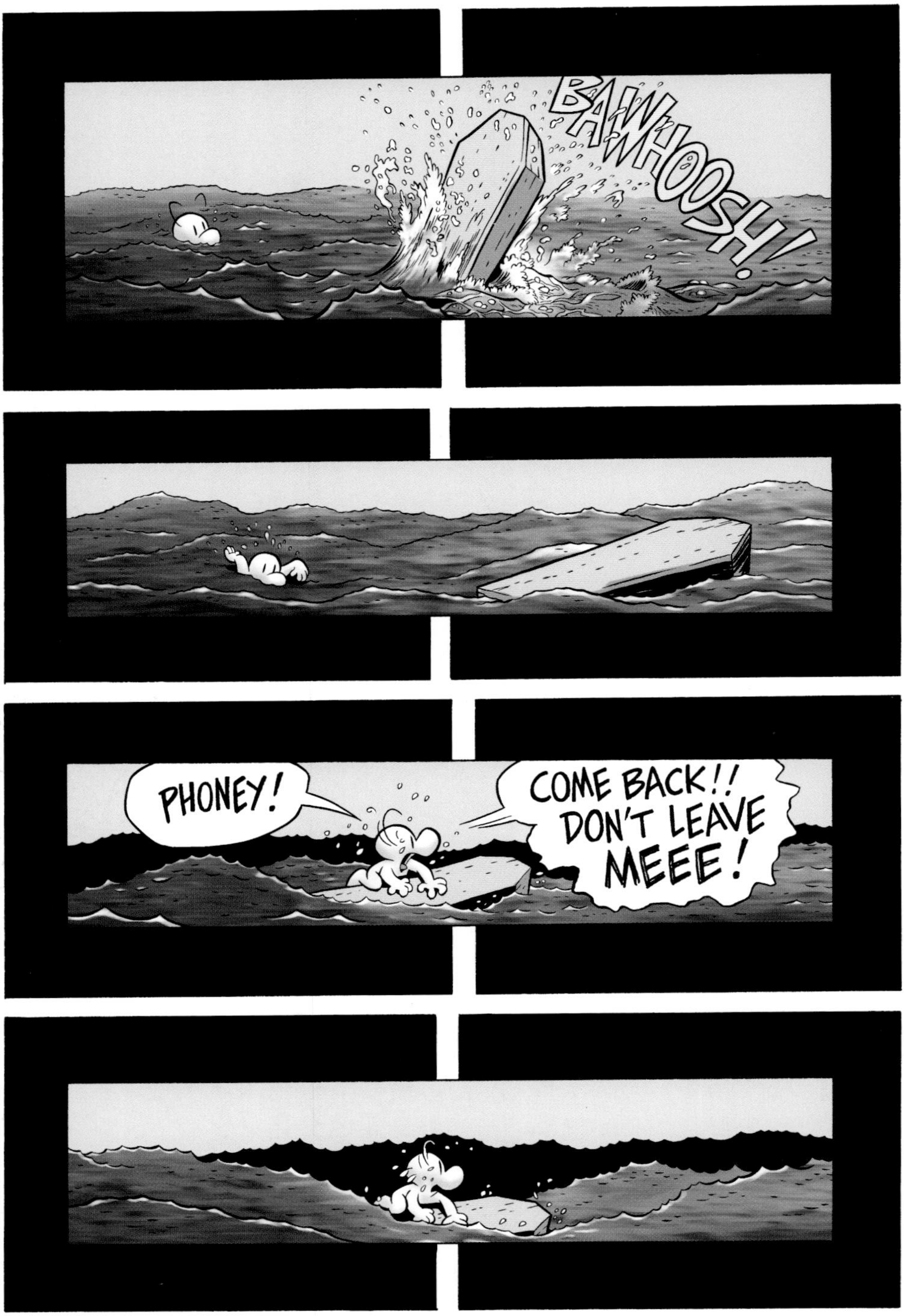
BAWHOOSH!
PHONEY!
COME BACK!! DON'T LEAVE MEEE!

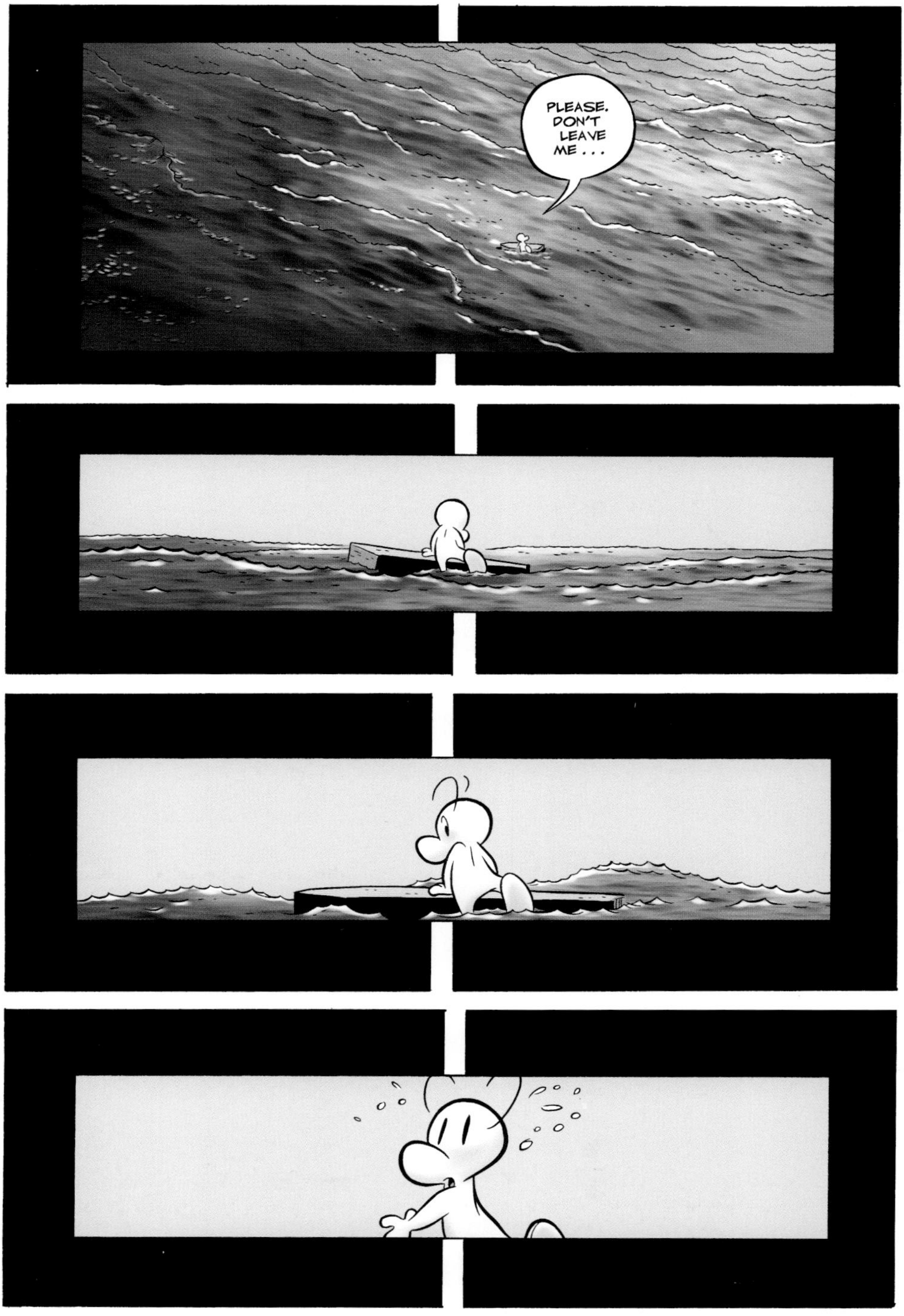
PLEASE. DON'T LEAVE ME . . .

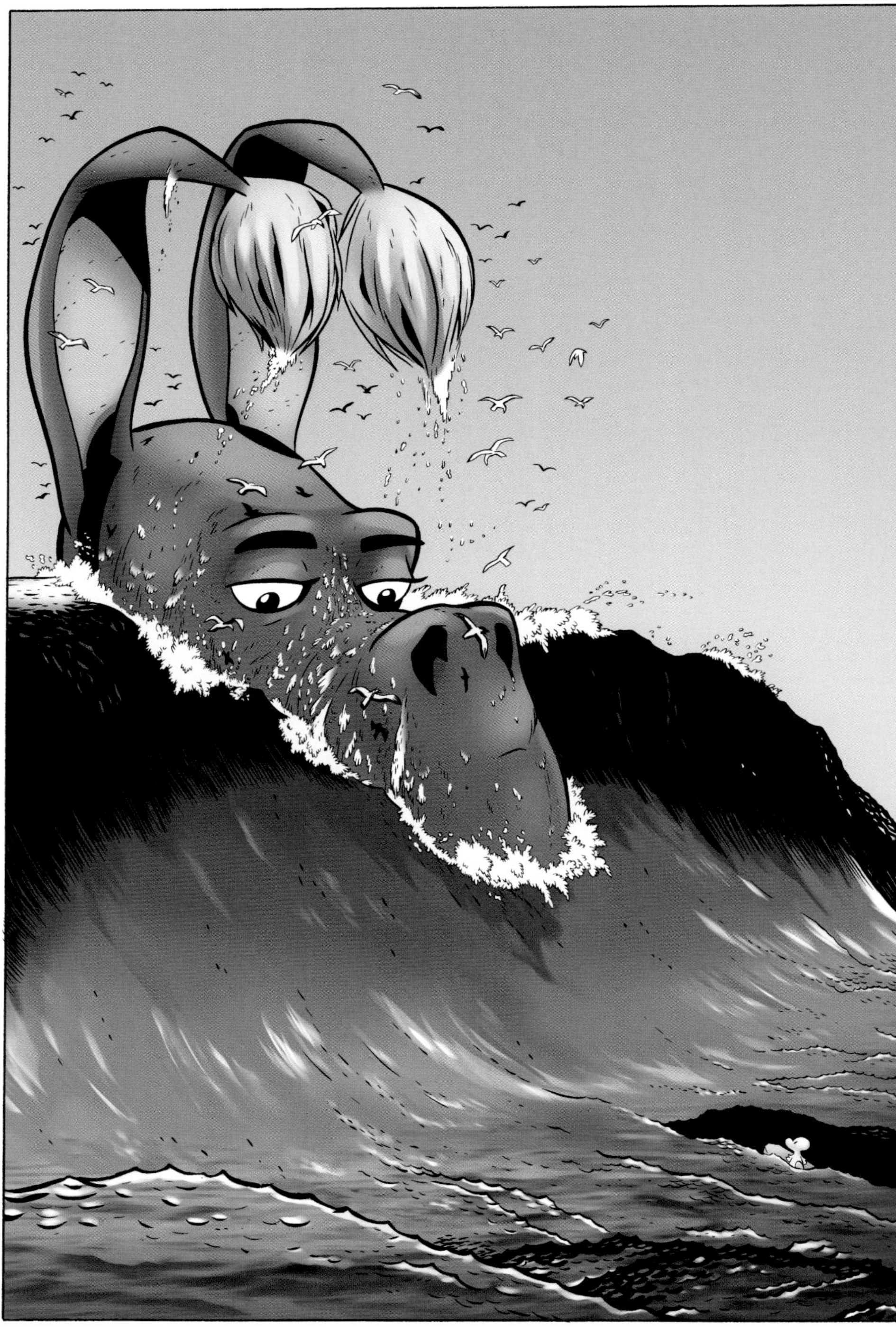

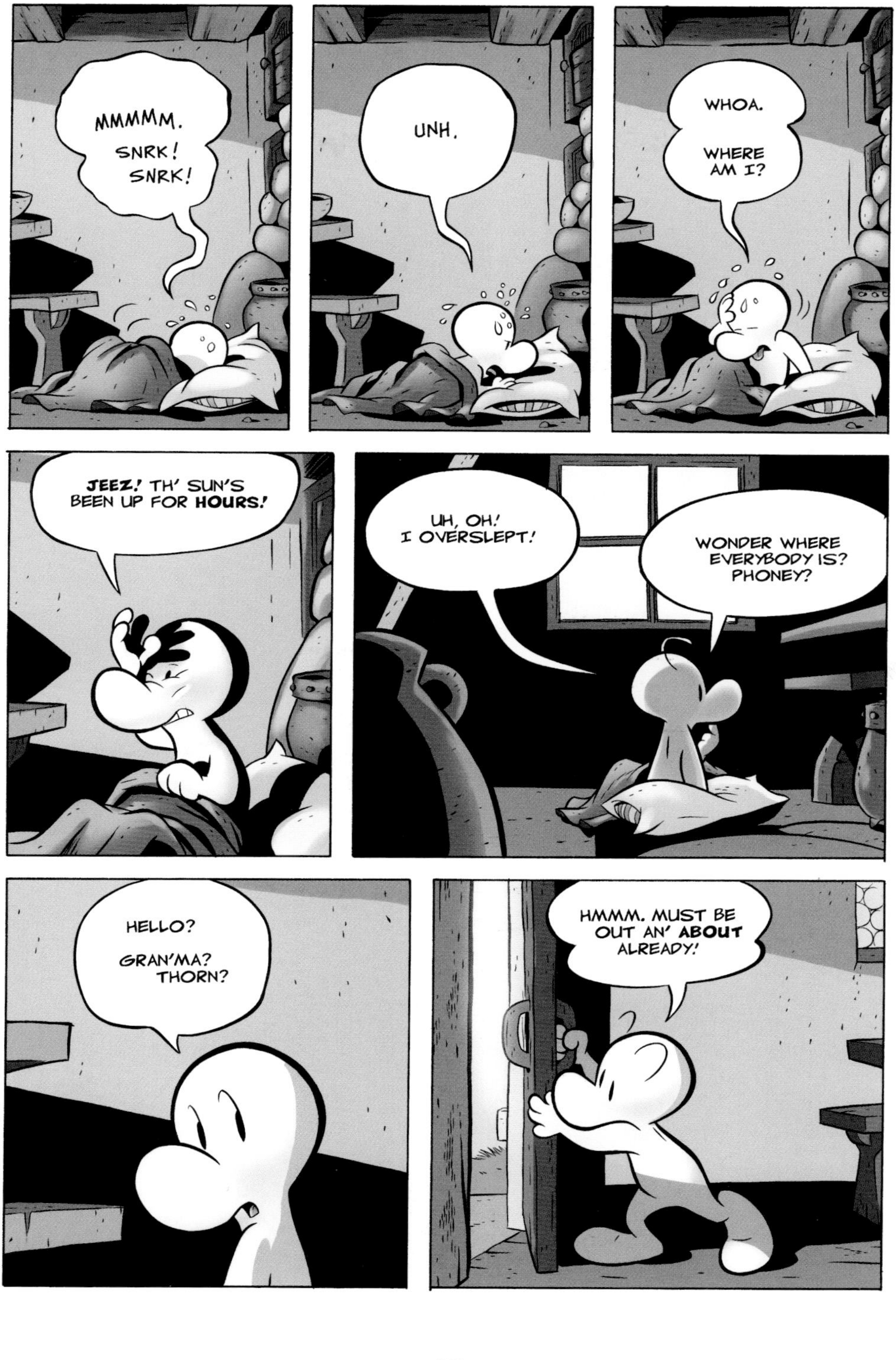
MMMMM.
SNRK! SNRK!
UNH.
WHOA.
WHERE AM I?
JEEZ! TH' SUN'S BEEN UP FOR HOURS!
UH, OH! I OVERSLEPT!
WONDER WHERE EVERYBODY IS? PHONEY?
HELLO?
GRAN'MA? THORN?
HMMM. MUST BE OUT AN' ABOUT ALREADY!

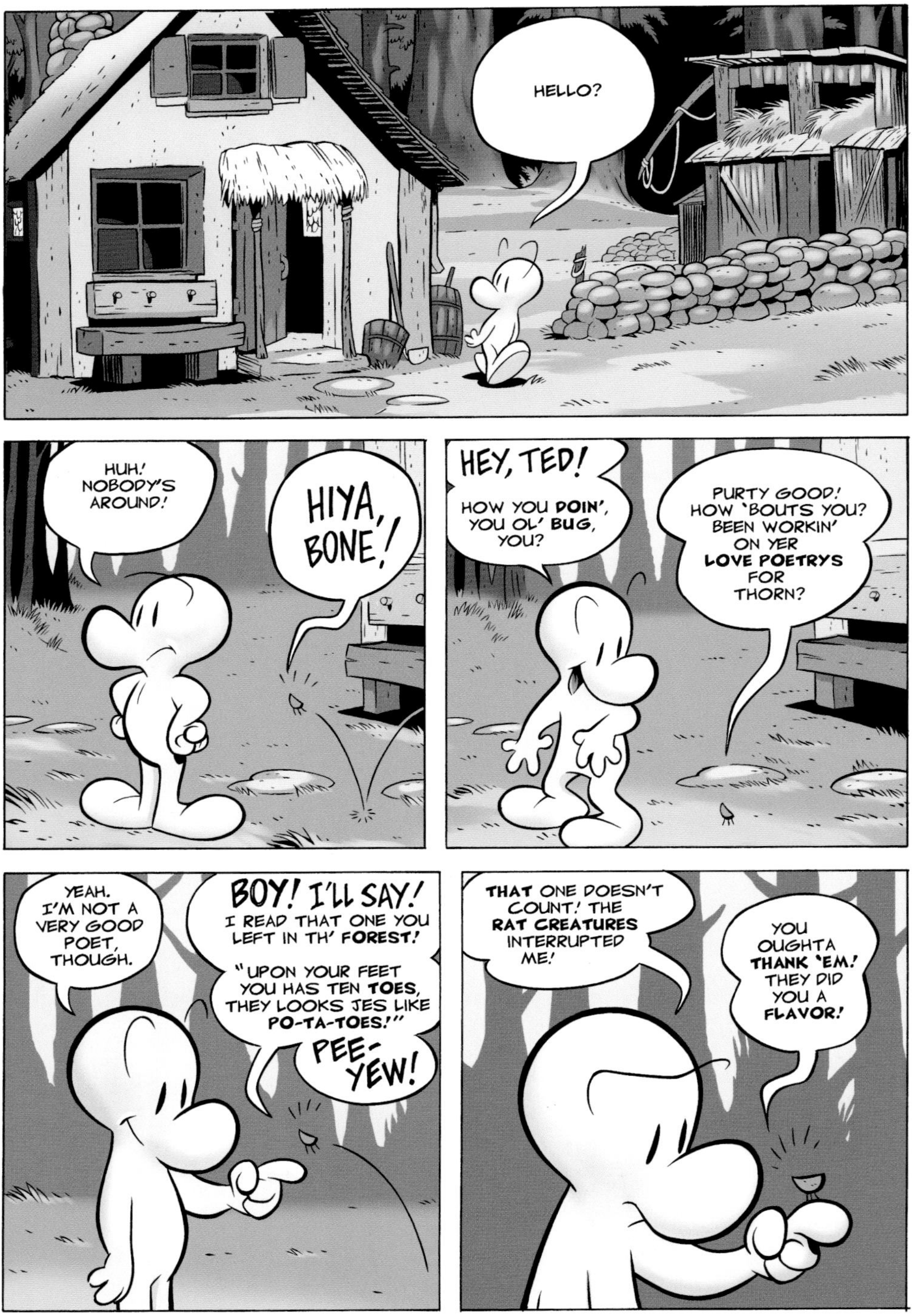
HELLO?
HUH! NOBODY'S AROUND!
HIYA, BONE!
HEY, TED!
HOW YOU DOIN', YOU OL' BUG, YOU?
PURTY GOOD! HOW 'BOUTS YOU? BEEN WORKIN' ON YER LOVE POETRYS FOR THORN?
YEAH. I'M NOT A VERY GOOD POET, THOUGH.
BOY! I'LL SAY! I READ THAT ONE YOU LEFT IN TH' FOREST!
"UPON YOUR FEET YOU HAS TEN TOES, THEY LOOKS JES LIKE PO-TA-TOES!"
PEE-YEW!
THAT ONE DOESN'T COUNT! THE RAT CREATURES INTERRUPTED ME!
YOU OUGHTA THANK 'EM! THEY DID YOU A FLAVOR!

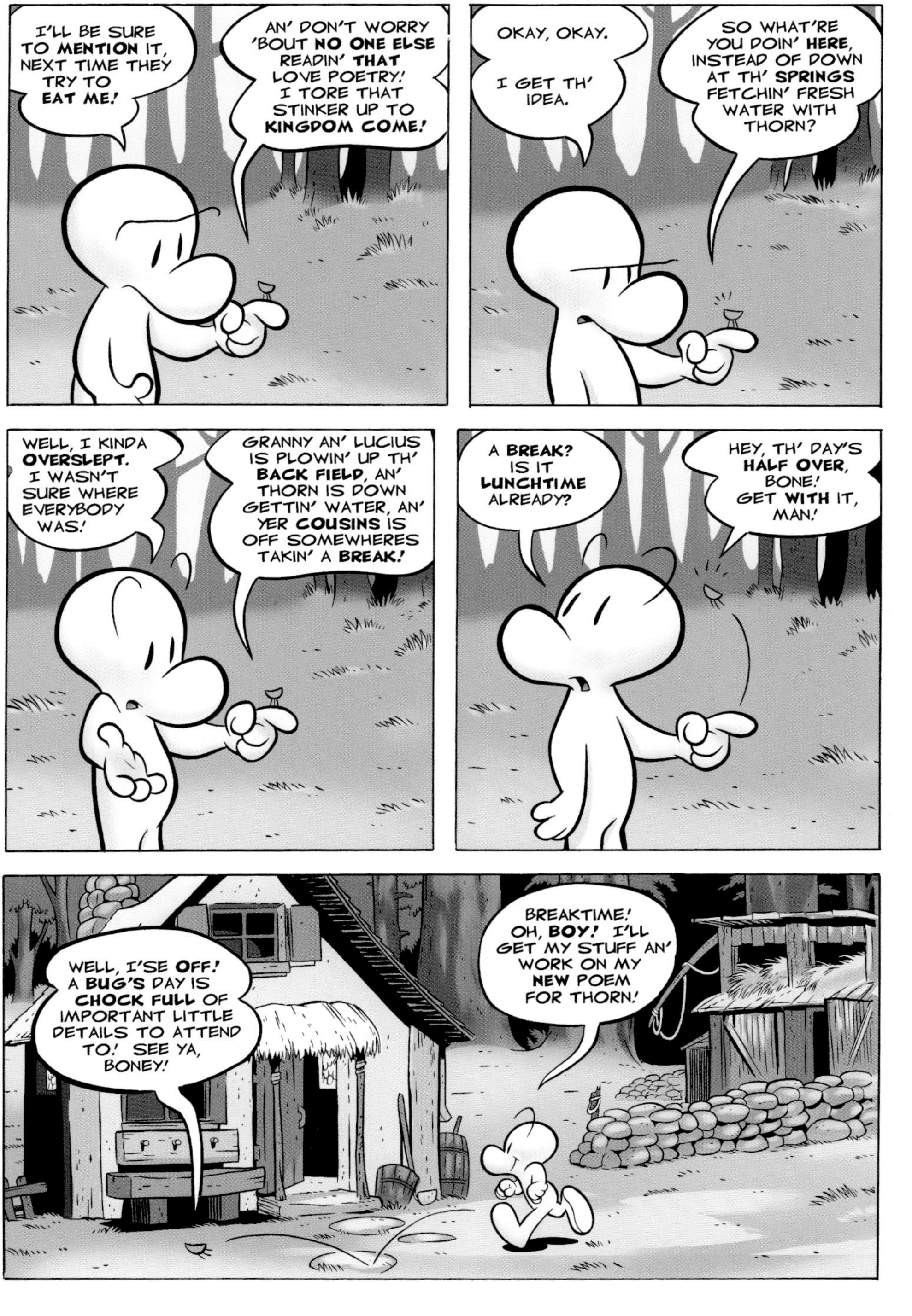
I'LL BE SURE TO MENTION IT, NEXT TIME THEY TRY TO EAT ME!
AN' DON'T WORRY 'BOUT NO ONE ELSE READIN' THAT LOVE POETRY! I TORE THAT STINKER UP TO KINGDOM COME!
OKAY, OKAY.
I GET TH' IDEA.
SO WHAT'RE YOU DOIN' HERE, INSTEAD OF DOWN AT TH' SPRINGS FETCHIN' FRESH WATER WITH THORN?
WELL, I KINDA OVERSLEPT. I WASN'T SURE WHERE EVERYBODY WAS!
GRANNY AN' LUCIUS IS PLOWIN' UP TH' BACK FIELD, AN' THORN IS DOWN GETTIN' WATER, AN' YER COUSINS IS OFF SOMEWHERES TAKIN' A BREAK!
A BREAK? IS IT LUNCHTIME ALREADY?
HEY, TH' DAY'S HALF OVER, BONE! GET WITH IT, MAN!
WELL, I'SE OFF! A BUG'S DAY IS CHOCK FULL OF IMPORTANT LITTLE DETAILS TO ATTEND TO! SEE YA, BONEY!
BREAKTIME! OH, BOY! I'LL GET MY STUFF AN' WORK ON MY NEW POEM FOR THORN!

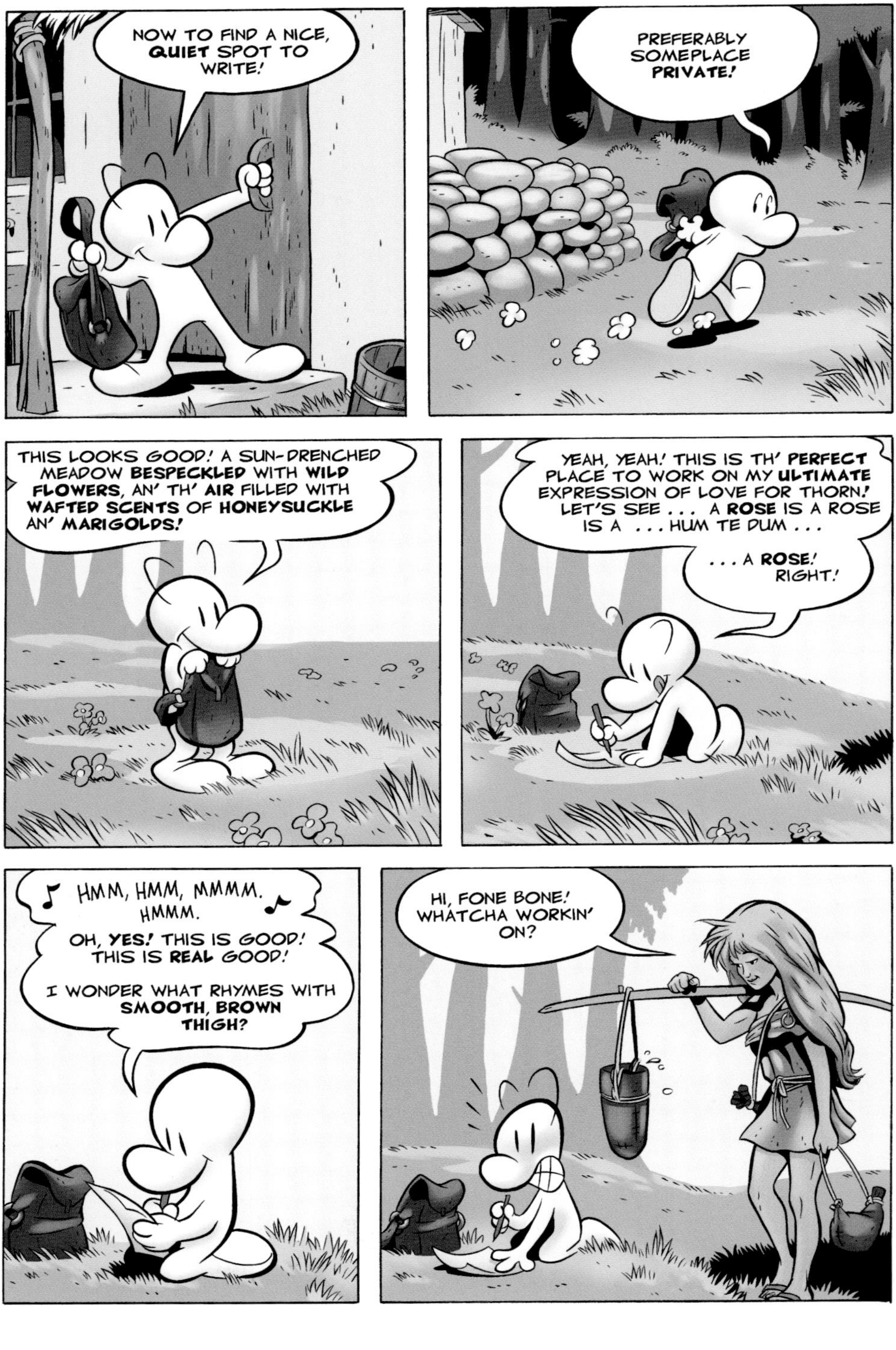
NOW TO FIND A NICE, QUIET SPOT TO WRITE!
PREFERABLY SOMEPLACE PRIVATE!
THIS LOOKS GOOD! A SUN-DRENCHED MEADOW BESPECKLED WITH WILD FLOWERS, AN' TH' AIR FILLED WITH WAFTED SCENTS OF HONEYSUCKLE AN' MARIGOLDS!
YEAH, YEAH! THIS IS TH' PERFECT PLACE TO WORK ON MY ULTIMATE EXPRESSION OF LOVE FOR THORN! LET'S SEE . . . A ROSE IS A ROSE IS A . . . HUM TE DUM . . .
. . . A ROSE! RIGHT!
HMM, HMM, MMMM. HMMM.
OH, YES! THIS IS GOOD! THIS IS REAL GOOD!
I WONDER WHAT RHYMES WITH SMOOTH, BROWN THIGH?
HI, FONE BONE! WHATCHA WORKIN' ON?

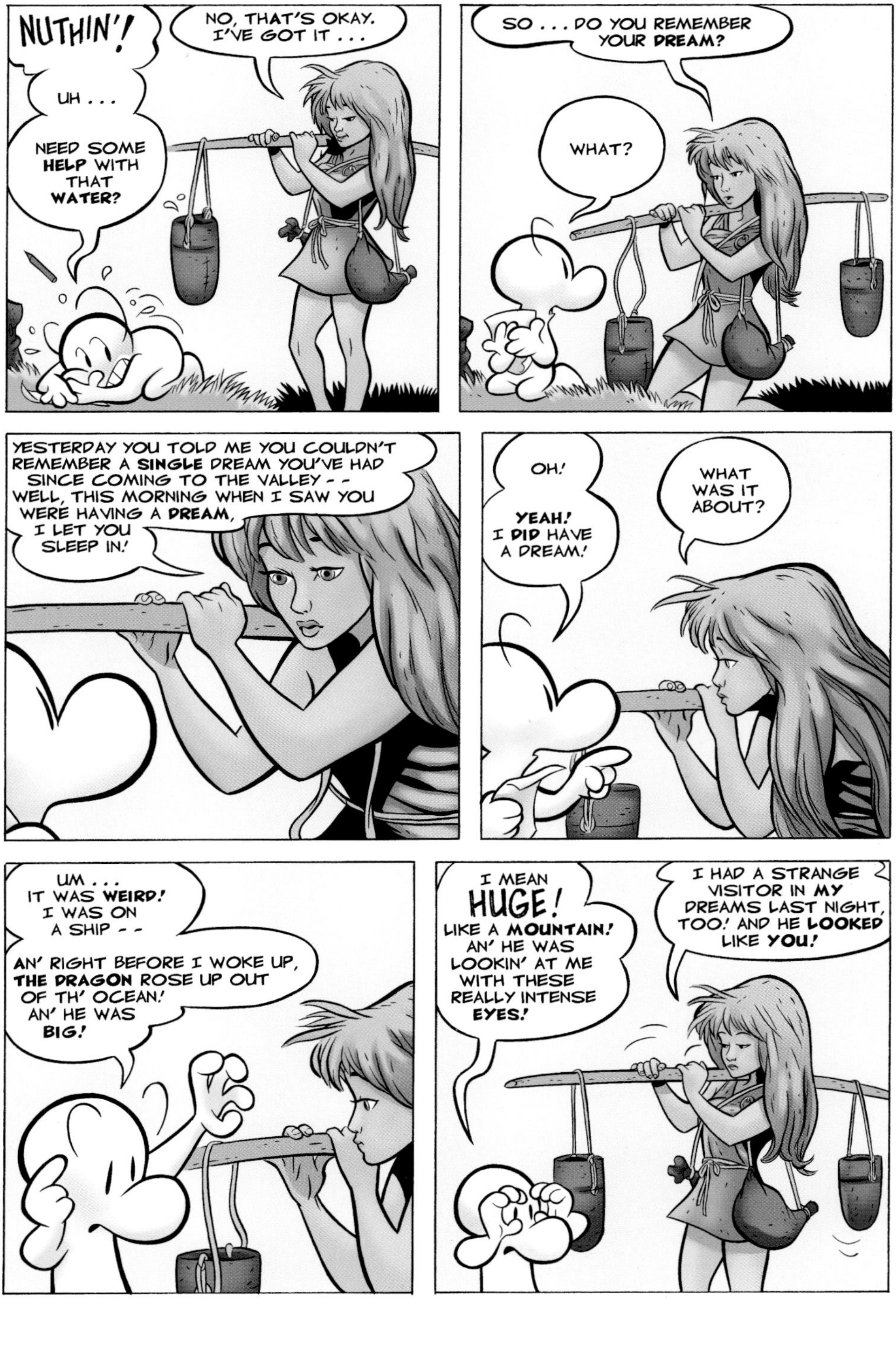
NUTHIN'!
UH . . .
NEED SOME HELP WITH THAT WATER?
NO, THAT'S OKAY. I'VE GOT IT . . .
SO . . . DO YOU REMEMBER YOUR DREAM?
WHAT?
YESTERDAY YOU TOLD ME YOU COULDN'T REMEMBER A SINGLE DREAM YOU'VE HAD SINCE COMING TO THE VALLEY - - WELL, THIS MORNING WHEN I SAW YOU WERE HAVING A DREAM,
I LET YOU SLEEP IN!
OH!
YEAH! I DID HAVE A DREAM!
WHAT WAS IT ABOUT?
UM . . . IT WAS WEIRD! I WAS ON A SHIP - -
AN' RIGHT BEFORE I WOKE UP, THE DRAGON ROSE UP OUT OF TH' OCEAN! AN' HE WAS BIG!
I MEAN HUGE! LIKE A MOUNTAIN! AN' HE WAS LOOKIN' AT ME WITH THESE REALLY INTENSE EYES!
I HAD A STRANGE VISITOR IN MY DREAMS LAST NIGHT, TOO! AN' HE LOOKED LIKE YOU!

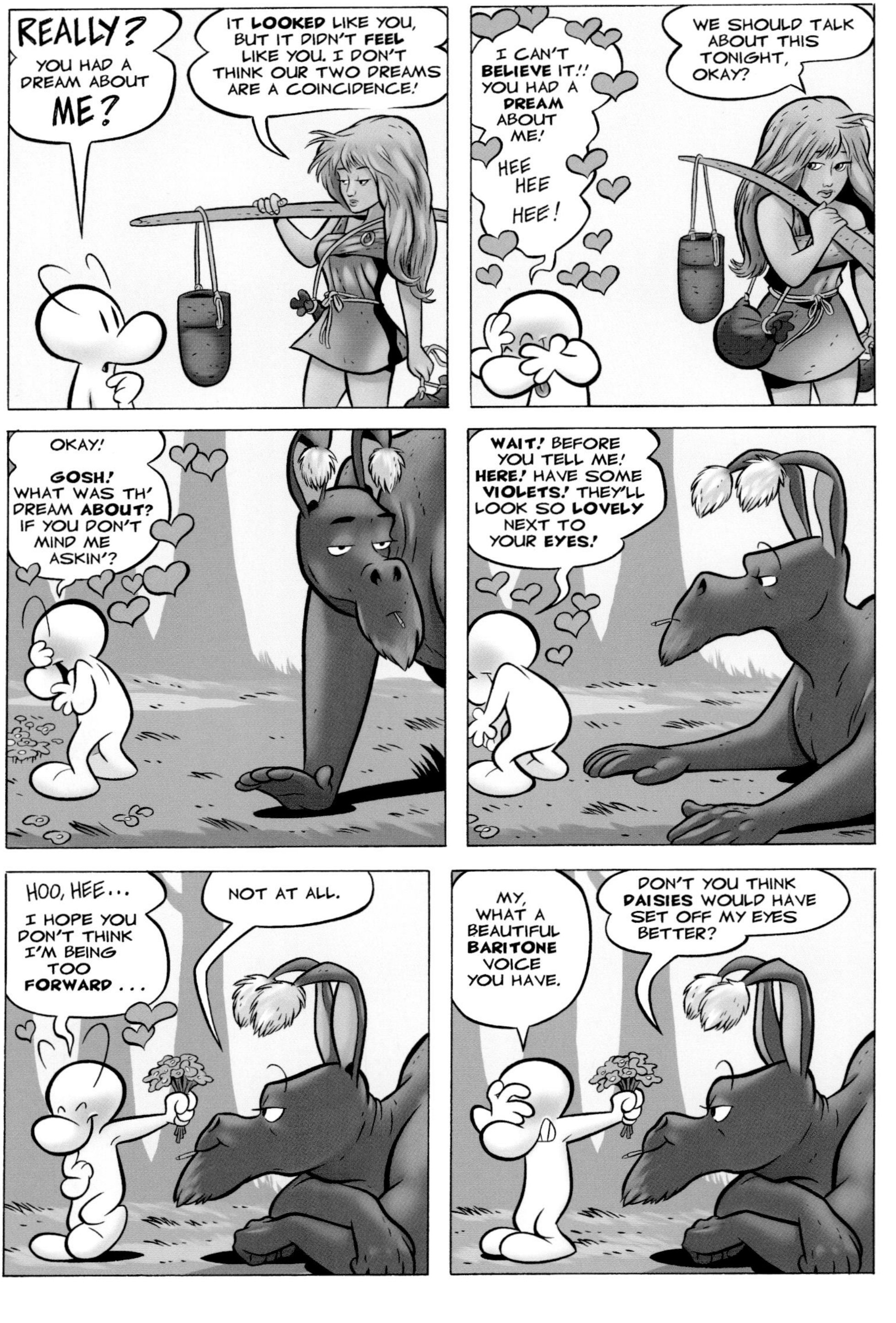
REALLY? YOU HAD A DREAM ABOUT ME?
IT LOOKED LIKE YOU, BUT IT DIDN'T FEEL LIKE YOU. I DON'T THINK OUR TWO DREAMS ARE A COINCIDENCE!
I CAN'T BELIEVE IT!! YOU HAD A DREAM ABOUT ME! HEE HEE HEE!
WE SHOULD TALK ABOUT THIS TONIGHT, OKAY?
OKAY! GOSH! WHAT WAS TH' DREAM ABOUT? IF YOU DON'T MIND ME ASKIN'?
WAIT! BEFORE YOU TELL ME! HERE! HAVE SOME VIOLETS! THEY'LL LOOK SO LOVELY NEXT TO YOUR EYES!
HOO, HEE... I HOPE YOU DON'T THINK I'M BEING TOO FORWARD...
NOT AT ALL.
MY, WHAT A BEAUTIFUL BARITONE VOICE YOU HAVE.
DON'T YOU THINK DAISIES WOULD HAVE SET OFF MY EYES BETTER?

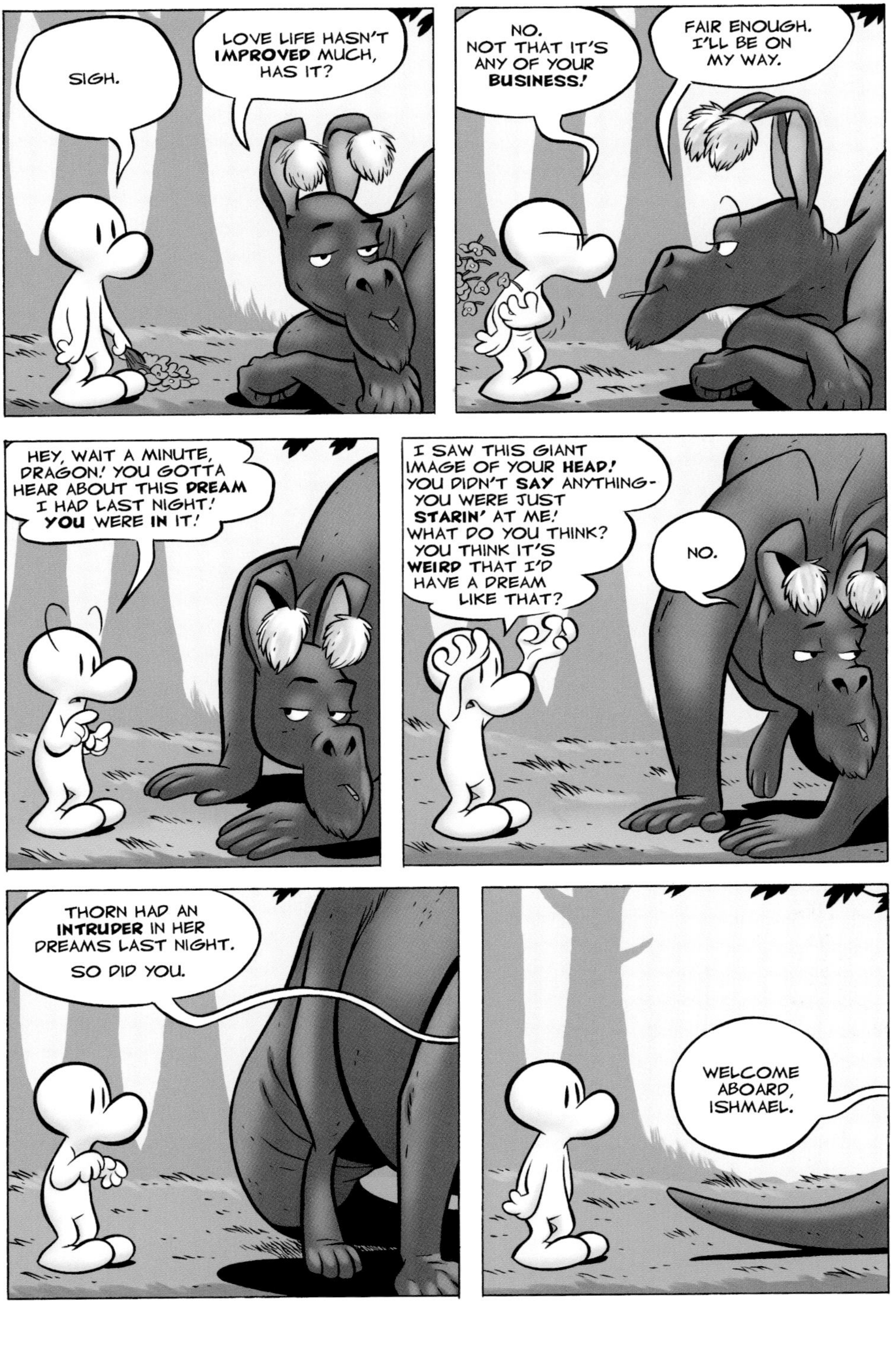
SIGH.
LOVE LIFE HASN'T IMPROVED MUCH, HAS IT?
NO. NOT THAT IT'S ANY OF YOUR BUSINESS!
FAIR ENOUGH. I'LL BE ON MY WAY.
HEY, WAIT A MINUTE, DRAGON! YOU GOTTA HEAR ABOUT THIS DREAM I HAD LAST NIGHT! YOU WERE IN IT!
I SAW THIS GIANT IMAGE OF YOUR HEAD! YOU DIDN'T SAY ANYTHING- YOU WERE JUST STARIN' AT ME! WHAT DO YOU THINK? YOU THINK IT'S WEIRD THAT I'D HAVE A DREAM LIKE THAT?
NO.
THORN HAD AN INTRUDER IN HER DREAMS LAST NIGHT.
SO DID YOU.
WELCOME ABOARD, ISHMAEL.

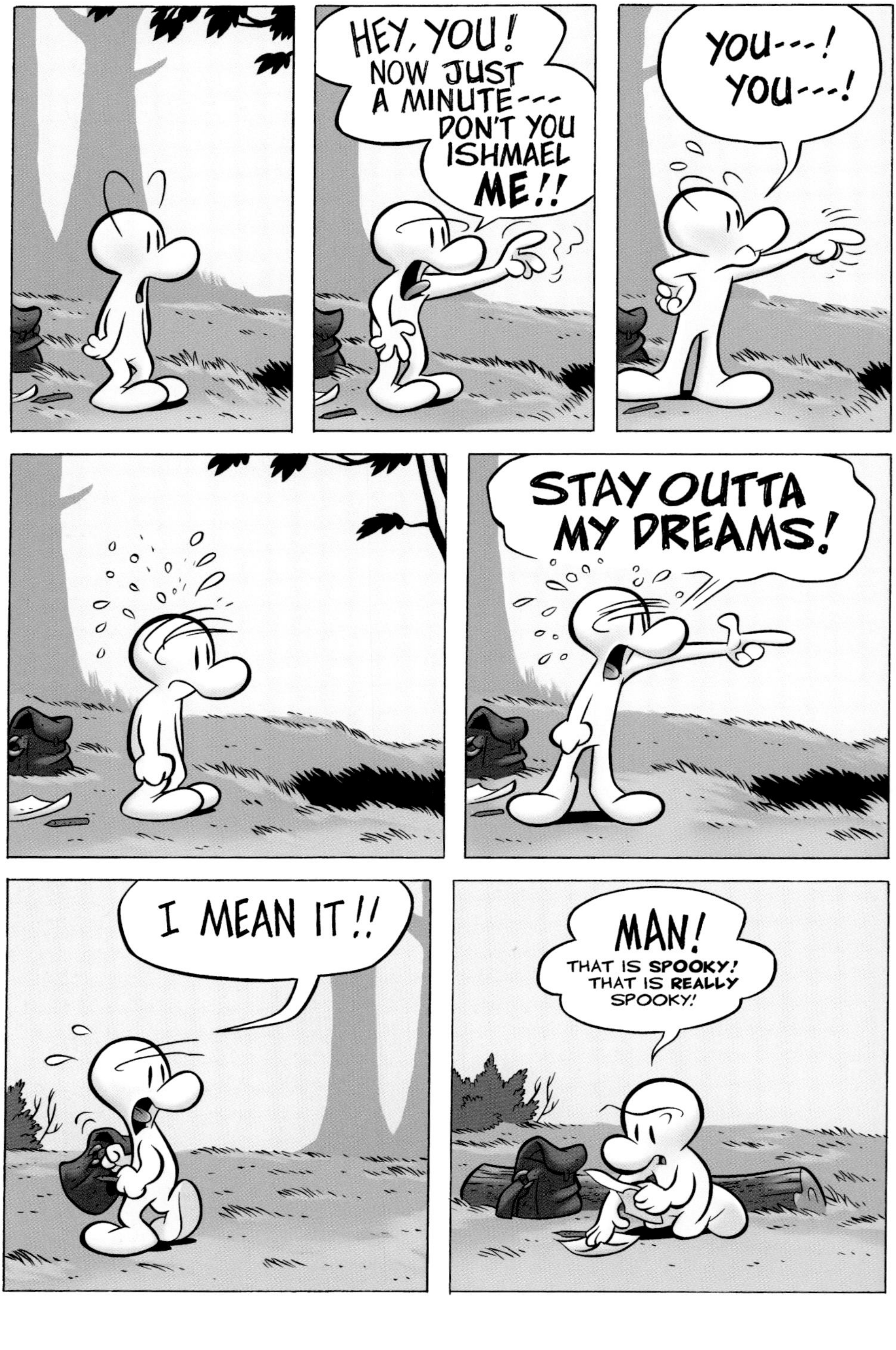
HEY, YOU! NOW JUST A MINUTE--- DON'T YOU ISHMAEL ME!!
YOU---! YOU---!
STAY OUTTA MY DREAMS!
I MEAN IT!!
MAN! THAT IS SPOOKY! THAT IS REALLY SPOOKY!

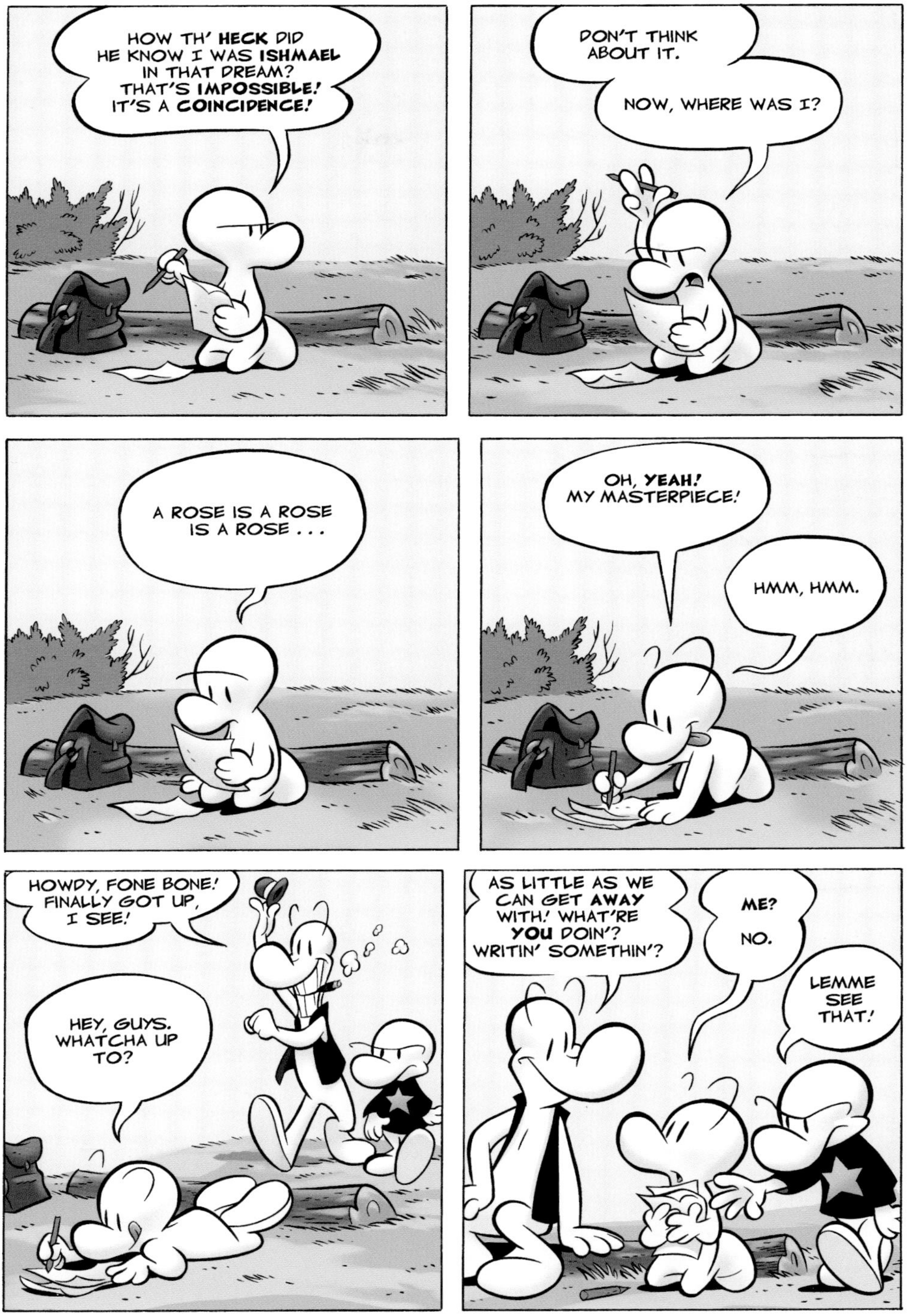
HOW TH' HECK DID HE KNOW I WAS ISHMAEL IN THAT DREAM? THAT'S IMPOSSIBLE! IT'S A COINCIDENCE!
DON'T THINK ABOUT IT.
NOW, WHERE WAS I?
A ROSE IS A ROSE IS A ROSE . . .
OH, YEAH! MY MASTERPIECE!
HMM, HMM.
HOWDY, FONE BONE! FINALLY GOT UP, I SEE!
HEY, GUYS. WHATCHA UP TO?
AS LITTLE AS WE CAN GET AWAY WITH! WHAT'RE YOU DOIN'? WRITIN' SOMETHIN'?
ME?
NO.
LEMME SEE THAT!

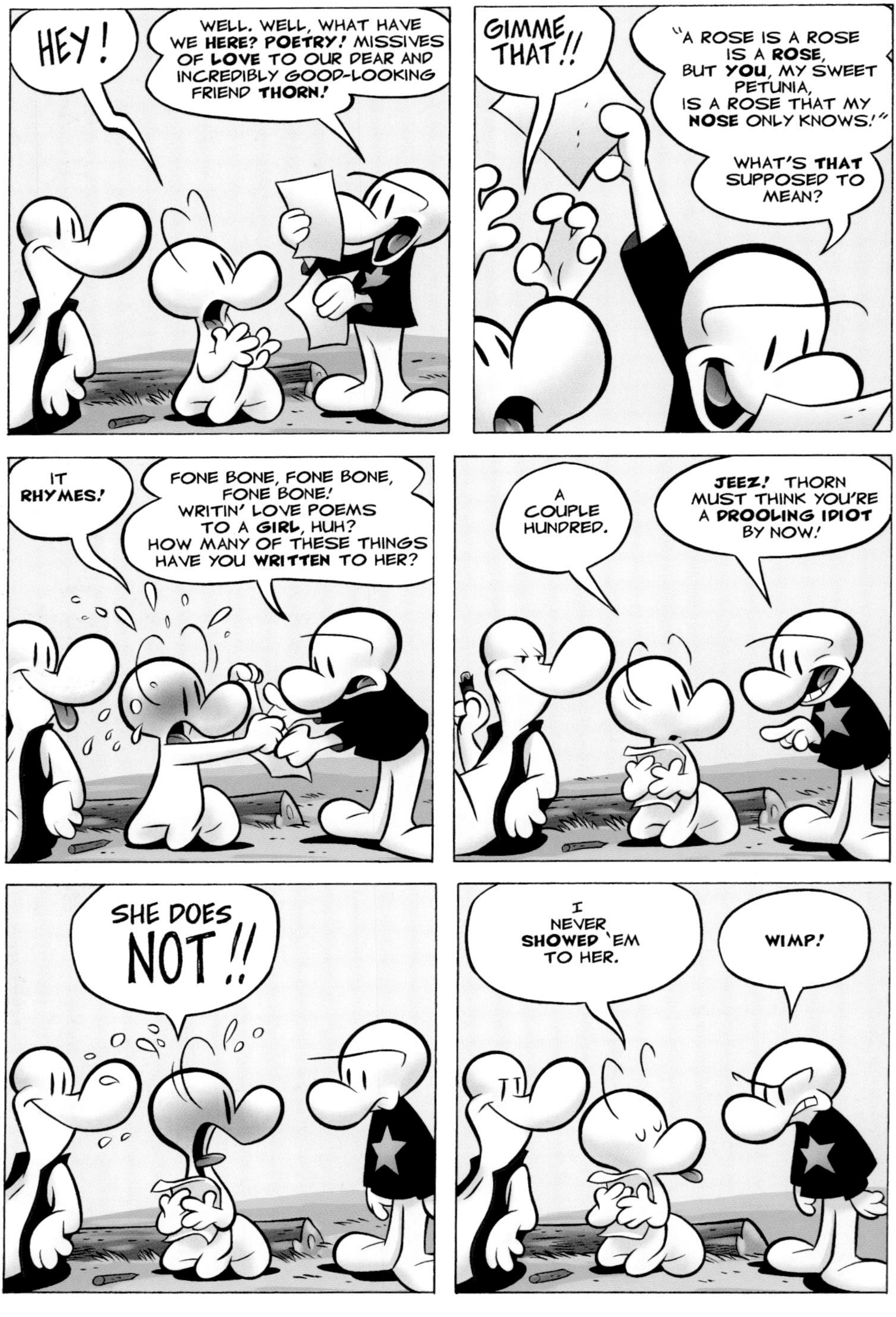
HEY!
WELL. WELL, WHAT HAVE WE HERE? POETRY! MISSIVES OF LOVE TO OUR DEAR AND INCREDIBLY GOOD-LOOKING FRIEND THORN!
GIMME THAT!!
"A ROSE IS A ROSE IS A ROSE, BUT YOU, MY SWEET PETUNIA, IS A ROSE THAT MY NOSE ONLY KNOWS!"
WHAT'S THAT SUPPOSED TO MEAN?
IT RHYMES!
FONE BONE, FONE BONE, FONE BONE! WRITIN' LOVE POEMS TO A GIRL, HUH? HOW MANY OF THESE THINGS HAVE YOU WRITTEN TO HER?
A COUPLE HUNDRED.
JEEZ! THORN MUST THINK YOU'RE A DROOLING IDIOT BY NOW!
SHE DOES NOT!!
I NEVER SHOWED 'EM TO HER.
WIMP!

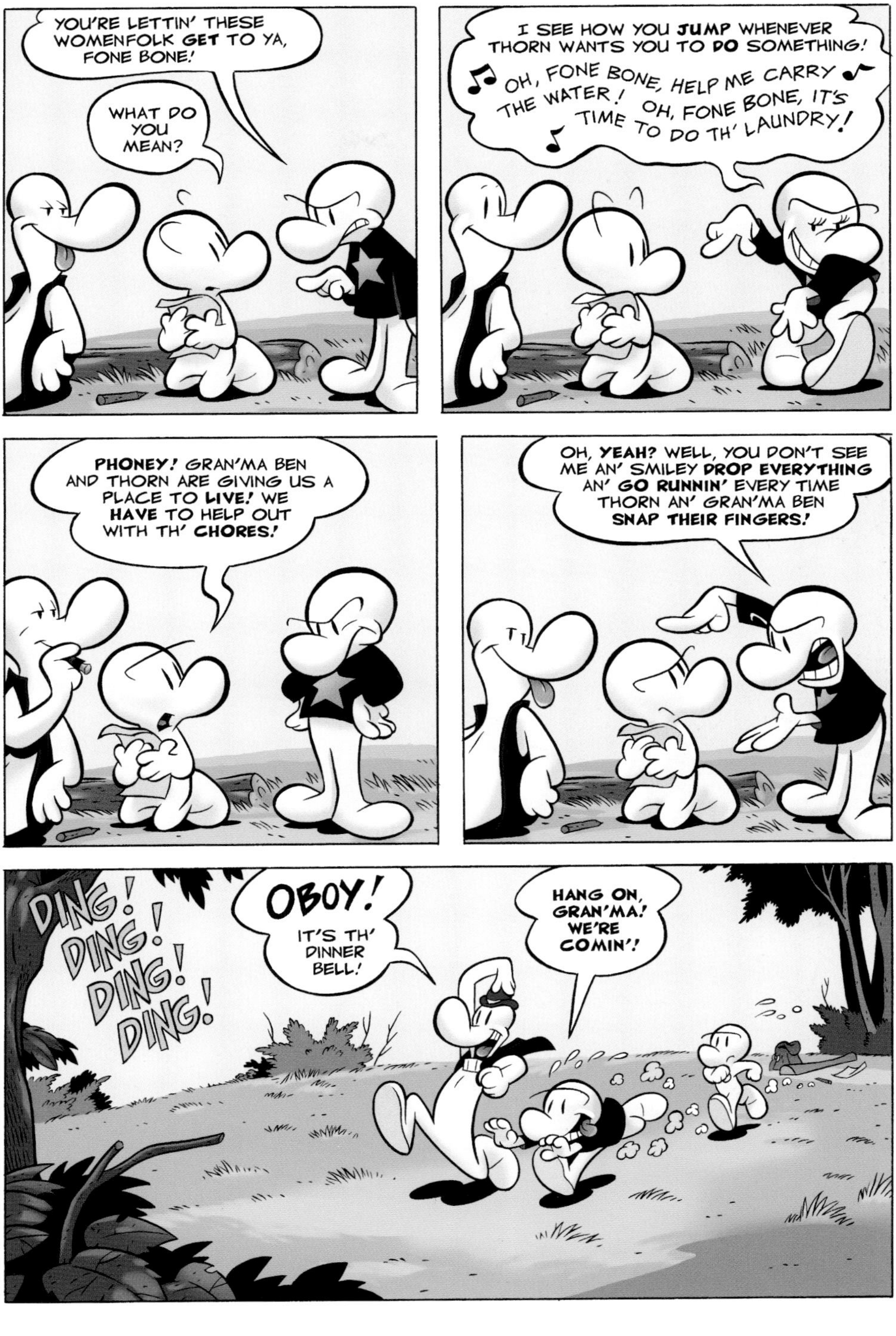

YOU'RE LETTIN' THESE WOMENFOLK GET TO YA, FONE BONE!
WHAT DO YOU MEAN?
I SEE HOW YOU JUMP WHENEVER THORN WANTS YOU TO DO SOMETHING!
OH, FONE BONE, HELP ME CARRY THE WATER! OH, FONE BONE, IT'S TIME TO DO TH' LAUNDRY!
PHONEY! GRAN'MA BEN AND THORN ARE GIVING US A PLACE TO LIVE! WE HAVE TO HELP OUT WITH TH' CHORES!
OH, YEAH? WELL, YOU DON'T SEE ME AN' SMILEY DROP EVERYTHING AN' GO RUNNIN' EVERY TIME THORN AN' GRAN'MA BEN SNAP THEIR FINGERS!
DING! DING! DING! DING!
OBOY!
IT'S TH' DINNER BELL!
HANG ON, GRAN'MA! WE'RE COMIN'!

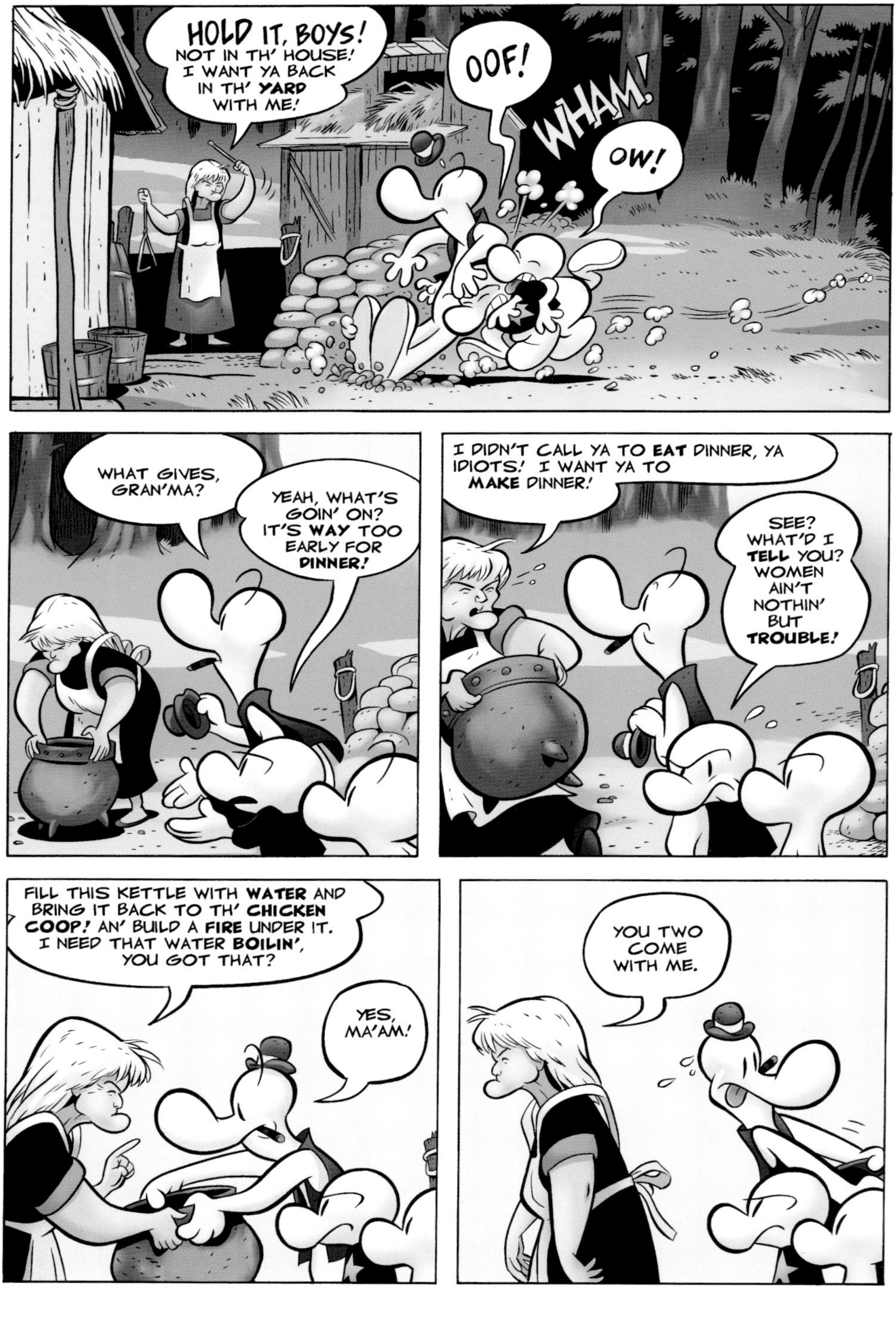
HOLD IT, BOYS! NOT IN TH' HOUSE! I WANT YA BACK IN TH' YARD WITH ME!
OOF!
WHAM!
OW!
WHAT GIVES, GRAN'MA?
YEAH, WHAT'S GOIN' ON? IT'S WAY TOO EARLY FOR DINNER!
I DIDN'T CALL YA TO EAT DINNER, YA IDIOTS! I WANT YA TO MAKE DINNER!
SEE? WHAT'D I TELL YOU? WOMEN AIN'T NOTHIN' BUT TROUBLE!
FILL THIS KETTLE WITH WATER AND BRING IT BACK TO TH' CHICKEN COOP! AN' BUILD A FIRE UNDER IT. I NEED THAT WATER BOILIN', YOU GOT THAT?
YES, MA'AM!
YOU TWO COME WITH ME.

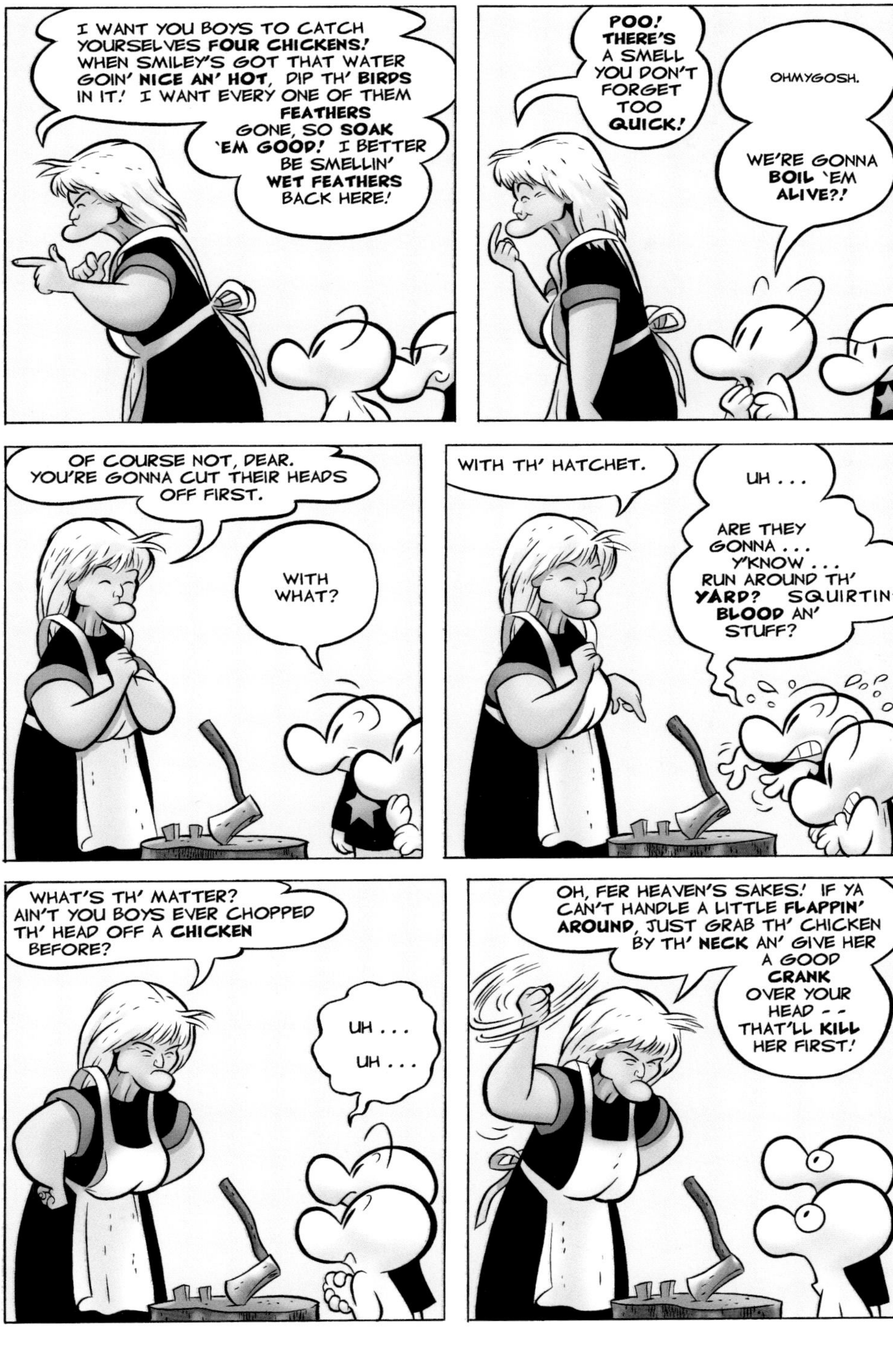
I WANT YOU BOYS TO CATCH YOURSELVES FOUR CHICKENS! WHEN SMILEY'S GOT THAT WATER GOIN' NICE AN' HOT, DIP TH' BIRDS IN IT! I WANT EVERY ONE OF THEM FEATHERS GONE, SO SOAK 'EM GOOD! I BETTER BE SMELLIN' WET FEATHERS BACK HERE!
POO! THERE'S A SMELL YOU DON'T FORGET TOO QUICK!
OHMYGOSH.
WE'RE GONNA BOIL 'EM ALIVE?!
OF COURSE NOT, DEAR. YOU'RE GONNA CUT THEIR HEADS OFF FIRST.
WITH WHAT?
WITH TH' HATCHET.
UH . . .
ARE THEY GONNA . . . Y'KNOW . . . RUN AROUND TH' YARD? SQUIRTIN' BLOOD AN' STUFF?
WHAT'S TH' MATTER? AIN'T YOU BOYS EVER CHOPPED TH' HEAD OFF A CHICKEN BEFORE?
UH . . .
UH . . .
OH, FER HEAVEN'S SAKES! IF YA CAN'T HANDLE A LITTLE FLAPPIN' AROUND, JUST GRAB TH' CHICKEN BY TH' NECK AN' GIVE HER A GOOD CRANK OVER YOUR HEAD -- THAT'LL KILL HER FIRST!

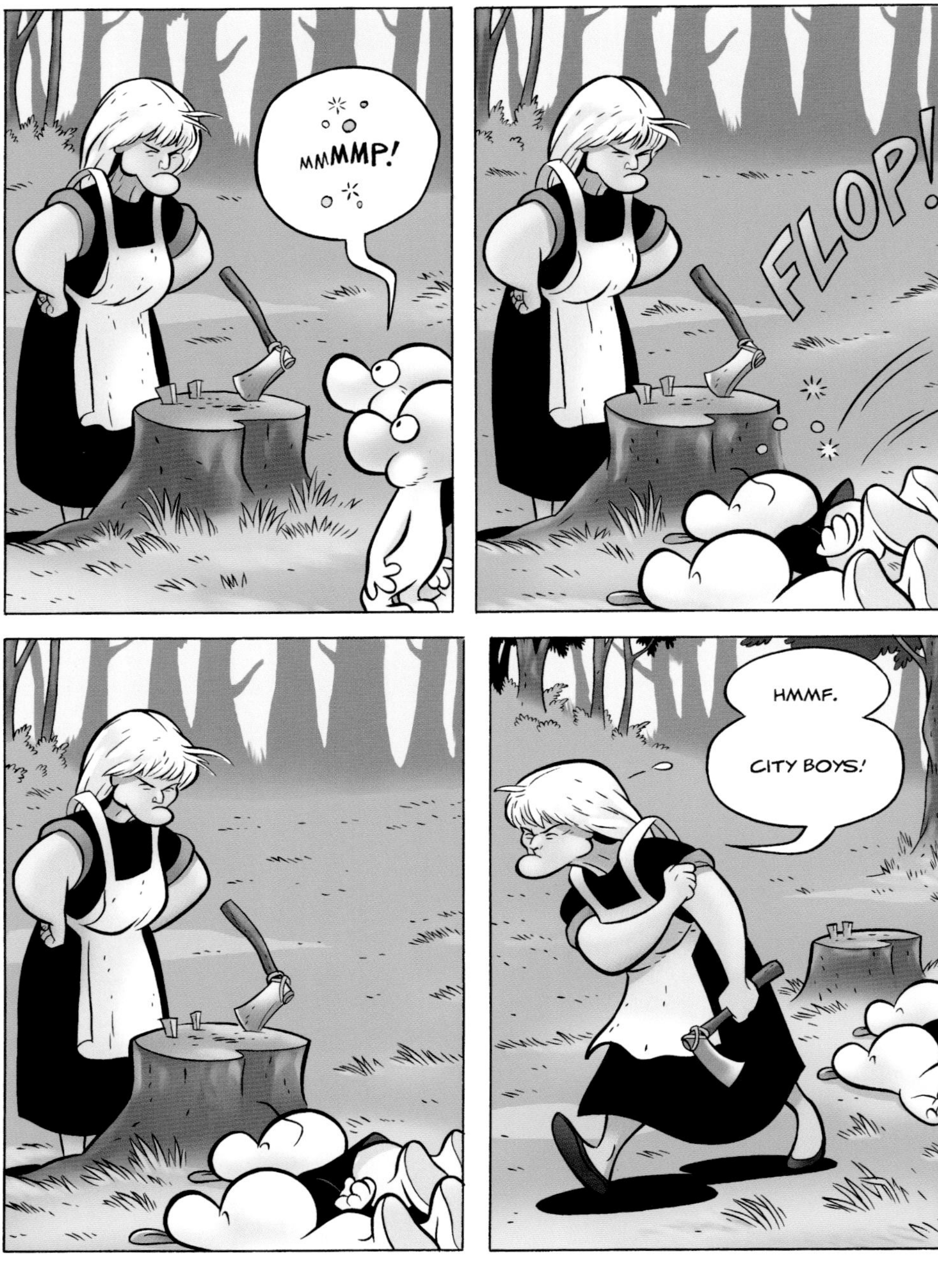
MMMMP!
FLOP!
HMMF.
CITY BOYS!

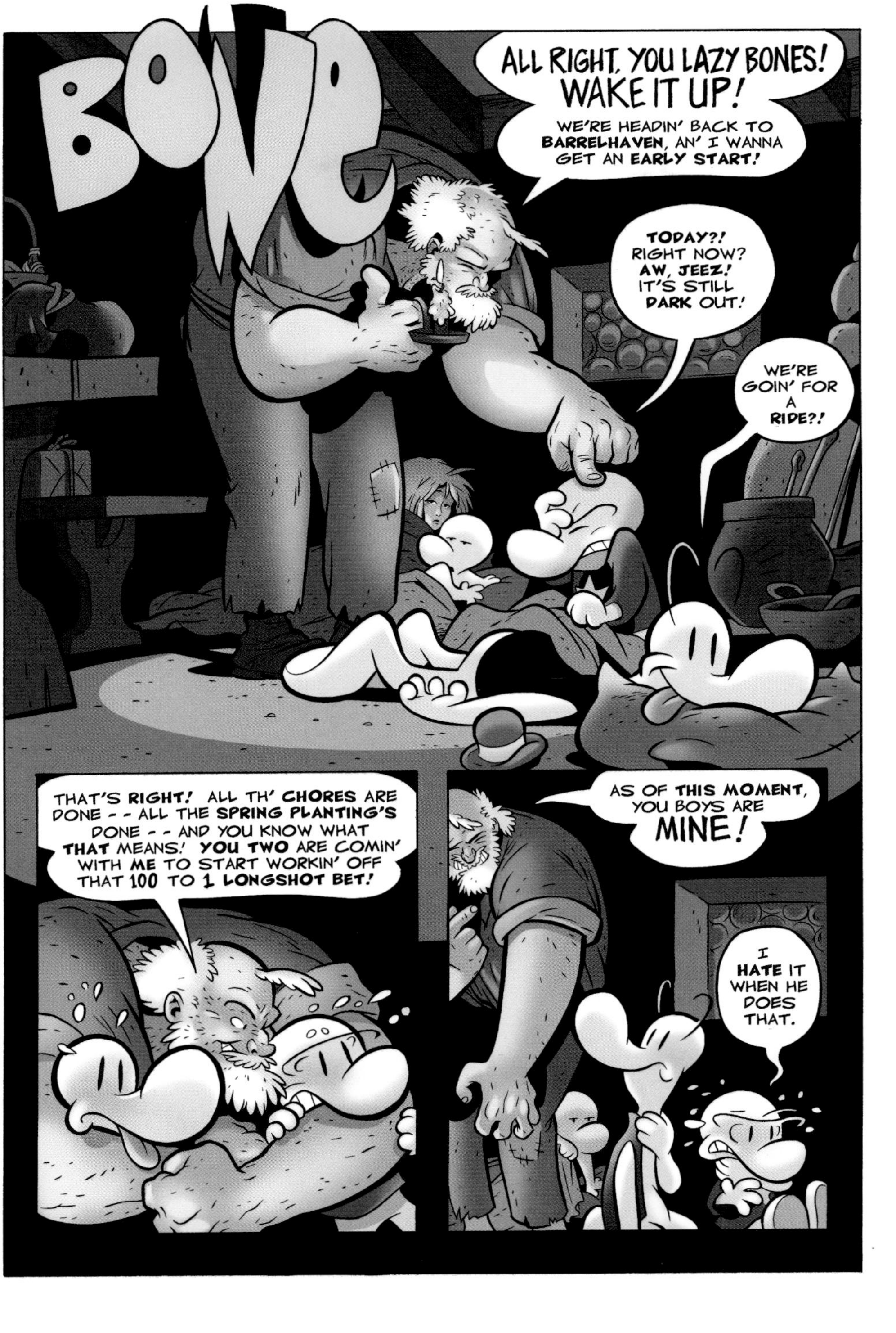
BONE
ALL RIGHT, YOU LAZY BONES! WAKE IT UP! WE'RE HEADIN' BACK TO BARRELHAVEN, AN' I WANNA GET AN EARLY START!
TODAY?! RIGHT NOW? AW, JEEZ! IT'S STILL DARK OUT!
WE'RE GOIN' FOR A RIDE?!
THAT'S RIGHT! ALL TH' CHORES ARE DONE - - ALL THE SPRING PLANTING'S DONE - - AND YOU KNOW WHAT THAT MEANS! YOU TWO ARE COMIN' WITH ME TO START WORKIN' OFF THAT 100 TO 1 LONGSHOT BET!
AS OF THIS MOMENT, YOU BOYS ARE MINE!
I HATE IT WHEN HE DOES THAT.

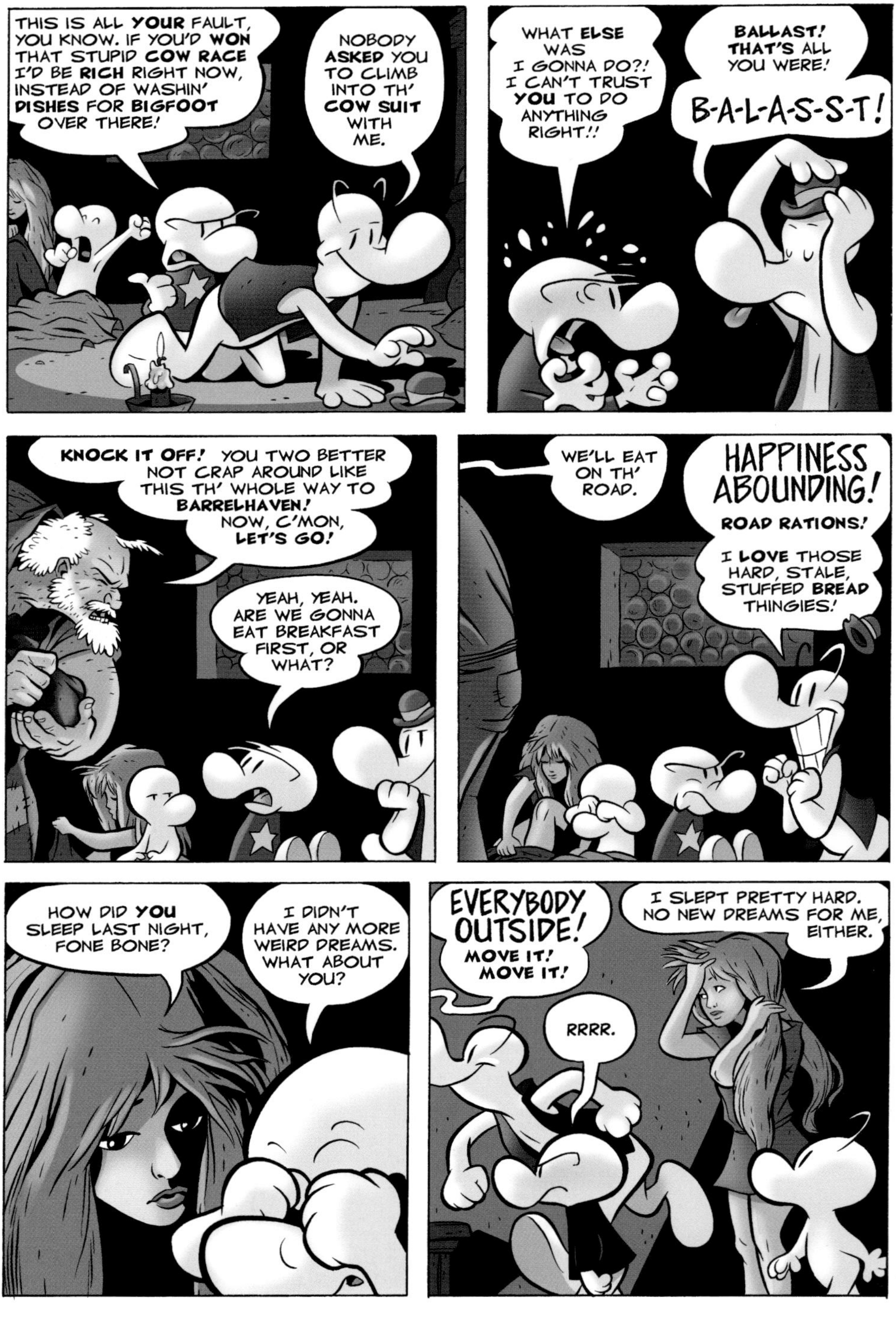
THIS IS ALL YOUR FAULT, YOU KNOW. IF YOU'D WON THAT STUPID COW RACE I'D BE RICH RIGHT NOW, INSTEAD OF WASHIN' DISHES FOR BIGFOOT OVER THERE!
NOBODY ASKED YOU TO CLIMB INTO TH' COW SUIT WITH ME.
WHAT ELSE WAS I GONNA DO?! I CAN'T TRUST YOU TO DO ANYTHING RIGHT!!
BALLAST! THAT'S ALL YOU WERE!
B-A-L-A-S-S-T!
KNOCK IT OFF! YOU TWO BETTER NOT CRAP AROUND LIKE THIS TH' WHOLE WAY TO BARRELHAVEN! NOW, C'MON, LET'S GO!
YEAH, YEAH. ARE WE GONNA EAT BREAKFAST FIRST, OR WHAT?
WE'LL EAT ON TH' ROAD.
HAPPINESS ABOUNDING!
ROAD RATIONS!
I LOVE THOSE HARD, STALE, STUFFED BREAD THINGIES!
HOW DID YOU SLEEP LAST NIGHT, FONE BONE?
I DIDN'T HAVE ANY MORE WEIRD DREAMS. WHAT ABOUT YOU?
EVERYBODY OUTSIDE!
MOVE IT! MOVE IT!
I SLEPT PRETTY HARD. NO NEW DREAMS FOR ME, EITHER.
RRRR.

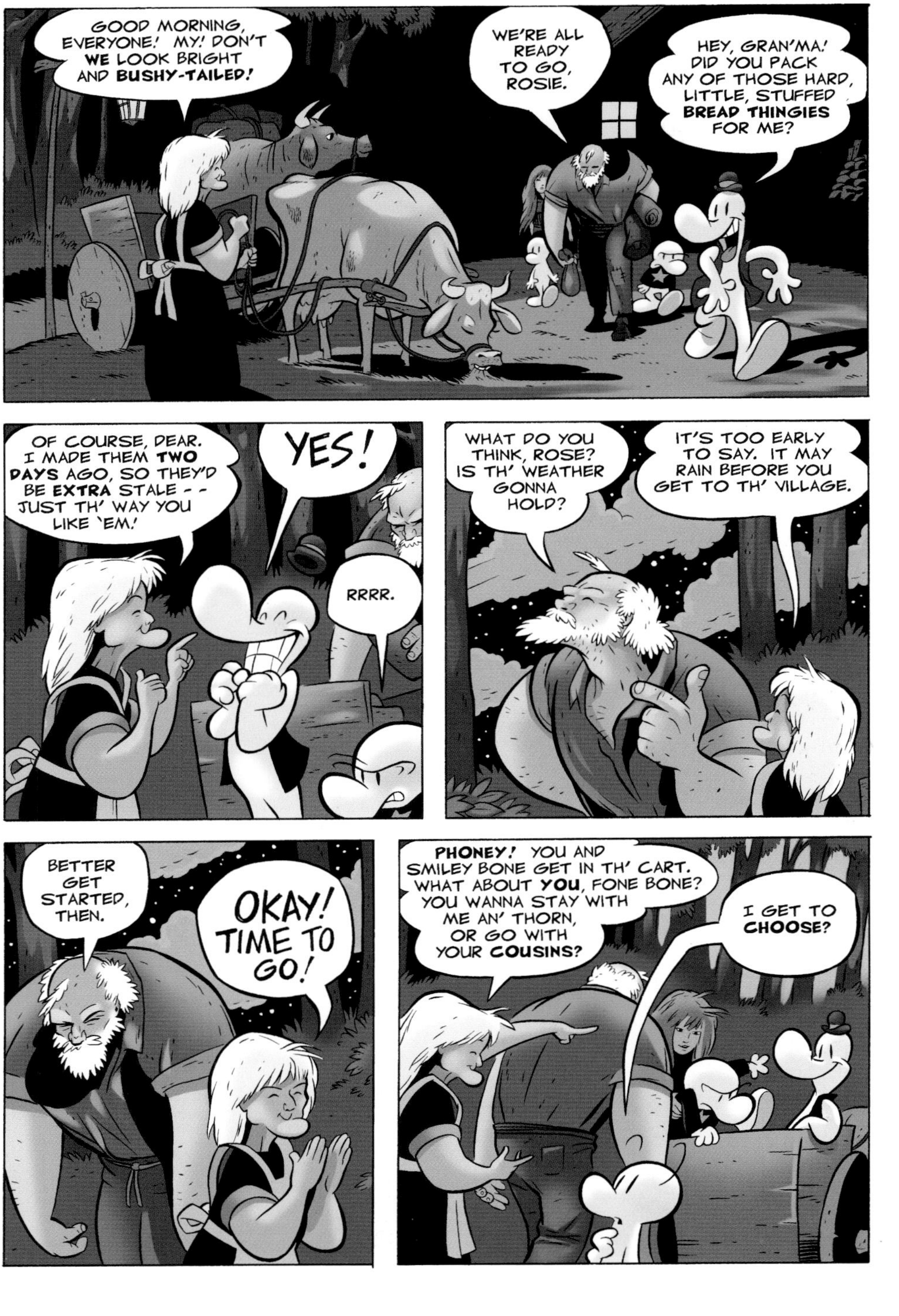
GOOD MORNING, EVERYONE! MY! DON'T WE LOOK BRIGHT AND BUSHY-TAILED!
WE'RE ALL READY TO GO, ROSIE.
HEY, GRAN'MA! DID YOU PACK ANY OF THOSE HARD, LITTLE, STUFFED BREAD THINGIES FOR ME?
OF COURSE, DEAR. I MADE THEM TWO DAYS AGO, SO THEY'D BE EXTRA STALE -- JUST TH' WAY YOU LIKE 'EM!
YES!
RRRR.
WHAT DO YOU THINK, ROSE? IS TH' WEATHER GONNA HOLD?
IT'S TOO EARLY TO SAY. IT MAY RAIN BEFORE YOU GET TO TH' VILLAGE.
BETTER GET STARTED, THEN.
OKAY! TIME TO GO!
PHONEY! YOU AND SMILEY BONE GET IN TH' CART. WHAT ABOUT YOU, FONE BONE? YOU WANNA STAY WITH ME AN' THORN, OR GO WITH YOUR COUSINS?
I GET TO CHOOSE?

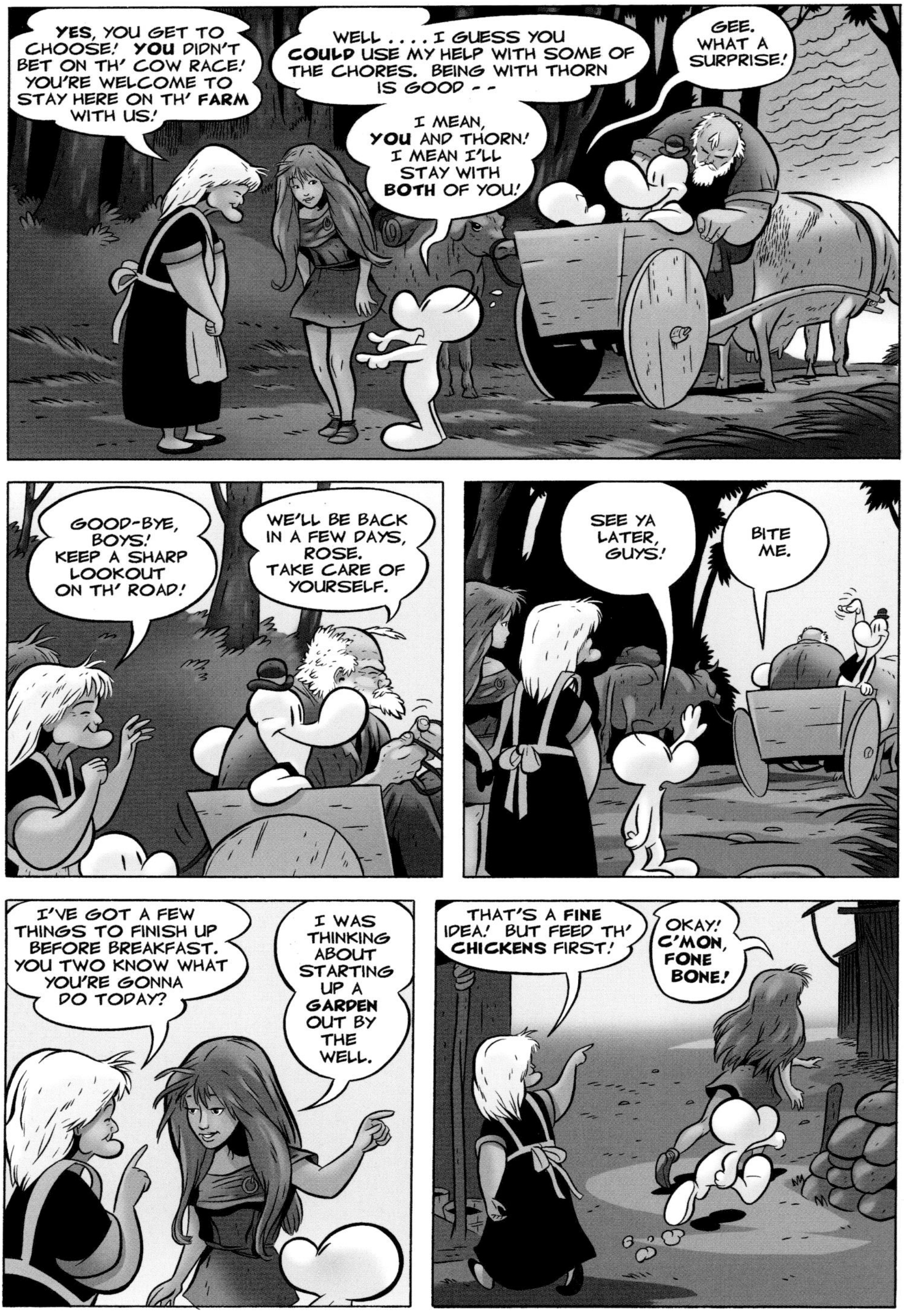
YES, YOU GET TO CHOOSE! YOU DIDN'T BET ON TH' COW RACE! YOU'RE WELCOME TO STAY HERE ON TH' FARM WITH US!
WELL . . . . I GUESS YOU COULD USE MY HELP WITH SOME OF THE CHORES. BEING WITH THORN IS GOOD - -
I MEAN, YOU AND THORN! I MEAN I'LL STAY WITH BOTH OF YOU!
GEE. WHAT A SURPRISE!
GOOD-BYE, BOYS! KEEP A SHARP LOOKOUT ON TH' ROAD!
WE'LL BE BACK IN A FEW DAYS, ROSE. TAKE CARE OF YOURSELF.
SEE YA LATER, GUYS!
BITE ME.
I'VE GOT A FEW THINGS TO FINISH UP BEFORE BREAKFAST. YOU TWO KNOW WHAT YOU'RE GONNA DO TODAY?
I WAS THINKING ABOUT STARTING UP A GARDEN OUT BY THE WELL.
THAT'S A FINE IDEA! BUT FEED TH' CHICKENS FIRST!
OKAY! C'MON, FONE BONE!

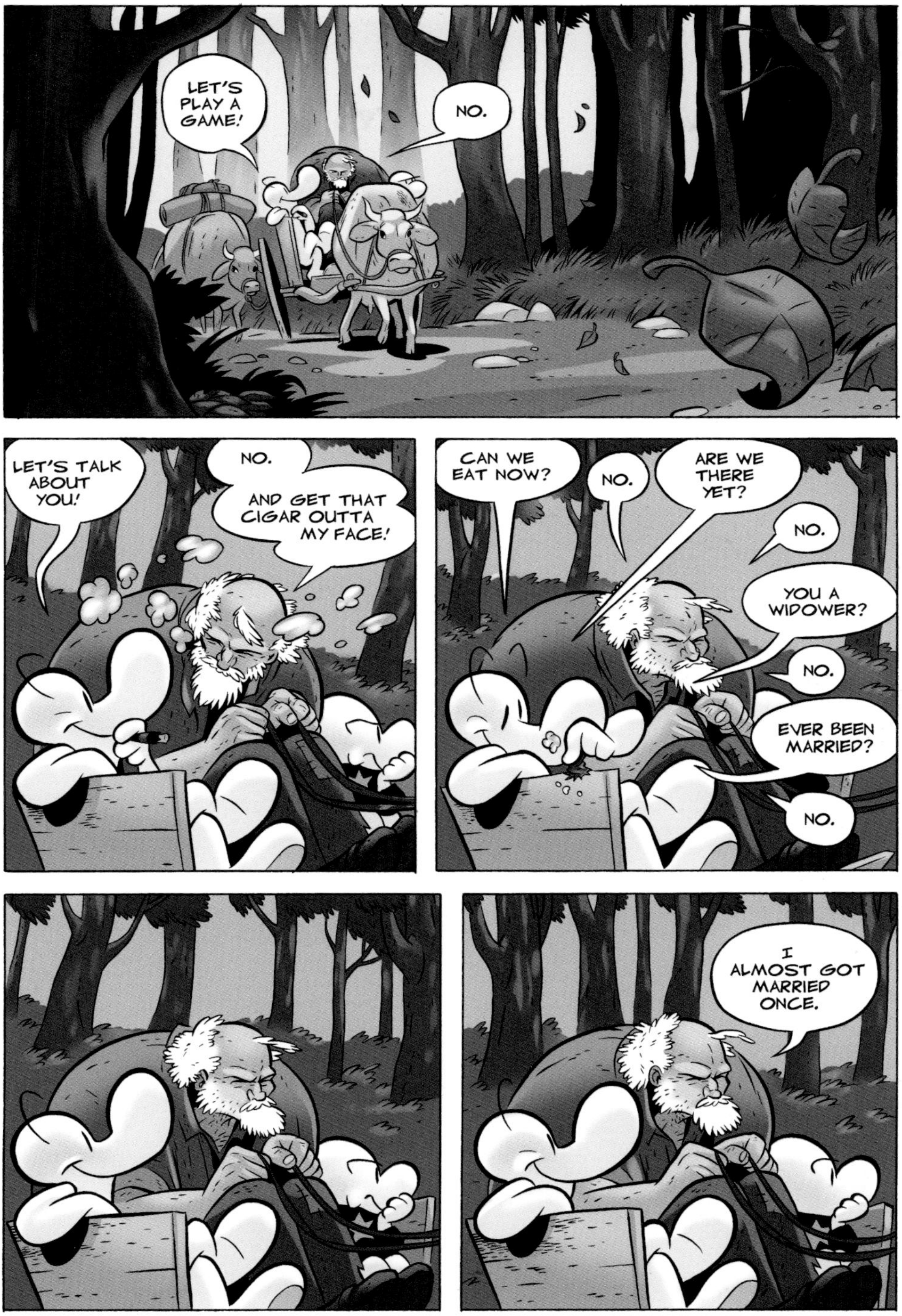
LET'S PLAY A GAME!
NO.
LET'S TALK ABOUT YOU!
NO.
AND GET THAT CIGAR OUTTA MY FACE!
CAN WE EAT NOW?
NO.
ARE WE THERE YET?
NO.
YOU A WIDOWER?
NO.
EVER BEEN MARRIED?
NO.
I ALMOST GOT MARRIED ONCE.

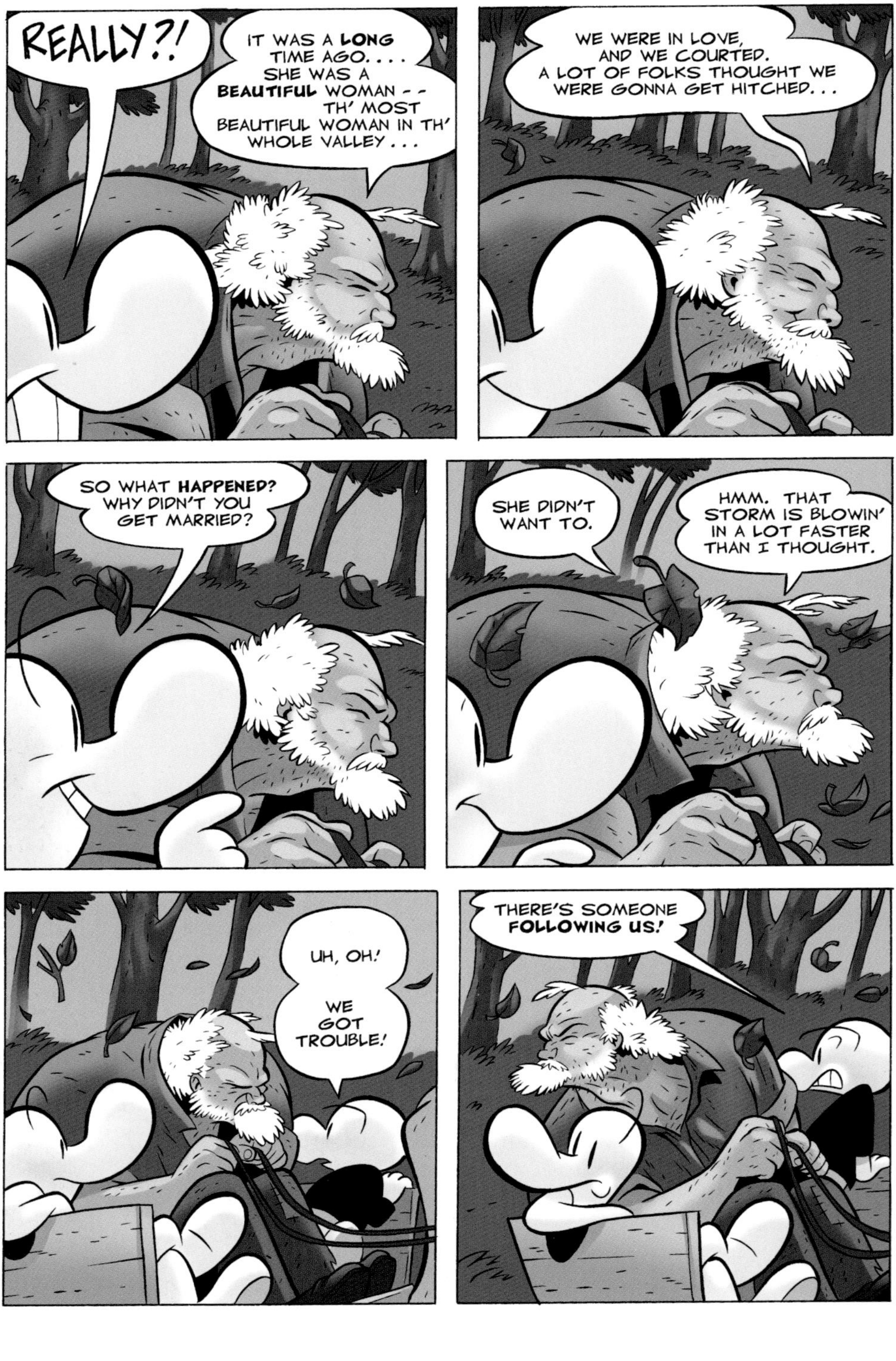
REALLY?!
IT WAS A **LONG** TIME AGO. . . . SHE WAS A **BEAUTIFUL** WOMAN - - TH' MOST BEAUTIFUL WOMAN IN TH' WHOLE VALLEY . . .
WE WERE IN LOVE, AND WE COURTED. A LOT OF FOLKS THOUGHT WE WERE GONNA GET HITCHED. . .
SO WHAT **HAPPENED?** WHY DIDN'T YOU GET MARRIED?
SHE DIDN'T WANT TO.
HMM. THAT STORM IS BLOWIN' IN A LOT FASTER THAN I THOUGHT.
UH, OH!
WE GOT TROUBLE!
THERE'S SOMEONE **FOLLOWING US!**

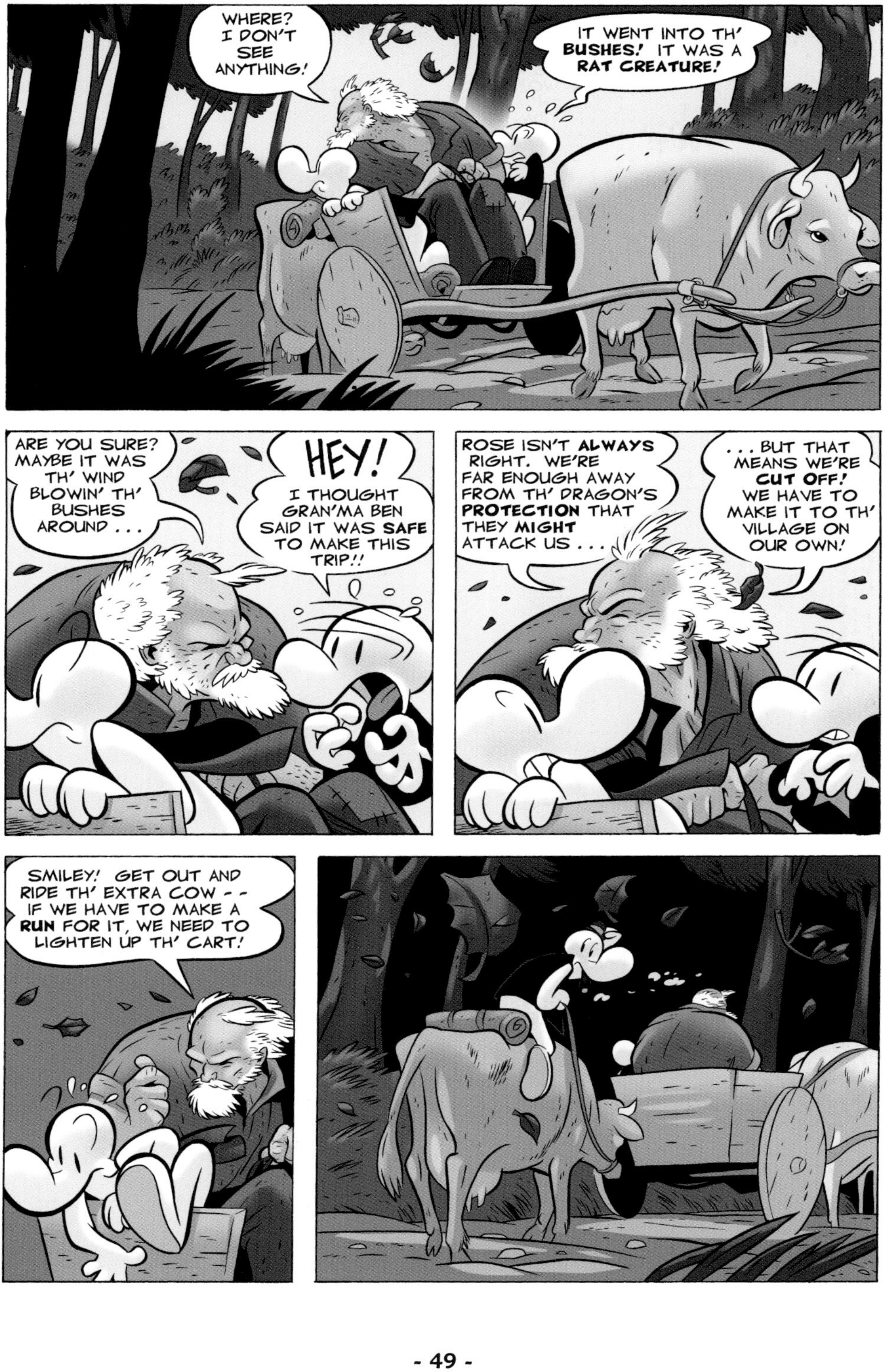
WHERE? I DON'T SEE ANYTHING!
IT WENT INTO TH' BUSHES! IT WAS A RAT CREATURE!
ARE YOU SURE? MAYBE IT WAS TH' WIND BLOWIN' TH' BUSHES AROUND . . .
HEY! I THOUGHT GRAN'MA BEN SAID IT WAS SAFE TO MAKE THIS TRIP!!
ROSE ISN'T ALWAYS RIGHT. WE'RE FAR ENOUGH AWAY FROM TH' DRAGON'S PROTECTION THAT THEY MIGHT ATTACK US . . .
. . . BUT THAT MEANS WE'RE CUT OFF! WE HAVE TO MAKE IT TO TH' VILLAGE ON OUR OWN!
SMILEY! GET OUT AND RIDE TH' EXTRA COW - - IF WE HAVE TO MAKE A RUN FOR IT, WE NEED TO LIGHTEN UP TH' CART!

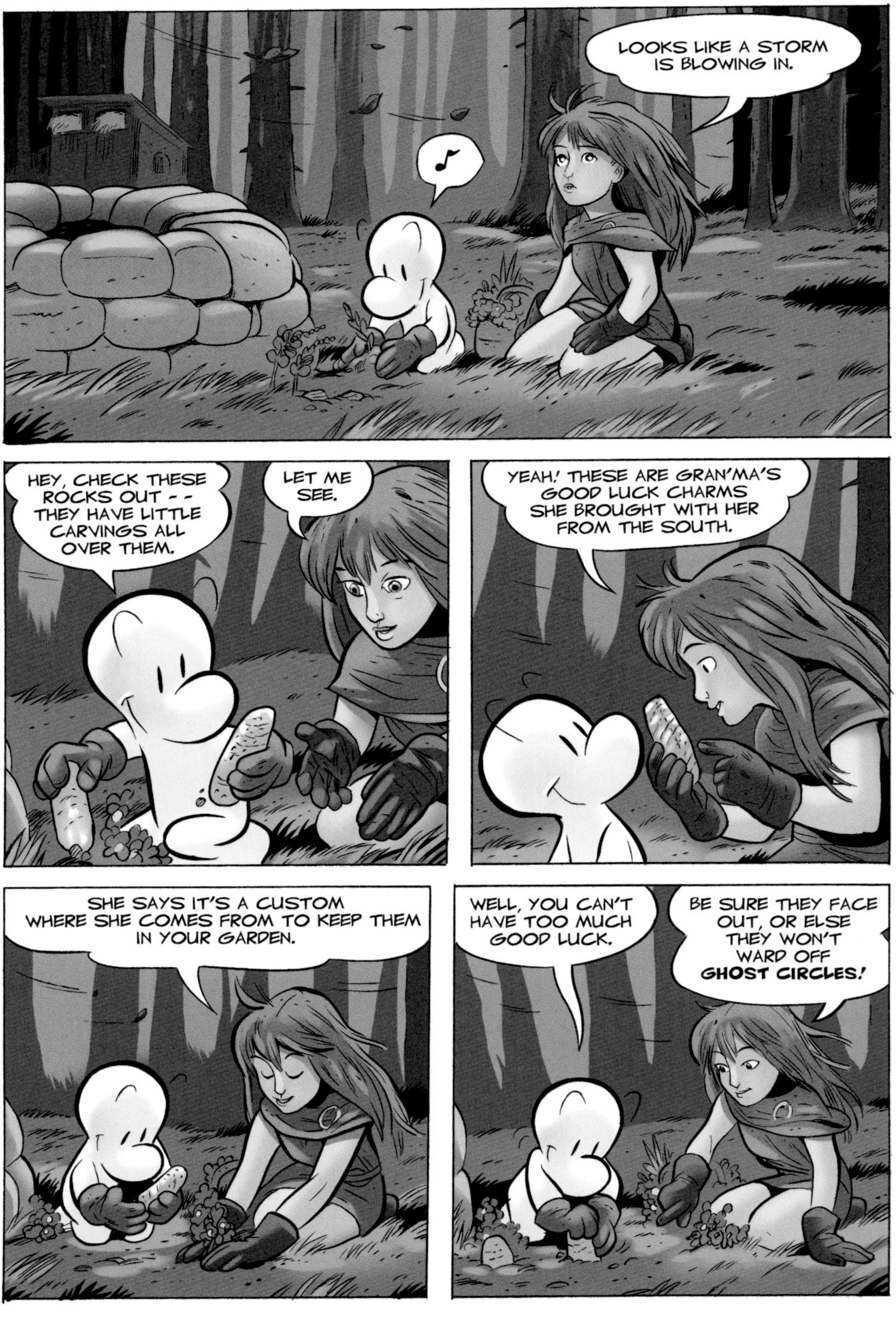
LOOKS LIKE A STORM IS BLOWING IN.
HEY, CHECK THESE ROCKS OUT - - THEY HAVE LITTLE CARVINGS ALL OVER THEM.
LET ME SEE.
YEAH! THESE ARE GRAN'MA'S GOOD LUCK CHARMS SHE BROUGHT WITH HER FROM THE SOUTH.
SHE SAYS IT'S A CUSTOM WHERE SHE COMES FROM TO KEEP THEM IN YOUR GARDEN.
WELL, YOU CAN'T HAVE TOO MUCH GOOD LUCK.
BE SURE THEY FACE OUT, OR ELSE THEY WON'T WARD OFF GHOST CIRCLES!

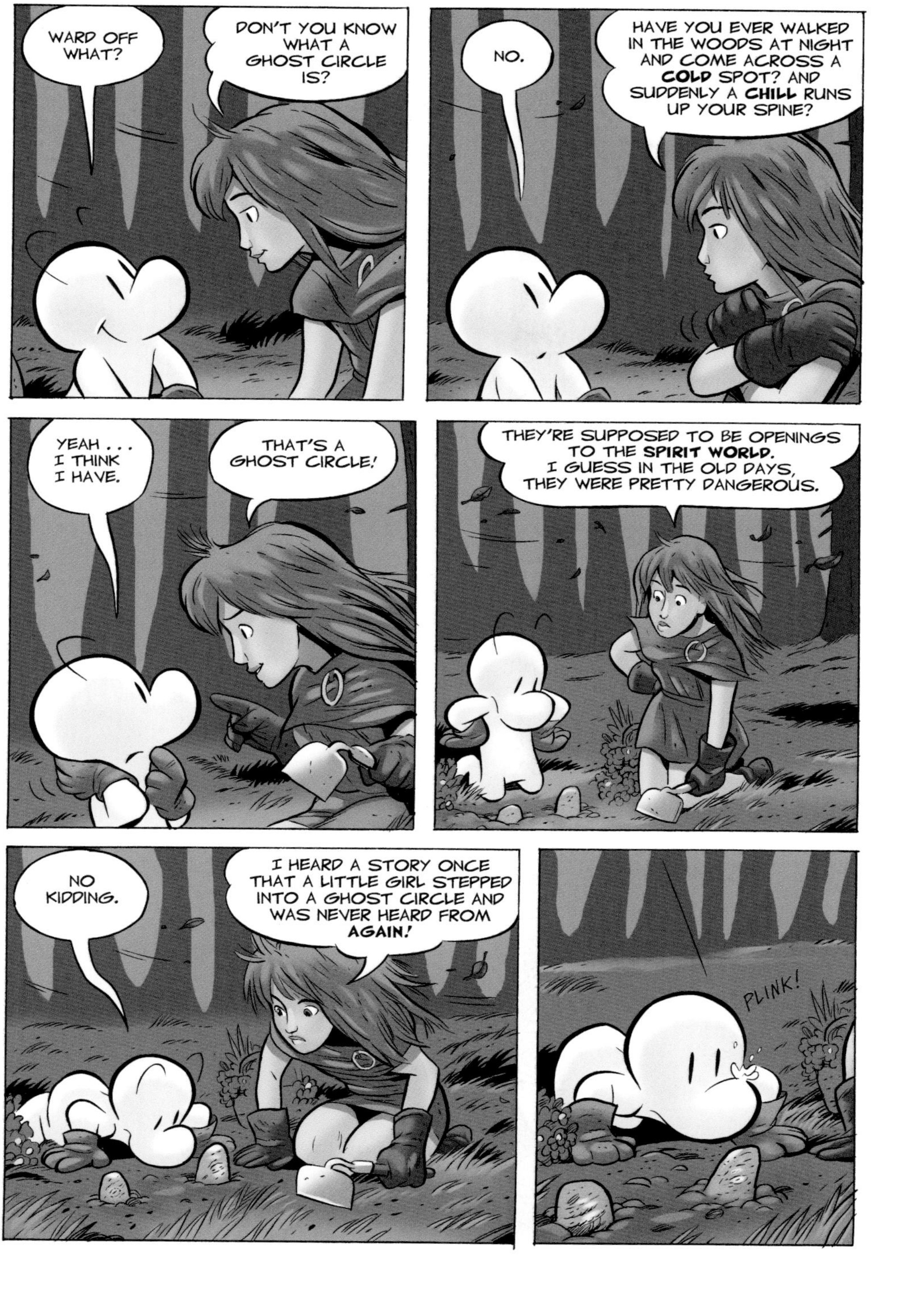
WARD OFF WHAT?
DON'T YOU KNOW WHAT A GHOST CIRCLE IS?
NO.
HAVE YOU EVER WALKED IN THE WOODS AT NIGHT AND COME ACROSS A COLD SPOT? AND SUDDENLY A CHILL RUNS UP YOUR SPINE?
YEAH . . . I THINK I HAVE.
THAT'S A GHOST CIRCLE!
THEY'RE SUPPOSED TO BE OPENINGS TO THE SPIRIT WORLD. I GUESS IN THE OLD DAYS, THEY WERE PRETTY DANGEROUS.
NO KIDDING.
I HEARD A STORY ONCE THAT A LITTLE GIRL STEPPED INTO A GHOST CIRCLE AND WAS NEVER HEARD FROM AGAIN!
PLINK!

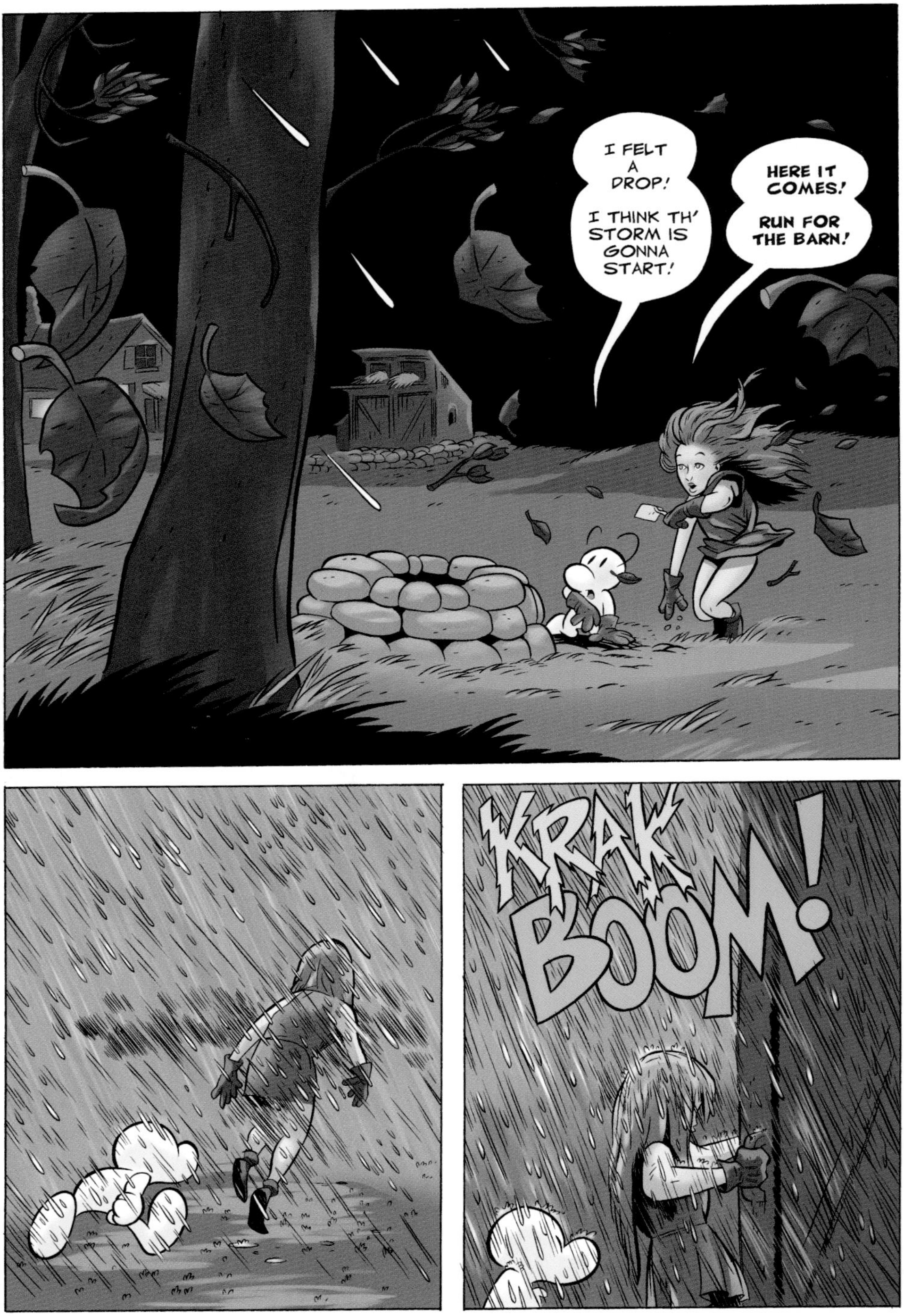
I FELT A DROP! I THINK TH' STORM IS GONNA START!
HERE IT COMES! RUN FOR THE BARN!
KRAK BOOM!

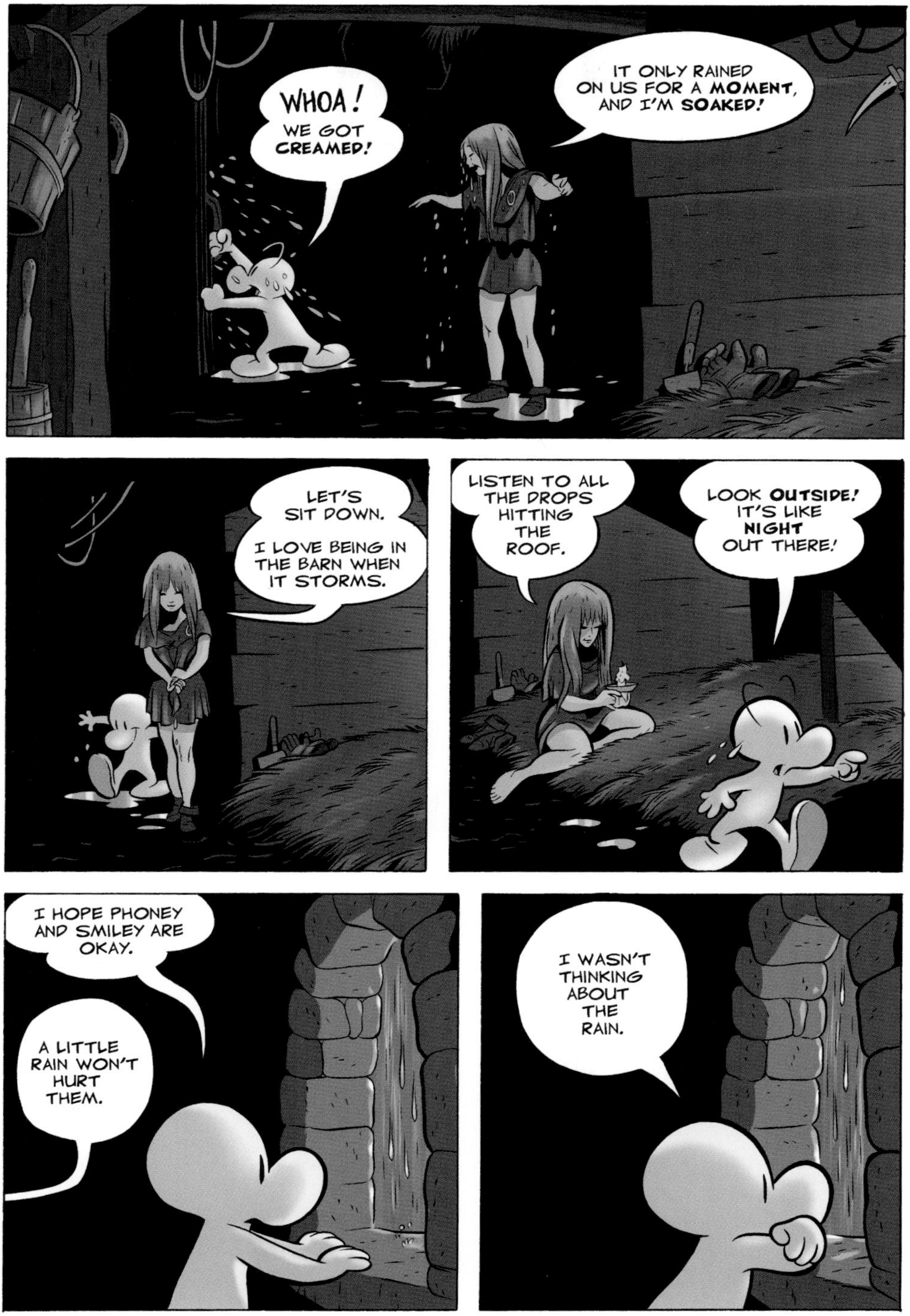
WHOA! WE GOT CREAMED!
IT ONLY RAINED ON US FOR A MOMENT, AND I'M SOAKED!
LET'S SIT DOWN.
I LOVE BEING IN THE BARN WHEN IT STORMS.
LISTEN TO ALL THE DROPS HITTING THE ROOF.
LOOK OUTSIDE! IT'S LIKE NIGHT OUT THERE!
I HOPE PHONEY AND SMILEY ARE OKAY.
A LITTLE RAIN WON'T HURT THEM.
I WASN'T THINKING ABOUT THE RAIN.

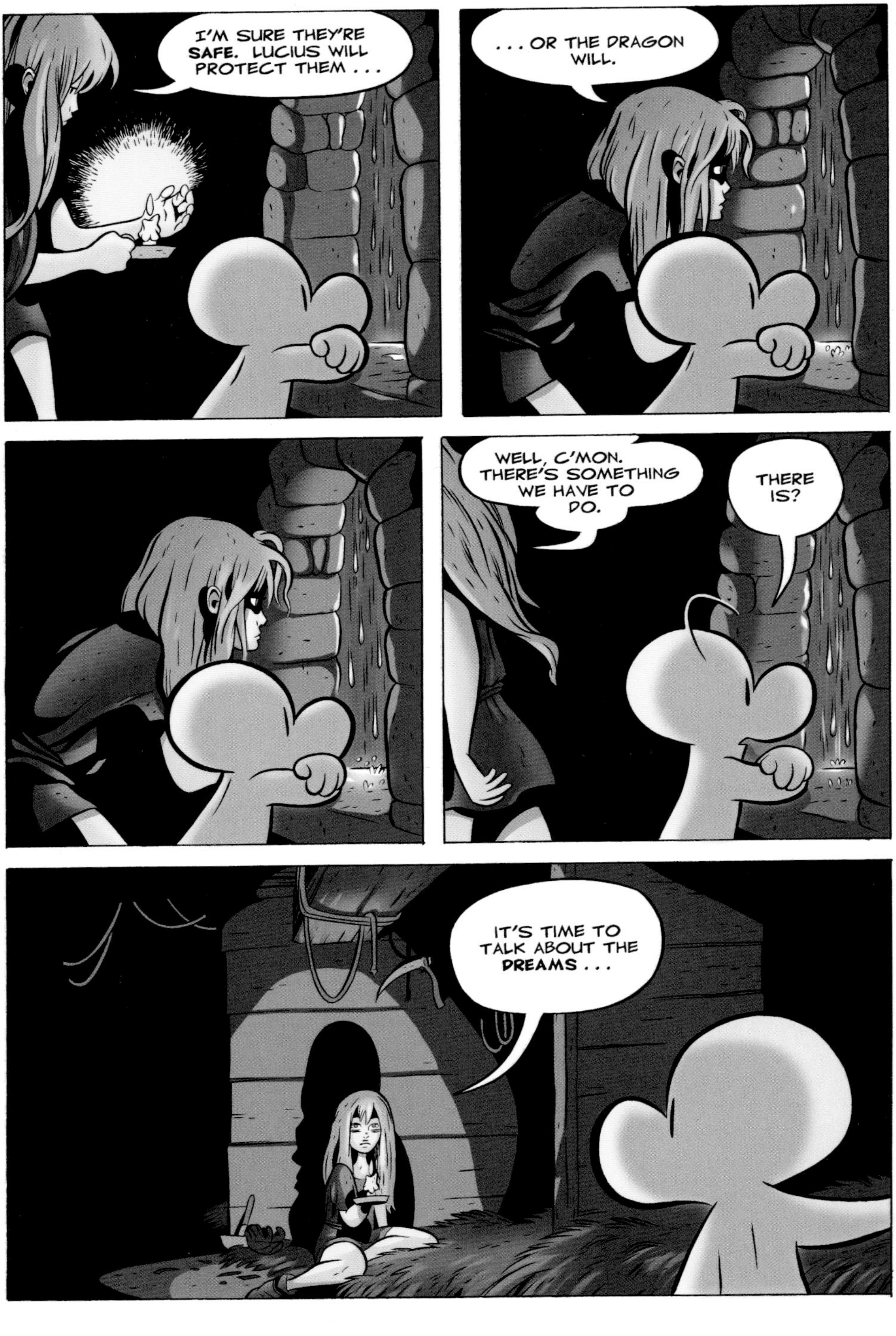
I'M SURE THEY'RE SAFE. LUCIUS WILL PROTECT THEM . . .
. . . OR THE DRAGON WILL.
WELL, C'MON. THERE'S SOMETHING WE HAVE TO DO.
THERE IS?
IT'S TIME TO TALK ABOUT THE DREAMS . . .

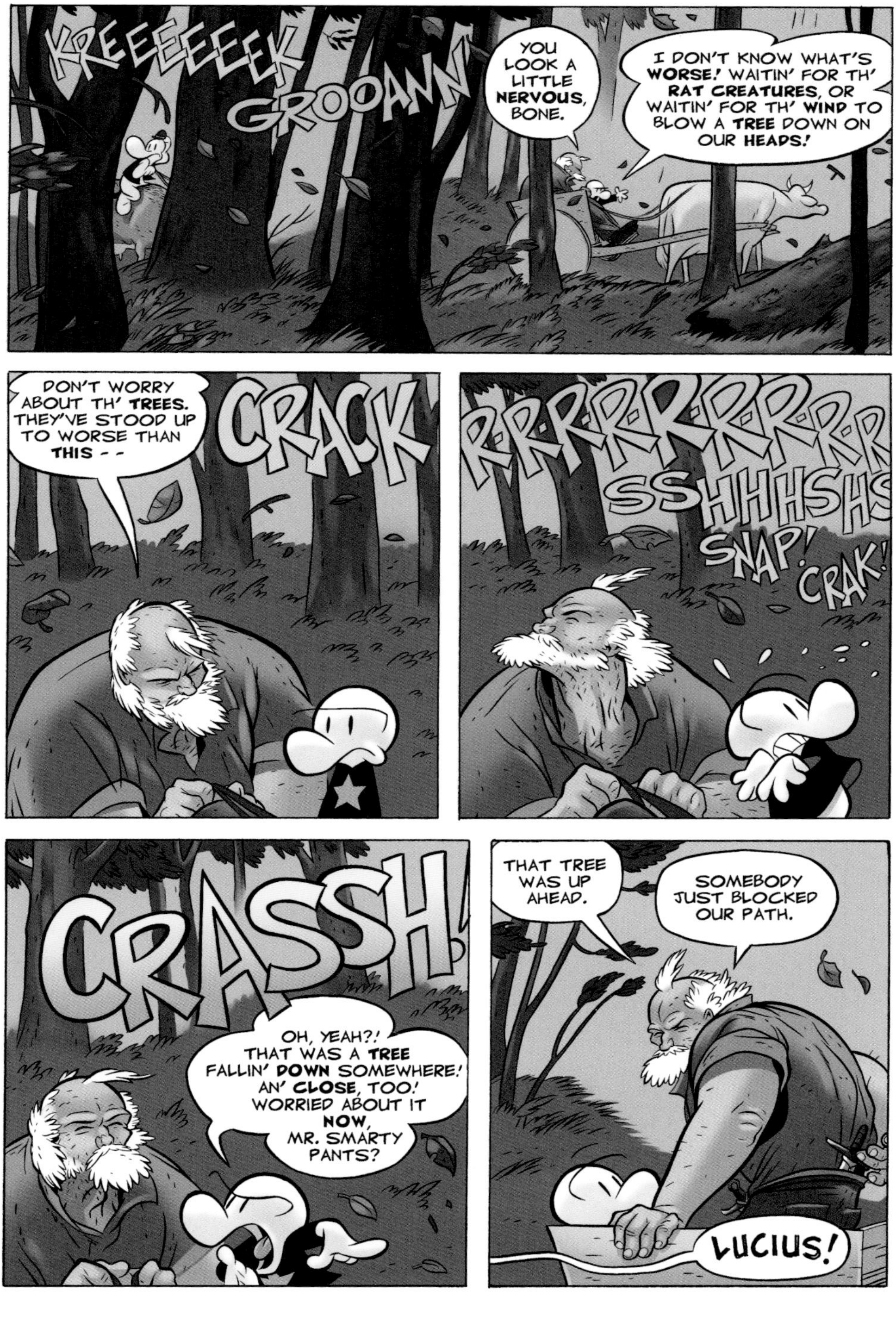
KREEEEEEK
GROOANN
YOU LOOK A LITTLE NERVOUS, BONE.
I DON'T KNOW WHAT'S WORSE! WAITIN' FOR TH' RAT CREATURES, OR WAITIN' FOR TH' WIND TO BLOW A TREE DOWN ON OUR HEADS!
DON'T WORRY ABOUT TH' TREES. THEY'VE STOOD UP TO WORSE THAN THIS - -
CRACK
R-R-R-R-R-R-R-R-R-R-R
SSHHHSHS
SNAP!
CRAK!
CRASSH!
OH, YEAH?! THAT WAS A TREE FALLIN' DOWN SOMEWHERE! AN' CLOSE, TOO! WORRIED ABOUT IT NOW, MR. SMARTY PANTS?
THAT TREE WAS UP AHEAD.
SOMEBODY JUST BLOCKED OUR PATH.
LUCIUS!

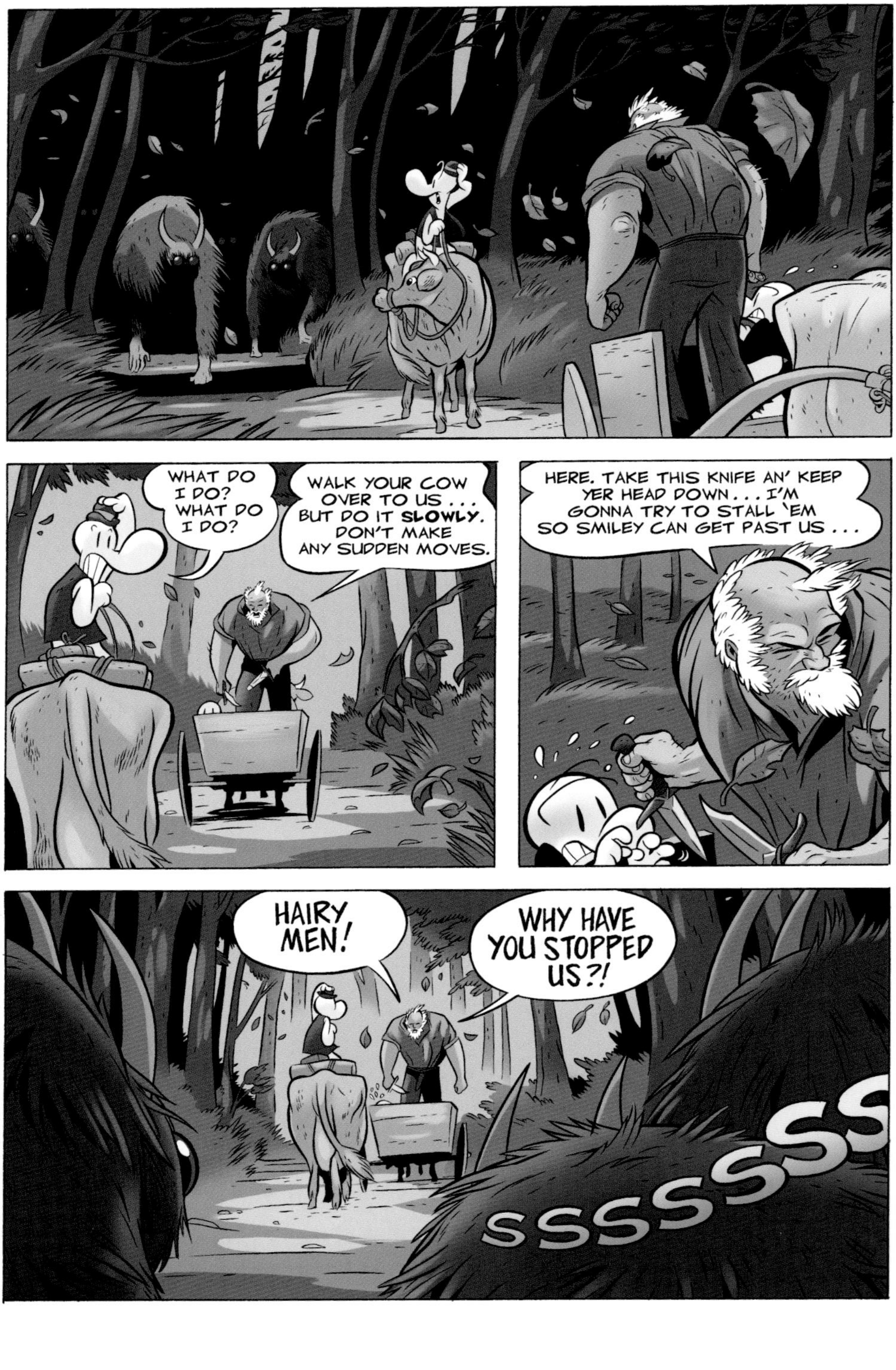
WHAT DO I DO? WHAT DO I DO?
WALK YOUR COW OVER TO US . . . BUT DO IT SLOWLY. DON'T MAKE ANY SUDDEN MOVES.
HERE. TAKE THIS KNIFE AN' KEEP YER HEAD DOWN . . . I'M GONNA TRY TO STALL 'EM SO SMILEY CAN GET PAST US . . .
HAIRY, MEN!
WHY HAVE YOU STOPPED US?!
SSSSSSSSSS

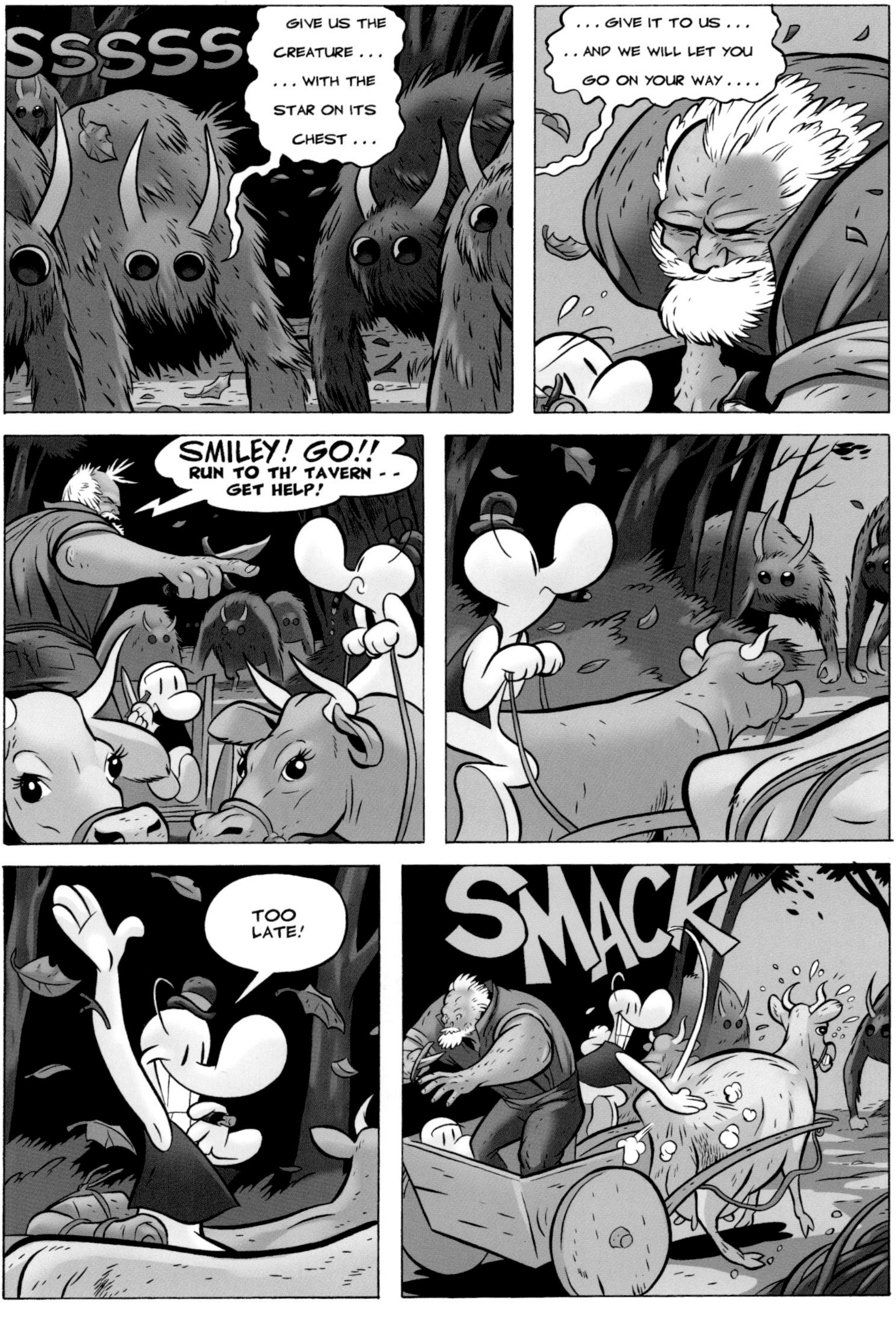
SSSSS
GIVE US THE CREATURE . . . . . . WITH THE STAR ON ITS CHEST . . .
. . . GIVE IT TO US . . . . . AND WE WILL LET YOU GO ON YOUR WAY . . . .
SMILEY! GO!! RUN TO TH' TAVERN - - GET HELP!
TOO LATE!
SMACK

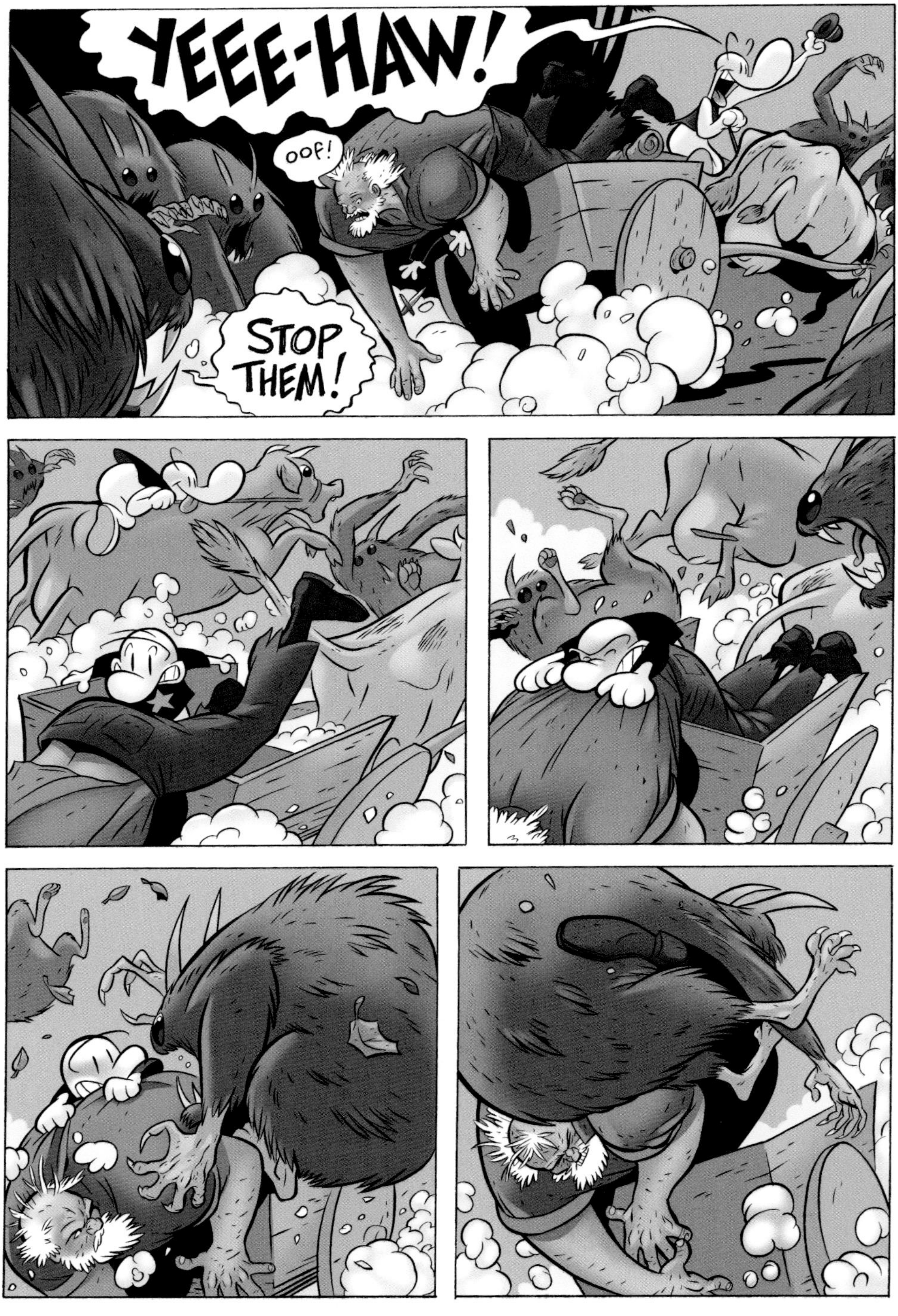
YEEE-HAW!
OOF!
STOP THEM!

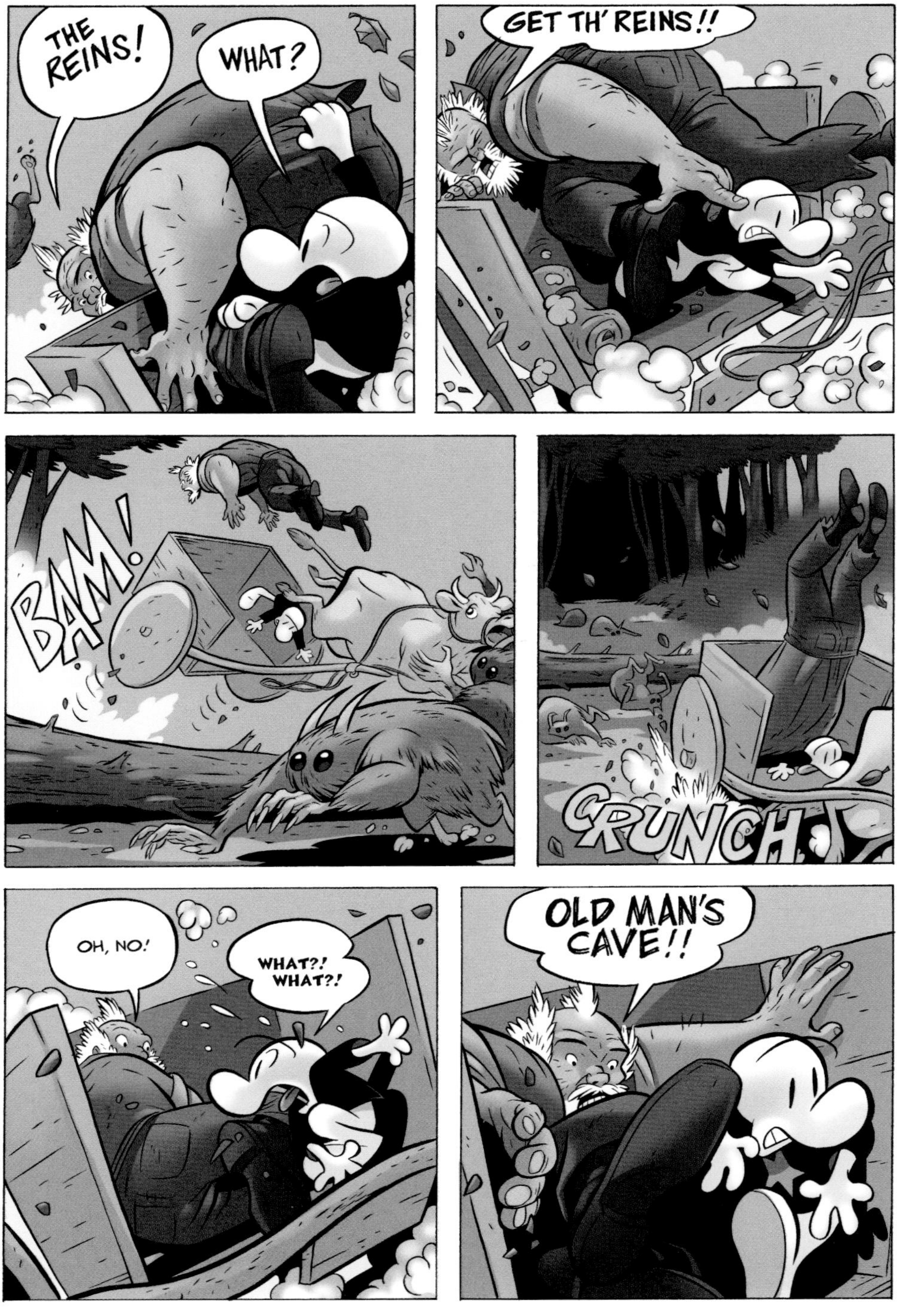
THE REINS!
WHAT?
GET TH' REINS!!
BAM!
CRUNCH
OH, NO!
WHAT?! WHAT?!
OLD MAN'S CAVE!!

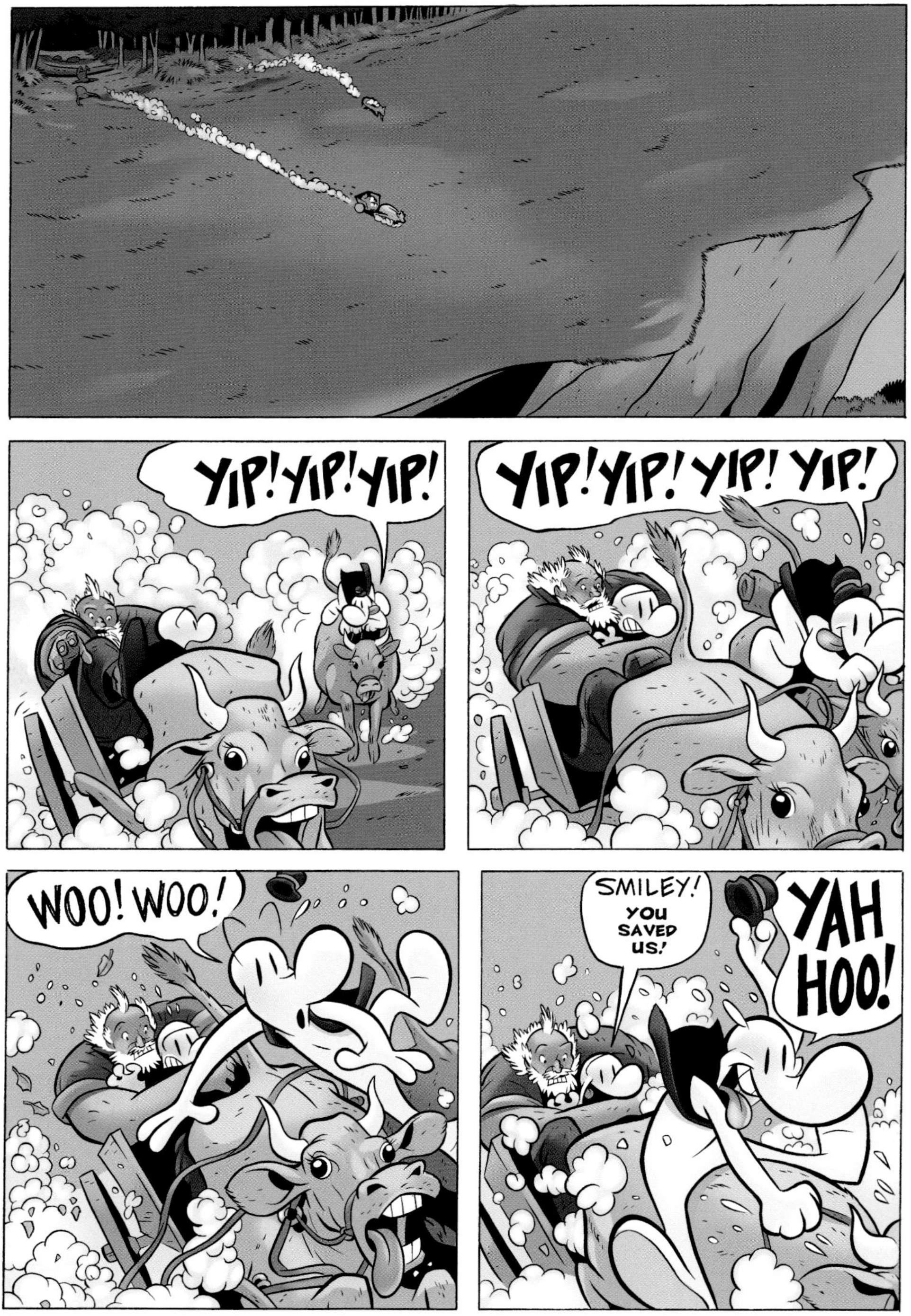
YIP! YIP! YIP!
YIP! YIP! YIP! YIP!
WOO! WOO!
SMILEY! YOU SAVED US!
YAH HOO!

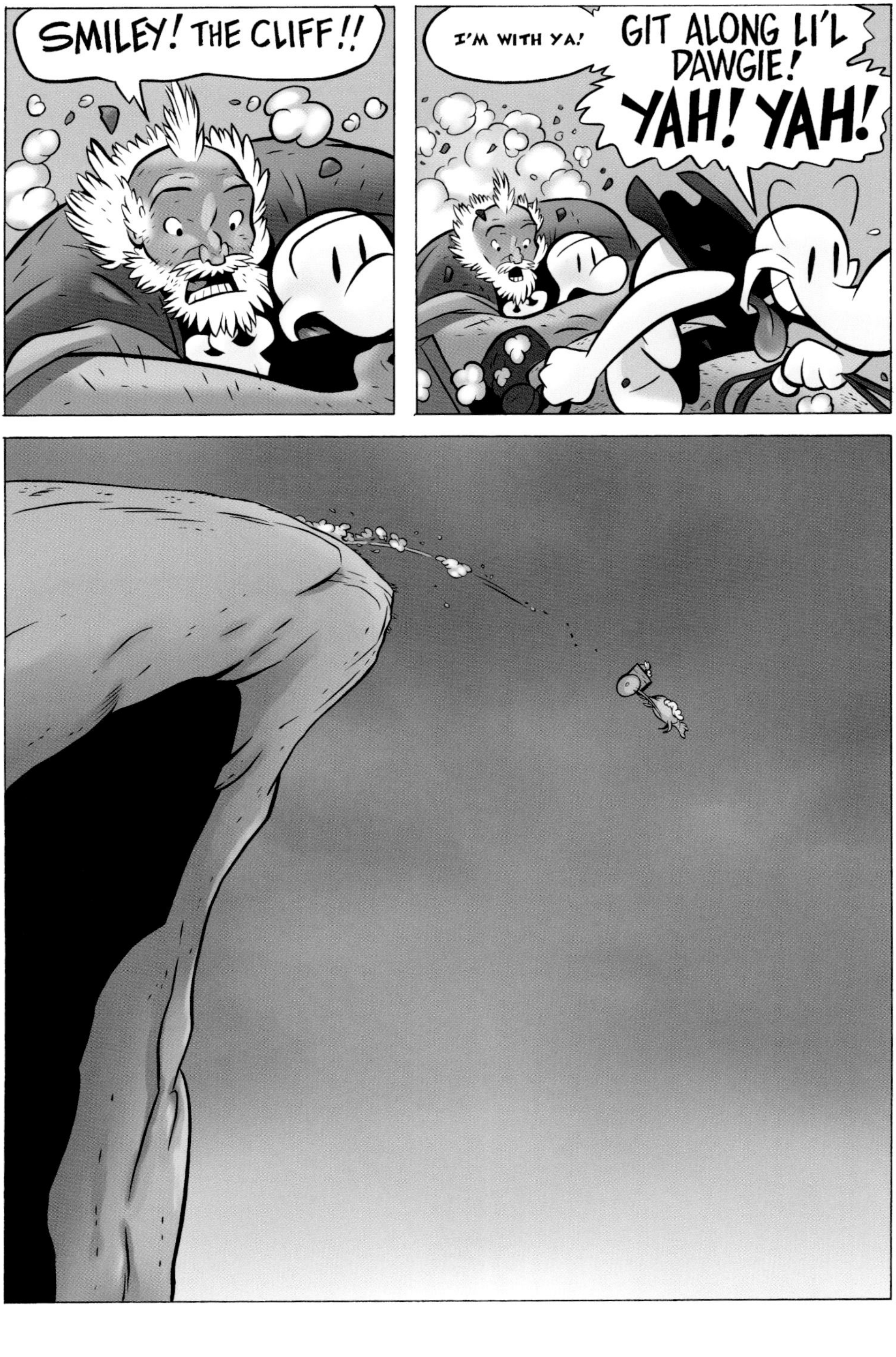
SMILEY! THE CLIFF!!
I'M WITH YA!
GIT ALONG LI'L DAWGIE! YAH! YAH!

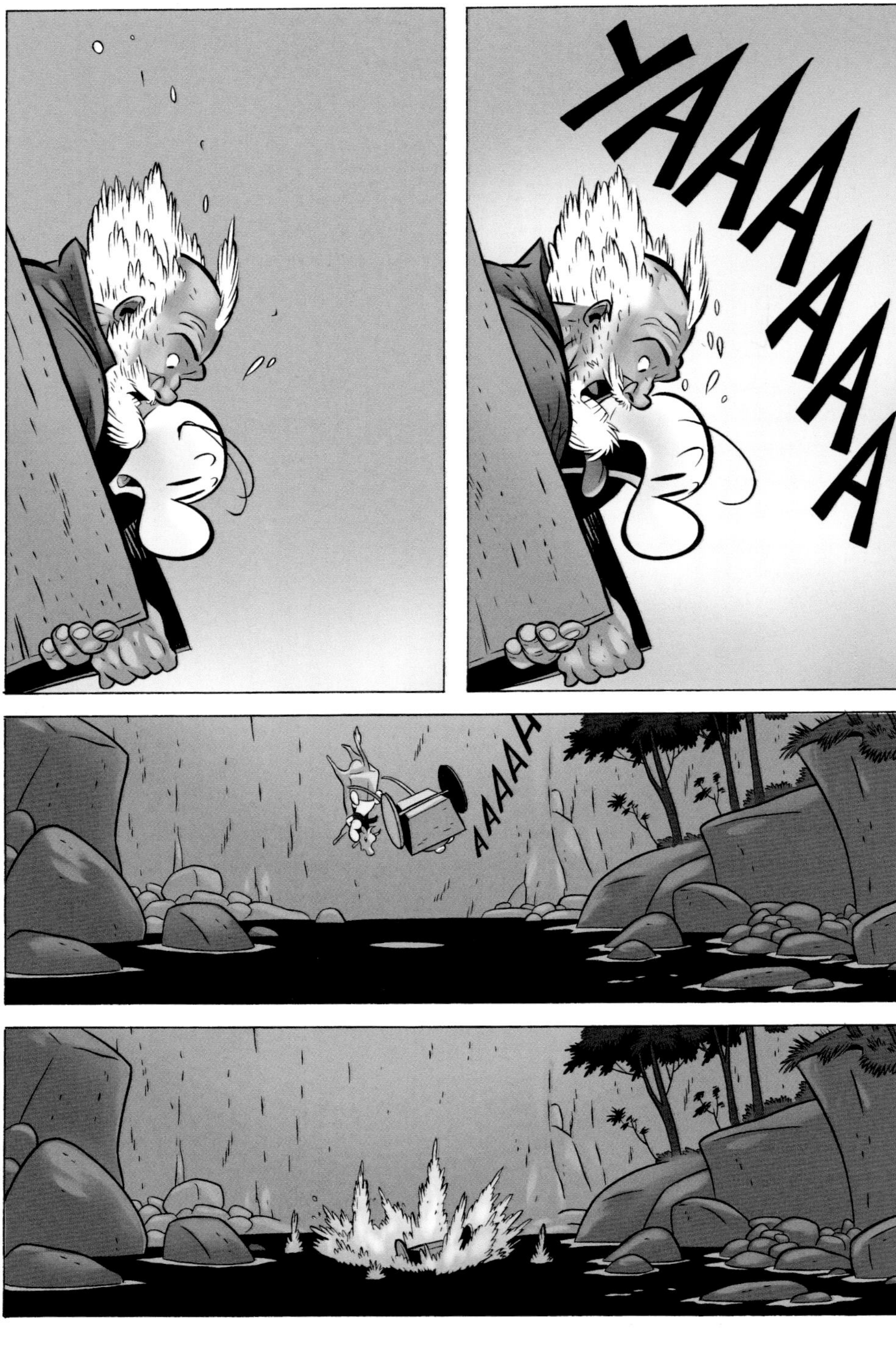
YAAAAAAA
AAAAA

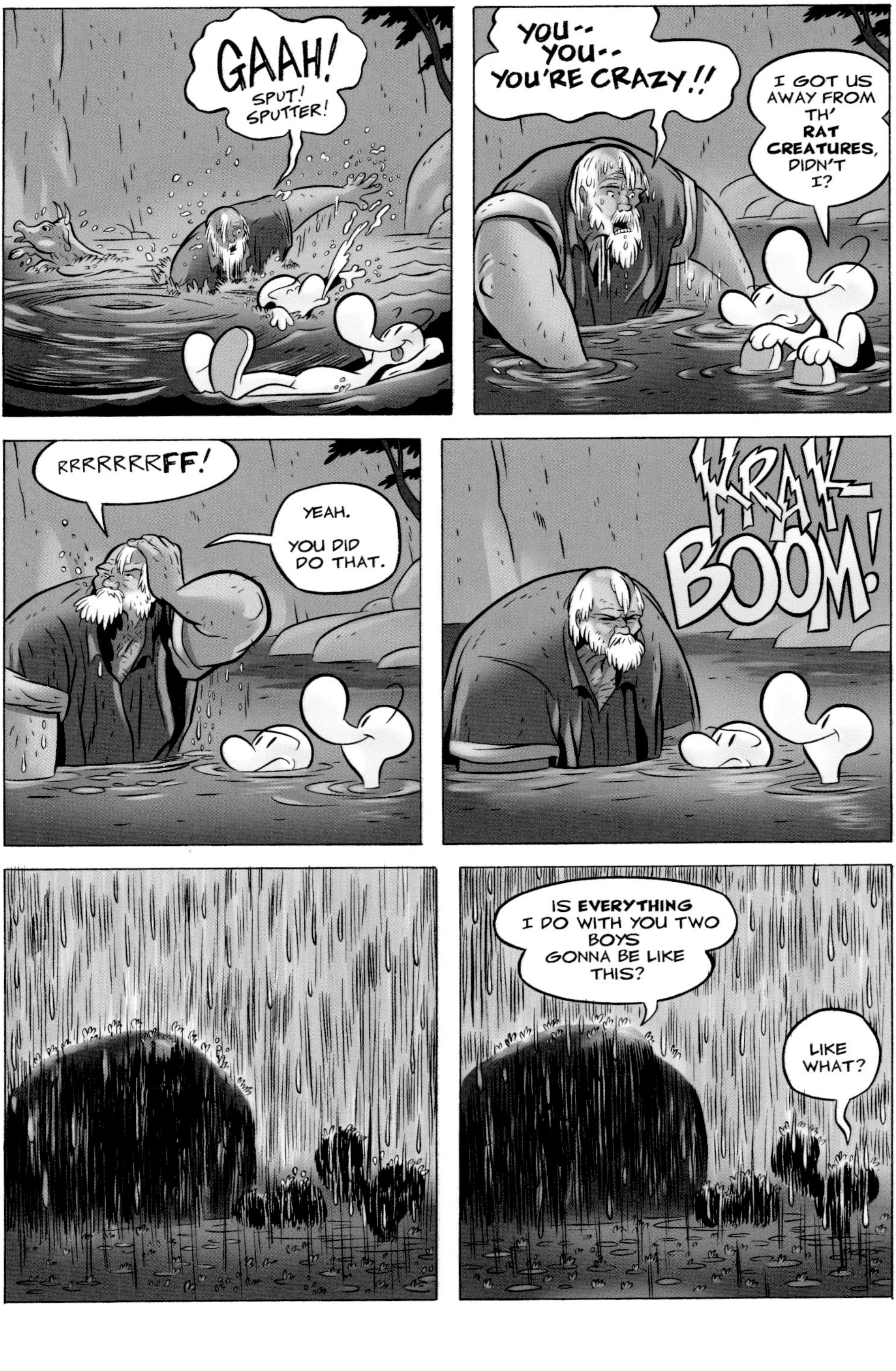
GAAH!
SPUT! SPUTTER!
YOU-- YOU-- YOU'RE CRAZY!!
I GOT US AWAY FROM TH' RAT CREATURES, DIDN'T I?
RRRRRRRFF!
YEAH.
YOU DID DO THAT.
KRAK BOOM!
IS EVERYTHING I DO WITH YOU TWO BOYS GONNA BE LIKE THIS?
LIKE WHAT?

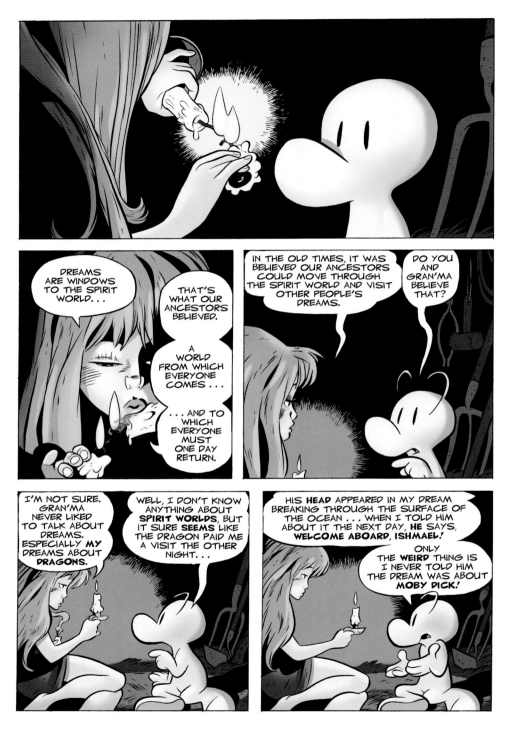

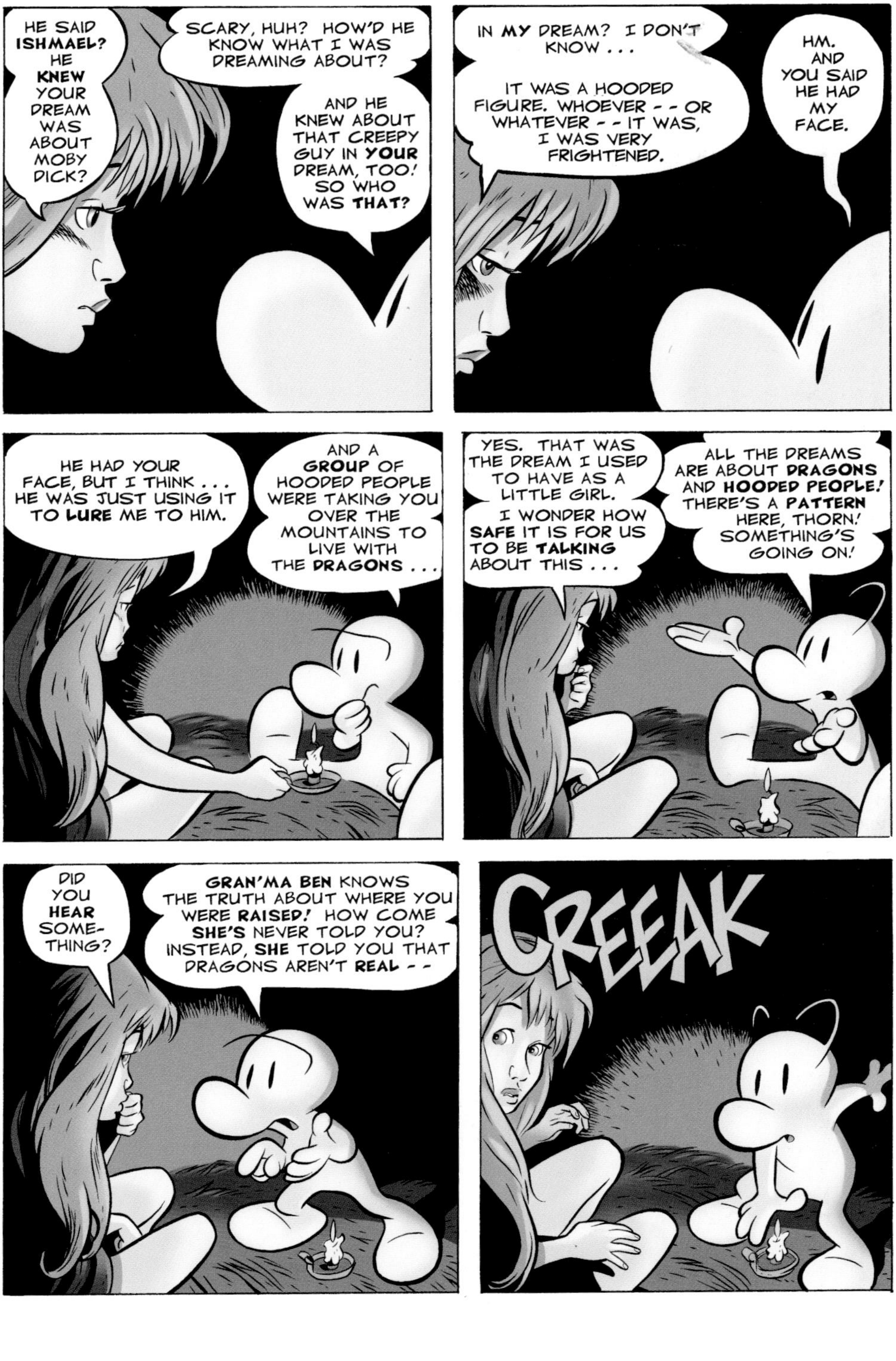
HE SAID ISHMAEL? HE KNEW YOUR DREAM WAS ABOUT MOBY DICK?
SCARY, HUH? HOW'D HE KNOW WHAT I WAS DREAMING ABOUT?
AND HE KNEW ABOUT THAT CREEPY GUY IN YOUR DREAM, TOO! SO WHO WAS THAT?
IN MY DREAM? I DON'T KNOW . . .
IT WAS A HOODED FIGURE. WHOEVER - - OR WHATEVER - - IT WAS, I WAS VERY FRIGHTENED.
HM. AND YOU SAID HE HAD MY FACE.
HE HAD YOUR FACE, BUT I THINK . . . HE WAS JUST USING IT TO LURE ME TO HIM.
AND A GROUP OF HOODED PEOPLE WERE TAKING YOU OVER THE MOUNTAINS TO LIVE WITH THE DRAGONS . . .
YES. THAT WAS THE DREAM I USED TO HAVE AS A LITTLE GIRL.
I WONDER HOW SAFE IT IS FOR US TO BE TALKING ABOUT THIS . . .
ALL THE DREAMS ARE ABOUT DRAGONS AND HOODED PEOPLE! THERE'S A PATTERN HERE, THORN! SOMETHING'S GOING ON!
DID YOU HEAR SOME-THING?
GRAN'MA BEN KNOWS THE TRUTH ABOUT WHERE YOU WERE RAISED! HOW COME SHE'S NEVER TOLD YOU? INSTEAD, SHE TOLD YOU THAT DRAGONS AREN'T REAL - -
CREEAK

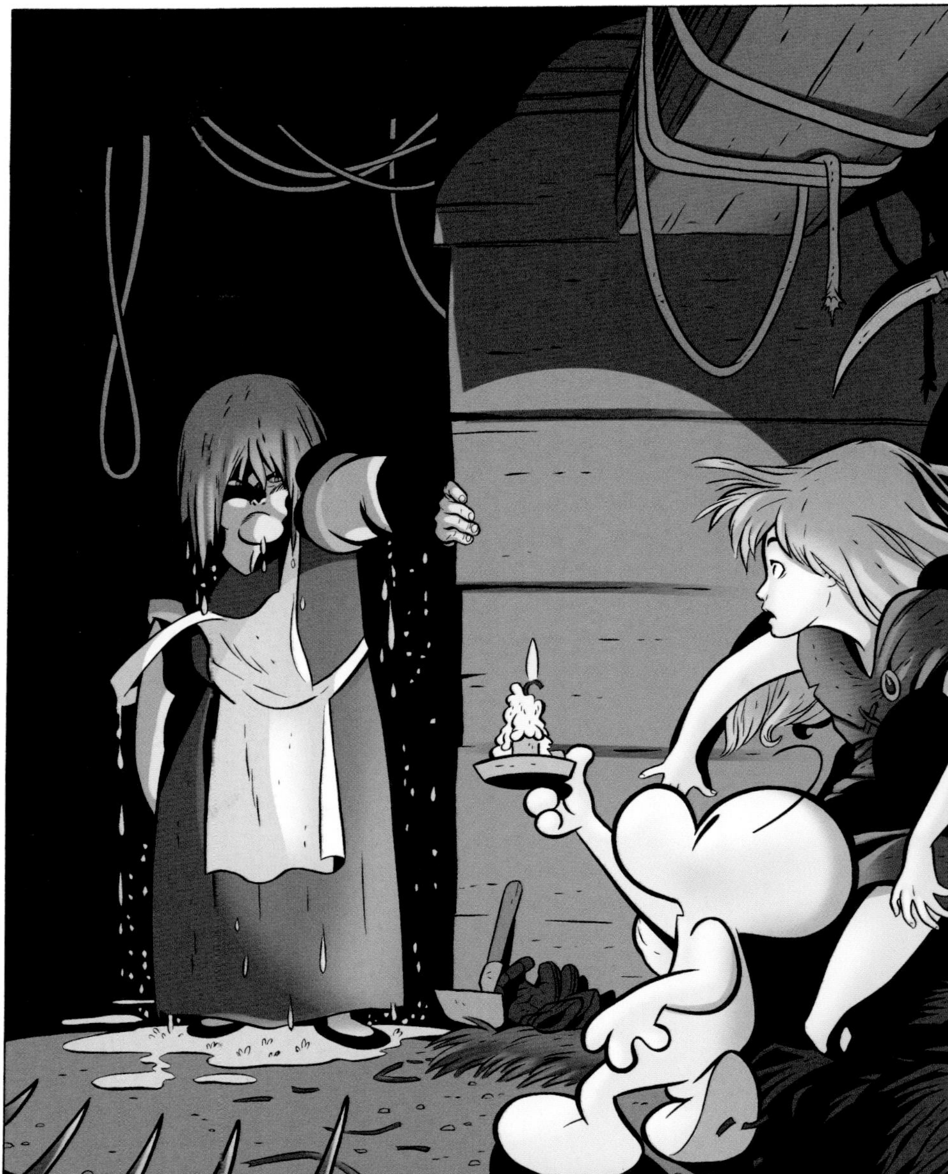

CHAPTER FOUR DOUBLE OR NOTHING

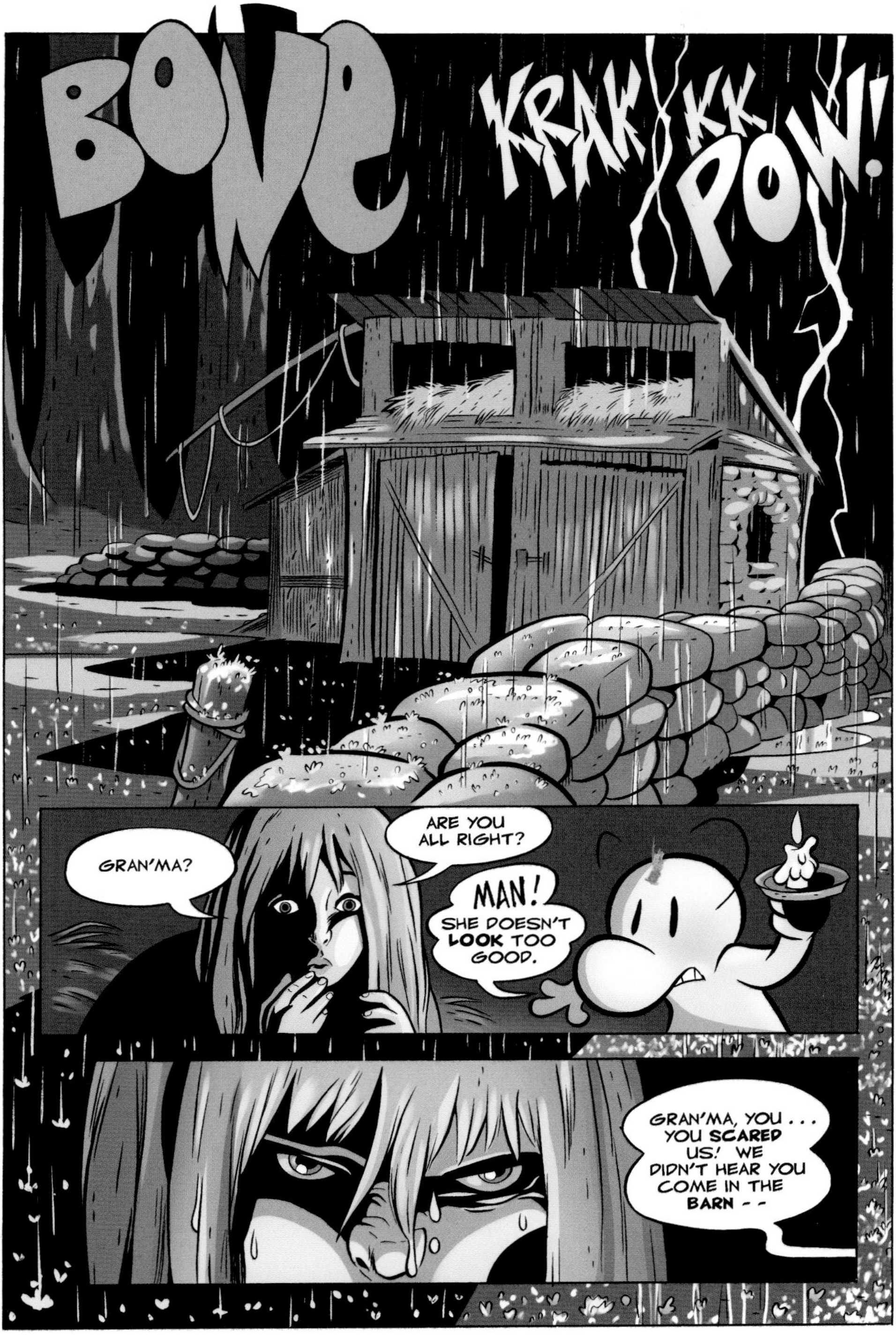
BONE
KRAK KK POW!
GRAN'MA?
ARE YOU ALL RIGHT?
MAN! SHE DOESN'T LOOK TOO GOOD.
GRAN'MA, YOU . . . YOU SCARED US! WE DIDN'T HEAR YOU COME IN THE BARN - -

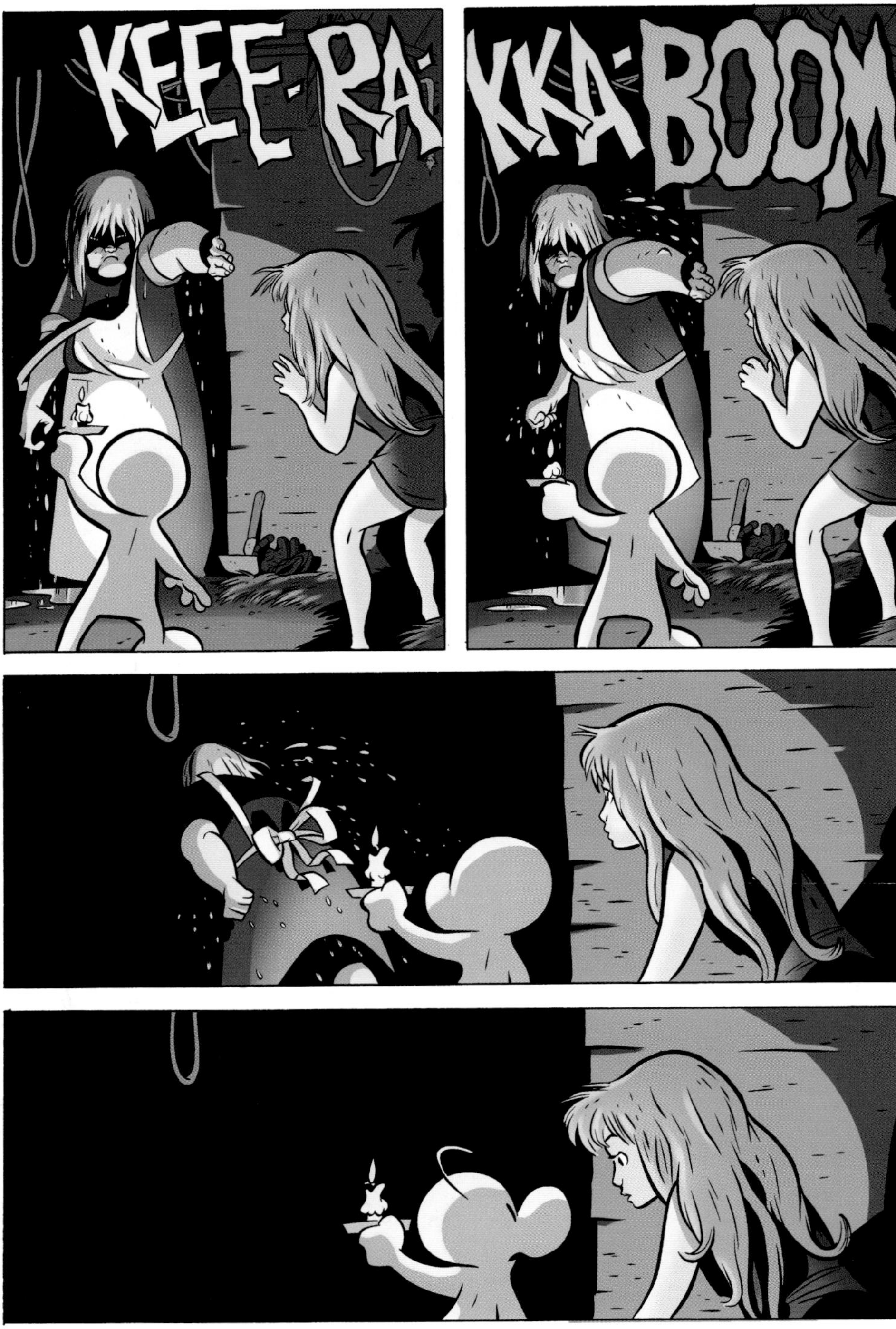
KEEE-RA-KKA-BOOM

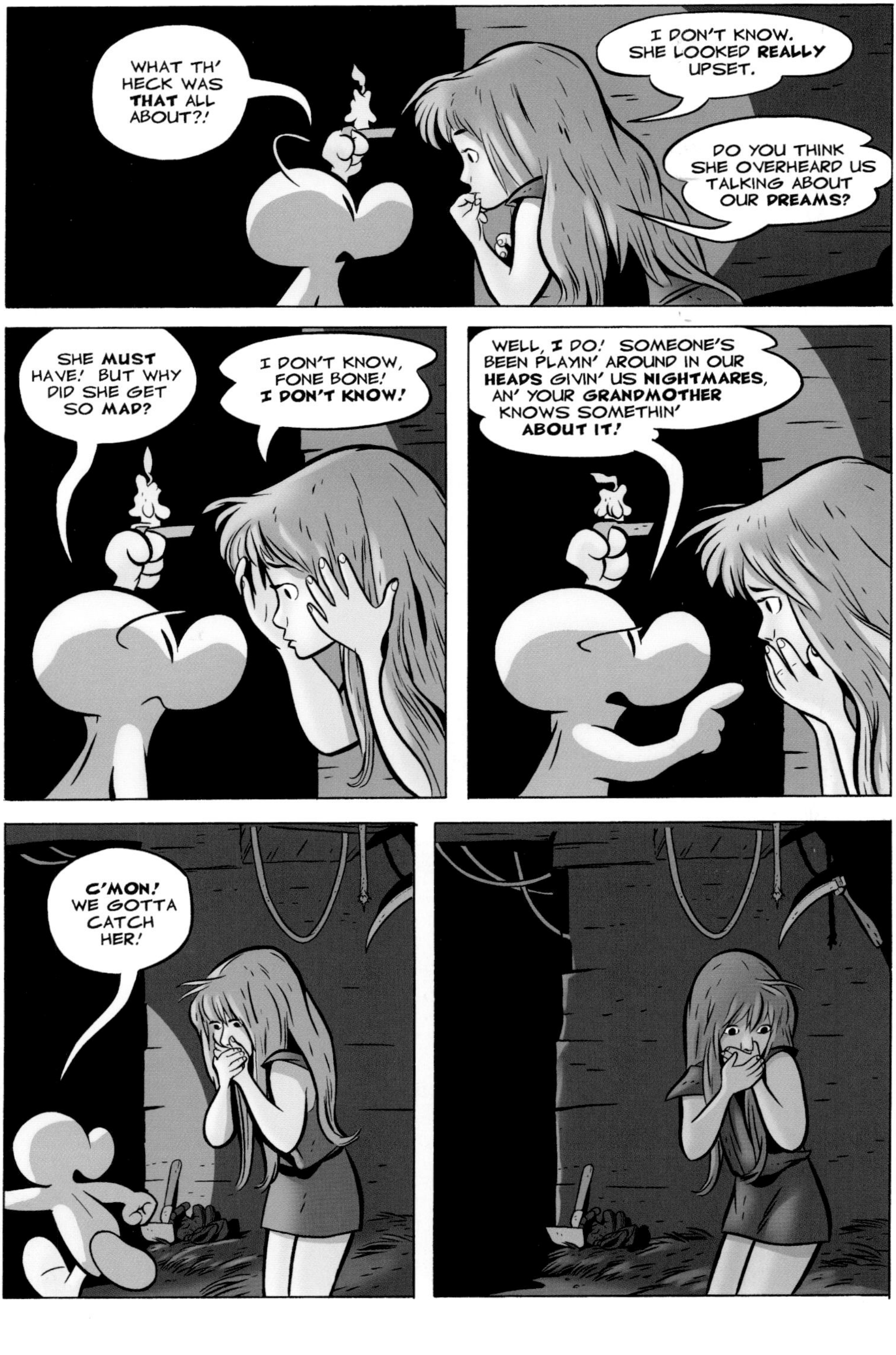
WHAT TH' HECK WAS THAT ALL ABOUT?!
I DON'T KNOW. SHE LOOKED REALLY UPSET.
DO YOU THINK SHE OVERHEARD US TALKING ABOUT OUR DREAMS?
SHE MUST HAVE! BUT WHY DID SHE GET SO MAD?
I DON'T KNOW, FONE BONE! I DON'T KNOW!
WELL, I DO! SOMEONE'S BEEN PLAYIN' AROUND IN OUR HEADS GIVIN' US NIGHTMARES, AN' YOUR GRANDMOTHER KNOWS SOMETHIN' ABOUT IT!
C'MON! WE GOTTA CATCH HER!

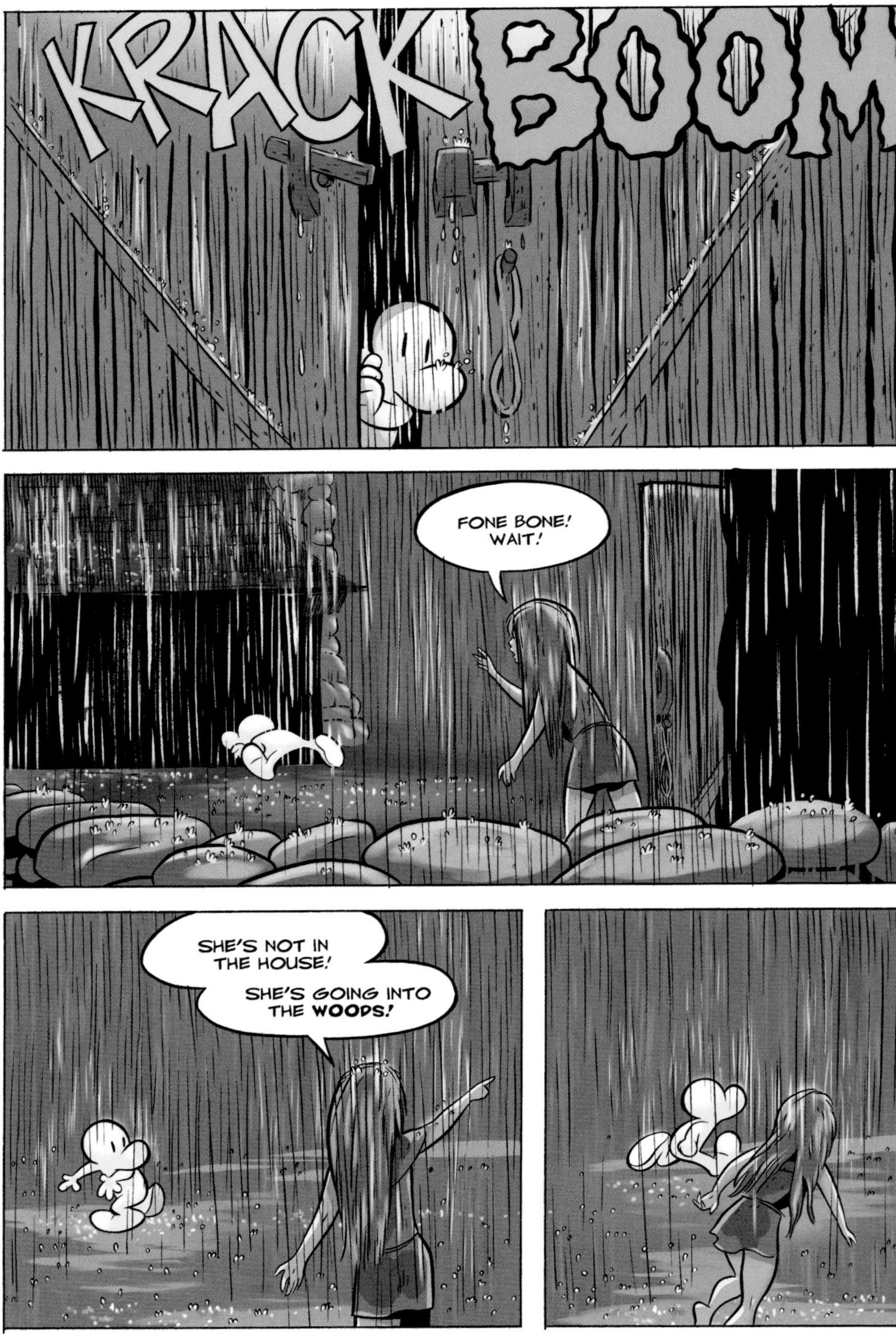
KRACK BOOM
FONE BONE! WAIT!
SHE'S NOT IN THE HOUSE!
SHE'S GOING INTO THE WOODS!

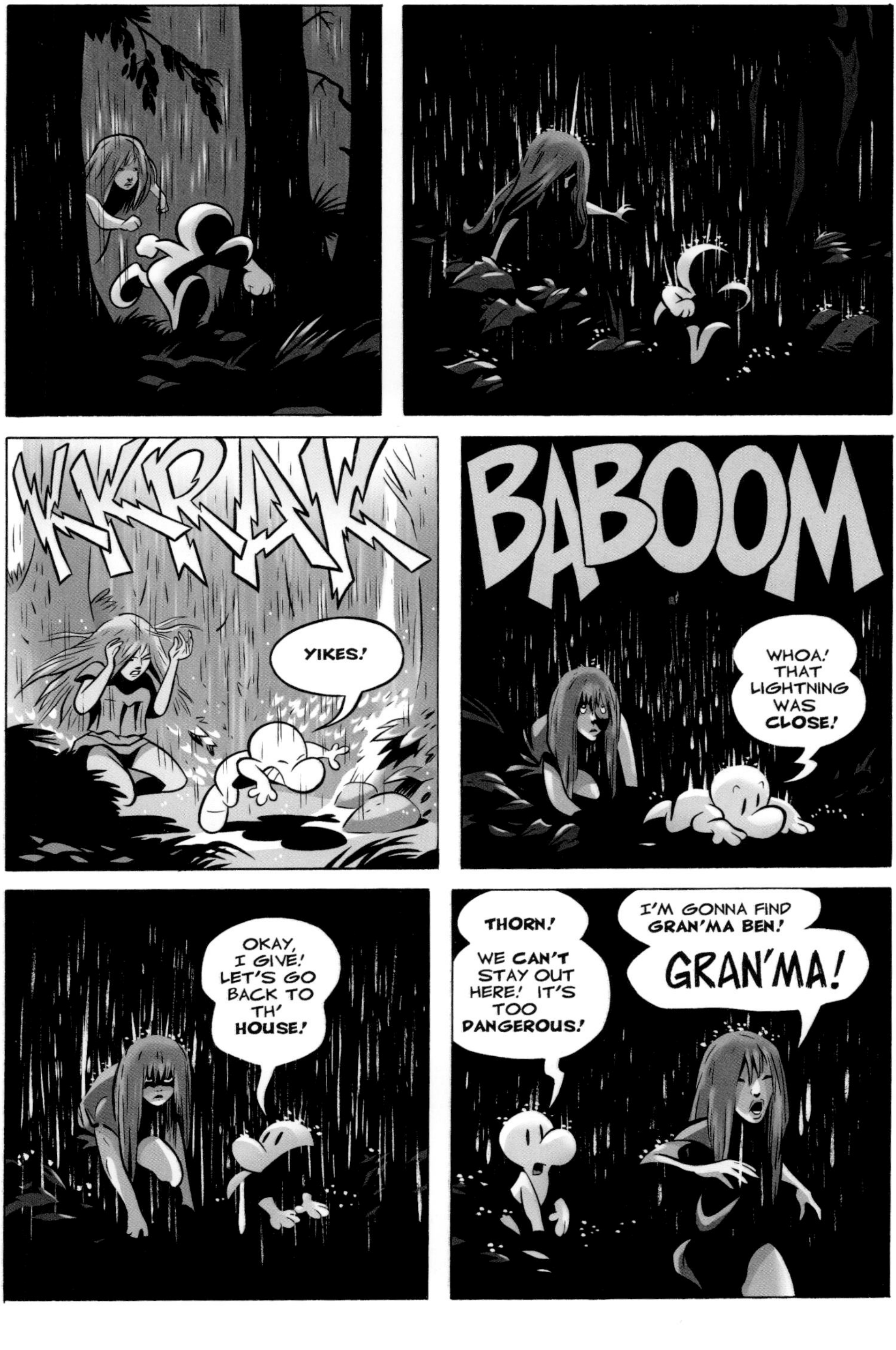
KKRAK
YIKES!
BABOOM
WHOA! THAT LIGHTNING WAS CLOSE!
OKAY, I GIVE! LET'S GO BACK TO TH' HOUSE!
THORN!
WE CAN'T STAY OUT HERE! IT'S TOO DANGEROUS!
I'M GONNA FIND GRAN'MA BEN!
GRAN'MA!

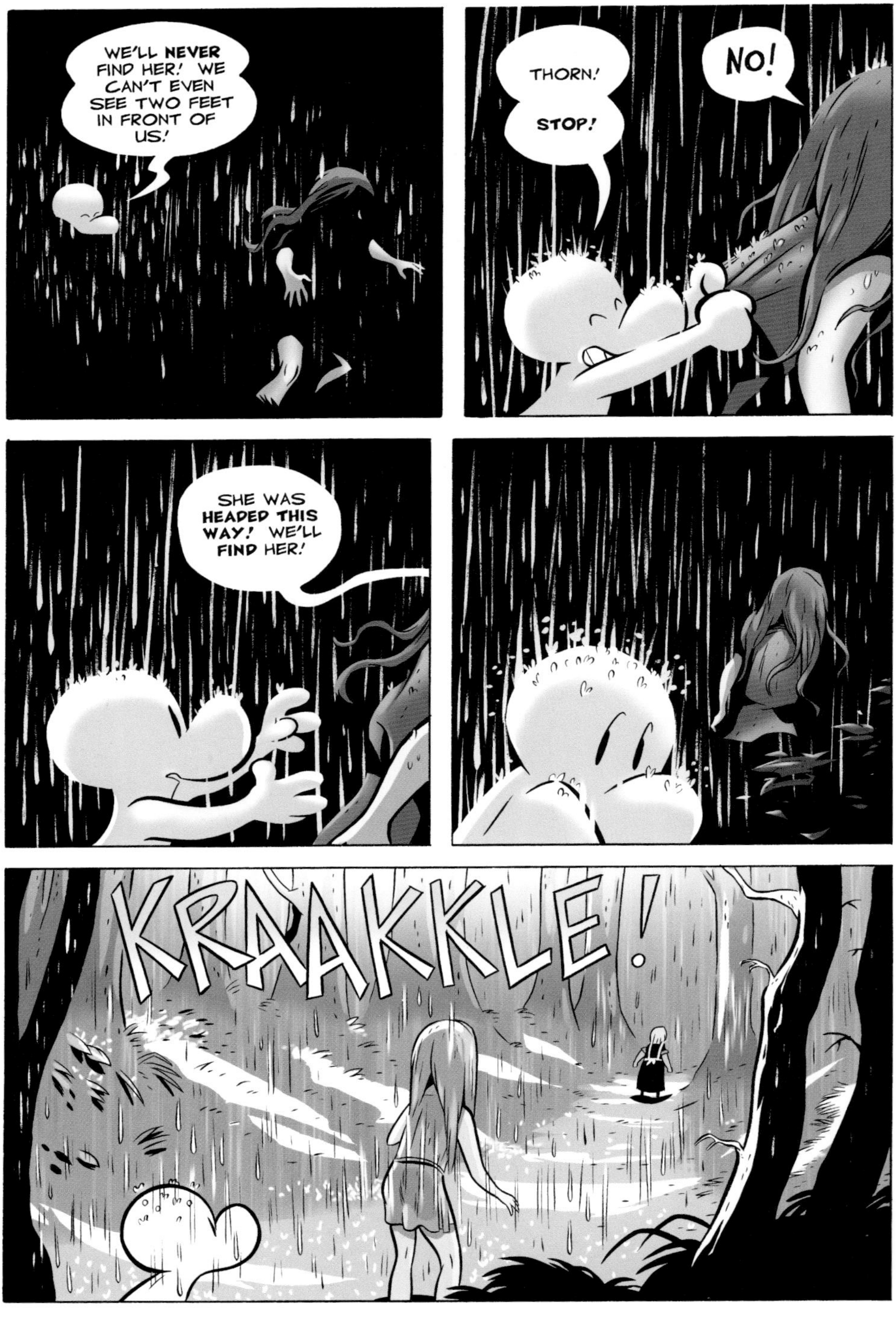
WE'LL **NEVER** FIND HER! WE CAN'T EVEN SEE TWO FEET IN FRONT OF US!
THORN!
STOP!
NO!
SHE WAS **HEADED THIS WAY!** WE'LL **FIND** HER!
KRAAKKLE!

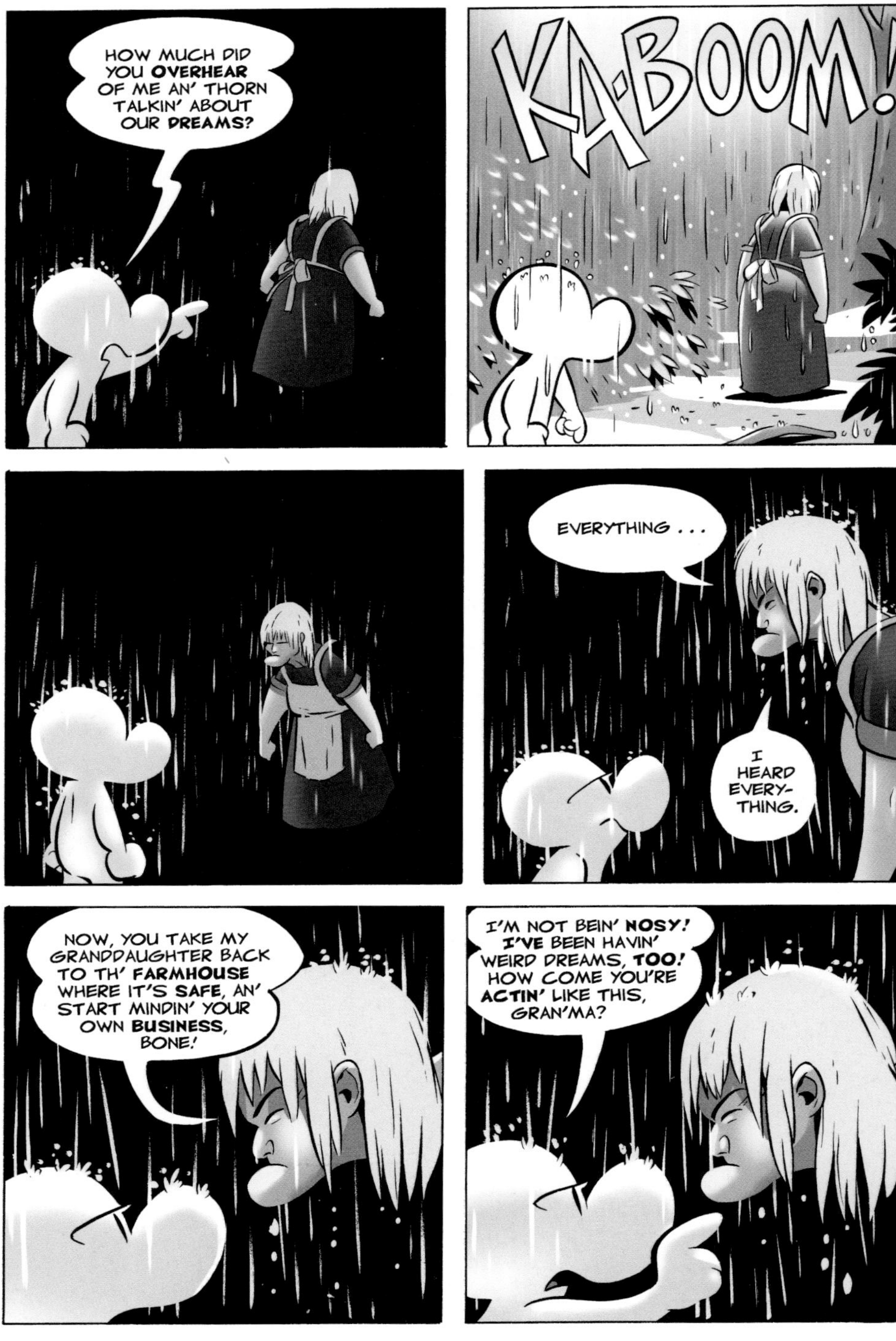
HOW MUCH DID YOU **OVERHEAR** OF ME AN' THORN TALKIN' ABOUT OUR **DREAMS?**
KA-BOOM!
EVERYTHING . . .
I HEARD EVERY-THING.
NOW, YOU TAKE MY GRANDDAUGHTER BACK TO TH' **FARMHOUSE** WHERE IT'S **SAFE**, AN' START MINDIN' YOUR OWN **BUSINESS**, BONE!
I'M NOT BEIN' **NOSY! I'VE** BEEN HAVIN' WEIRD DREAMS, **TOO!** HOW COME YOU'RE **ACTIN'** LIKE THIS, GRAN'MA?

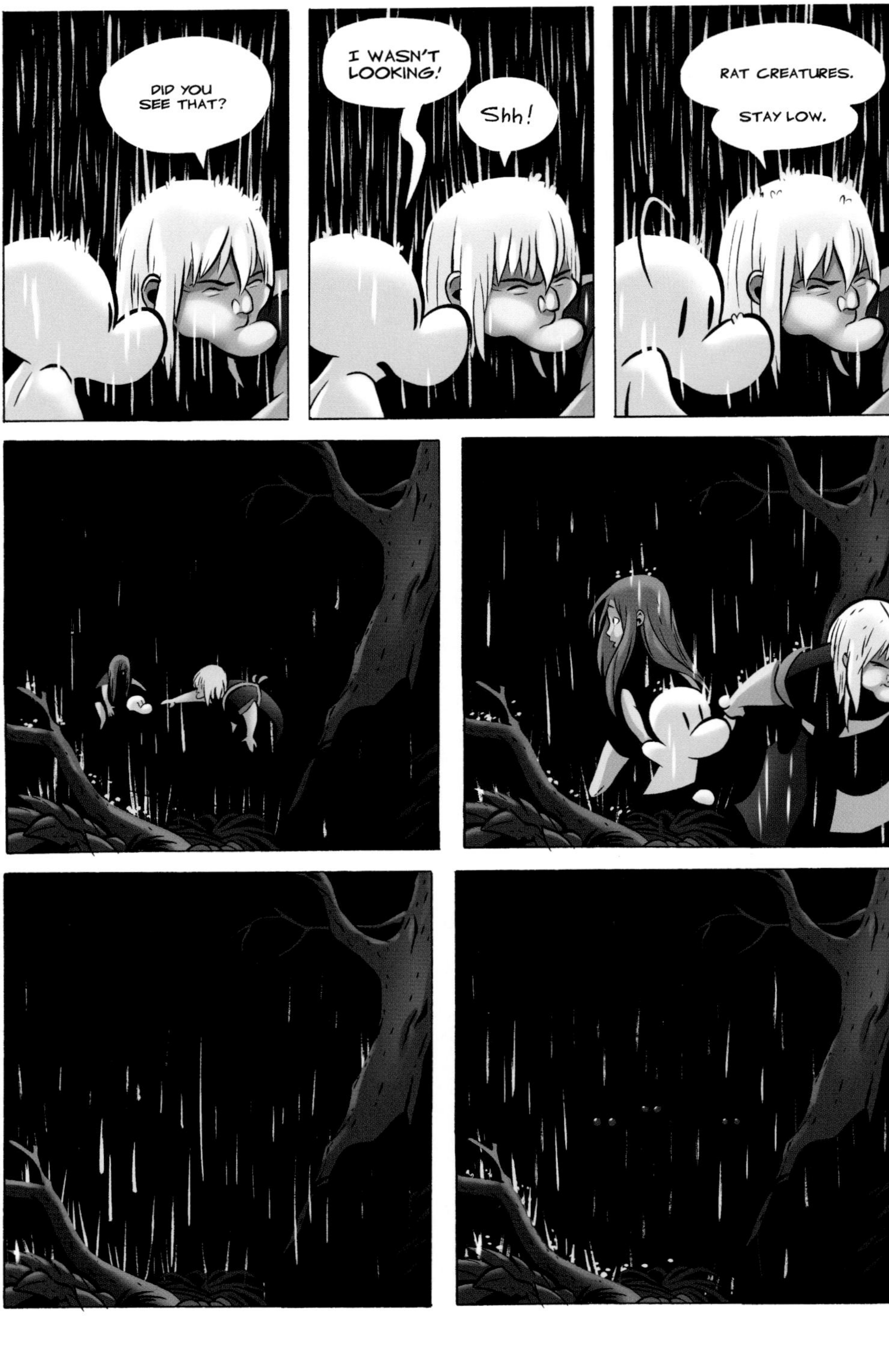
DID YOU SEE THAT?
I WASN'T LOOKING!
Shh!
RAT CREATURES.
STAY LOW.

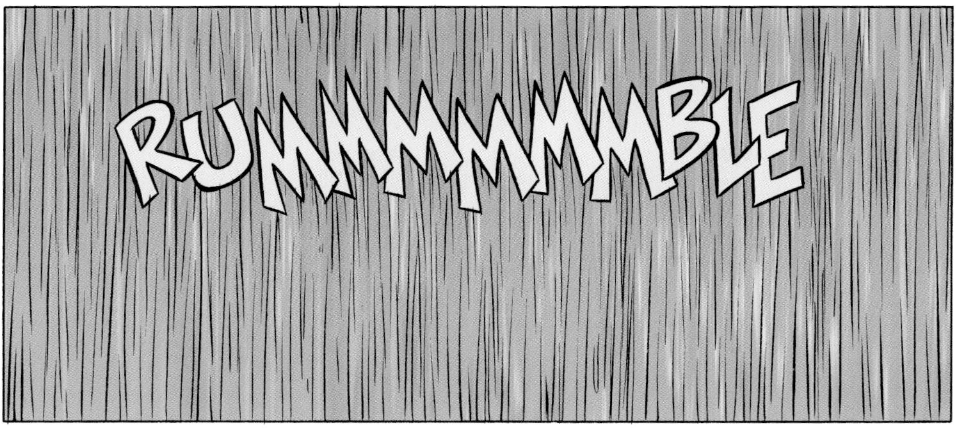
RUMMMMMMBLE

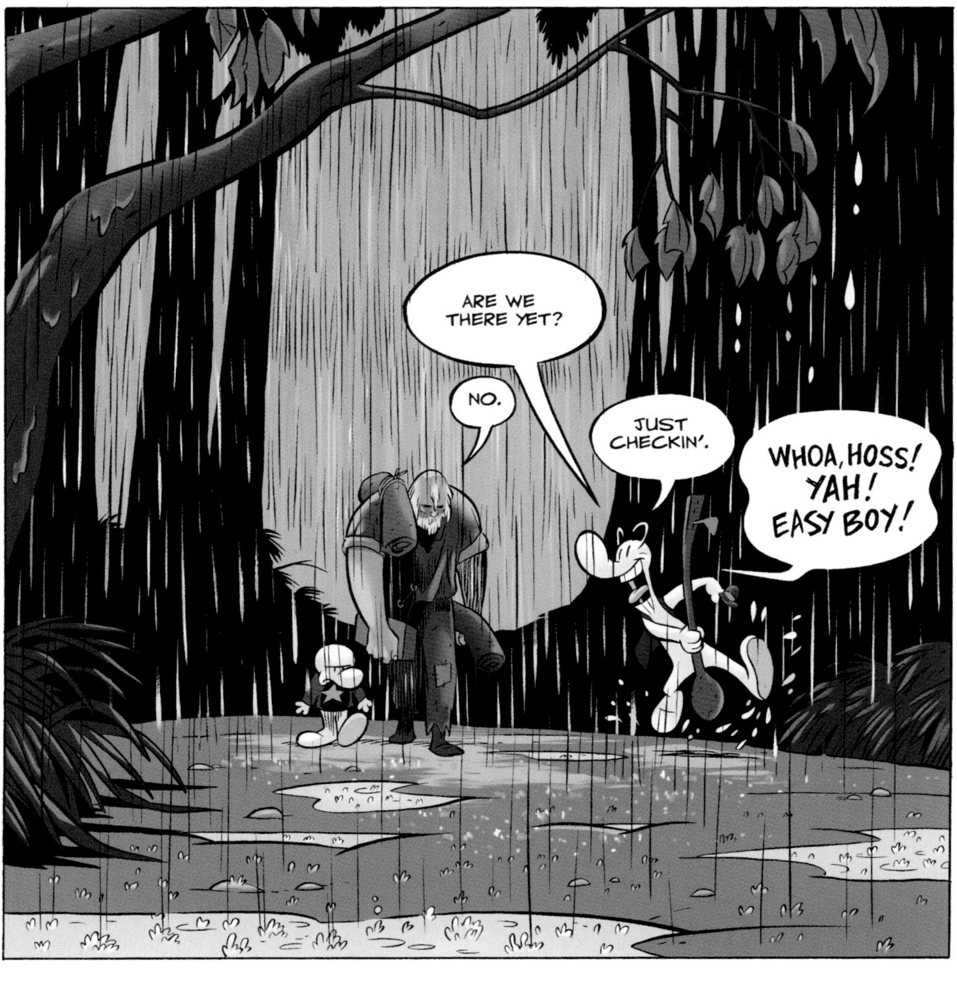
ARE WE THERE YET?
NO.
JUST CHECKIN'.
WHOA, HOSS! YAH! EASY BOY!

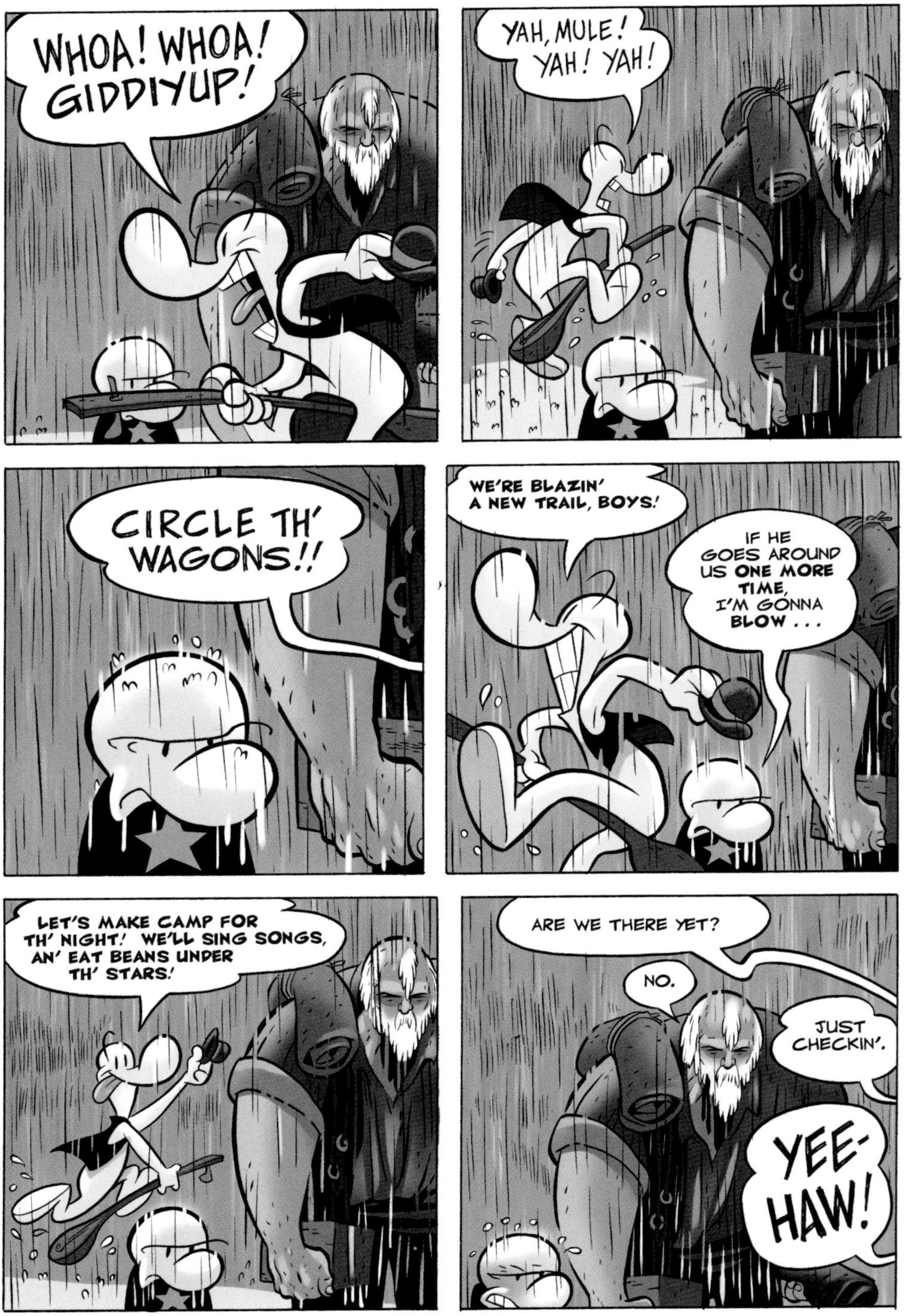
WHOA! WHOA! GIDDIYUP!
YAH, MULE! YAH! YAH!
CIRCLE TH' WAGONS!!
WE'RE BLAZIN' A NEW TRAIL, BOYS!
IF HE GOES AROUND US ONE MORE TIME, I'M GONNA BLOW . . .
LET'S MAKE CAMP FOR TH' NIGHT! WE'LL SING SONGS, AN' EAT BEANS UNDER TH' STARS!
ARE WE THERE YET?
NO.
JUST CHECKIN'.
YEE-HAW!

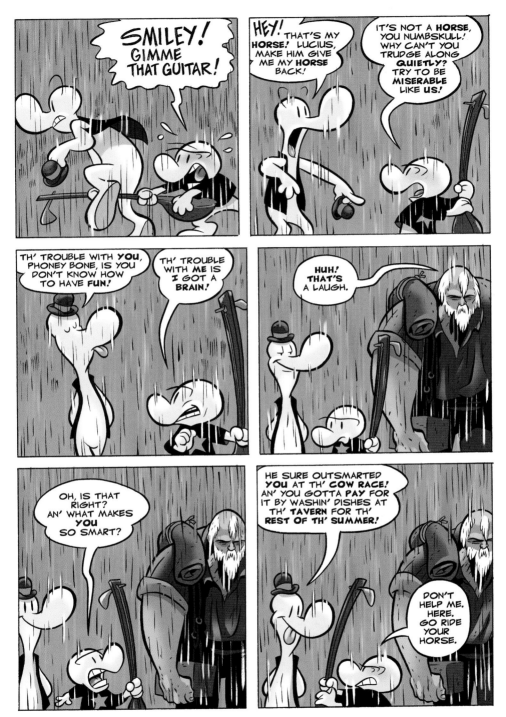

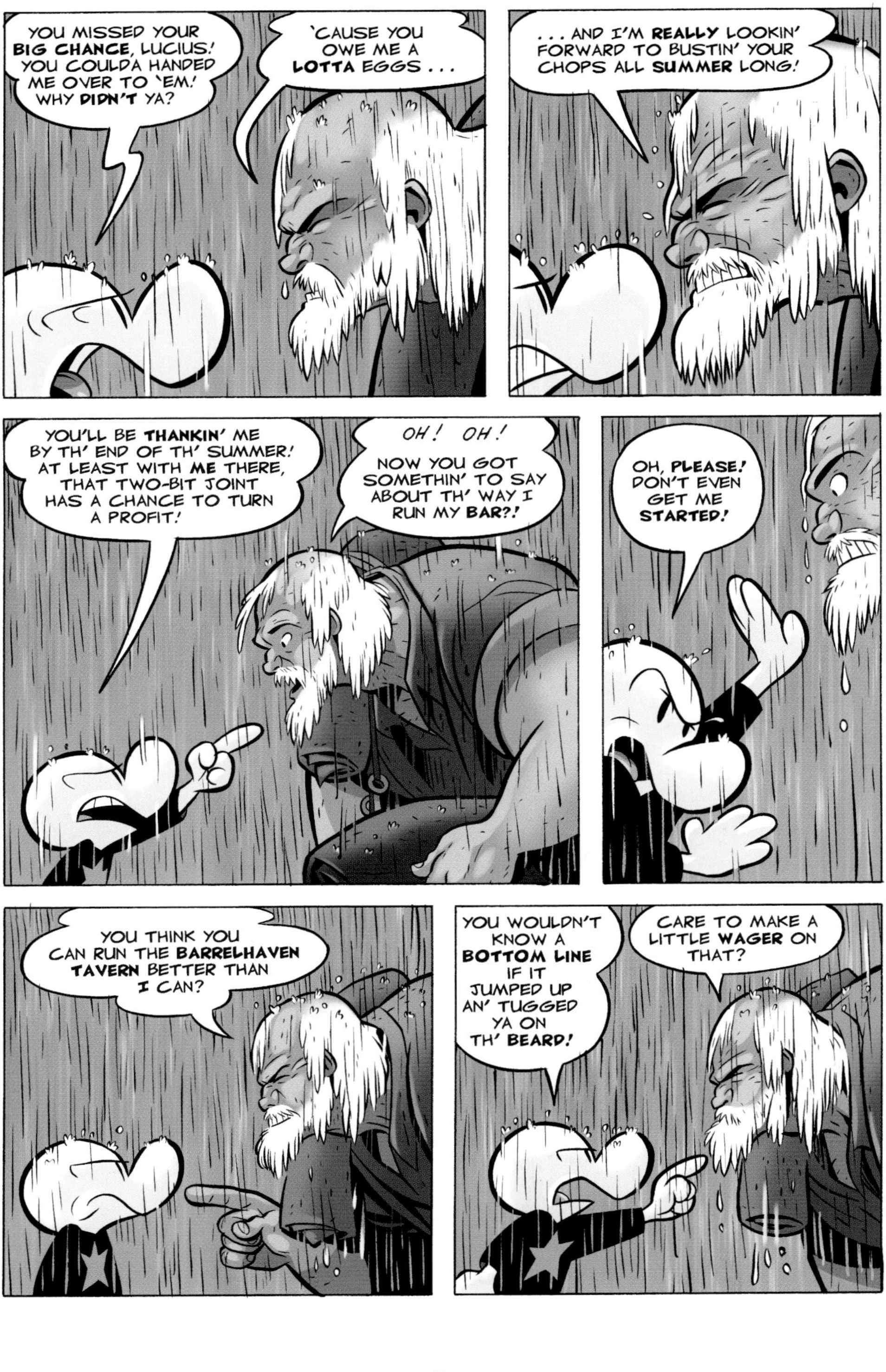
YOU MISSED YOUR BIG CHANCE, LUCIUS! YOU COULDA HANDED ME OVER TO 'EM! WHY DIDN'T YA?
'CAUSE YOU OWE ME A LOTTA EGGS . . .
. . . AND I'M REALLY LOOKIN' FORWARD TO BUSTIN' YOUR CHOPS ALL SUMMER LONG!
YOU'LL BE THANKIN' ME BY TH' END OF TH' SUMMER! AT LEAST WITH ME THERE, THAT TWO-BIT JOINT HAS A CHANCE TO TURN A PROFIT!
OH! OH!
NOW YOU GOT SOMETHIN' TO SAY ABOUT TH' WAY I RUN MY BAR?!
OH, PLEASE! DON'T EVEN GET ME STARTED!
YOU THINK YOU CAN RUN THE BARRELHAVEN TAVERN BETTER THAN I CAN?
YOU WOULDN'T KNOW A BOTTOM LINE IF IT JUMPED UP AN' TUGGED YA ON TH' BEARD!
CARE TO MAKE A LITTLE WAGER ON THAT?

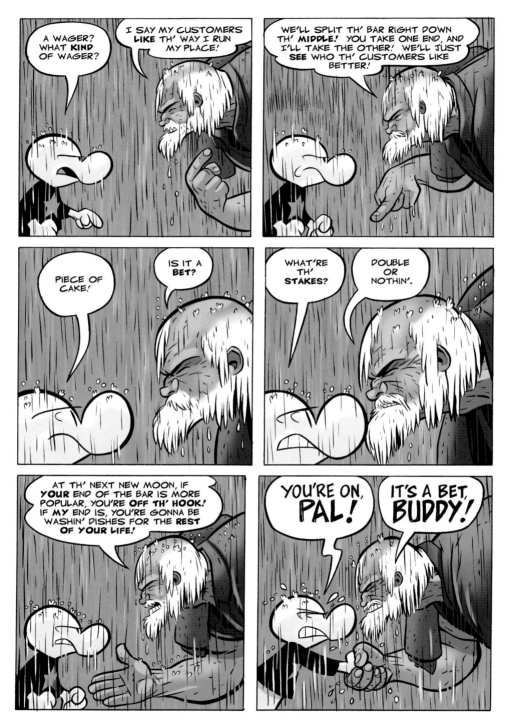

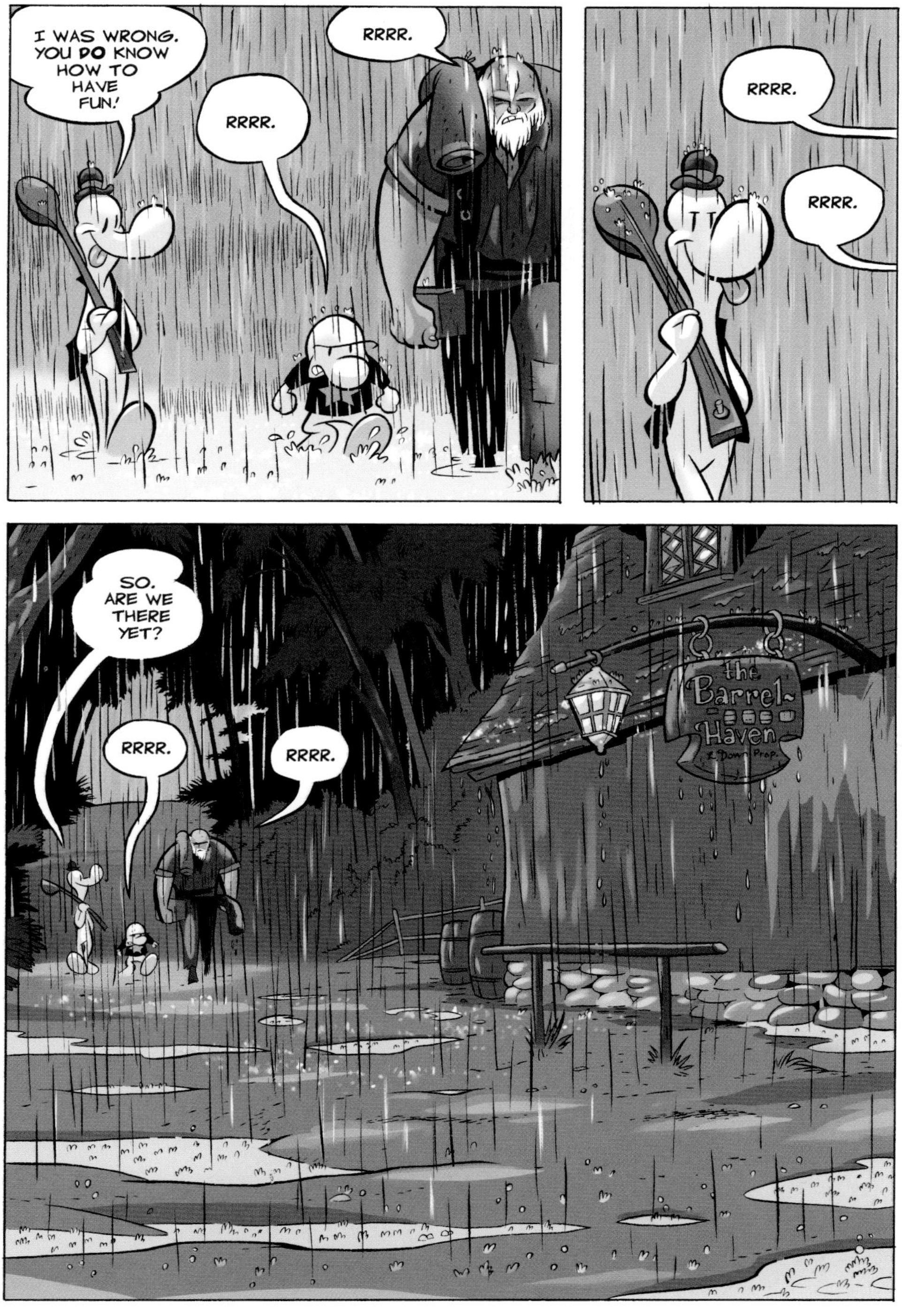
I WAS WRONG. YOU **DO** KNOW HOW TO HAVE FUN!
RRRR.
RRRR.
RRRR.
RRRR.
SO. ARE WE THERE YET?
RRRR.
RRRR.
the Barrel Haven

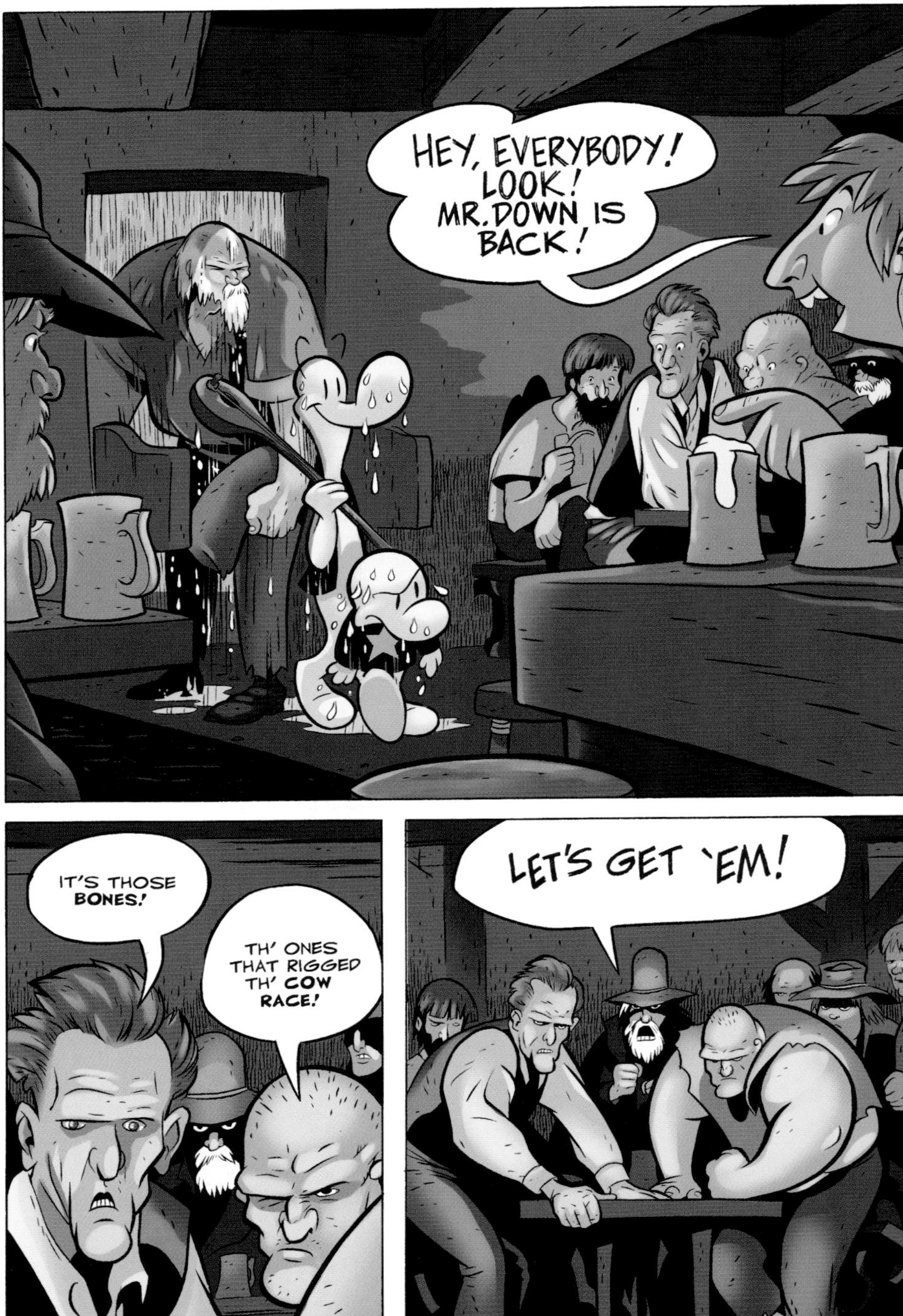
HEY, EVERYBODY! LOOK! MR. DOWN IS BACK!
IT'S THOSE BONES!
TH' ONES THAT RIGGED TH' COW RACE!
LET'S GET 'EM!

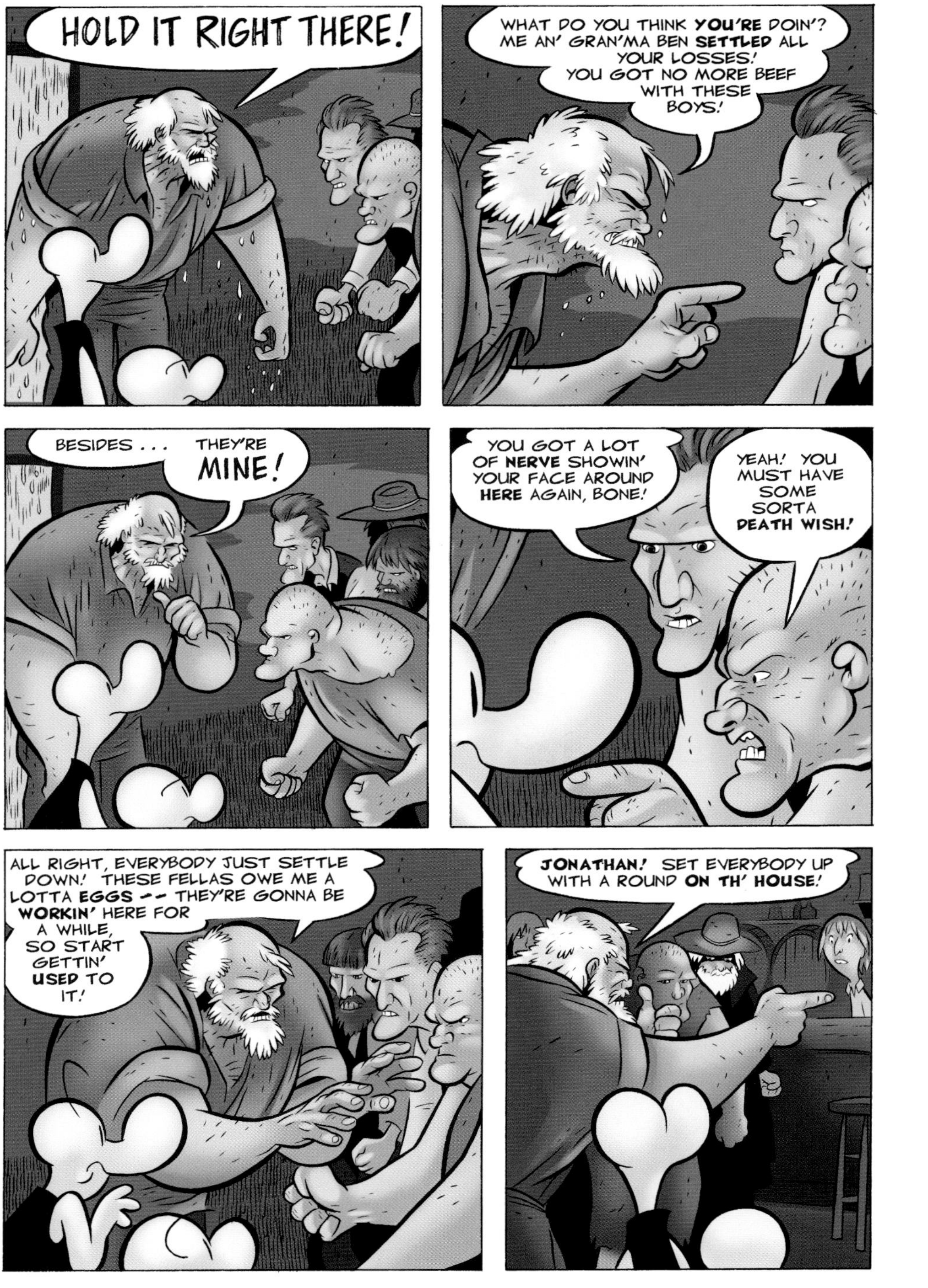
HOLD IT RIGHT THERE!
WHAT DO YOU THINK YOU'RE DOIN'? ME AN' GRAN'MA BEN SETTLED ALL YOUR LOSSES! YOU GOT NO MORE BEEF WITH THESE BOYS!
BESIDES . . . THEY'RE MINE!
YOU GOT A LOT OF NERVE SHOWIN' YOUR FACE AROUND HERE AGAIN, BONE!
YEAH! YOU MUST HAVE SOME SORTA DEATH WISH!
ALL RIGHT, EVERYBODY JUST SETTLE DOWN! THESE FELLAS OWE ME A LOTTA EGGS -- THEY'RE GONNA BE WORKIN' HERE FOR A WHILE, SO START GETTIN' USED TO IT!
JONATHAN! SET EVERYBODY UP WITH A ROUND ON TH' HOUSE!

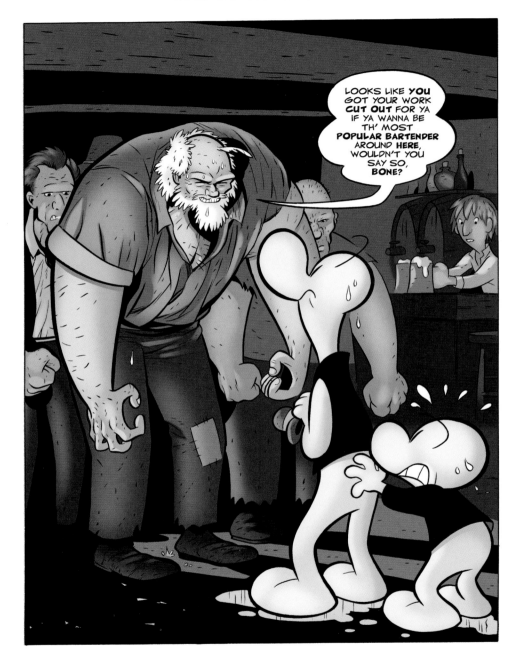

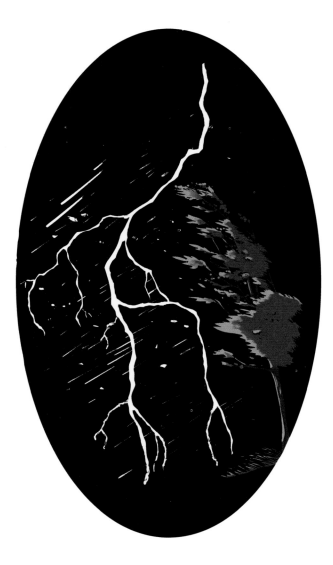

CHAPTER FIVE EYES OF THE STORM

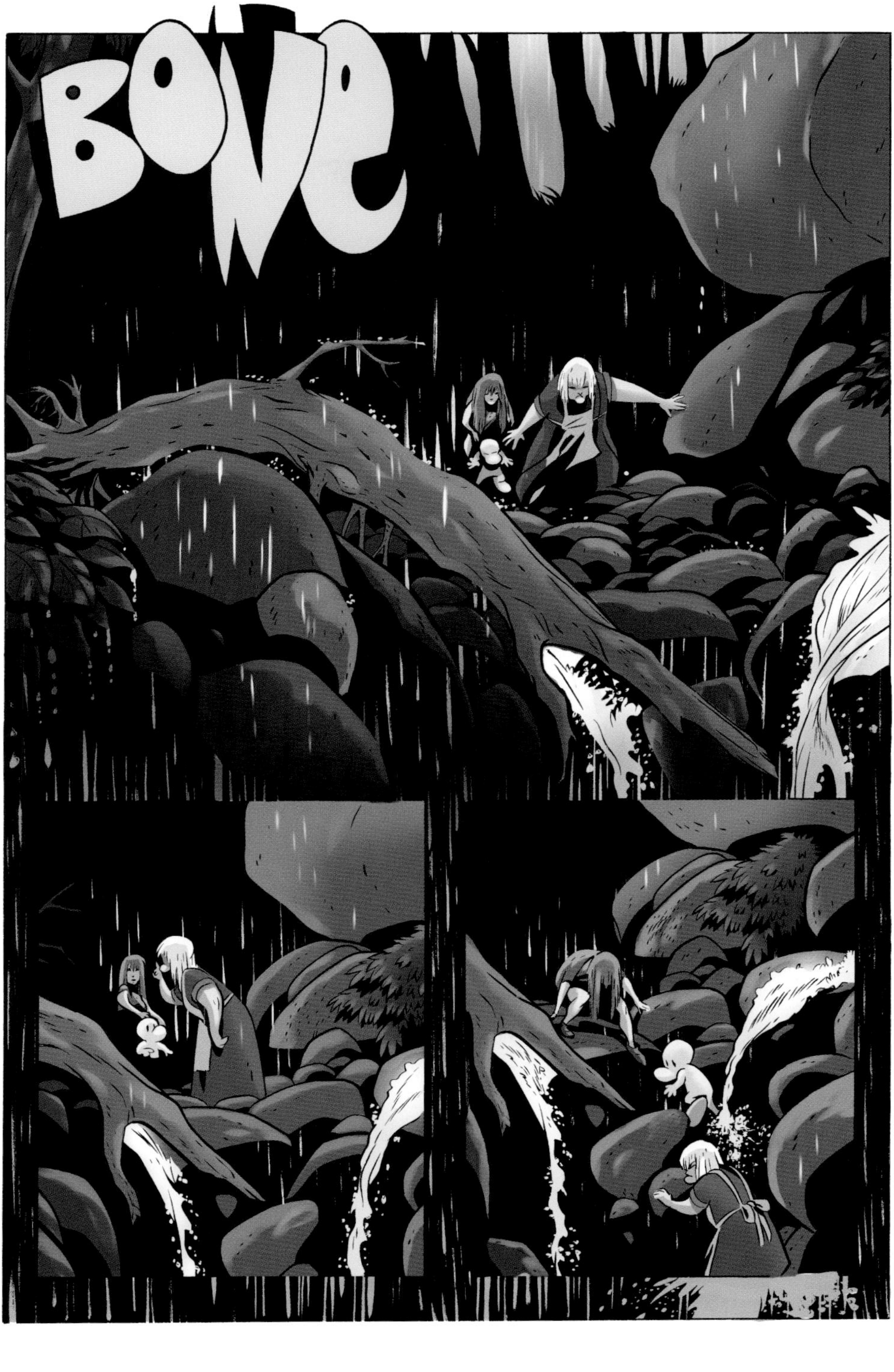
BONE

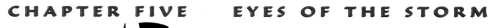

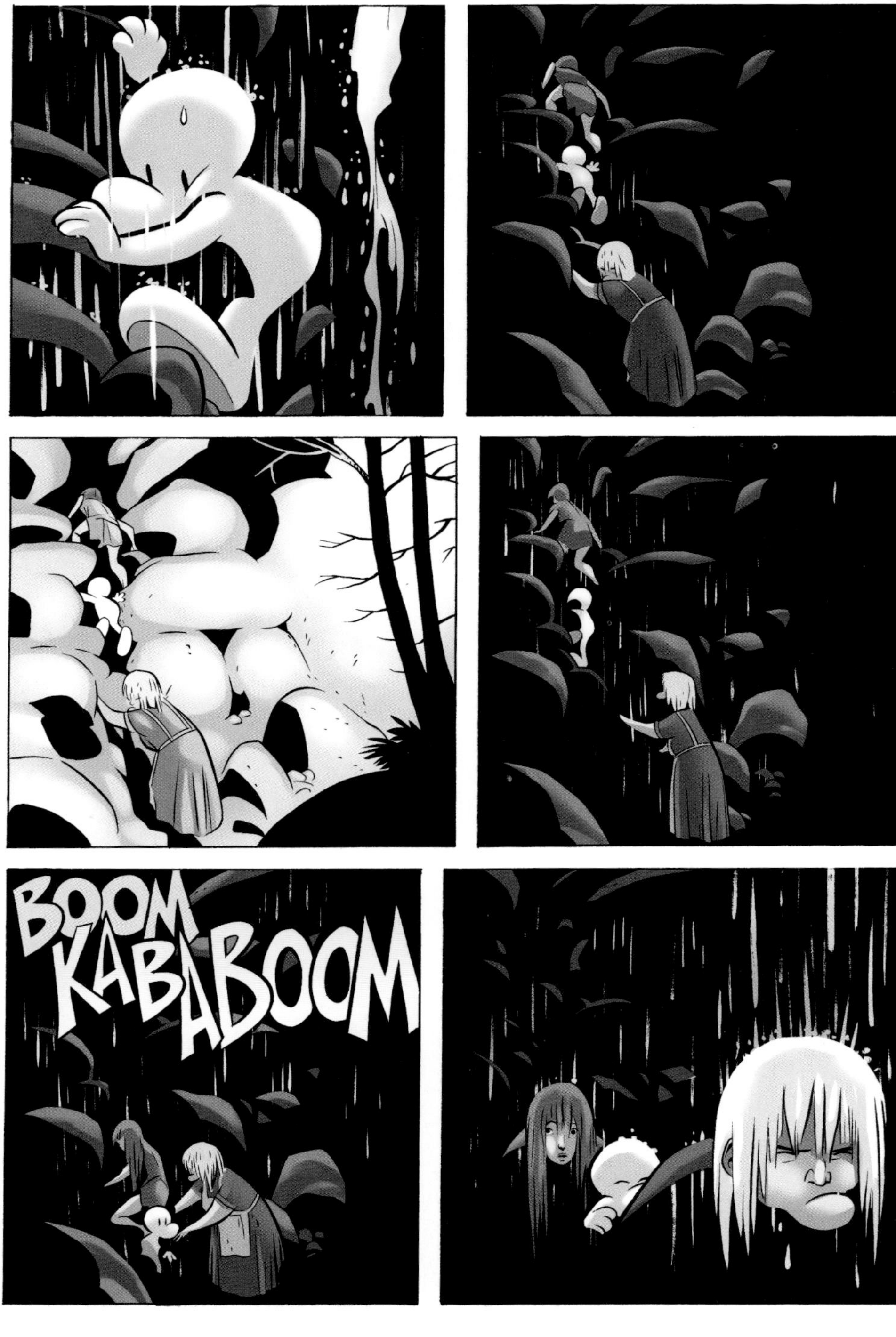
BOOM
KABABOOM

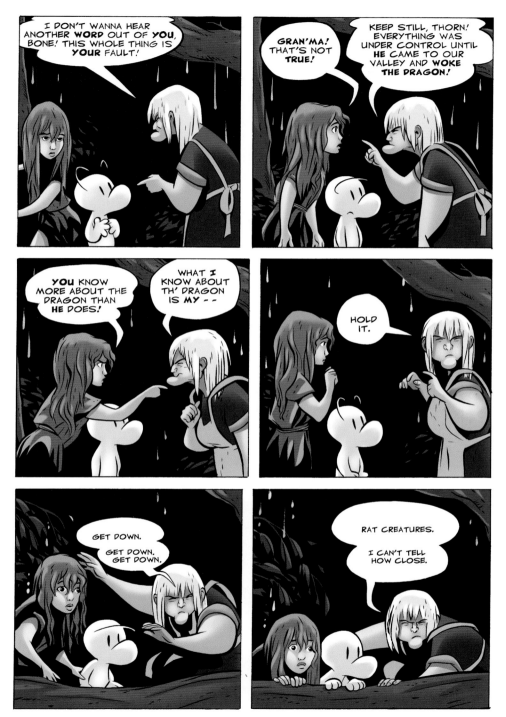

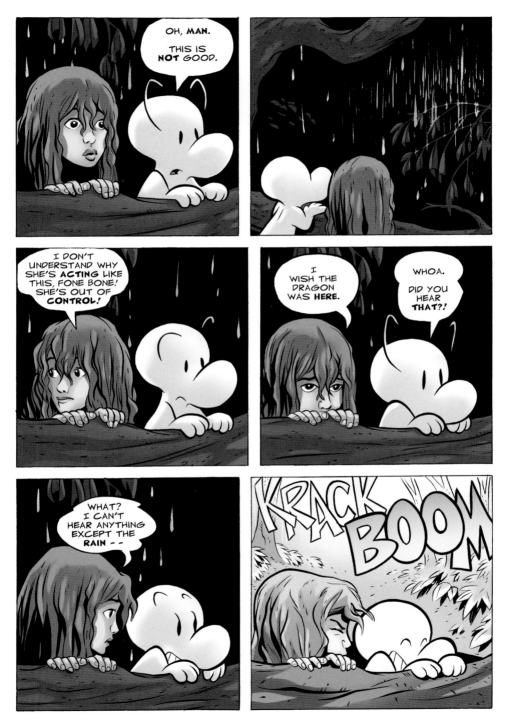

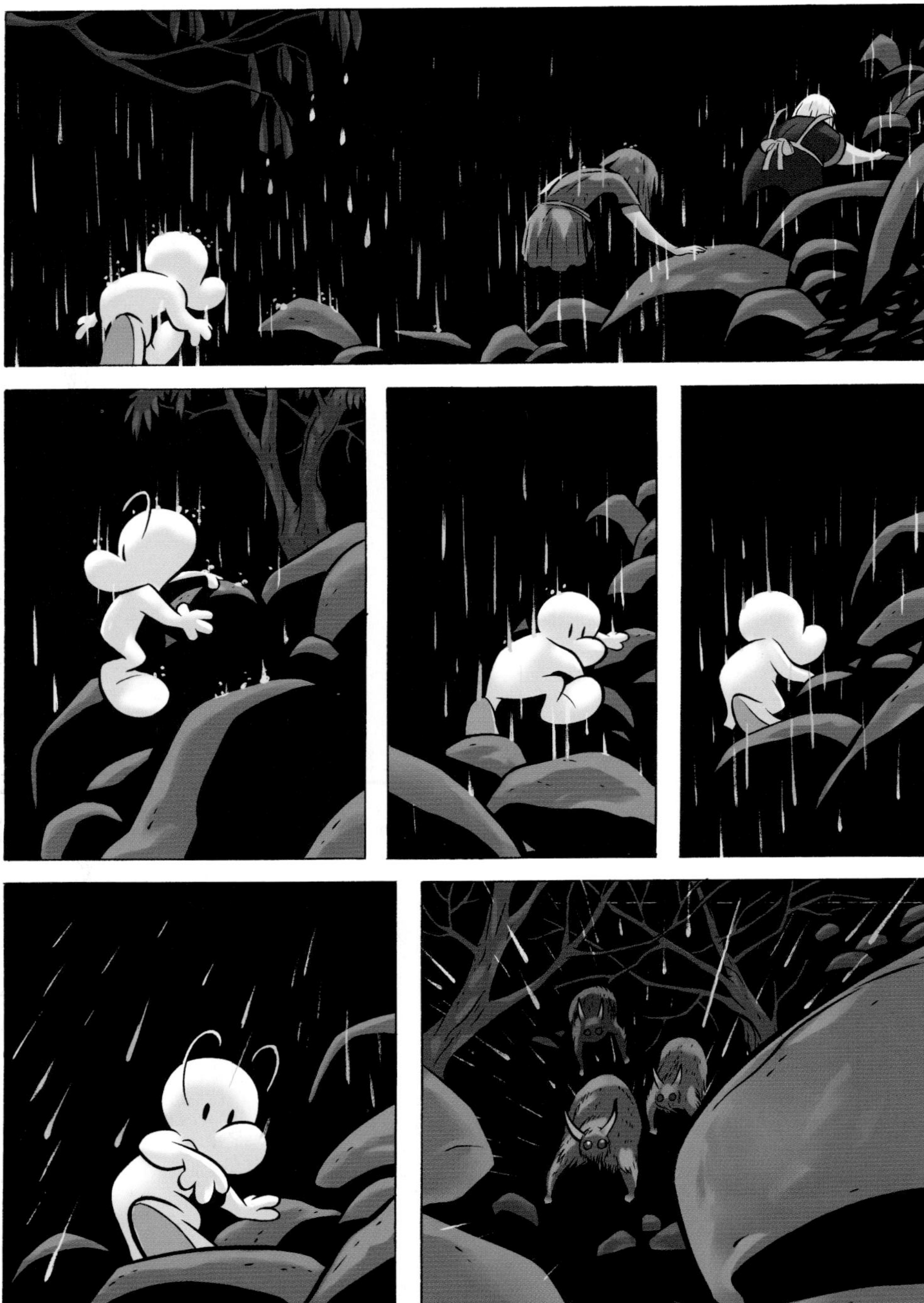

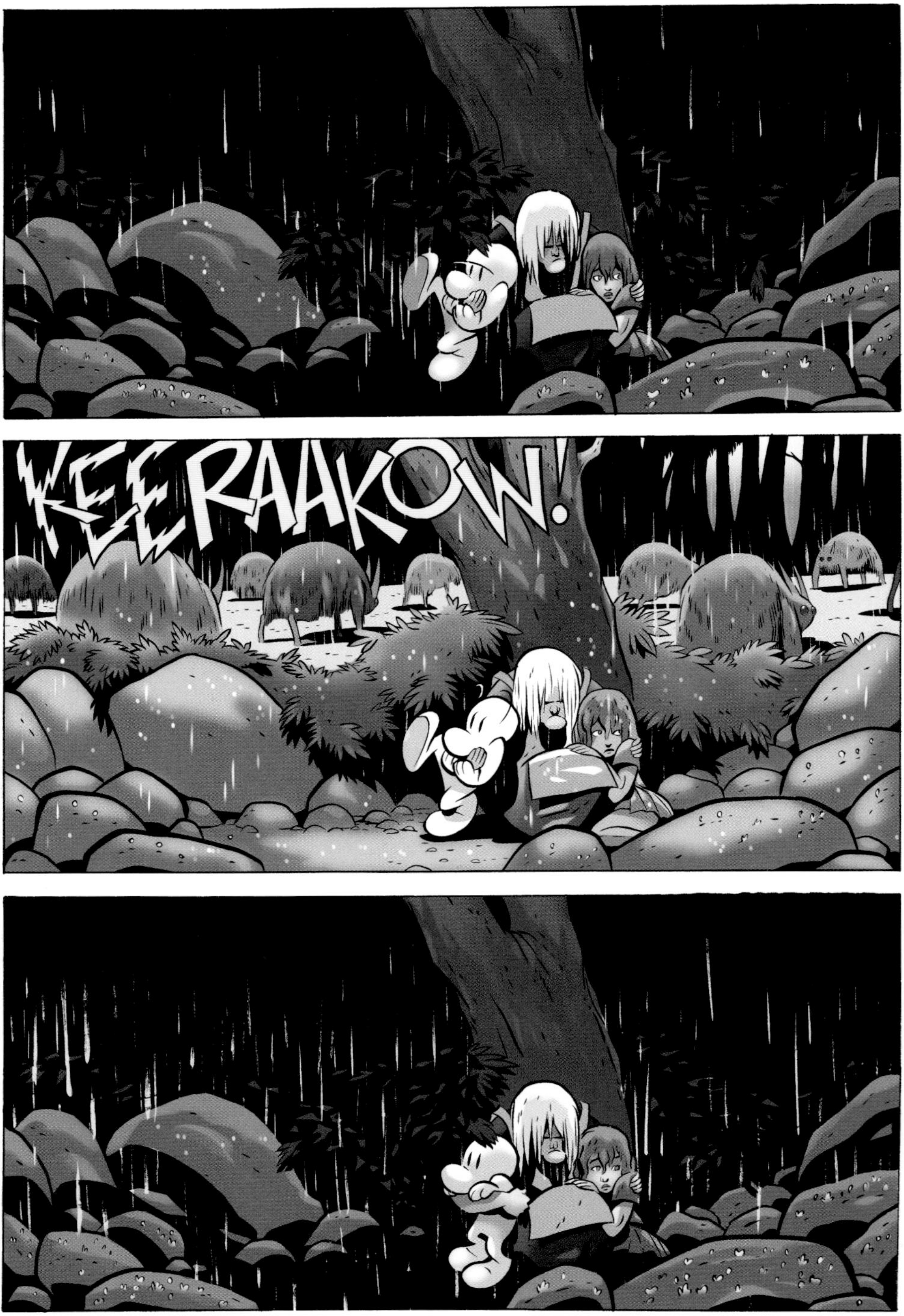
KEERAAKOW!

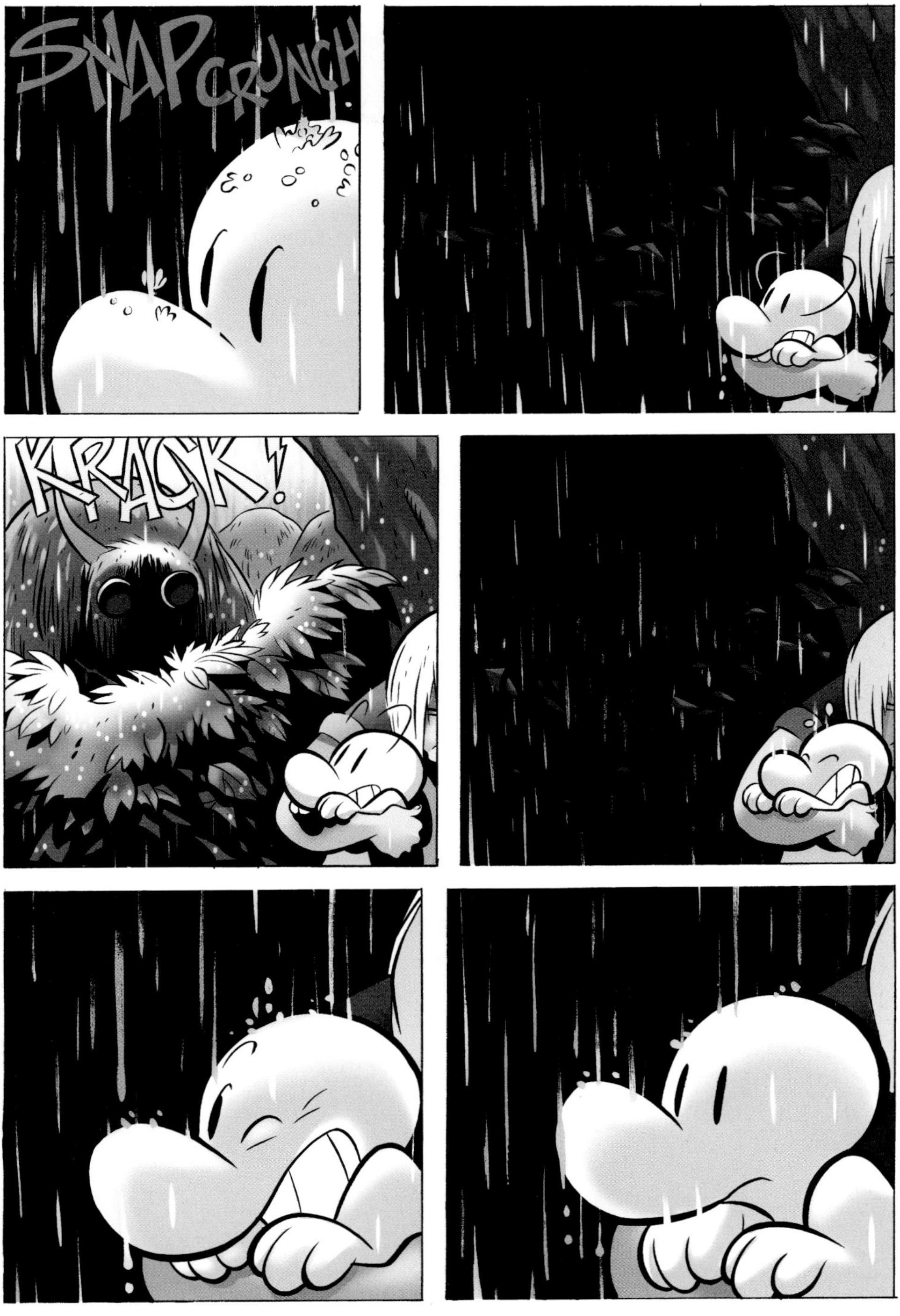
SNAP CRUNCH
KRACK!

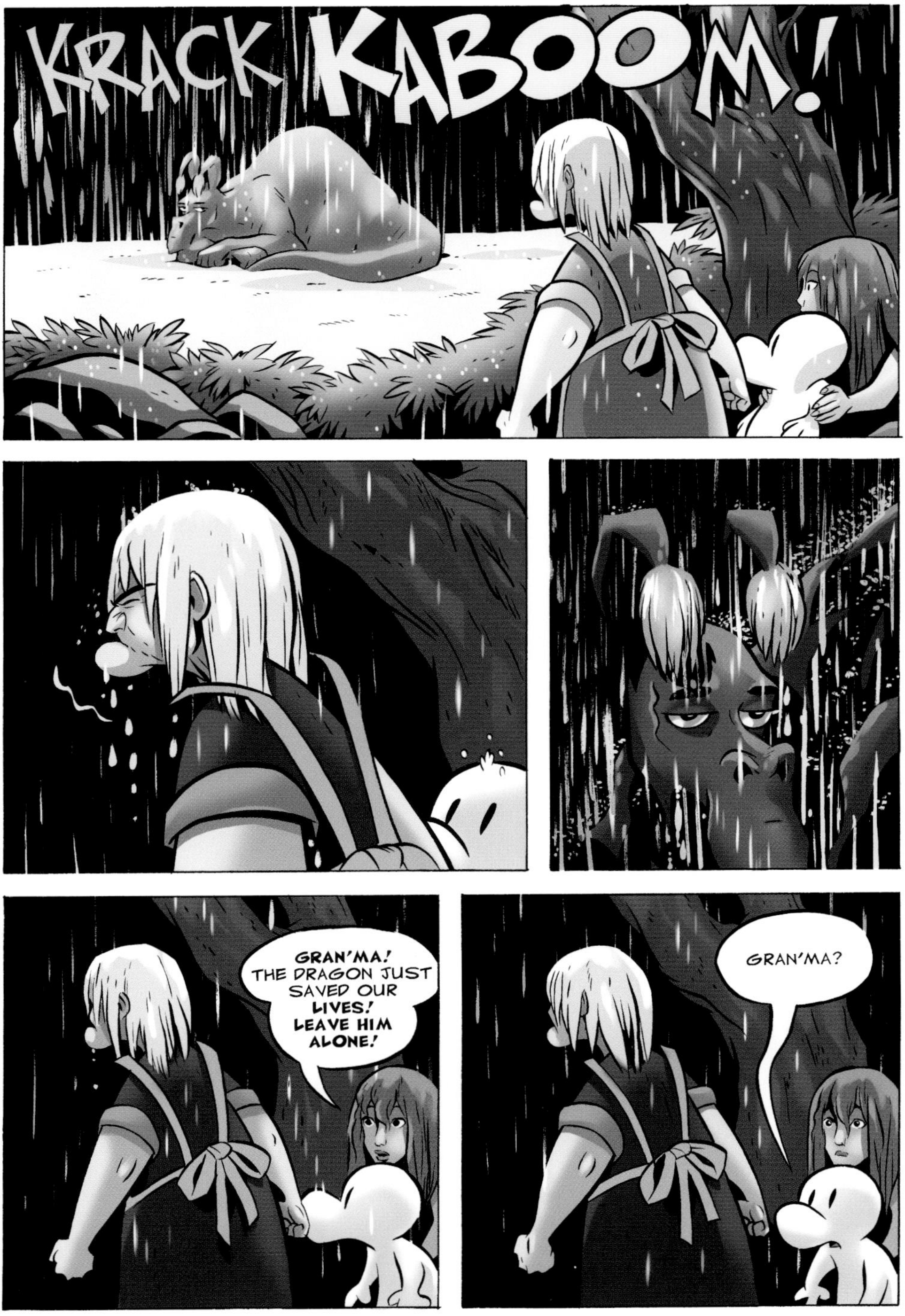
KRACK KABOOM!
GRAN'MA! THE DRAGON JUST SAVED OUR LIVES! LEAVE HIM ALONE!
GRAN'MA?

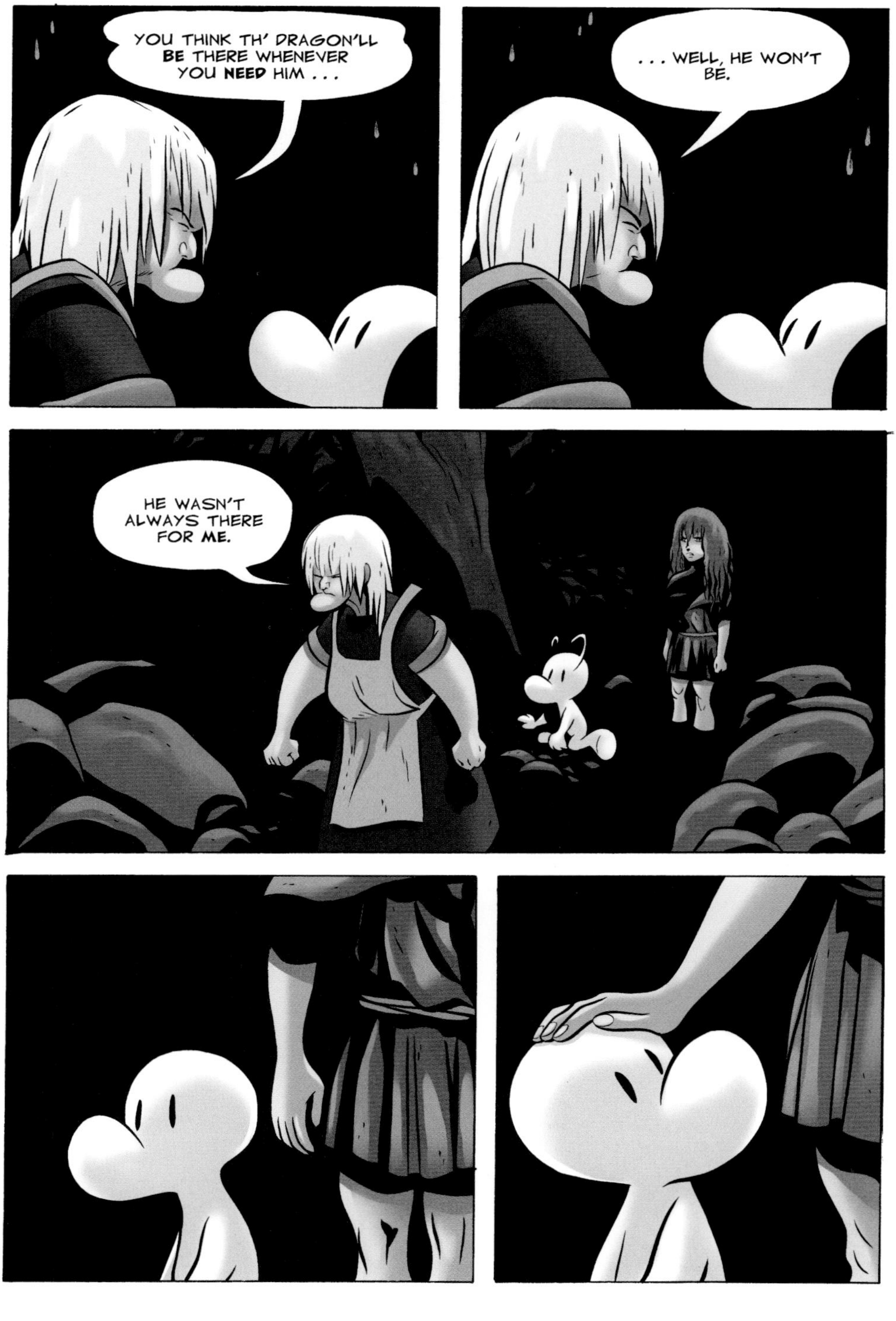
YOU THINK TH' DRAGON'LL BE THERE WHENEVER YOU NEED HIM . . .
. . . WELL, HE WON'T BE.
HE WASN'T ALWAYS THERE FOR ME.

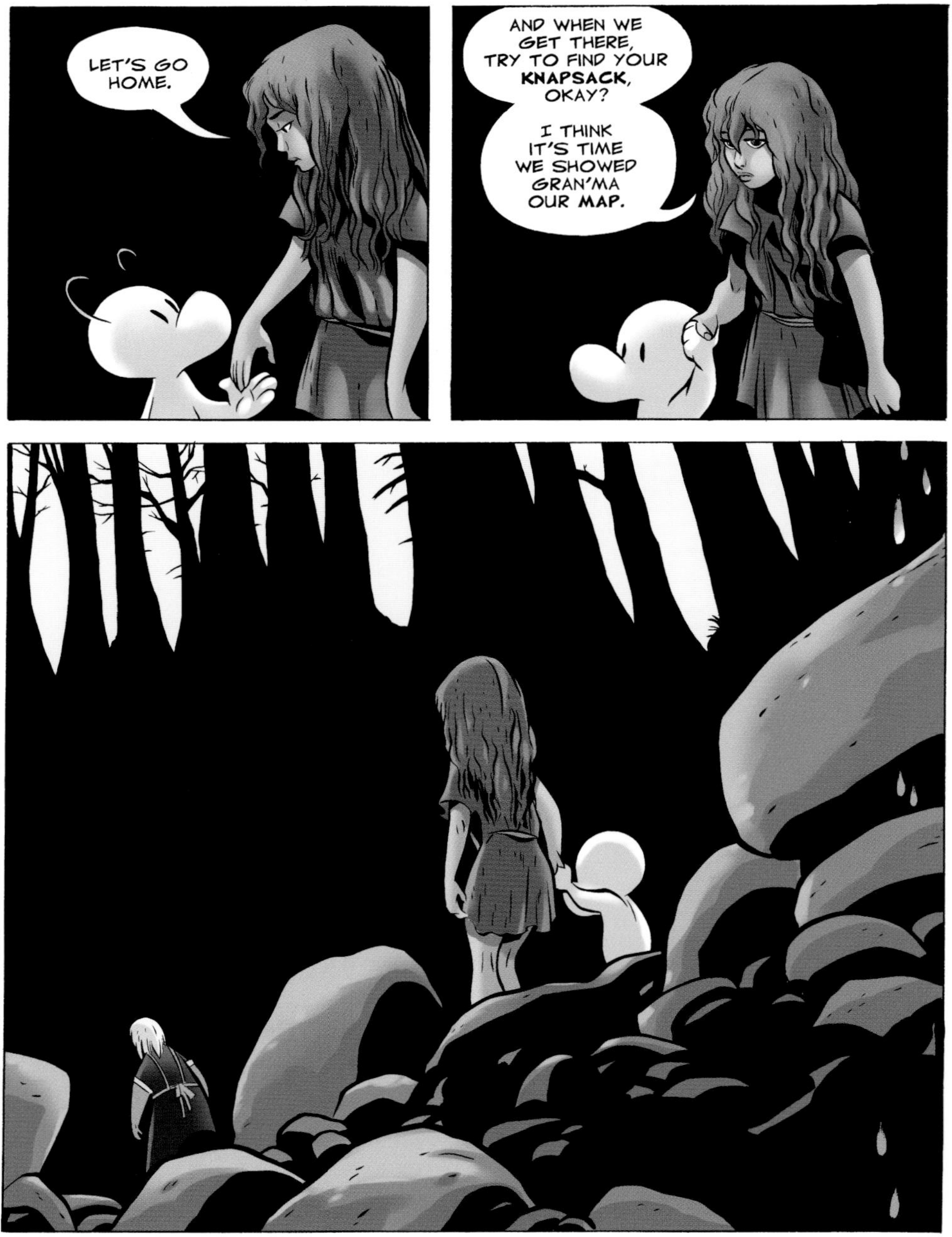
LET'S GO HOME.
AND WHEN WE GET THERE, TRY TO FIND YOUR KNAPSACK, OKAY?
I THINK IT'S TIME WE SHOWED GRAN'MA OUR MAP.

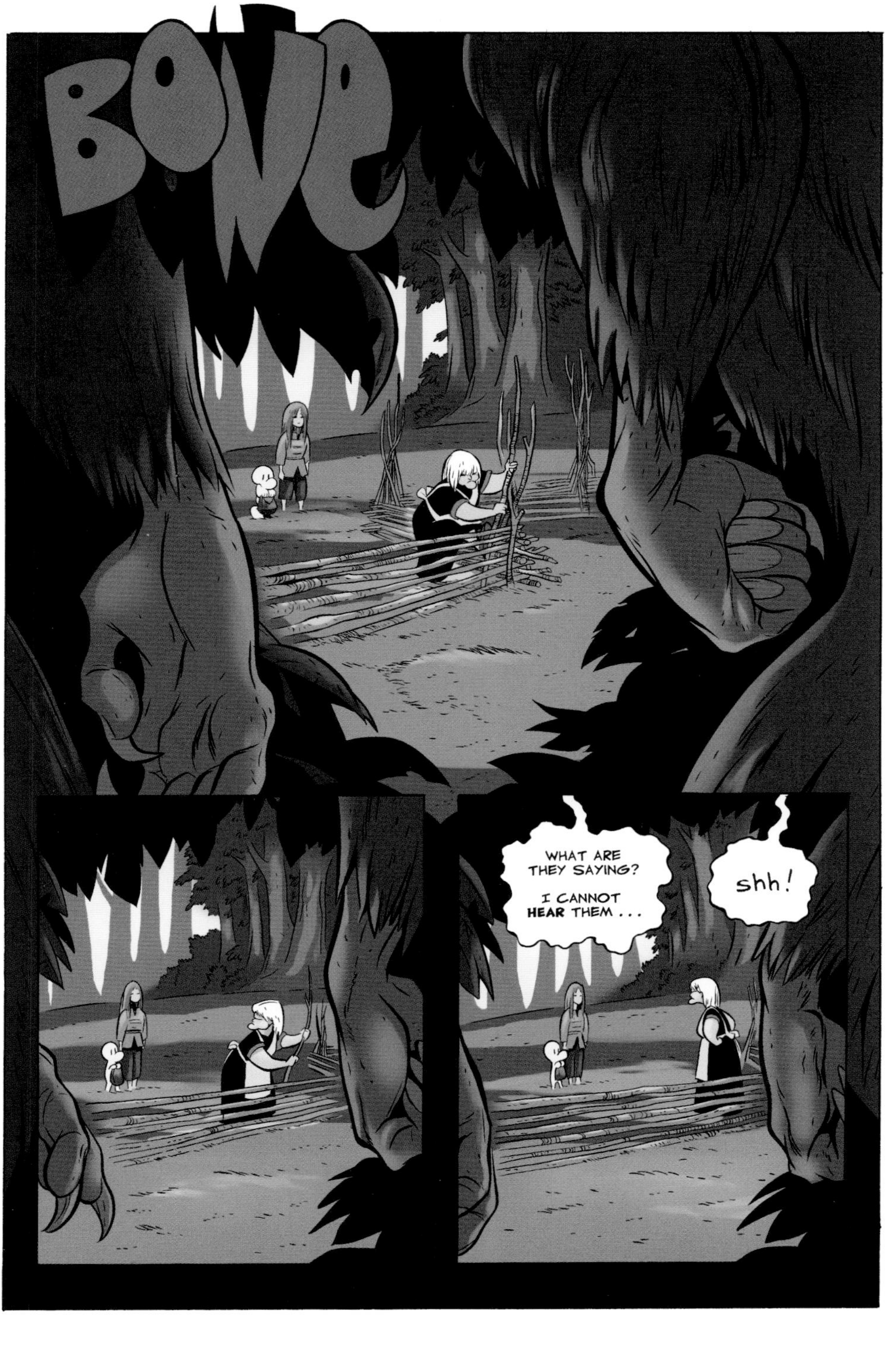
BONE
WHAT ARE THEY SAYING? I CANNOT HEAR THEM . . .
shh!

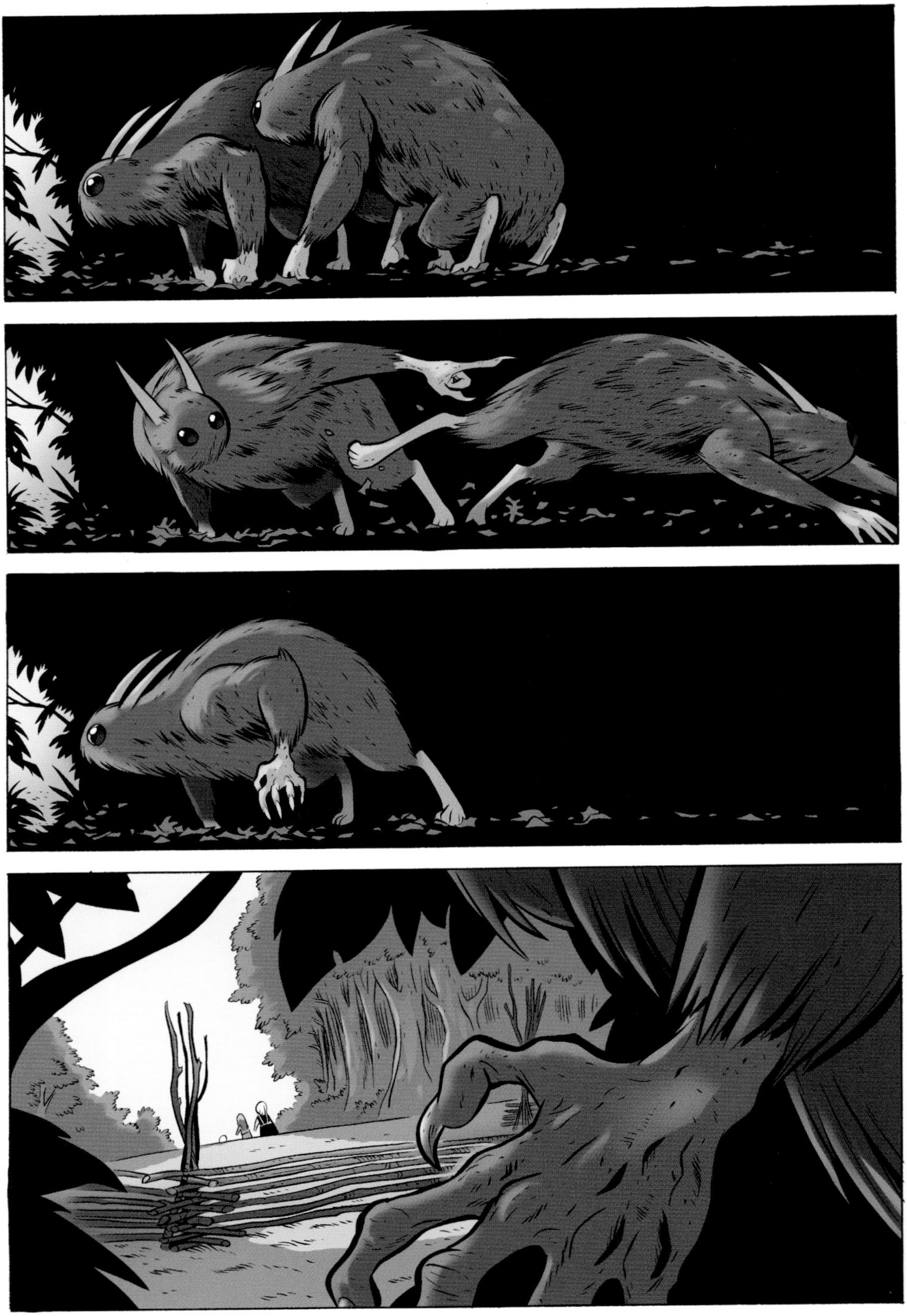

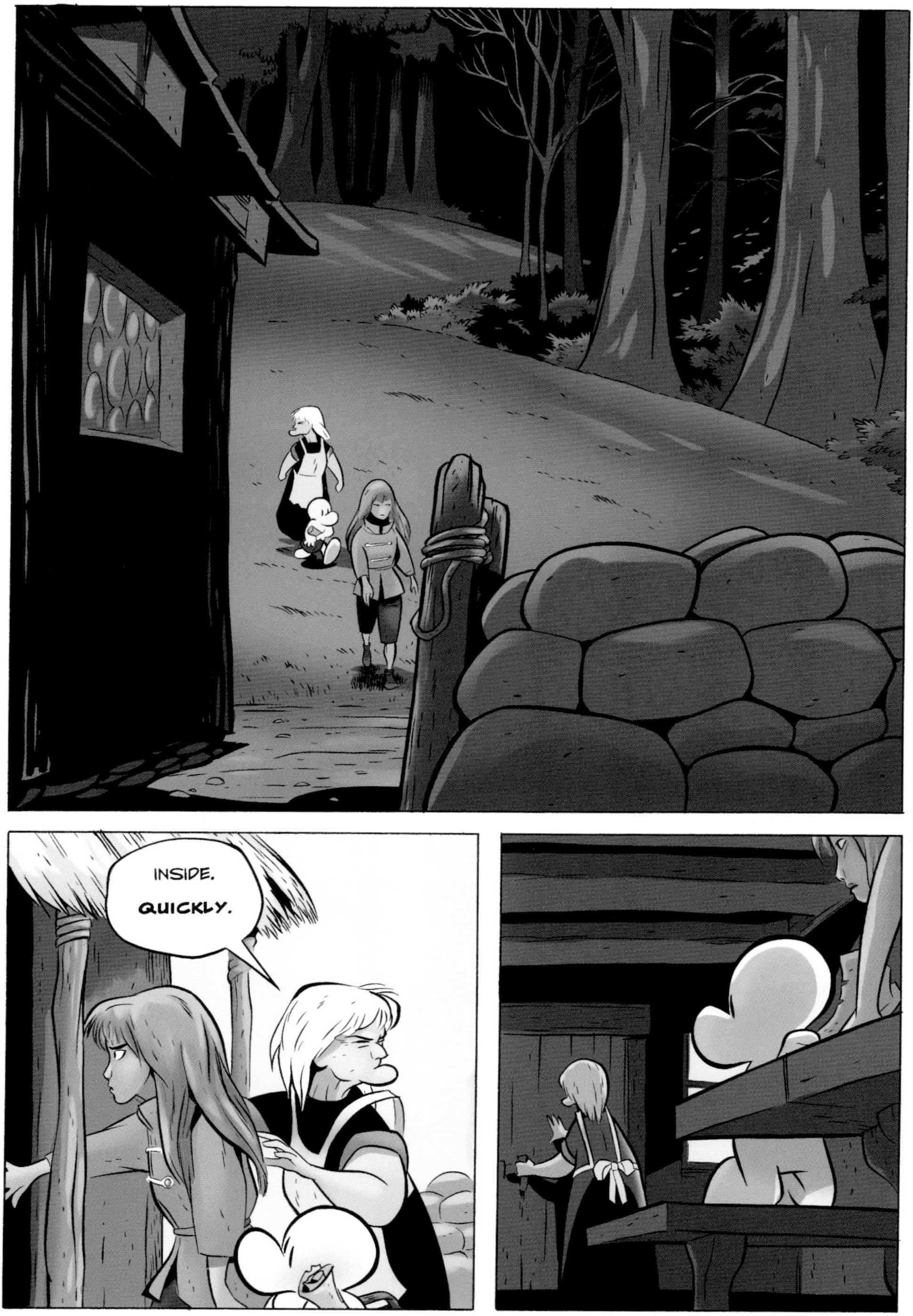
INSIDE.
QUICKLY.

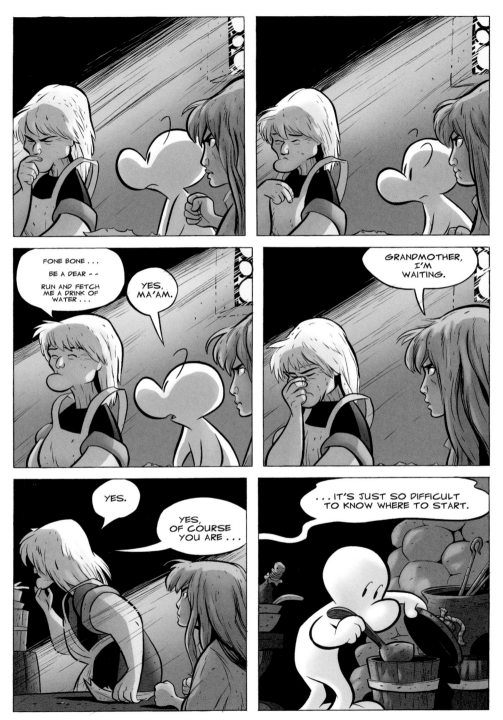

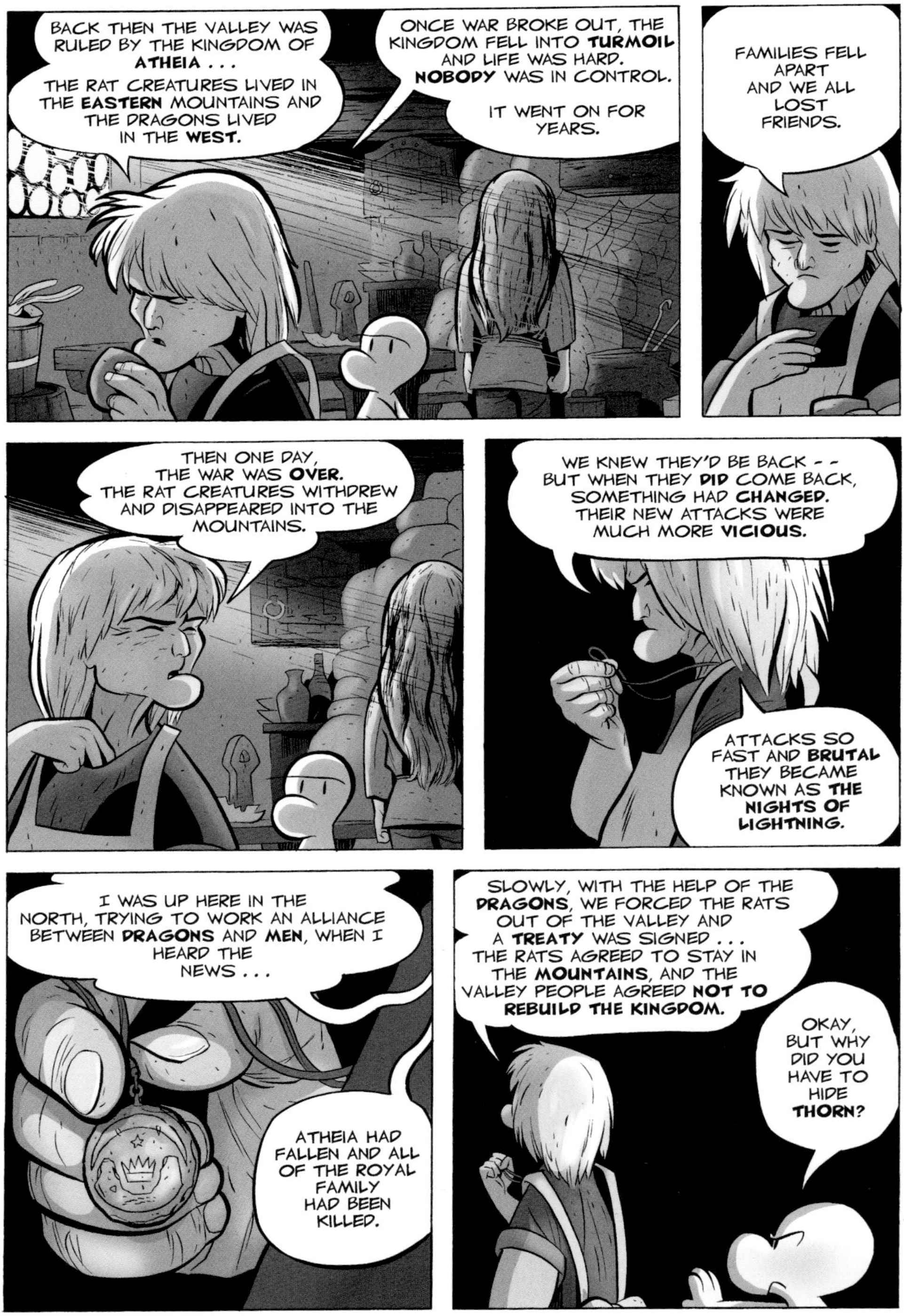
BACK THEN THE VALLEY WAS RULED BY THE KINGDOM OF ATHEIA . . .
THE RAT CREATURES LIVED IN THE EASTERN MOUNTAINS AND THE DRAGONS LIVED IN THE WEST.
ONCE WAR BROKE OUT, THE KINGDOM FELL INTO TURMOIL AND LIFE WAS HARD. NOBODY WAS IN CONTROL.
IT WENT ON FOR YEARS.
FAMILIES FELL APART AND WE ALL LOST FRIENDS.
THEN ONE DAY, THE WAR WAS OVER. THE RAT CREATURES WITHDREW AND DISAPPEARED INTO THE MOUNTAINS.
WE KNEW THEY'D BE BACK - - BUT WHEN THEY DID COME BACK, SOMETHING HAD CHANGED. THEIR NEW ATTACKS WERE MUCH MORE VICIOUS.
ATTACKS SO FAST AND BRUTAL THEY BECAME KNOWN AS THE NIGHTS OF LIGHTNING.
I WAS UP HERE IN THE NORTH, TRYING TO WORK AN ALLIANCE BETWEEN DRAGONS AND MEN, WHEN I HEARD THE NEWS . . .
ATHEIA HAD FALLEN AND ALL OF THE ROYAL FAMILY HAD BEEN KILLED.
SLOWLY, WITH THE HELP OF THE DRAGONS, WE FORCED THE RATS OUT OF THE VALLEY AND A TREATY WAS SIGNED . . .
THE RATS AGREED TO STAY IN THE MOUNTAINS, AND THE VALLEY PEOPLE AGREED NOT TO REBUILD THE KINGDOM.
OKAY, BUT WHY DID YOU HAVE TO HIDE THORN?

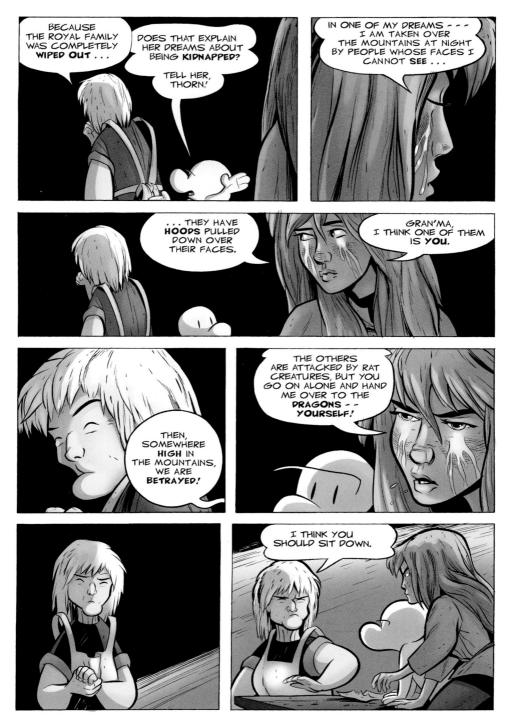

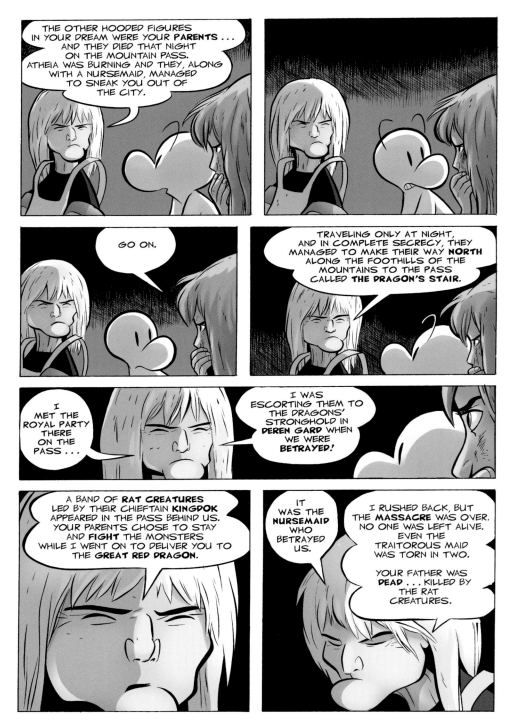

THE OTHER HOODED FIGURES IN YOUR DREAM WERE YOUR **PARENTS** ... AND THEY DIED THAT NIGHT ON THE MOUNTAIN PASS. ATHEIA WAS BURNING AND THEY, ALONG WITH A NURSEMAID, MANAGED TO SNEAK YOU OUT OF THE CITY.

GO ON.

TRAVELING ONLY AT NIGHT, AND IN COMPLETE SECRECY, THEY MANAGED TO MAKE THEIR WAY **NORTH** ALONG THE FOOTHILLS OF THE MOUNTAINS TO THE PASS CALLED **THE DRAGON'S STAIR.**

I MET THE ROYAL PARTY THERE ON THE PASS ...

I WAS ESCORTING THEM TO THE DRAGONS' STRONGHOLD IN **DEREN GARD** WHEN WE WERE **BETRAYED!**

A BAND OF **RAT CREATURES** LED BY THEIR CHIEFTAIN **KINGDOK** APPEARED IN THE PASS BEHIND US. YOUR PARENTS CHOSE TO STAY AND **FIGHT** THE MONSTERS WHILE I WENT ON TO DELIVER YOU TO THE **GREAT RED DRAGON.**

IT WAS THE **NURSEMAID** WHO BETRAYED US.

I RUSHED BACK, BUT THE **MASSACRE** WAS OVER. NO ONE WAS LEFT ALIVE. EVEN THE TRAITOROUS MAID WAS TORN IN TWO.

YOUR FATHER WAS **DEAD** ... KILLED BY THE RAT CREATURES.

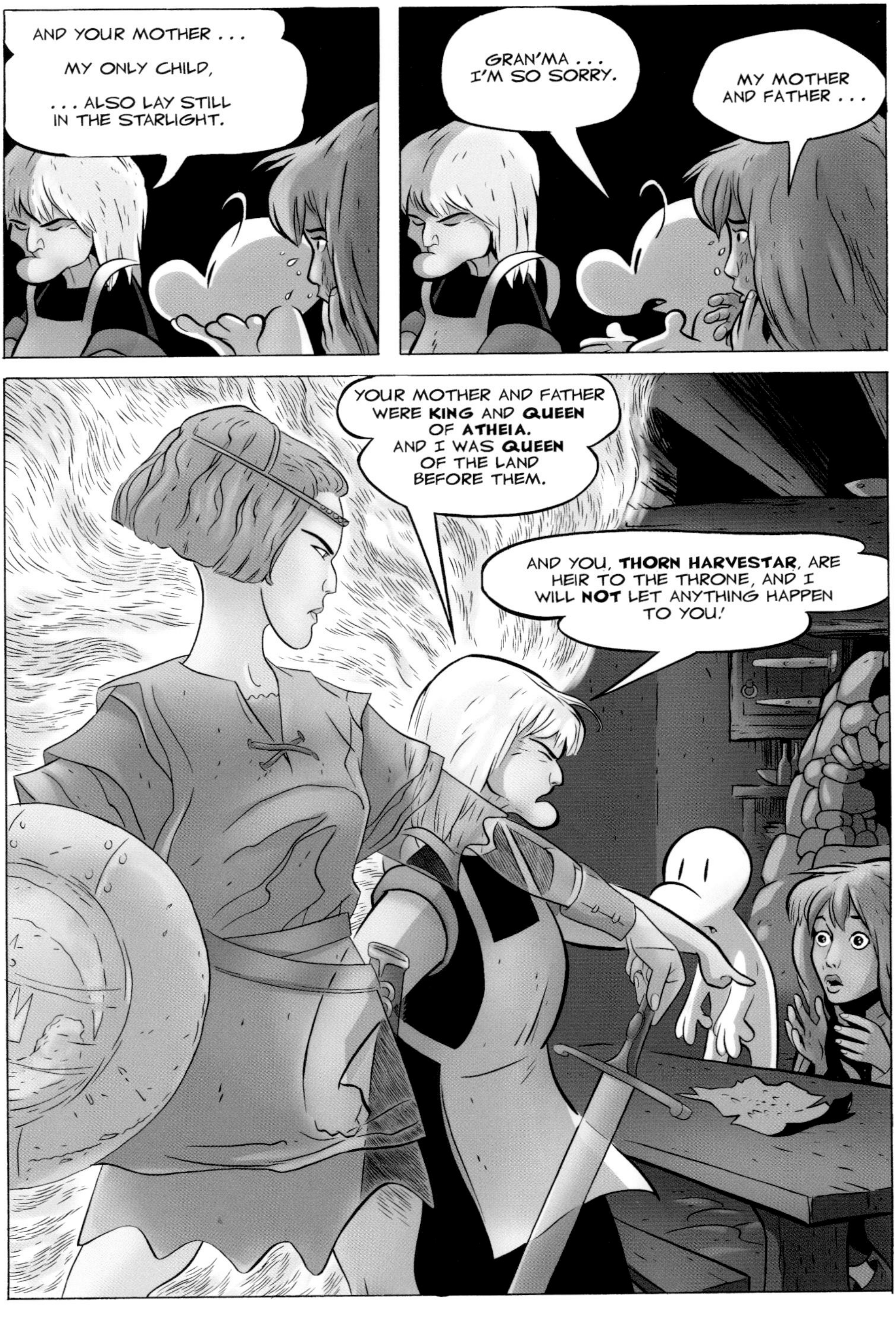
AND YOUR MOTHER . . .
MY ONLY CHILD,
. . . ALSO LAY STILL IN THE STARLIGHT.
GRAN'MA . . . I'M SO SORRY.
MY MOTHER AND FATHER . . .
YOUR MOTHER AND FATHER WERE KING AND QUEEN OF ATHEIA. AND I WAS QUEEN OF THE LAND BEFORE THEM.
AND YOU, THORN HARVESTAR, ARE HEIR TO THE THRONE, AND I WILL NOT LET ANYTHING HAPPEN TO YOU!

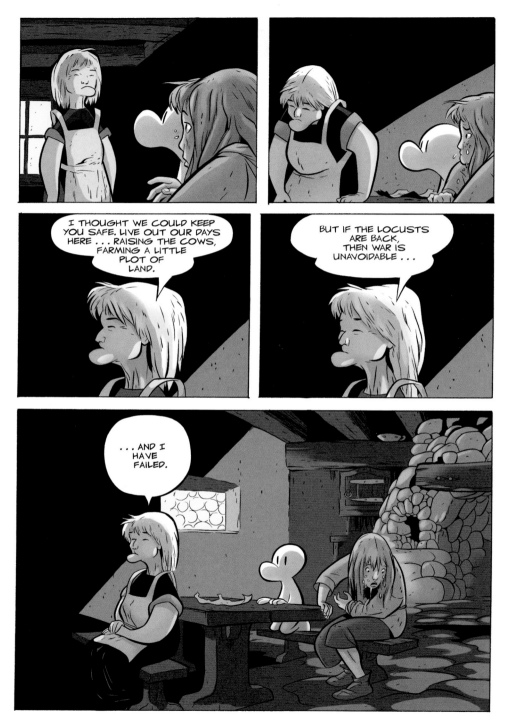

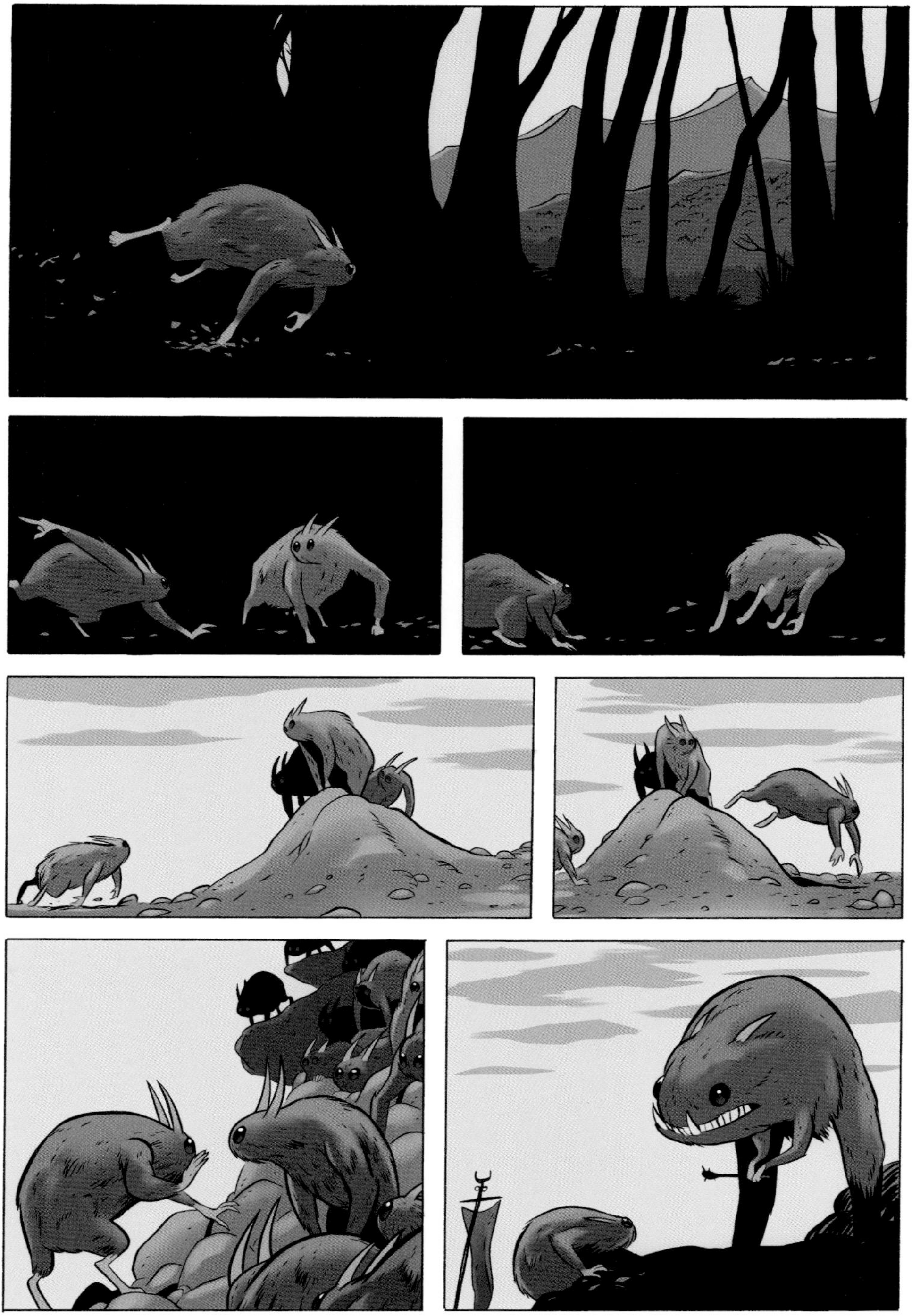

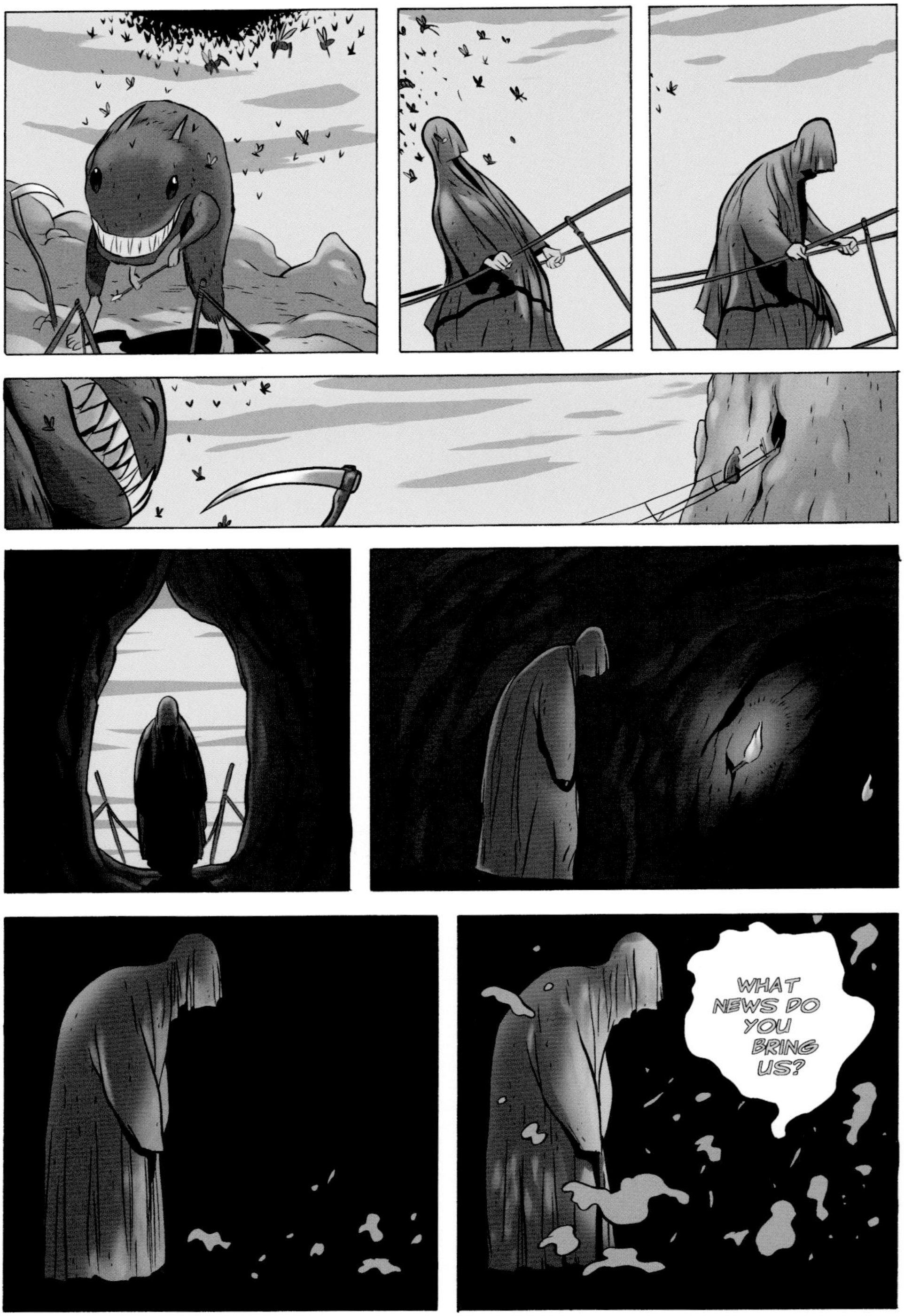
WHAT NEWS DO YOU BRING US?

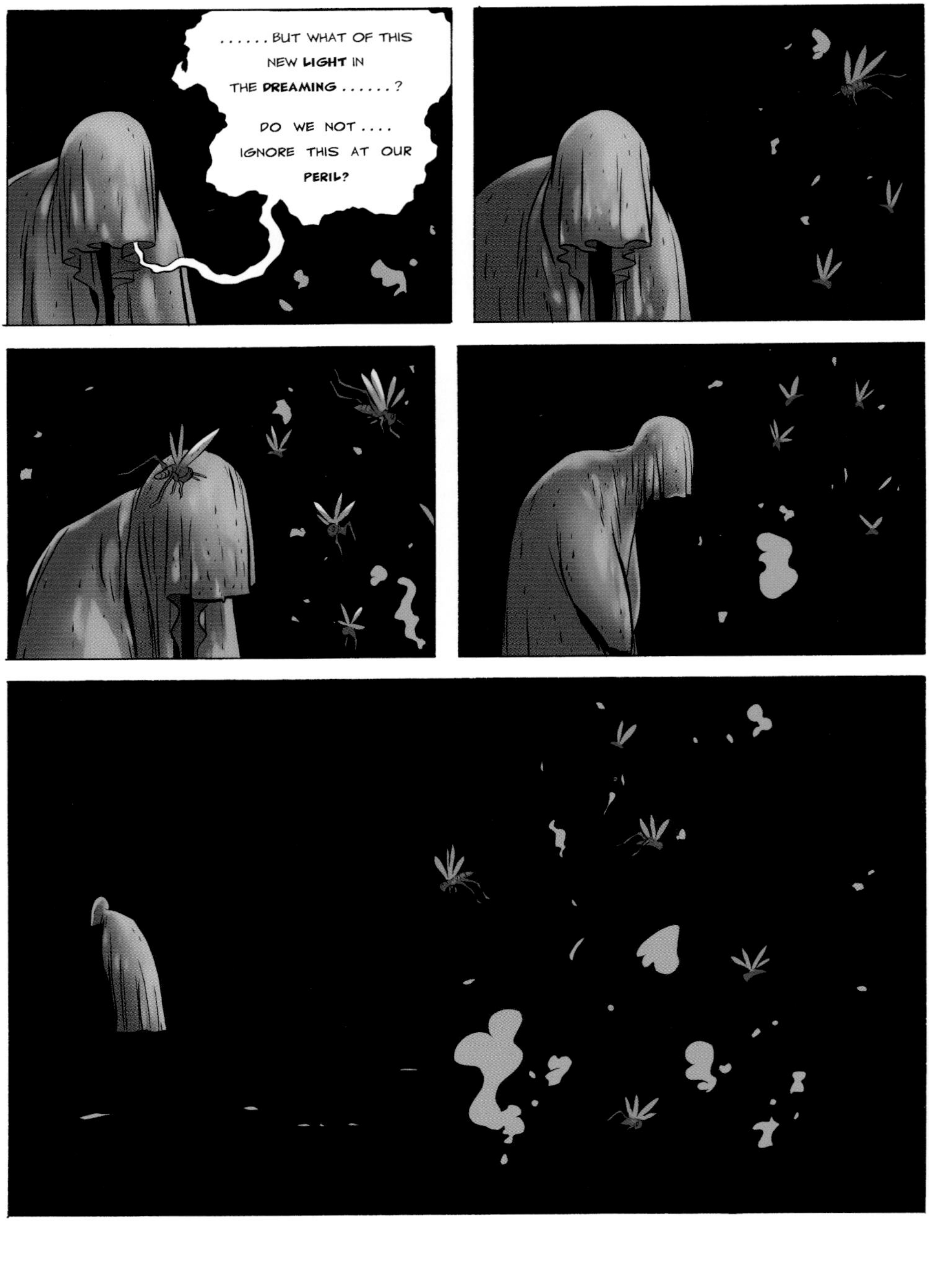
......BUT WHAT OF THIS NEW LIGHT IN THE DREAMING......?
DO WE NOT.... IGNORE THIS AT OUR PERIL?

GRR!

RR!

RRR!

OKAY, NOW THAT **THAT'S** SETTLED, I WANNA TELL YA ABOUT THIS LITTLE **CONTEST** WE'RE GONNA HAVE . . .

. . . THESE TWO - -

KILL 'EM!

!

RIP THEIR HEADS OFF!

BACK OFF OR I START SWINGIN'!

HERE'S TH' DEAL, SEE? AS LONG AS PHONEY BONE AN' HIS COUSIN SMILEY BONE ARE **WORKIN'** HERE, NOBODY LAYS A **FINGER** ON 'EM OR THEY ANSWER TO **ME!** **CLEAR?!**

CLEAR.

ALL RIGHT THEN.

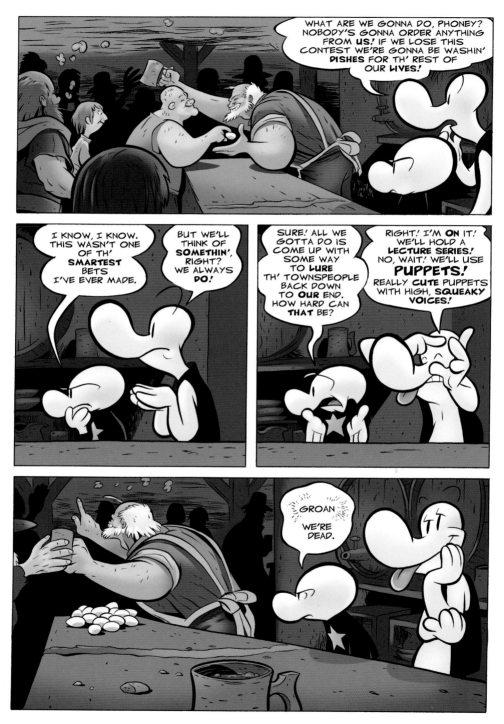

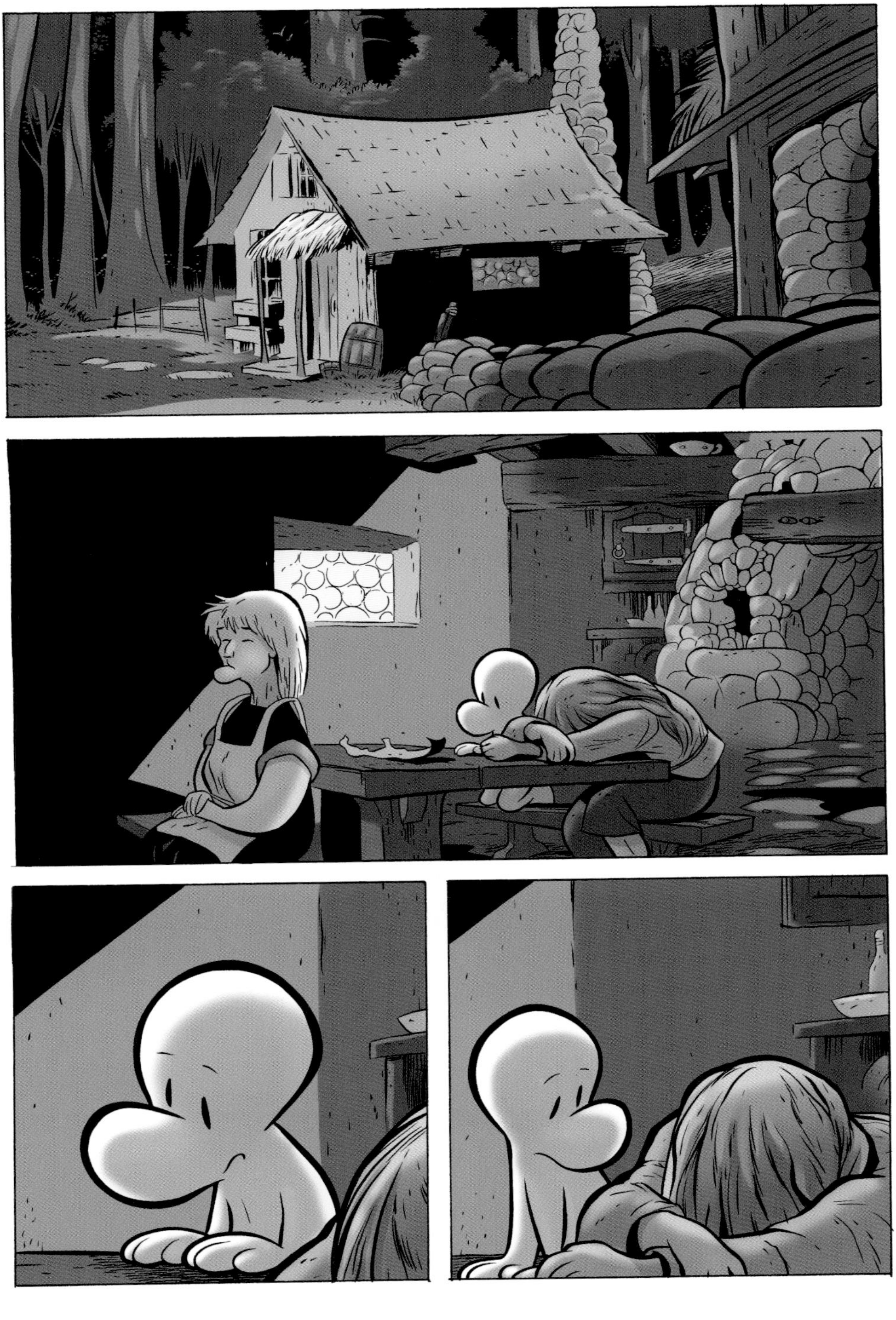

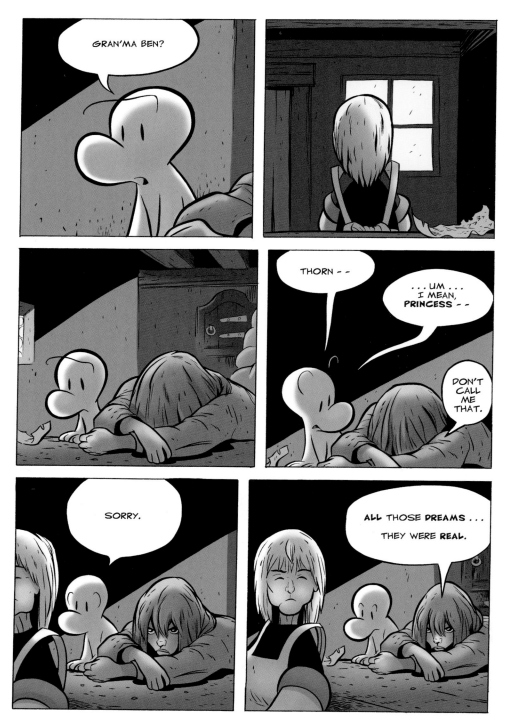

DREAMS

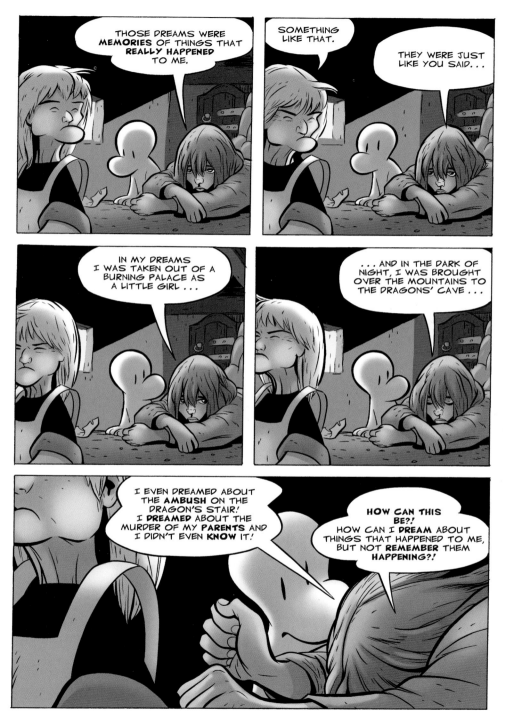

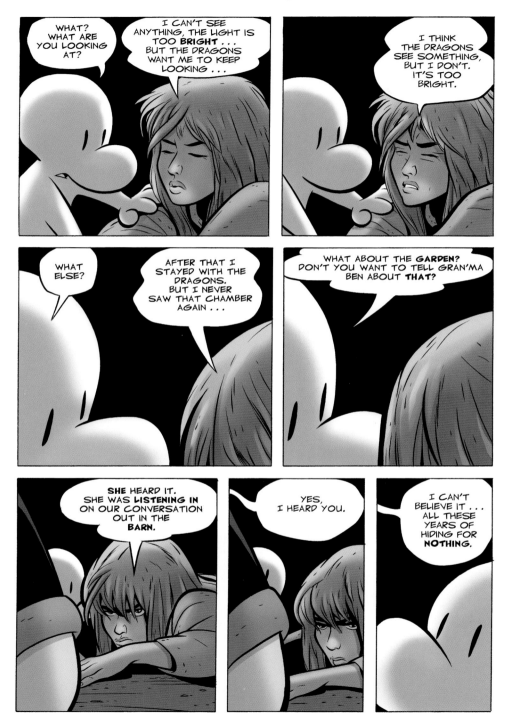

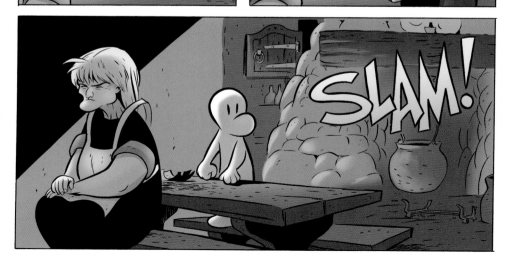

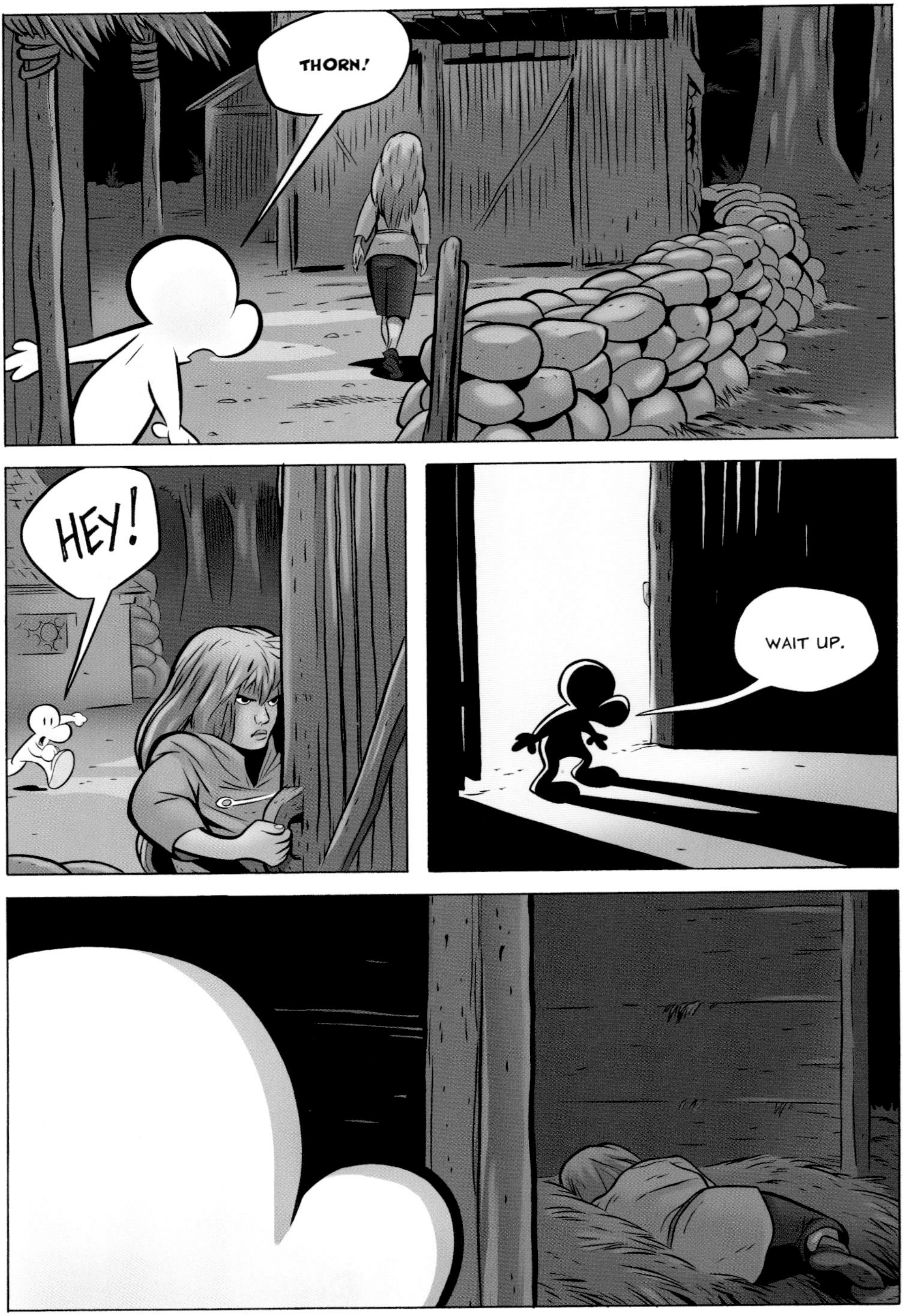
THORN!
HEY!
WAIT UP.

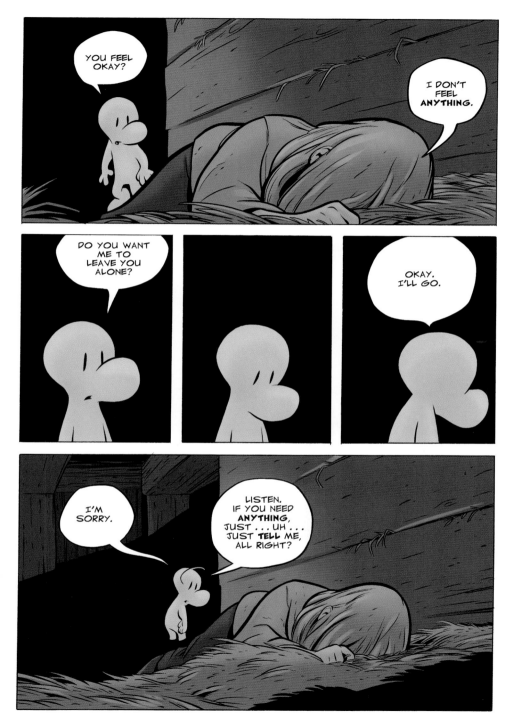

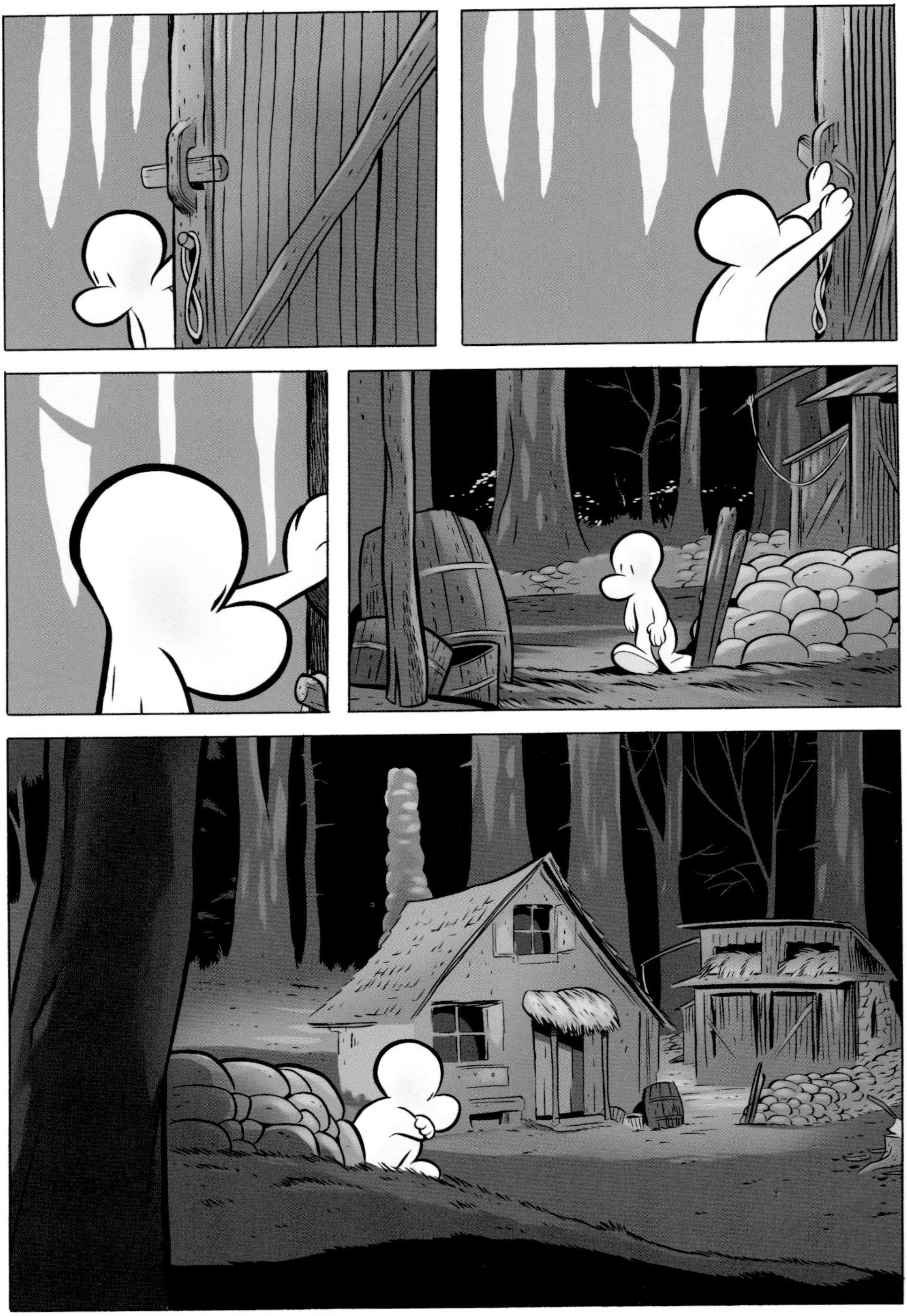

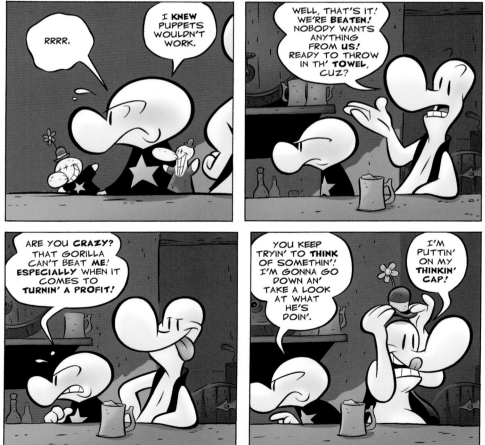

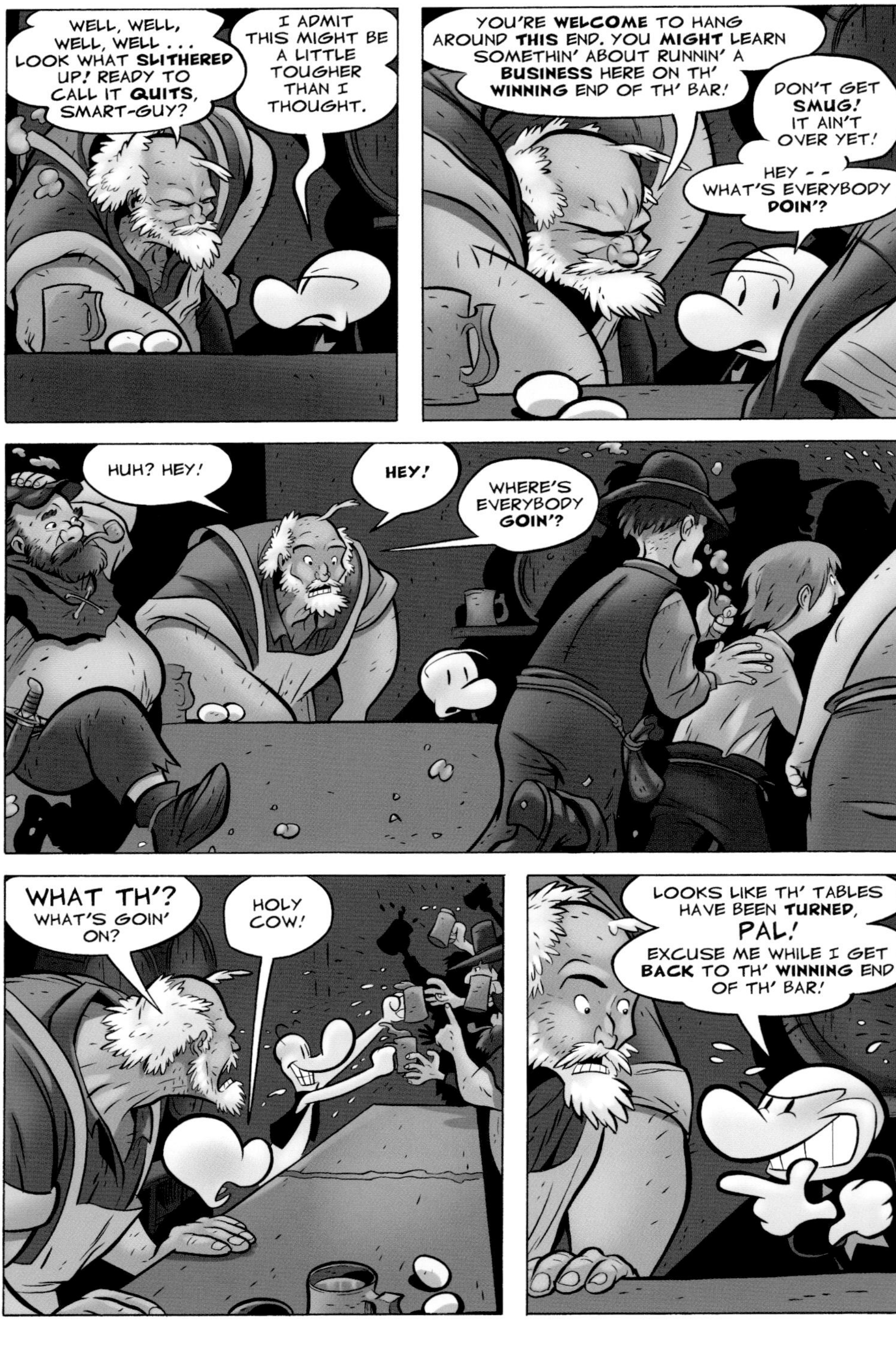
WELL, WELL, WELL, WELL . . . LOOK WHAT SLITHERED UP! READY TO CALL IT QUITS, SMART-GUY?
I ADMIT THIS MIGHT BE A LITTLE TOUGHER THAN I THOUGHT.
YOU'RE WELCOME TO HANG AROUND THIS END. YOU MIGHT LEARN SOMETHIN' ABOUT RUNNIN' A BUSINESS HERE ON TH' WINNING END OF TH' BAR!
DON'T GET SMUG! IT AIN'T OVER YET!
HEY - - WHAT'S EVERYBODY DOIN'?
HUH? HEY!
HEY!
WHERE'S EVERYBODY GOIN'?
WHAT TH'? WHAT'S GOIN' ON?
HOLY COW!
LOOKS LIKE TH' TABLES HAVE BEEN TURNED, PAL! EXCUSE ME WHILE I GET BACK TO TH' WINNING END OF TH' BAR!

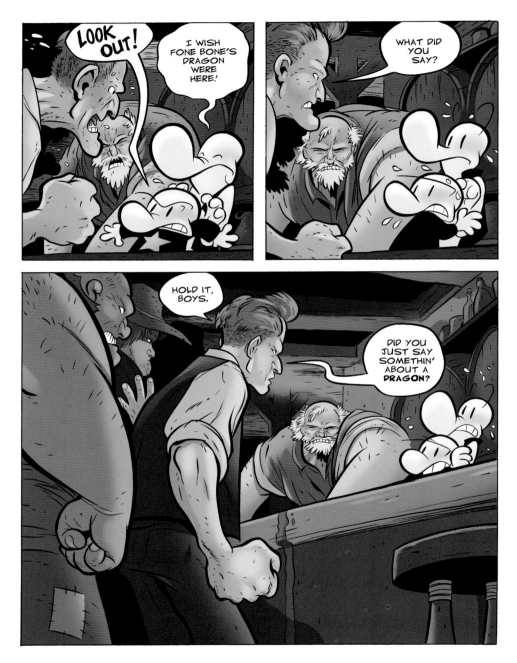

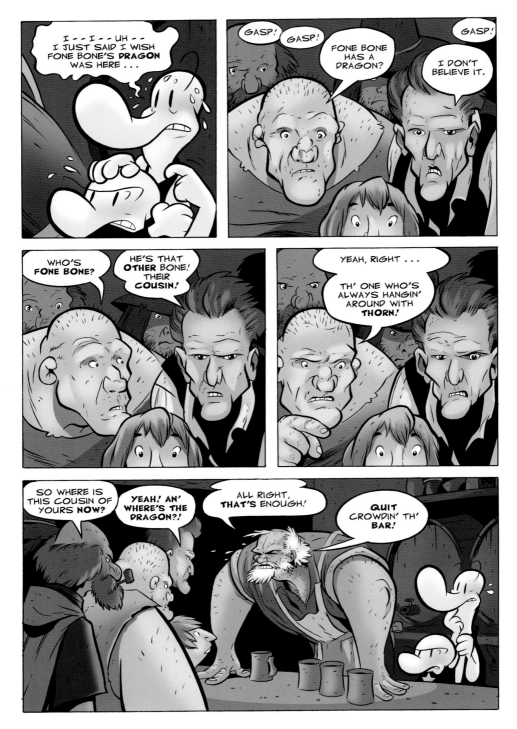

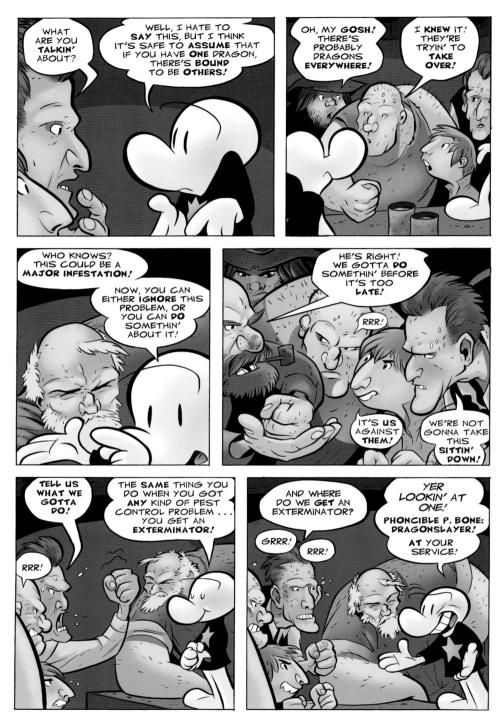

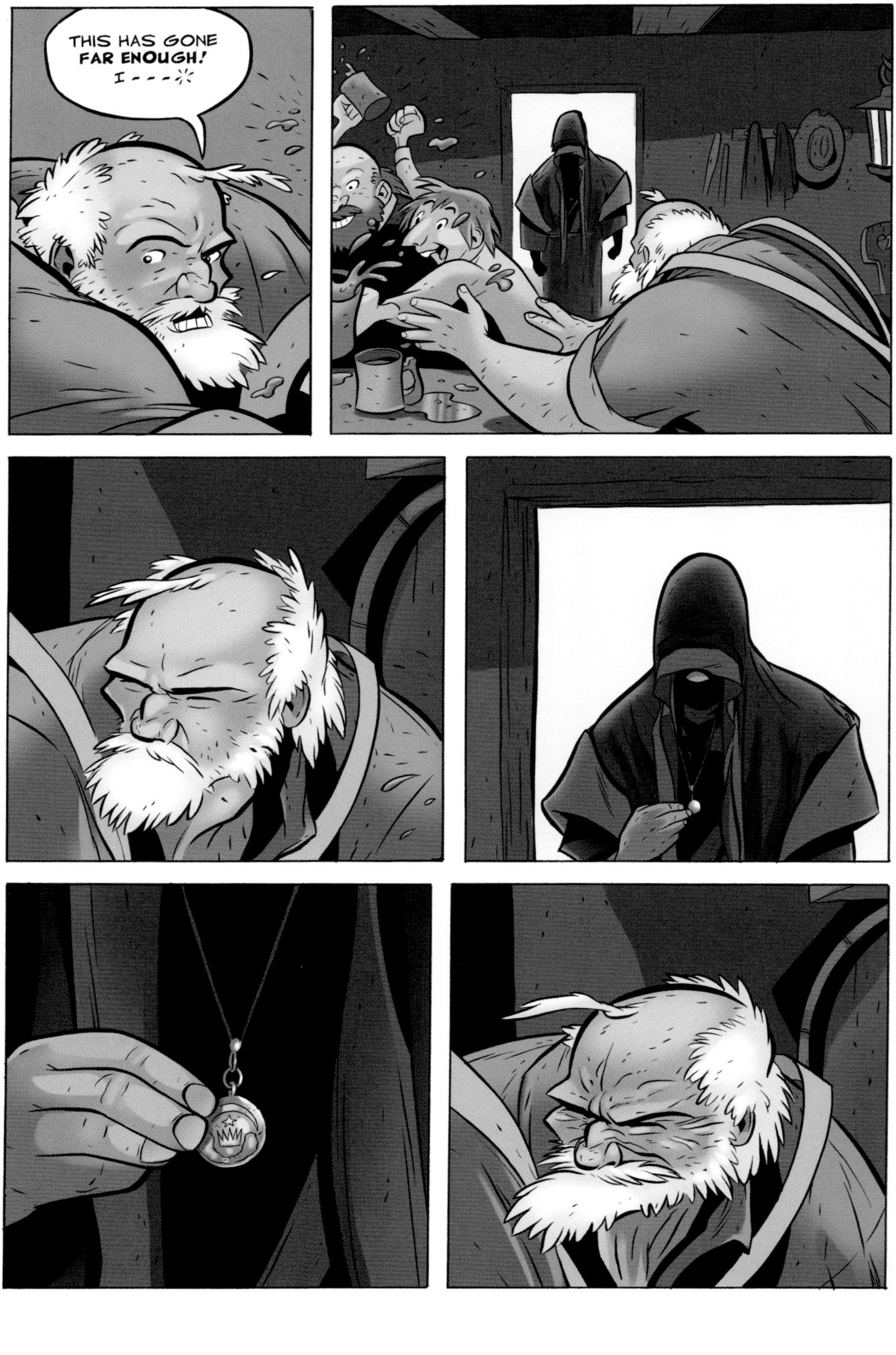
THIS HAS GONE
FAR ENOUGH!
I----

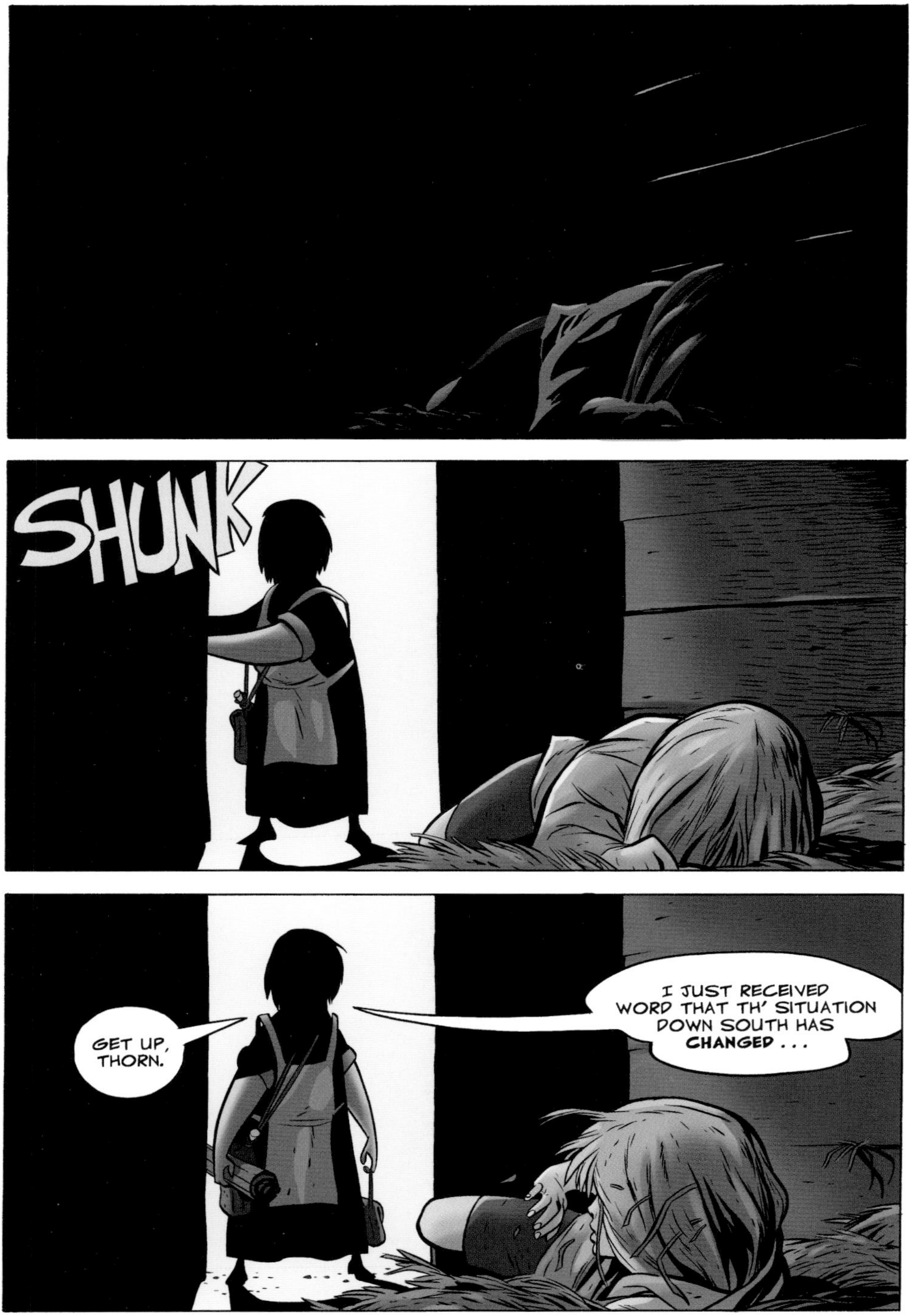
SHUNK
GET UP, THORN.
I JUST RECEIVED WORD THAT TH' SITUATION DOWN SOUTH HAS **CHANGED . . .**

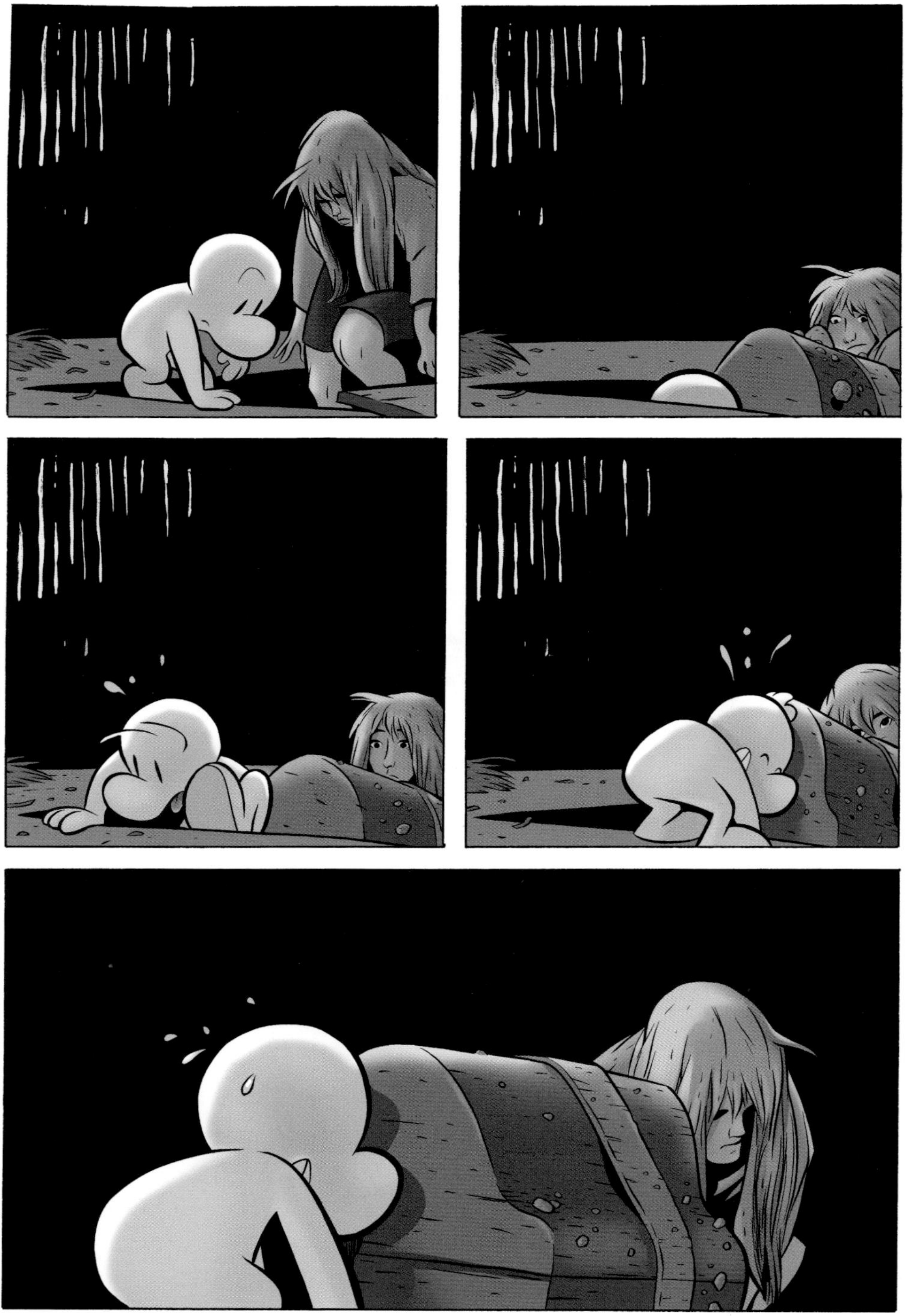

YOU GOT IT? GOOD!
OKAY, STEP BACK.

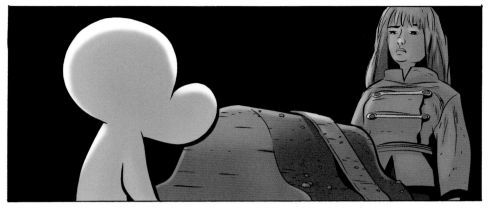

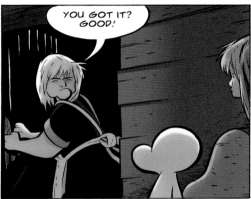

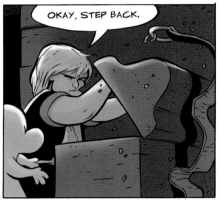

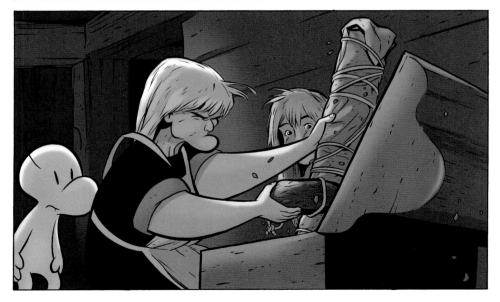

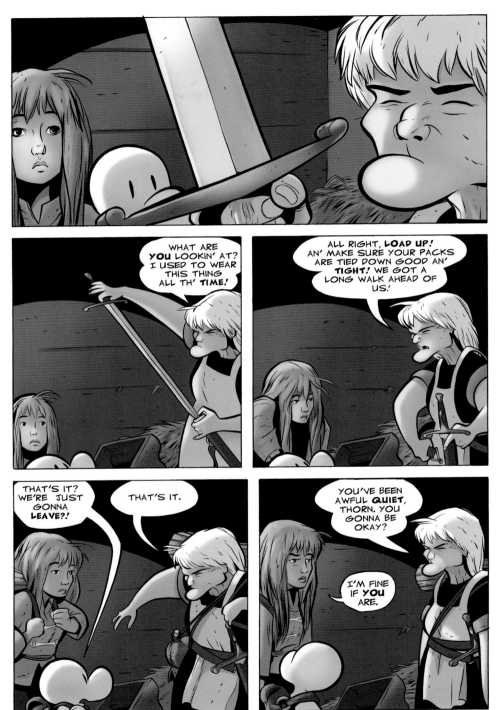

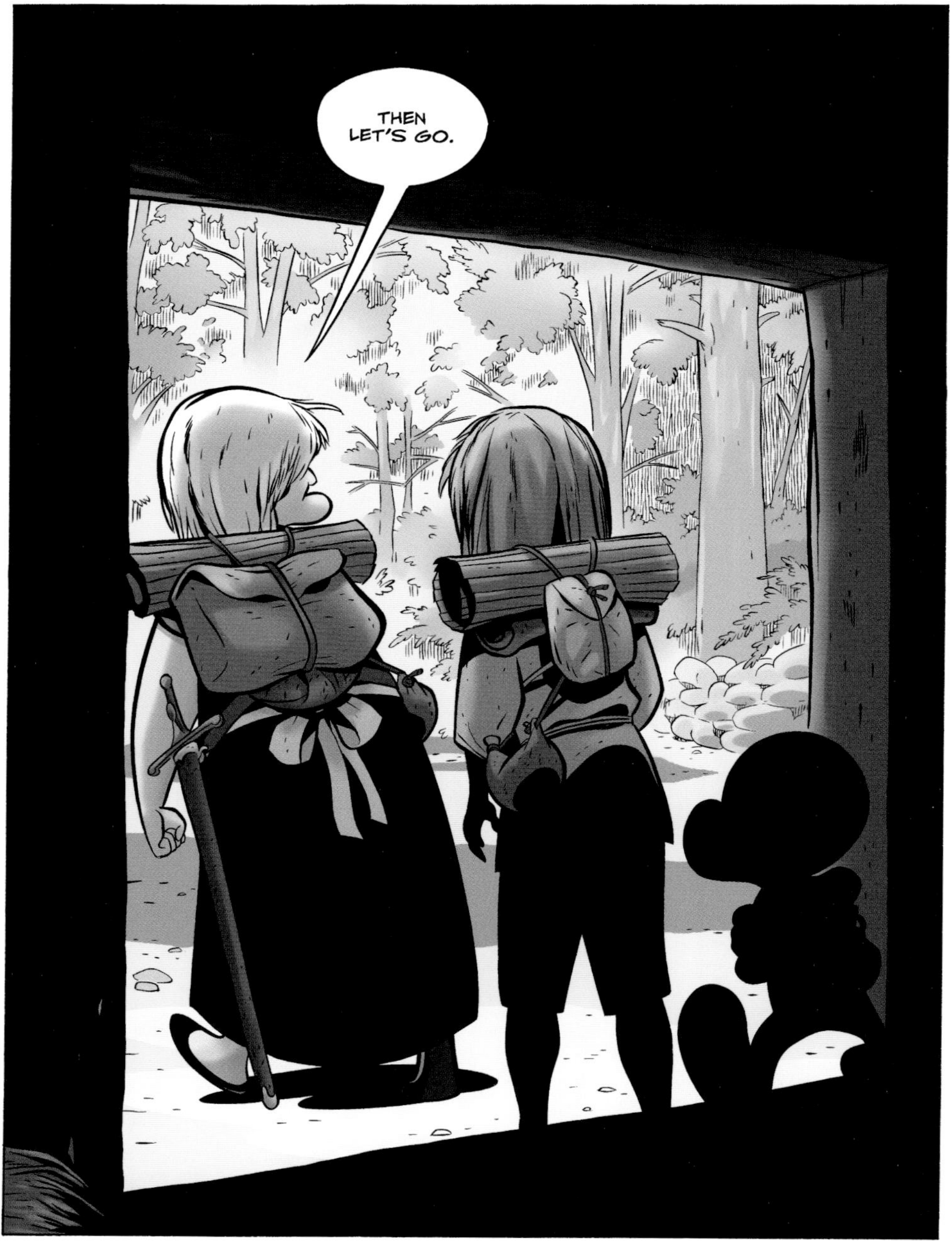
THEN LET'S GO.

...TO BE CONTINUED.

About JEFF SMITH

JEFF SMITH was born and raised in the American Midwest and learned about cartooning from comic strips, comic books, and watching animated shorts on TV. After four years of drawing comic strips for The Ohio State University's student newspaper and co-founding Character Builders animation studio in 1986, Smith launched the comic book *BONE* in 1991. Between *BONE* and other comics projects, Smith spends much of his time on the international guest circuit promoting comics and the art of graphic novels.

More about *BONE*

An instant classic when it first appeared in the U.S. as an underground comic book in 1991, *BONE* has since garnered 38 international awards and sold a million copies in 15 languages. Now, Scholastic's GRAPHIX imprint is publishing full-color graphic novel editions of the nine-book *BONE* series. Look for the continuing adventures of the Bone cousins in *The Dragonslayer*.